ALSO BY CALEB STEPHENS

If You Lie

The Girls in the Cabin

What Waits Below

If Only a Heart and Other Tales of Terror

YOU'LL NEVER KNOW

A PSYCHOLOGICAL THRILLER

CALEB STEPHENS

THRILLERSCAPE PRESS

For Jen – my always and forever.

Invisible threads are the strongest ties.

–FRIEDRICH NIETZSCH

PART ONE
THE OPENING

CHAPTER 1

GRANT

"I think we're lost," I say.

"We're fine," Avery replies with a wink, her hand resting loose on the wheel of our white Jeep Cherokee as it rumbles up the rugged road. The Uncompahgre National Forest presses in around us, shadows flickering over the hood, the mountains rising ahead, looking ominous and indifferent.

"How did you hear about this hike again?" I ask.

"I found it on Reddit," Avery says.

My eyebrows rise. "Reddit? Seriously?"

She shrugs. "What? It had a thousand upvotes."

I laugh. I can't help it. My wife is easygoing like that. To her, every moment is a cause for adventure—which I love, but right now I want her to pull over. I need to check the map. The road has split three times already, and I lost cell service miles back.

"Are you sure about that?" I ask. "Reddit also thinks birds aren't real."

"That's not true," she says with a grin. It's a weapon she uses against me frequently. Anytime we have a disagreement, all she has to do is smile: fight over.

"It is, I swear. Look it up."

She returns her gaze to the road. "The thread did say the trail's a little hard to find."

"I'd say it's more than a little hard to find. Here, let me see if I can figure out where we are." I retrieve my phone and try, knowing full well I won't be able to get a signal. The forest is growing thicker by the minute, the trees crowding in on either side of the road like silent sentinels, attempting to block out the sky. "Actually, can you pull over for a second? We might need to turn around."

"No, we don't. We're good. Look." She points, and I spot the gutted remains of the structure ahead. It's the landmark Avery told me to be on the lookout for when we first pulled off the highway—a cabin ravaged by a long-ago fire. It means we only have another quarter mile to go. Still, I can't help but feel a twinge of dread at seeing a building that looks like a blackened skeleton half swallowed by the trees sitting out here in the middle of nowhere.

Avery pops an eyebrow. "Okay, you can admit it now."

"Admit what?" I ask, pretending not to know what she's talking about.

"You know exactly what."

"Fine," I say with an exaggerated huff. "You were right."

"And?"

"And I was wrong. We're not lost. Better?"

Her smile widens. "Much."

A few minutes later, we break from the trees and into a clearing that takes my breath away. The horizon is drenched in a spectacular wave of color. Mountains spring up around us everywhere I look, all of them dressed in vivid suits of blue and green. The peaks climb toward the sky in a dizzying array of granite crags and vertical pitches that are so beautiful they almost look artificial. Living in Durango, I'm used to gorgeous scenery, but nothing like this. The view is stunning. For a moment, it feels like we've been transported to Switzerland.

"Wow," I mutter, hypnotized. "This is amazing."

"So beautiful," Avery echoes as we reach the lot.

She pulls off the road and parks near a sign indicating the trailhead. I'm about to get out and take it all in when she reaches over and lays a hand on my knee. "Wait a second. I have something for you." She slides a small box from the pocket in the door and hands it to me. It's a present, fully wrapped and topped with a white bow.

"Did I forget an anniversary?" I ask, surprised. "What's this all about?"

She laughs. "Open it and find out."

I do exactly that, expecting to see a book or new wallet, but instead find myself staring at a framed photo. At first, I don't understand what I'm looking at. It's nothing but a black canvas with a white blob in the center that—

Oh my god.

The image takes shape and the world outside the car turns to a smear of color. None of it exists—the sky, the mountains, the trees— all of it is gone in an instant. The only thing that matters is what I'm clutching in my palms. The picture isn't of a blob but rather of a head rounding down into a face with a small bump of a nose. Lower, I can just make out a belly sprouting two little legs and an arm caught in what looks like a wave. Because it *is* a wave—I'm looking at a hand growing five little fingers.

"Is this real?" I whisper in awe.

Avery doesn't reply. I look up to find her crying, tears spilling over her cheeks in silent streams. She nods. "Look at the bottom corner."

When I do, I see the baby's stats—a length of nearly six centimeters and an estimated age of twelve weeks. The name Avery Wilson is stamped above them, along with a date. The ultrasound was taken two days ago.

I try to speak, but I can't. I'm unable to push the words past the lump in my throat.

"It's real, Grant," she says. "I'm pregnant."

"But ... how?" It's the only question I can think to ask because Avery can't get pregnant. What I'm looking at is impossible.

"Honestly, I don't know," she says. "My gynecologist thinks it's a miracle."

I continue to stare at the photo in a daze. A father. I'm going to be *a father*.

Me, Grant Wilson.

I'm going to be responsible for shaping a new life.

"Hey, breathe."

Avery's fingertips graze my cheek, and I realize I'm shaking. Words pour from my mouth in a jumbled mush of sound. "I don't ... I thought ... I mean ... wait, how long have you ..."

"Known?" The corners of her lips kick up into a pair of dimples. "A while. A little over two months."

I gawk at her. "And you're just telling me this *now?*"

"I wanted to make sure it was going to stick first." A sliver of fear flashes across her face and her lips firm. "It still might not. We're not out of the woods, yet."

"I still can't believe this," I say, rubbing my forehead. It must have happened in Napa. I relive the vacation in a flash of heat. Our honeymoon. A bougie, sun-splashed week full of luxury and four-star cuisine. And sex. Lots and lots of sex.

A laugh bubbles up her throat, and she wipes her eyes. "Oh, you'd better believe it. We're going to have a family."

"I'm going to be a dad," I mumble in a daze.

"Yes, you are," she says, laying her head on my shoulder. "Get ready."

When I don't move, she takes hold of my chin and pulls my face toward hers. "Hey, it's going to be fine. We're in this together. You're going to be a great father."

"You really think so?" I manage.

"Yes. Now, come on. I want to get this hike in while I still can."

She gets out, and I follow, the summer sun warming my skin the second I step outside. A gentle breeze ruffles my hair and drifts over my skin.

I'm going to be a father.

"Hey," Avery says, wagging a bottle of sunscreen at me from the other side of the car. "Can you help me with this?"

"Of course." I make my way over to her and she presses the bottle into my palm as she pulls her auburn hair over her shoulder. Besides her smile, her hair was the first thing I noticed when I bumped into her nearly a year ago. Hair so red it stole my breath. As did her eyes. They're this beautiful shade of light green I immediately lost myself in. One look, and I knew I was in trouble.

"Make sure you get my neck," she says.

I don't. I spin her around instead. She starts to protest, but I lean in and kiss her. Her lips soften, and we remain there, lost in each other for a blissful moment, until she places a hand on my chest and pushes me back with a grin. "Save your energy for the hike. There will be plenty of time for that later."

"Fine," I groan, but I don't step back. Instead, I reach up and brush my thumb over her cheek.

Her nose crinkles as she looks at me. "What?"

"I can't wait to do this with you."

"Well, let's go, then," she says, eyeing the trail.

"No." I lower my palm to her stomach and hold it there. *"This."*

She slides her fingers over mine. "Me too." With a final squeeze, she snatches the bottle of sunscreen and raises it. "Now put this on."

"Yes, ma'am," I say with a chuckle.

After I'm done, we circle to the back of the Jeep. Avery pops the hatch and swings it up. Lying inside is a backpack stuffed with several bottles of water, two bags of trail mix, and a pair of long-sleeved shirts for both of us in case any clouds blow in.

"Here." She tucks the car keys into the backpack and hands it to me. "This is yours to carry."

"Of course," I say, shouldering it. "So how many miles is this hike, anyway? Wait, are you even okay to hike? What did the doctor say about exercise?"

She rolls her eyes. "I'm pregnant. Women do it all the time. I'll be fine."

"I know. It's just—"

The sound of an engine cuts me off. We turn together in time to see a black van with tinted windows roll out of the trees. I groan. I knew this was coming; a place like this is far too beautiful to keep to ourselves. Still, I'd dared to hope.

"Let's get going," Avery says. "Maybe we can beat them up the trail."

I don't move. I simply stand there, staring at the van as it barrels toward us. It's paint-chipped and covered in rust, the shocks squealing as the tires bounce up and down. The sound is at odds with the peace of this place. And the vehicle is going fast. Too fast. A slash of annoyance cuts through me when it rips to a stop a few feet away, covering us in a thick plume of dust and exhaust.

I cover my mouth and cough. "What the hell?"

Avery takes my hand and tugs. "Seriously, let's go."

But I still don't move. For some reason, I can't stop staring at the idling vehicle with its battered, black body and dark windows. It's ugly and doesn't look like the kind of car a typical hiker would drive. Something about it feels wrong.

Avery pulls harder. "Grant …"

"Okay, yeah, this is getting weird." I'm about to turn and follow her, when the passenger side door bangs open, and a man steps out. He's big and dressed all in black. Black shoes, black pants, black shirt, black gloves. A black ski mask.

And in his hand, pointing at us, is a black gun.

CHAPTER 2

GRANT

My blood turns to ice. My existence becomes a series of micro-sensations: the gooseflesh rippling over my arms, every hair rising. The acrid smell of exhaust invading my nostrils and pooling at the root of my tongue. Avery's hand squeezing mine, my palm going slick with sweat.

The rattle and cough of the engine.

The waves of dread stitching up my spine.

Time as it slows and turns to syrup.

Questions rip through my head like bullets: What the fuck is happening? Who is this guy? And what does he want from us? Why is he standing *here* of all places, in the middle of this gorgeous natural oasis, holding a gun?

I don't have time to consider the answers before he says, "Get in the van."

"*What?*" I reply, stunned.

Through the mask, the man's eyes turn to slits. Blue eyes. Eyes that feel like icepicks as they narrow on me. "Are you deaf?" he asks. "I said, get in the van."

I glance at Avery in disbelief. Her eyes are blinking open and shut like she's taking little pictures, trying to work out what's happening one image at a time, her face pale.

"Why?" I ask, turning my attention back to the man.

He laughs but there's no humor in the sound, only menace. "How about we all sit down and I'll fill you in over a cup of coffee. Are you kidding me? Get in the fucking van or I'll shoot you both!"

A voice like speaker static hisses from the back of my mind: *Don't do it, Grant. Do it, and you're both dead.* Not that we have a choice. If we don't do what he says, he'll kill us. I'm positive he isn't bluffing. There's no good outcome here.

"Okay," I say, guiding Avery closer to me. "Just take it easy. We'll do what you say."

"Not you," he says, his gaze shifting from me to Avery. "Her."

Her. The word smashes through my skull like a cannonball. *He means Avery. This man intends to take my wife.*

I step in front of Avery and slowly raise my hands. "That's not happening."

"It's not up to you."

"She's not going anywhere without me."

"Grant ..." Avery whispers behind me, but I don't turn around. I keep my focus centered on the man.

"You're not taking her," I say.

He tilts his head and regards me, his eyes narrowing to two blue flames. His grip on the gun firms, and he steps forward and levels it at my head.

My eyes screw shut a second before he fires.

My ears explode. The sound that follows is like a power drill burning through my skull. A high, piercing shriek. One I shouldn't be able to hear because I should be dead. But I'm not.

I'm alive.

How am I still alive?

Because it was a warning shot. He must have moved the gun before he pulled the trigger.

My eyelids click open, and I try to make sense of what's happening.

The man is standing right in front of me now, barking words I can't hear through the ringing in my ears. His voice is a muffled throb. It's like he's standing above me, yelling down through ten feet of water.

I shake my head and try to clear the cobwebs. Pop my jaw. "I can't hear you," I say.

It does nothing. His eyes are two electric pools of anger. His entire body is a snarl. I vaguely register Avery's fingertips brushing my arm from behind. I can't let this man take her.

"Don't do this," I plead. "You can have our car. My wallet. Whatever you want, it's yours."

He shakes his head, his gaze coming to rest on Avery.

"No," I say. "*No.* Please listen to me. I can get you money if that's what you want. I just need—"

Before I know what's happening, he slams the butt of the revolver straight into my temple.

My head snaps toward my shoulder.

White lights wheel through my vision.

Sparks firework and hiss in my brain.

My knees buckle, and I crash down. My teeth clack together when I hit the ground, the taste of warm metal flooding my mouth. The tang of iron and copper. Flecks whirl through my vision, and I know I'm seconds away from passing out. But then I hear the scream and the world comes rushing back.

"Grant!"

Avery's scream.

I wince and roll over, see the man dragging her toward the van.

No, no, no, no ...

I plant one hand on the ground and force myself to my knees. Reality flickers in and out in waves. A sticky warmth covers my cheek. Blood. It doesn't matter. Not the fire raging in my temple or the nausea greasing my gut. Not the way I sway like a tree when I take to my feet and nearly topple over. The only thing that matters is saving Avery.

I lurch forward. I will kill this man. I will turn whatever face lies beneath his mask to pulp. I don't care if he shoots me. He's not taking my wife.

But then my vision clears, and I stop. He's no longer pointing the gun at me. He's pointing it at Avery, the barrel planted squarely against the side of her head.

My rage snuffs out in an instant. I raise my palms in a silent plea. Because I know that this man, whoever he is, is capable of violence. He's already proven it. I have no doubt he'll pull the trigger if I take another step.

"Take me," I beg.

The man doesn't say anything. He just stares at me with two ice-colored eyes that look like shards of glass ready to cut. And then he speaks: "Don't follow us. Don't contact the police. Go back to your Airbnb and you'll receive further instructions. If you go anywhere else, or you tell anyone about what happened here"—his eyes tick toward Avery—"we'll kill her. You have one hour. Don't make us wait."

We. Us. Because someone else is driving. I didn't even register that fact until now. All of my logic washed away the second this man stepped out of the van holding death in his hand. I peer past him and try to see who's behind the wheel but all I can make out is the vague outline of someone else.

"Toss your phone into the van," the man orders.

With shaking fingers, I pull it from my pocket and lob it through the open door. The gun swings from Avery's temple and comes to rest on me before arcing right. He fires twice: *Crack! Crack!* One of the tires on the Jeep explodes.

When I look back to Avery, she's pressing a hand to her belly.
Oh god, the baby.

The thought is like a switchblade planted between my eyes—a bright splinter of pure panic. Because whoever these people are, they aren't just taking my wife.

They're also taking my child.

My eyes lock with Avery's. Tears stream down her cheeks. Her face is bone white. She says something I can't hear over the roar of the engine as the man pulls her inside. But I recognize the words. I see them in the way her mouth widens and the tip of her tongue lightly taps her upper row of her teeth. I feel them in the shape of her lips when they round into a soft O a second before the door slams shut.

I love you.

And then she's gone.

CHAPTER 3

GRANT

I run after the van, my eyes hungry for a license plate, or anything I might be able to use to identify the vehicle later. Any distinguishing marks or scratches. There's none. The back of the van is all dirt and rust, the bumper bare metal—no plate. And then it's gone, disappearing into the trees.

I stop and suck air, feeling like my bones will turn to gelatin, like my organs will dissolve, and I'll splash to the earth as a gutless sack of meat.

This isn't happening, this isn't happening, this isn't happening …
But it *is* happening.

My wife is gone, and my child is gone. The child I didn't know I had until this morning—everything I love in this world, ripped away from me in the span of a few minutes by a stranger wearing a black mask.

And you can't stand here a second longer thinking about it!

My body comes to life. I move. I sprint for the Jeep and climb inside. Go for the keys—which aren't there. *Shit, where are they?* My mind vapor locks. I scan the cup holders, the dash, yank open the glove box, and stop. Avery was driving. She had them.

And they have her.

Oh, god.

My heart slams against my ribs. I can't breathe. Can't think.

And then I remember.

The backpack! She put them in the backpack!

I spot it through the windshield, the lime-green Osprey day pack lying on the ground right where the man knocked me down.

Go! Go! Go!

I push back through the door, race toward it, and tear it open with shaking hands. My fingertips are numb as I rip the zippers down and peel the compartments wide. I yank out the bags of trail mix and bottles of water, pull free a bunch of electrolyte pouches and granola bars, searching for the only thing that counts. The one thing that isn't there.

The keys. Where are the keys?

Behind me, the thrum of the van's engine fades in a series of burps and gurgles. When it snuffs out entirely, I'm overcome by a wave of panic that threatens to blow every fuse in my brain and send me spiraling into a full-on mental breakdown.

Find them!

I grab the bag and turn it over, shaking it until the key fob falls from a side pocket and hits the ground, I cry out in relief and take it. Then I'm sprinting back to the Jeep as fast as my legs will carry me. I leap into the driver's seat, slam the door, and stab the ignition button. The engine roars to life. My hands hit the steering wheel, my foot the gas pedal—and I smash it down.

The Jeep surges forward with a violent shudder. The hood lurches right. I fight for control and ease off the gas.

The tire! Shit!

I punch the dash so hard it bloodies my knuckles. If I still had my phone, I might be able to find a signal and call for help, tell someone what happened to Avery. But even if I could make a call, I wouldn't. The man with the ice for eyes was no liar. That much was blindingly clear. He was telling the truth. He'll kill my wife if I contact anyone else—especially the police. Of that, I have no doubt.

And I have an hour. That's it. One single hour to make it back to the Airbnb on three tires instead of four. An hour is what it took for us to reach this place. So how the fuck am I supposed to make it back to the rental in that amount of time with a flat? Sure, I could change it if I had a spare, but I don't. I used it to repair a flat last year and, like an idiot, never put the spare back in the trunk. It's lying on a storage rack in my garage, covered in boxes, completely useless.

Which leaves the option of running—tearing through the meadow and sprinting down the mountain like a madman. I want to. I nearly do. But even in my heightened state of anxiety, I know it would be a foolish choice. I'll never make it, not without stopping for breaks. No, the Jeep is still my best, and fastest, bet to reach the highway. I need to drive.

So I do, and it's maddening how slow I have to go as I roll through the meadow and back into the forest. How carefully. Every time I press the gas too hard, the steering wheel jerks to the right and jars my hands. Every time I hit a bump or a rut, the Cherokee vibrates and rattles like a bomb exploded beneath the chassis. It's all I can do to keep the car from plowing straight into a tree.

It can't happen. If it does, I'll never reach the highway. My heart claws at my ribs in panic. There's no way I'll get back to the Airbnb in time, but it's not like I have another choice. All I can do is drive.

And drive. And drive. And drive.

The world outside passes by in a perpetual loop of branches, road, trees, and sky. The mountains leer through the leaves, no longer looking majestic but sinister. A jagged row of hulking giants watching as I crawl ever down. I barely see them. All I can think about is my wife.

Images fill my mind. Avery, lying bound on the floor of the van with her ankles and wrists knotted in thick coils of rope. Avery, crying through a grease-soaked gag for help as the man in the mask crouches above her and tells her to shut her mouth. The harsh smack of his palm against her cheek when she doesn't. Avery shaking her head as he tears off her shirt, her pants ...

An avalanche of goosebumps pours down my arms. *Jesus.* Avery doesn't possess a mean bone in her body. She doesn't deserve this. She's the best person I know. A kind person. *My* person. And someone else has her now. Why?

I drive faster, my anxiety hitting DEFCON 1 levels. Blood hammers my ears. The axles squeal and grind. Every bump in the road feels like a mountain, every rut a canyon. I don't know how much longer the bare metal rim beneath the flat tire will stay in a circle, but I pray it lasts long enough for me to reach the highway.

Because I'm coming, Avery. I'm coming.

The road splits and then splits again. At this point, I have no idea which way the van went, much less know which way I should go. I scrub my memory for landmarks, for any detail I recognize. A broken branch or a stray pile of rocks. Something that will tell me I'm going the right way.

There's nothing. The only thing I remember from the trip up is the burned-out cabin. That's it, and I already passed it miles ago. Now everything is an endless parade of trees, dirt, rocks, and sky. Like on the way up here, there's no one around, no cars, no one to flag down and beg for a ride. Only the forest thick with pine trees and the never-ending dirt road in front of me that's barely a road at all. It doesn't matter. Nothing matters except getting down.

The corners are the worst. Each one is a monumental effort spent white-knuckling the steering wheel and jamming the brakes—which are getting spongier by the second. I ignore them and coax the Jeep lower foot by miserable foot. I practically coo at it, telling the car it can do this, whispering that it's strong enough, fast enough. I need the distraction, need to focus on anything other than the scent of burning rubber and metal. It's the smell of death. *Avery's* death if I can't get back to the Airbnb in time.

One hour. That's all I have.

And it's already been twenty minutes.

My temple throbs. Blood drips down my neck and warms the collar of my shirt. A headache thunders at the base of my skull. I probably have a concussion, but I'll live. And my injury is the least of my concerns right now. My mind is locked on one thing and one thing only: what will happen to Avery if I can't reach the house in time? I don't know the answer. But I do know this: it won't be good. And it will be my fault.

Stop it, I tell myself. *Focus.*

That's all I can do. Focus. If I do anything else, I'll wind up stranded on the side of the road or overturned in a ditch. And then I see it—a thin strip of gray asphalt curling through the trees like a miracle. It's a sight that fills me with a desperate hope.

The highway.

I hammer the gas and push the Jeep faster, skidding around the corners, ignoring the gyrations in the steering wheel. The hood bucks up and down through the windshield, obscuring my view. It feels like I'm in the middle of a rodeo, doing everything I can to remain on top of the angry bull. The car won't last much longer at this pace, but I don't care. If I wreck, I'll bail out and leave the thing behind. From here, I can run.

That's the thought that barrels through my head—*You made it down, you did it, Grant!*—as I round the final corner, going so fast I don't register the fact that the brakes are no longer working until it's too late.

CHAPTER 4

GRANT

I rocket toward the highway—and the semi-truck that I can tell doesn't see me yet.

It won't see me until I clear the trees. *Oh fuck, oh fuck,* I think, slamming the brake pedal to the floor. It's useless. I'll be obliterated in another thirty feet. I need to find another way to slow down, I need to—

Down shift!

My hand hits the gearshift a millisecond after the thought. The engine whines as the RPMs kick higher. I shift again—from second gear to first. And then I'm ripping onto the asphalt and cranking the steering wheel right. The nose of the Jeep kicks two feet into the lane before I'm able to wrestle the vehicle onto the shoulder. A horn bellows as the semi roars past in a massive rush of wind, so close it leaves the vehicle shaking.

It's shaking like I'm shaking. *Holy shit.*

The Jeep drifts to a stop, and I put it in park and sit there gripping the steering wheel so hard my fingers leave indents in the rubber. I nearly just died. But I didn't. I'm somehow still alive, and I need to find a way back to the Airbnb ASAP. I need to get out and flag down a car for a ride. I'm about to do exactly that—my hand drifting toward the door—when motion in the rearview mirror catches my attention. Relief pours through me.

Police lights. A cop. They can help—

The relief vanishes in an instant. *Don't contact the police.*

Fuck!

I stare at the cruiser as the door cracks open and the cop gets out. He's tall with brown hair and wide shoulders. He strolls my way, touching the Jeep's trunk when he passes, taking note of the car. By the time he reaches me, I've already got my window down.

"Close call there," he says, leaning in. "You okay?"

"Yes," I manage, even though my heart is beating in my throat.

"You don't look okay. You're bleeding."

"What? Where? I—"

"By your ear."

I finger the spot and remember the warmth I felt dripping down my face after being pistol whipped.

"Oh that. Yeah, I ... must have hit my head when I swerved out of the way of that semi. I didn't realize it was bleeding, though. Must have hit it harder than I realized. But I'm okay."

"You sure?" he asks, taking stock of me. "That's a pretty decent cut."

"Yeah, fine."

"What happened there, anyway?" the cop asks.

"My front tire blew out."

He glances at it, then looks back. "You hit a pothole or something?"

I run a hand over my face and try to swallow my anxiety. This is already taking way too long. "Honestly, I'm not sure. It was fine one minute, gone the next."

"Yeah, that can happen sometimes. These mountain roads get hairy. Where you coming from?"

"I was ..." I stop, don't finish the sentence—*on a hike with my wife.* The one thing I can't do is bring up Avery while talking to this guy, and here I am about to do exactly that in the space of a few minutes. I take a breath and start again. "Just on a hike."

He flattens his lips, his eyes ticking toward the glove box. "License, registration, and insurance, please."

Feeling sick, I retrieve them and pass them through the window. He takes them and examines my license.

"Grant Wilson—that you?"

"Yes," I say, gritting my teeth. I really need this guy to move it along.

You have anything to drink today, Mr. Wilson?"

"Jesus, what? No. I told you I was on a hike. That's it. And I'm in a bit of a hurry."

His eyebrows stitch together, and I mentally kick myself.

Keep your cool, Grant, you idiot. The last thing you need to do right now is piss this guy off.

For a second, I think it's too late—that he's about to ask me to step out of the vehicle for a roadside sobriety test, but instead he says, "Hang tight. I'll be right back."

And then he's gone, slowly striding back toward his cruiser. I watch him go, pulling a sliver of cheek between my teeth to keep from screaming. I know *right back* means ten minutes at least. Probably longer. He'll have to enter all of my information into his computer system and make sure everything checks out. Which it will. Of course, it will. But that doesn't change the fact that every second he takes doing it is another second I'm stuck sitting here on the side of the road instead of getting back to the Airbnb like I'm supposed to.

Not that I can do that anyway—because the Jeep is completely fucked.

Just like me.

I watch five minutes tick past and then another ten before the officer returns. He hands me the documents.

"Okay, you're all good. But I'm going to need you to call a tow truck. This thing is undriveable. There's no way you'll get a new tire on that rim. Looks like you dinged it up pretty bad. I'll wait with you until the tow gets here. Make sure traffic sees you."

"No," I reply a little too fast. "I don't have time for that. I really need to get home."

"Like I said, you can't drive your car like this."

I fucking know that! I want to shout. *My wife was just abducted!* I clench and unclench my fists. "Here's the deal, Officer ..."

"Gunn."

I stare at him wordlessly. *Gunn?* Because of course I'm talking to a cop named after his weapon. It would almost be funny in any other situation, but right now it only adds to my growing sense of unease. A quick glance at the dash tells me it's 1:23 p.m. It was right around 12:40 when I left. I have exactly seventeen minutes left to get back to the rental.

"Officer Gunn, I can't wait here. I need to call an Uber or a taxi."

He chuckles. "Yeah, you won't find transportation like that up here. You'll need to wait for a tow."

Tendrils of panic slide through my chest. I rage at him silently. *Goddammit!* Things can't get any worse than this. But they can. The voice of the man in the mask scrapes through my head. *Don't contact the police. Tell anyone what happened, and we'll kill her.* I need to jar this guy out of standard operating procedure, and I need to do it *now*. But I can't unload on him. If I do, I'll wind up in a jail cell and Avery will wind up dead. Which means the only option I have left is to lie.

"Look," I say, "the truth is I'm on vacation with my sister. She's back at our rental, and she called me and said she isn't feeling well. That's why I was driving so fast. I need to get back to the house and make sure she's okay. It's a bit of an emergency."

"Want me to send an ambulance over?"

Heat floods my cheeks. "No, don't do that. She's ... not well."

"Yeah, like you just said."

I clench my jaw. "Mentally, I mean. She has … problems. If you send an ambulance to the house, it will freak her out. She might hurt herself." The lies are flowing quicker now, piling up faster than I can handle. I need to wrap this up before it gets too tangled. "So that's why I can't wait around for a tow."

He massages his chin which is seeded in scruff, his mud-colored gaze pinned on me. I know he's analyzing me, assessing whether or not I'm telling the truth. It takes every ounce of my willpower not to look away.

Finally, he sighs. "I just had to land traffic duty today, didn't I? Listen, I'll give you a ride if you promise to call a tow truck on the way. You can't leave your car up here like it is. It's a safety hazard."

The offer hits me like a cinder block to the face. I have to take him up on it—I don't have another choice—but there's no way I can roll up to the Airbnb in a police car. They might be watching.

They could be watching now.

They might already know I'm talking to a cop. Jesus. I have zero idea what I'm up against. But I can't sit here with my thumb up my ass and wait for a tow truck to show up, either. I need to go, and I need to go right now.

With a shaky breath, I get out of the Jeep.

CHAPTER 5

GRANT

"Is this the right house?" Officer Gunn asks.

I nod. It is, and it's a miracle I even remembered it. I didn't give him a fake address when he asked. I wasn't able to look one up without my phone, which I said I forgot in the Jeep. I had to borrow his to call the goddamn tow truck. And even if I had been able to come up with a different spot for him to drop me off, it wouldn't have worked. I don't have the time. It's 1:46 p.m. and I'm already six minutes late. All I can do is pray no one is watching the place, because if they are …

Don't go there, I tell myself. *Just get inside.*

"Thanks," I say to Gunn, moving to get out.

"Why don't I come check on your sister and make sure she's okay?"

"No," I say a little too quickly. "No, she'll be fine now that I'm here. Thanks again for the ride." And then I'm gone, pushing out of the cruiser and sprinting up the driveway toward the door—which is wide open.

And not just open. The glass panes are shattered along with the sidelights, the wood splintered, the frame bowed like someone kicked it in.

Because someone did, I realize with a chill. That's exactly what happened.

What's inside is worse.

I stop the second I enter, too stunned to move. The couch is shredded. Ribbons of stuffing foam through gills cut into the cushions. The ottoman is overturned, the coffee table broken. The floor is strewn in a violent constellation of shattered glass. But that isn't what holds my attention. What immediately draws my gaze is the long crimson arrow glistening on the carpet, pointing toward the hall.

Blood. That's all I can think as I move closer to it. They painted the carpet with Avery's blood. *Oh god.* And then the fumes hit—harsh and sharp—and I exhale in relief. Not blood. Spray paint. And fresh. Whoever did this hasn't been gone for long—if they're gone at all.

"What happened here?"

I nearly jump out of my skin at the voice. When I spin around, I see Gunn pushing inside with a frown. I look behind him, and the sight of his squad car still parked in the street sends me spiraling. It can't be out there, and he can't be in here. *Fuck.*

"I don't know," I manage to stutter.

"Where's your sister?" he asks.

His question doesn't register for a moment, but then I remember my cover story. "I'm ... not sure."

He squints at me and then the arrow. The squint deepens. He draws his weapon and edges past me. "Stay here."

I don't. I drift after him instead, both of us moving into the hall, where more arrows soak the carpet. But not just the carpet. They're painted on the walls and ceiling as well. Dozens of them—every one angling toward the master bedroom at the end of the hall. The door is shut, spray-painted with a bright red X that ties my throat in a knot.

What does it mean? Is Avery lying behind that door?

Gunn slows and places a single finger to his lips as I near, his face pure stone. I can tell he's pissed I followed him, but I don't care. Whatever lies inside is too important to miss.

Don't move, he mouths as he turns the doorknob.

I nod.

He thrusts the door open and disappears inside, sweeping his gun left to right. He's only gone for a few seconds, but it feels like ten minutes have passed by the time he returns. His face is still grim, his eyes wide and alert, but he's no longer on edge like he was a moment ago.

He holsters his gun and steps aside. "It's clear. No one's in here. But you need to see this."

I move past him and freeze for the second time since walking into the house. A phone lies in the center of the bed, outlined in a blood-red circle. Above it, painted in all caps on the duvet, is an order.

DIAL THE NUMBER.

"What the hell is going on here?" Gunn asks.

I ignore him and snap up the phone. When I do, I realize that despite the demanding words bleeding all over the comforter, I don't know what number to call. I'm missing something. I scan the bed-spread again and spot the business card. It's lying where the phone was a second earlier. I grab it and stare at the ten digits stamped on the front in black ink—a phone number. That's it. Nothing else.

Gunn takes a step closer, the crease between his eyes now so deep it might as well be a canyon. "You need to level with me right now, Grant. What's going on?"

"Listen to me," I hiss. "I'll explain everything in a second. But I have to make this call first, and the person on the other end of the line cannot know you are here. Because if they do, they're going to hurt someone very important to me."

It stings as I say it. Gunn shouldn't be here. There could be cameras in the house. Avery's abductors could be watching us right now. Hell, they could be hiding *in* the house for all I know. Or seconds away from shooting my wife. There are too many variables to consider at this point, and the only one I control is still clutched in my hand.

"Put it on speaker," Gunn says as I punch in the number.

"Not a word," I reiterate, glaring at him. "Not a sound."

He nods, and I hit the call button.

The phone rings twice before a voice fills the line. It's deep and gruff, mechanical, two words spilling through the speaker like gargled rocks.

"You're late."

CHAPTER 6

"Where is she? Where's my wife?" The words burn up my throat with hot urgency.

No reply comes. My pulse thumps hard in my ears. "Answer me!"

Officer Gunn raises a hand and levels it with his chest, then lowers it an inch. The message is clear. *Stay calm.*

When the response finally comes, it's distorted, full of static. "Why are you late?"

I grit my teeth, my rage rising. This is the asshole who ripped my wife away from me at gunpoint along with my unborn child—a baby that's no less than a miracle. The same man who shot my tire and gave me the impossible task of getting back here in one hour. And now he's asking why I'm late? If I could reach through the phone and strangle him, I would. But Gunn is right. I can't do anything that will further endanger Avery. So, I force myself to dial it back a notch. "You made it difficult. Put my wife on the line."

"You aren't the one in control here. You don't give the orders."

"What do you want?"

"Four million."

"What?"

"If you want to see your wife again, you will transfer four million dollars to the account listed on the back of the card in the next five minutes."

My knees buckle. It feels like I've been punched. So, it *is* about money. "I ... don't have access to that kind of cash."

"Agreed, you have access to three point nine million, to be exact."

I stand there reeling, fighting for balance. He shouldn't know this. No one should. A while back, Avery and I had decided to transfer most of our retirement into Bitcoin and Ethereum. It was a risky move, but we'd both agreed crypto was the future of finance—a decentralized system not controlled by massive institutions that can fail at any moment. A bet that cryptocurrency was not only safer than the stock market, but here to stay and would allow us to retire years sooner than we would be able to otherwise. A bet that had already gone wildly in our favor.

And someone found out.

I swallow hard and flip the card over. There's a QR code printed on the back.

Gunn watches me with wide eyes as the voice drawls on, impossibly deep. "Scan the code with the phone, log in to your account, and transfer the funds."

"I need to talk to Avery first. How do I know she's safe?"

"You have four minutes."

Shit. My brain goes into overdrive. It's not as simple as that. I can't just log in and transfer the money. The account requires dual-factor authentication, which means a code will be sent to my email or my phone to verify I'm the one who's actually signing on. It's not usually a big deal, but I don't have my phone. My phone is gone.

But my laptop isn't.

I search for it and spot it resting on the side table. I'm about to move for it when Gunn steps in front of me and mimes covering the phone. When I do, he leans in and whispers, "You can't do this. There's no guarantee they'll release your wife if you give them what they want. If they get the cash, there's a good chance they'll kill her anyway. You need to stall until I can get my people involved. You're the one with the leverage here. Don't give it away."

It's true—I am. I have what they want. But they have what I need, what I literally can't live without. I move my hand and speak into the phone. "Can we slow down for a minute and talk about this? Just let me speak to Avery first. How do I know she's still alive?"

"Mr. Wilson," the voice says, "I fear you aren't taking this situation seriously enough. Let me assure you that if you don't transfer the money in the next three minutes, I will fill your wife's head with every bullet left in my gun."

"If you do, you won't get a cent."

"Do you think you're special?" the voice snaps back. "We have a long list of targets. You're only one of them. We'll simply kill your wife and move on. Go ahead and test me. Find out what happens."

My heart stops. "Okay, okay. Give me a second."

I move. I push past Gunn toward the laptop and hit the power button. The machine whirs, taking an impossibly long time to load before the screen blinks and comes to life. I raise the business card and bring the QR code into focus through the phone's camera, then click on the link that pops up. The exchange appears on the cellphone's screen. I enter my credentials and, as I expected, am required to confirm my account. I open Chrome on my laptop and surf to Gmail. The message is waiting for me, looking sinister in my inbox. *Click this button to confirm your device.*

"Two minutes," the voice says.

A hand hits my shoulder. I startle and find Gunn staring at me with eyes that are wide in warning. He shakes his head. *Don't do this.*

But I have to. It isn't his wife who was abducted. It isn't his child whose life is on the line. He doesn't have anything to lose, unlike me. Right now, my entire world hangs in the balance. And if I don't do this, it could all be wiped away in an instant.

I click the button to confirm the phone and my account loads: $3,886,554.23. A transfer window appears a second later—one populated with a crypto wallet string I don't recognize. A series of digital characters ready to swallow every cent Avery and I have ever worked for.

I type in the amount, bring my thumb toward the green transfer button, and hesitate. Once I do this, once I submit the transfer, I'll never be able to recover the funds. Transferring crypto isn't the same as sending a wire. With a wire you can sometimes get your money back if needed. Not with Bitcoin or Ethereum. Once you send crypto to someone, it's gone. And as Gunn pointed out, so is my leverage.

"One minute," the voice says. "Transfer the money."

I close my eyes and swallow. I can't do it. Not yet. I have to know. "Put my wife on the phone."

"Forty seconds. Transfer the funds."

"No, not until I speak to Avery." My ribs tighten as I say it. But I have to know. I *have* to.

"You're playing a very dangerous game, Mr. Wilson. I won't ask again."

"And I won't transfer a fucking dime if you don't let me talk to my wife first!" The words pour out of me in a hot rush, my rage resurfacing, my absolute frustration at how powerless I am right now. But I won't send them a cent until I know she's still alive. "Put her on!"

The line goes silent, and my world turns to molasses. Every second that passes feels like a noose cinching tighter around Avery's neck. And not just hers, but mine too. Because if this doesn't work, if this man doesn't let me speak to her, if he actually carries through with his threat to kill her, I'll never forgive myself. I'll never be able to let it go.

No response comes. His breath leaks through the phone in a distorted hiss.

In. Out. In. Out. In.

My heart rages in my chest. My head swells with panic.

Put her on! Put her on! Put her on!

Finally, a sharp rustling sound floods the phone and I hear a new voice. "G-Grant ... is that you?" The tone is frail and broken—a feather lost in a gust of wind—but it's Avery's. Relief pours through me. She's alive, and I still have a chance to save her.

"Are you okay?" I ask, my voice shaking. "Did they hurt you?"

"Grant, I'm so scared."

"I'm going to find you, baby. I swear I'm not going to let them—"

A rattle cuts me off, followed by a choking gasp, then the robotic voice is back, slicing straight into my ear. "There. Now transfer the *fucking* money!"

And I do.

CHAPTER 7

But not all of the money.

"It's done," I say.

A cold silence fills the line. Then: "This isn't the amount we agreed on."

"We didn't agree on anything," I hiss.

"Your wife is dead."

A wave of pure terror rolls down my spine. "Wait—*wait!*" I plead. "I'll give you the rest, but not before I get Avery back alive." It's a gamble. A hedge they don't actually have the long list of abduction targets lined up they say they do. Compared to my wife, the money means absolutely nothing. I'd gladly transfer every dollar if it meant getting Avery back safe—which is the problem. That *if.* Gunn is right. There's no guarantee that will happen. And now that I've given them a million and a half, they know I'll play ball. They'll want the rest.

Sweat beads on my forehead as I wait for his reply. My entire world will come down to what he says next.

After what feels like an eternity, he speaks. "Fine. We are not unreasonable people. We will provide you with a location. You will meet us at this location in exactly thirty minutes. Once you are there, you will transfer the remainder of your account to us. If you give us the money, we will return your wife unharmed."

The floor rocks beneath my feet, and I nearly topple over. It worked.

"But listen carefully," the voice drones, impossibly deep. "The same rules apply. If you tell anyone about this, if you contact the authorities or try to seek help in any way, your wife dies. If you don't transfer the rest of the money when you get to the location we provide, your wife will die. If you're late to the exchange, your wife dies. This time, there will be no second chances."

"Hold on," I say, trying to stall, but it's too late; the line is already dead.

Gunn is staring at me when I look up, the corners of his eyes creased with concern. "You need to level with me right now."

I take a deep breath and attempt to swallow my panic. At this point there's no longer any reason to lie, not when he's already involved. I speak rapidly, moving through the day as quickly as I can, starting with the van. I tell him about the men inside and how they assaulted me and took Avery. I tell him how they told me to return here within an hour and then made it next to impossible by shooting out the front tire of my Jeep. And then I tell him how they forbade me to talk to the police.

"Which is why I lied to you in the first place," I finish. "You aren't supposed to know any of this."

His mouth widens in reply, but before he can speak the phone vibrates in my palm. I glance at the screen. A text message. It's a location pin. I tap it, and Google Maps opens to a blue and green square full of topography and squiggled roads. I pass the phone to Gunn. "Where is this?"

He studies it for a moment, flattening his lips in concentration. "Mason's Quarry. I know the place. It's condemned. A party spot for the kids." He hands the phone back to me and it buzzes with another text. Two words: Thirty minutes. It's two o'clock on the nose. I show Gunn. Then I start past him.

He grabs my elbow. "Wait. I need to call this in first."

I shake free, heat flooding my cheeks. "Did you not hear a word I said? You can't do that!"

"I already did."

"When?" I ask, stunned.

"When I saw your front door was kicked in. But one extra cop won't be enough to handle a situation like this."

"They'll kill her for sure." I suddenly feel unsteady on my feet.

Gunn claps his hand on my shoulder. "Hey, stay with me. They won't. These guys aren't that sophisticated. Think about it. If they were, they'd already know I was here. But they didn't. Which means no one has eyes on us right now. And they damaged your car, which made it more difficult for you to do what they wanted. They obviously haven't fully thought this through. They sound like amateurs. But amateurs can still be dangerous. We need backup."

"We don't have time to wait for backup!"

"We don't have to." Gunn nods at the window, and I turn in time to see another squad car pulling into the driveway. Despite what he said, this new development rattles me. Gunn's probably right. Avery's kidnappers must not be surveilling the house, but seeing this second cruiser feels like setting off a smoke signal and screaming for them to take notice. I'm so lost in the thought it takes me a moment to realize Gunn is still talking about radioing in for more support. More cops.

I spin to face him. "No! This is my wife we're talking about here. They might be amateurs, but you didn't see the guy who took Avery. If we roll up to this place in a bunch of squad cars, they'll kill her for sure!"

I blow past him and this time he doesn't try to stop me. The second cop is climbing out of his car when I walk outside.

"Grant," Gunn says, hurrying to catch up. "This is Officer Holston."

He's young, early twenties if I were to guess, with close-cropped blond hair and muscular arms. I nod at him, but the kid doesn't return the gesture. He just glares. And something about his eyes makes me shiver. They're flat and empty.

"What's the situation?" he asks, turning to Gunn.

"I'll explain on the way," Gunn says. "Leave your car. We'll take mine. Come on."

"Where we going?" Holston asks.

"Did I not just say I'll explain on the way? Now move your ass."

Holston grumbles something about Gunn being the boss and follows us toward Gunn's cruiser. We get in. Gunn and Holston take the front while I slip into the back. I search for the clock the second Gunn cranks the engine. It glows to life on the dash: 2:03 p.m. We have twenty-seven minutes, and I already feel the weight of every single one. We need to *go*.

Gunn reaches for the radio instead.

I lean forward in alarm. "Don't! They could have a police scanner."

"They would have heard me before if they did," Gunn replies.

"It doesn't matter," I say, noting the silver band on Gunn's ring finger. "I don't want to put Avery in any more danger than she's already in. I can see you're married. What would you do if it were your wife in this situation? Would you be willing to risk her life on an assumption, too?"

Gunn hesitates.

"My wife is pregnant," I add. "It's too dangerous."

He returns the radio to the dash. The clock reads 2:05 p.m.

"Will someone tell me what the hell is going on?" Holston asks.

"We have a hostage situation," Gunn replies. "This man's wife was abducted earlier today."

"Wow, seriously?"

I can't help but note the excitement in the kid's voice, like Gunn just told him today was Christmas morning instead of the worst day of my life.

"Yes, we need to get to Mason's Quarry by two-thirty for an

exchange." He hits the gas, and we tear down the street. "Who else is on shift today besides us?"

"Only John. Craig's off."

"Shit," Gunn mutters. "What about Mark?"

"Mark's on PTO this week. Disneyland with the family."

Gunn shakes his head. "Call dispatch. Have Cathy get ahold of John and tell him to get his ass up to the quarry. Same with Craig. I don't care what he's doing."

I tense. "You just said you wouldn't call it in."

"I didn't say shit," Gunn replies, his eyes catching mine in the rearview mirror. "Look, I won't use the radio, but there's no way I'm not alerting the station. We aren't trained for this kind of thing. We're a small department. We're going to need as much support as we can get." His gaze shifts to Holston. "Make the call. Tell Cathy to keep it off the air. Have her use her phone. Tell her John and Craig need to bring their personal vehicles. No squad cars. And tell her they need to call your mobile as soon as they're on their way."

Holston pulls out his cellphone and dials, and I sit there hyperventilating as he relays what Gunn said. By the time he hangs up, he's wearing a frown. "Bad news. Craig's up at Alta Lake fishing. He's completely out of pocket. Cathy said she can probably get John to the quarry, but he's right in the middle of a nasty domestic at the moment. She said it's going to be a bit."

The back of Gunn's neck reddens. "Fuck."

"What's the plan? Do we wait?" Holston asks.

"No. We go to the quarry. But we make a stop first."

My eyes hit the clock again: 2:08 p.m. "We don't have time to make a stop!"

Gunn glances over his shoulder. "You said it yourself. We can't go up there in a cop car. We need to switch it out. My house is close. Same with the quarry. We'll make it if we hurry."

It takes another five minutes to reach Gunn's house, which is a white one-story ranch tucked away in a neighborhood right off the highway. The place is set a ways back from the road, so I'm thankful when he tells me the GMC Yukon parked on the street is his. It means we won't need to waste time pulling it out of the garage.

We swap cars, and by the time we're in the Yukon, it's 2:16 and my mind is nothing more than a fuse burning toward 2:30. Fourteen minutes left.

"How far away is this place?" I ask as Gunn smokes back onto the highway.

He lays on the horn and tears around a truck blocking our path. "About ten minutes. I know it pretty well. Here's what's going to happen. When we get to the quarry, Officer Holston and I are going to get out. The pin they dropped is in the middle of a clearing overlooking the pit. There's cover nearby, a bunch of trees where we can take position. Grant, we'll get out, and you'll keep driving. The clearing is easy to see. You can't miss it. If they ask you where you got the car, lie to them. Say you stole it. Whatever. I don't think it will matter to these guys as long as they get their money. As soon as you have your wife, we'll take them down."

My eyes burn as he continues to speak, the highway turning to a blurry strip of asphalt through the windshield. I'm running on fumes at this point, barely able to focus. All I can think about, all I keep seeing, is Avery's expression and the way her lips moved with those final words as she was ripped into the van. *I love you.*

"Hey, it's going to be okay," Gunn says, looking at me in the rear-view mirror. "We won't let them get away with this. I promise."

I can only nod and pray he's right.

CHAPTER 8

We arrive with five minutes to spare, the SUV skidding to a stop in front of a fence with a yellow metal sign tacked to it that reads:

**WARNING
THIS PROPERTY IS CONDEMNED.
KEEP OUT!**

The gate hangs open, a lock dangling uselessly from a chain around the post.

"Looks like they're already here," Gunn says, taking note. "This is the only way in or out." He eases the Yukon forward and then brakes once he's past the fence. "No word from John yet?"

Holston shakes his head. "Nothing."

"Shit. Okay. You have your service weapon?"

Holston pulls the gun from his holster in answer.

"Good," Gunn says. "Let's go."

We get out, and I slip into the driver's seat as Gunn pulls open the hatch and grabs something. When he appears through the open passenger door he's holding a hunting rifle.

A slug of dread hits me. "What's that for?" I ask.

"To protect you and your wife if this doesn't go right." He points up the road. "The quarry is just over that ridge. Officer Holston will take a position behind those boulders there while I flank west into the trees. Grant, you keep driving and head for the clearing." He turns his attention to Holston. "Calvin, if this turns ugly, cover Grant. And if you see anyone coming back down that road but him, you stop them, understand?"

Holston nods.

Gunn's gaze narrows. "We arrest them if we can, but if they don't comply, you do whatever you need to do. The training wheels are off on this one. These people cannot get away."

Holston's face firms. "They won't. I'm ready for this."

"You better be. Now move!"

Holston spins around and nearly trips before racing up the road in a half crouch.

"You're going to need to delay them for a few minutes," Gunn says, eyeing me again. "I need some time to get into position. Shouldn't take long. Think you can do that?"

"Yes," I say, even though I have no clue how I will.

"Good. Now listen. If you see anything going sideways. If they look like they're going to hurt your wife, rub the back of your neck and I'll try to take them out. But Grant, if that happens, you need to get to her and then find cover. You cannot hesitate. I probably won't be able to tag them both, at least not right away."

"Got it." He doesn't need to say it. I won't hesitate. Not when it comes to Avery. "What about a gun? Should I take one?"

He shakes his head. "No. We don't want them to have any reason to view you as a threat. Don't worry. I'll be watching." He checks his watch. "Okay, you gotta go." He leans into the car and places a hand on my shoulder and gives it a squeeze. "You've got this."

An unexpected wave of gratitude rolls over me. The man doesn't have to be doing this. He's potentially putting his career—and his life—on the line. All to help me save Avery.

"Thank you," I say. "I owe you one."

His eyes soften. "No, you don't. I've got a wife and kids of my own. If I were in your shoes, I'd want someone to do the same thing." A hint of a smile plays over his lips. "But I will let you buy me a beer afterward."

I issue a single, nervous laugh. "Deal."

"Now go," he says. And then he's gone, hustling away with the rifle and vanishing into the trees.

I put the Yukon into gear and drive. Gravel crunches beneath the tires. A soft breeze drifts through the window as I grip the steering wheel and climb the road. When I pass Holston, he gives me a single nod. He doesn't look nearly as frightened as I feel, seems almost excited in a way, like he's looking forward to this. Something about his posture reminds me of a wolf stalking its prey—head low, weight shifted forward. He's probably been waiting for a moment like this where he thinks he can make his mark when in reality it could easily get him killed.

Don't be a hero, kid, I think.

I crest the hill and he slips from my mind, swallowed by the view. To the left of the road lies a vast open pit. Cliffs like teeth jut skyward from a table of unnaturally blue water far below. Piles of stone surround it along with mounds of gravel. The pit is so massive it looks like God himself reached down and tore free an immense scoop of earth. Skirting higher to the right of the road, I spot the clearing Gunn mentioned—a huge, flat patch of dirt overlooking the quarry. A charred fire ring sits at the center, surrounded by several rusted folding chairs. Beyond that, further back, there's nothing but trees.

And no van. *Where is the van?*

I accelerate and descend the road, then ease into the clearing and stop. Streamers of dust float past the windshield. I stare at the clock.

It's 2:30 sharp and I'm the only one here. There's no one else.

Anywhere.

What the fuck?

My pulse clicks higher. I push open the door and step outside to the smell of chalk and minerals, the wet must of earth. An empty beer can crunches beneath my shoe, and I kick it away. The quarry looks even deeper this close, the vertical walls of granite scarred by decades of machinery harvesting rock. I turn my attention to the trees—a dense thicket of cottonwood, pine, and aspen—and then spin a three-sixty and search for movement, for anything at all.

There's nothing. Just the trees and the quarry with the mountains rising beyond. I return my gaze to the road I traversed—the only way in or out. Isn't that what Gunn told me? That there was no other way to access this place? Which means they should already be here, just like Gunn said. The lock on the gate was cut. So why aren't they?

The answer hits like a bat to the face. *Shit.* They must have spotted us arriving, saw Gunn and Holston get out of the car with their weapons drawn. They saw and they fled. But that doesn't make sense, either. Again, only one way in or out, so we would have seen them leaving. And we didn't.

Goddammit. My head feels like it's full of smoke. I don't know what's happening. All I know is that coming up here with cops was a mistake. That has to be why the abductors aren't here. It *has* to be. Nothing else makes sense.

Which means I fucked up.

Which means Avery might already be dead.

I'm ready to crawl out of my skin, about to hop back into the car and round up Gunn and Holston when I hear the sound. The *same* sound I first heard this morning at the trail. The intermittent chug of an engine. It's soft at first, a rattle in the distance.

The van.

But it isn't coming from the road I descended. It's coming from the opposite direction a ways back from the clearing. It's hard to tell through the bright afternoon sun, but I can barely see the vehicle edging past a second bank of trees I didn't notice until now, planted farther back beyond an old equipment shed at the end of the quarry.

The van draws closer, rising and falling until it reaches the clearing and comes to a stop on the far side. I cup my hand to my forehead in an attempt to ward off the sun. Like before, it's hard to see much through the tinted windshield, but I can just make out the outline of the driver through glass.

Where is she? I think. *Where's Avery? Is she safe?*

The side door slides open with a loud *thwack!* and a masked man gets out. *The* man. The same guy who assaulted me earlier. The one who grabbed Avery. I can see it in the way he stands with his arms crossed and his shoulders squared. I can feel it in the heat of his gaze. A bolt of fury runs through me. I ball my hands into fists and take a step forward, but he raises two fingers and wags them side to side while shaking his head. Then he turns and leans into the van.

When he reappears, it's with Avery.

My legs fill with cement as he drags her from the vehicle and holds her in front of him.

Her hair looks matted and dirty, her eyes hidden behind a bank of weeping red strands. Her nose and mouth are concealed by a handkerchief which is knotted tight around her face, and her hands are bound behind her back. I can't make out anything else, but I can tell this: She's crying. It's evident in the way her chest is heaving up and down in little quaking shifts. She's scared. Beyond scared. Terrified.

I'll kill you for this, I think as I stare at the man. *I will fucking end you.*

The thought dies the second he plants his gun against her temple.

Something vibrates in my pocket—the phone. I grab it and raise it to my ear.

"Yeah."

"Transfer the rest of the money."

"Let her go first." Despite my anger, I manage to keep my voice steady.

"As soon as you transfer the money." The voice sounds like it's been run through a blender. It has to be the driver speaking, though I can't see enough of him to make out a phone pressed to his ear.

"How do I know you won't hurt her if I do?" I ask.

"You don't."

"Then you won't get anything."

The man falls silent, his breath rolling through the phone and into my ear like a mechanical tide. It wasn't the right thing to say; I pushed him too far, too fast. But I can't simply transfer the money, either. Not without guaranteeing Avery's safety first. And where is Gunn? He told me to delay, but has to be in position by now, right? It's been … I have no clue how long it's been, but surely long enough. Not that I can risk searching for him in the trees. That would give away the fact I'm here with support. All I can do is stare at the driver—who keeps staring directly back at me.

After what feels like a lifetime, he turns and barks something at the man holding Avery. The man nods and pulls the gun from her head and aims it vaguely in my direction, the barrel hovering a few inches from Avery's skull.

He fires.

The gunshot echoes off the granite walls like a thunderclap. The bullet pings a stone somewhere to my left. Avery lets out a high, piercing shriek that quickly turns to a low mournful wail. The cry is muffled through the handkerchief—a noise I've never heard her make. It's pure, unfiltered terror. All the blood in my body flushes to my feet.

"The next one goes in her brain."

I flinch at the voice, don't realize I'm still smashing the phone to my ear until I hear the words.

"Transfer the money NOW!"

The statement is physical, like a slap to the face. I can't delay any longer. I pull the phone from my ear, tap the screen, and load my account. What's left of my money—and Avery's—stares back at me in seven black digits. Two point four million, all of it about to disappear with a single flick of my finger. It's so much money—everything we were planning to use to slow down in a few years. To retire early. But right now money doesn't matter. Money can be replaced. Avery can't. It's not even a choice.

I tap the green transfer button, confirm the transaction, and watch the balance in the account evaporate. The screen changes to a confirmation: *Transaction complete.*

I crush the phone back to my ear. "You have it," I say.

But no one's there. The line is dead.

My gaze comes to rest on the man holding Avery. Nothing's changed. He still has the gun pressed to her head, his fingers roped in her hair. The driver shouts something at him and he stiffens. His jaw dips. His eyes hit mine. For a long, sick moment I think he's going to do exactly what Gunn said he'd do—take our money and kill Avery anyway. But he doesn't. He pistol whips her instead.

"No!" I cry.

I give the signal, rubbing the back of my neck as he lets go. Avery collapses in on herself like a ventriloquist's dummy. The man leaps back into the van and slams the door shut. And then I'm running, pounding toward her as the van spins in a U-turn, kicking up a giant rooster-tail of dust. From somewhere a thought hits, vague and distant: Gunn hasn't fired a single shot yet. Neither has Holston.

But I don't care.

All I'm focused on, all I can see, is my wife lying face down in the dirt with her hair spread around her in a halo of red. My voice gushes up my throat thick with panic the moment I reach her. "Avery! Oh, Jesus, Avery! Are you okay? Please, tell me you're okay!"

I skid to my knees and roll her over, run my hands behind her head. There's already a substantial knot rising beneath her hair, the skin hot and sticky with blood. My thoughts splinter and burst. *Check for a pulse!* I press two fingers against her neck. *Find her heartbeat!*

It's weak but *there,* fluttering like butterfly wings beneath my fingertips. Relief rolls through me as tears flood my eyes. She's *alive.* She's alive and I have her back.

I have you back, I think. *I finally have you back.*

She groans and coughs, fighting to breathe through the handkerchief still covering her mouth. I grab it and tug it lower.

And that's when my world fully disintegrates.

I gawk at the broad nose and too-thin lips, at the square chin and plump, rounded cheeks. *This isn't Avery.* The realization hits like a shotgun blast, so hard, I thump down onto the dirt. The woman lying on the ground in front of me is a stranger.

PART TWO
THE SACRIFICE

CHAPTER 9

Erie, Pennsylvania
Age Six

Reed Aldridge woke like he did most mornings—to the sound of his parents fighting.

"You have to be kidding me, Jack! It happened again? *Again?*"

His mom's voice shot into his room like a grenade. Reed sat up with a gasp, unsure if he'd actually heard her or if he'd been dreaming.

"After one month? A single, goddamn month? You are so fucking pathetic!"

Nope. Not dreaming. Real.

Something made of glass exploded down the hall. He plugged both fingers in his ears and hummed to himself in an attempt to drown out the sounds coming from the other side of the wall. Bad sounds. Scary sounds. Sounds he hoped would stop if he gave them a few minutes. They sometimes did if he waited long enough.

His mom shrieked.

His dad roared.

Something thudded against the floor. Another loud crash followed. The fights weren't always this bad, but they were always *there.*

And even when they weren't, one could break out at any time. It felt like living in the middle of a storm.

When it came to his parents, Reed had become an expert at reading their weather. Like all the times his dad slumped through the door after work looking wrung out and went straight for the beer. Reed knew better than to run to him for a hug on those days because he'd just be told to get out of the way. It was better to leave him alone. Or the times when his mom spent the day muttering to herself as she cleaned the house, talking about how dirty everything was. Those were bad days to ask for a cookie. His mom would tell him he didn't deserve one since he never picked up his toys.

Those weren't the worst days though. The worst days came when his mother didn't speak at all. Even Dad knew better than to bother her. On those days, he'd come home and head straight for the porch. He'd sit out there and set his empty beer bottles on the railing, and they'd grow by the hour. Reed knew if his dad cleaned them up before they hit five, things might blow over. If he didn't, well, they were all toast.

Last night there had been seven before Reed went to bed.

But that wasn't what worried Reed the most. Things had been bad for a while now. Mom and Dad had ignored each other for weeks. It seemed like all they could do was frown. They barely spoke, and when they did, it was to complain. Dad griped about their dinners and said all Mom did anymore was lay around and watch TV. Mom complained about money. She said they were broke and called his dad a loser. Reed didn't know what she meant by that. For the most part Reed thought his dad was great. Not so much when he was drinking, but he loved going to the park with his dad to play catch. And he took Reed fishing most weekends, which was fun. His mom never took him anywhere.

Reed wasn't sure what had set his parents off this time, but he was glad to be in his room. In here, his mom didn't slap his dad. In here, no one yelled. With the door shut, Reed could plug his ears and close his eyes and pretend his parents loved each other as much as he loved both of them. In his room, he could forget he knew them at all.

But not today. Not with how bad things sounded out there.

"Be a man for once and look at me when I talk to you!"

A crazy tone had crept into his mom's voice. She sounded like a rubber band about to snap, her pitch climbing higher and higher by the second. When she got like this, Reed knew there was only one thing that would calm her down.

Him.

Another shatter came from down the hall. A broken plate, maybe. Reed swallowed. He didn't want to go out there—nuh-uh, no way—but he had to. The last time he'd let his parents fight like this, his dad wound up at the hospital with a forehead full of stitches. This time he might wind up dead.

You can do this, he told himself. *Be brave.* That's what his dad always told him to do when he was scared. When they rode the Zipper at the carnival. When Reed took his turn at the plate to bat. When the moon ducked behind the clouds and painted his room in shadows that looked like monsters. *Be brave, Reed. Be brave.*

He pulled himself off of the bed and crept into the hall. He stopped near the living room and peeked around the corner before going in. It looked like a war zone. A lamp lay shattered on the floor. Two side tables were overturned in a shower of glass. The television was spider-webbed with cracks. A trail of milk leaked down the screen, weeping white tears onto the carpet. That scared him more than anything at all. The television—a sixty-inch Sony—was his dad's prized possession. The thing he loved more than life itself.

This was so bad.

Reed turned his attention to his mom. She stood in the center of the room and barked at his dad with her face twisted into a knot. Her lips were a hot slash of pink as she jabbed a red fingernail at him, stabbing the air in time with her words. "You are unbelievable! Just unbelievable! How, Jack? How do you lose three jobs in a single year? For fuck's sake, that has to be some kind of record!"

Dad sat on the couch and stared up at her with his face full of shock—eyes wide, lips parted, forehead tight.

"What the *hell* happened this time?" his mom screeched. "Out with it already!"

His dad mumbled something in response, but Reed couldn't hear it, could only stare at the pink strips of scalp shining through his thinning hair as he tilted his head forward and stared at his lap.

"What?" Reed's mother spat. "Speak up!"

His father returned his watery red gaze to hers. "I said, it wasn't my fault."

His mother scoffed. "It never is. Let me guess—the bottle just shoved its way into your mouth again and forced you to take a drink." She gazed at the three empties on the floor and then the fourth clutched in his dad's hand. That was bad, too. He never drank in the morning.

His eyes flashed. "I wasn't drinking!"

"That's a first."

"It was an accident."

"Explain." The way his mom said it—*Ex. Plain.*—in a slow growl, made it sound like she could barely squeeze the word past her teeth.

"I was backing up. There was a guy behind me. I didn't see him. That's it."

Reed didn't know much about his dad's job except that he drove a forklift. He complained about it every night, said it made his back hurt. Reed didn't understand that. How could it hurt his back? Didn't the forklift do all the lifting for you? Either way, Reed knew enough to know hitting someone with it wasn't good.

His mom set her hands on her hips. "You're shitting me. You ran someone over?"

His dad gave her a single nod then returned his gaze to the floor.

"Unbelievable. Do you have any idea the number of strings I had to pull to get you that job? *Any* idea? Max was the last one. I'm all out of favors, Jack. No one's going to hire you now. Not after this."

Reed knew his mother was talking about Max Tavish, the fat, bald man who never seemed to stop sweating and had eyes that looked like buttons. The only time they shined were when they looked at Reed's mom. It was like she was a bowl of ice cream to him—something he wanted to eat up. Reed thought it was weird. His dad never looked at his mom like that. He barely looked at her at all. But whatever. Max owned the meatpacking plant where his dad worked and had given his dad a job, which made him nice. He was also rich. Everyone in town knew that. And that was a good thing. Reed had thought maybe he could help his dad get rich too, and then his mom could finally stop whining about money all the time.

"I'll find something else," his dad said.

His mom laughed—a strange sound that sounded more like a sneeze. "No, you won't. When have you ever found a job on your own?"

"I'll find one."

"Who wants to hire a drunk?"

His dad shot up then, his face a deep blazing red like it had caught fire. He took a heavy step forward and shoved a finger in her face. "Call me a drunk one more time, Diane. See what happens."

She gasped and skittered back. Reed had never seen his Dad hit his mom before. But it looked like he might now. He even had his hand raised like he was going to. But then Mom crouched and seized one of the empty beer bottles from the floor and raised it over her head. "Go on and try it! See what happens!" Her arm tensed, and Reed knew right then and there she'd smack his dad with it if he didn't do something first.

He ran out of the hall toward her. "Mama, don't!"

She hesitated, and when she turned toward him, her face looked like a witch's mask. He let out a cry, the tears back. But then her face softened and Reed saw his mom again. His beautiful mother who read him stories about fuzzy creatures with horns that welcomed adventurous children to their island. Reed loved that version of his mother, loved the sound of her voice when she told him stories, loved her fingers ruffling his hair. *You're the best boy,* she told him when she was in a good mood.

But even in those rare moments, when he caught her smiling down at him like she was the sun and he was her only flower, he recognized the statement for what it was: A lie. He knew he was different than the other kids his age. The kids whose moms actually loved them and sent them to school wearing nice clothes while his always had a bunch of stains and holes. The kids who never had dirt on their cheeks or bits of food stuck in their hair. The same kids who looked at Reed and laughed anytime he passed by. They knew what Reed really was: a loser. Just like his dad.

His mom sighed and knelt in front of him. "What are you doing out here, Reed?"

He couldn't speak, not now that the tears had begun to flow.

"Go back to your room, okay?" she said in a tired tone.

Reed shook his head. "No! You'll hurt Dad again!"

The lines in her face deepened. The empty beer bottle slipped from her hand. She closed her eyes. "I can't do this anymore. Lord knows I've tried, but I can't." Her eyes clicked open then, and she reached out and cupped Reed's cheek. The smile she gave him was the saddest thing he'd ever seen, like she was growing old before his eyes. And then she pulled Reed into her arms and held him there for the longest time before standing and disappearing down the hall. When she returned half an hour later, it was with a suitcase that she tugged straight through their battered screen door.

Reed never saw her again.

CHAPTER 10

BAILEY

I sit on the vinyl bench, feeling threadbare after four hours of sleep, staring at the storm of children swirling like a hurricane in front of me. Ocean Island. No ocean, though. And no island. Just thirty thousand square feet of children's play equipment spreading out in front of me in a brilliant eyesore of neon green and stinging blue.

With a laugh, my son Noah peels from a nearby cluster of kids and races toward me. He slides to a stop a foot away and stands there, bouncing in place in front of my husband Ethan and me, electric with energy. His cheeks are tinged pink, the corners of his lips stained blue with remnants of the frosting from the cupcake he inhaled only minutes earlier.

"Mama, Mama! Luke said they have a ball pit! Can you believe it?"

"Come here," I say, licking my thumb before dabbing his lips. "Look at you. You're a mess."

"Hey, stop it!" he protests as Ethan chuckles.

"Never!" I pull him tighter and tickle him. Noah wriggles and attempts to break free, giggling as my fingers dance over his ribs. I release him and he straightens with a smile, his eyes sparkling.

"You're so silly, Mama."

"You'll never know how much I love you, Little Man," I say.

He shakes his head firmly, his smile growing wider. "Nuh-uh, you'll never know how much I love you!"

I tap his nose with my fingertip. "Nope, you'll never know how much I love *you*."

You'll never know is a game we play, usually at bedtime, to see who can say it last before I slip from his room. Noah won't go to sleep until I let him win.

He giggles and says, "Okay, I gotta go. Luke is waiting."

"Oh, is he now?" I follow his gaze toward a massive tub of red, blue, and yellow balls. Kids leap from the edges with spirited shrieks. A girl with butter-yellow hair plunges down a curving slide and slides face first into the tub like it's full of water. Noah's cousin stands next to it, clad in a pair of denim overalls, frantically waving his hands at Noah like a mini aircraft marshaller. Luke is five years old as of today, one year older than Noah. I can't help but smile.

"Can I go in the balls?" Noah asks.

"Of course you can go, buddy," Ethan says, biting back a laugh. "You can do whatever you want in here. You don't need our permission."

Noah's eyebrows climb a full inch, nearly disappearing beneath his straw-blond curls. "Weally?"

"Yes, *weally*," Ethan says. "Go on. Have fun."

With a cry of delight, Noah spins on his heel and races for Luke, weaving through the sea of children with reckless abandon.

"Anything he wants, huh?" I cock my head and study my husband. Freshly thirty, Ethan carries the look of someone five years his junior. He still has the round cheeks of a teenager and the same thick, acorn-colored bangs as when I originally met him, but his eyes are those of a man's—slightly hooded with the beginnings of crow's feet. Eyes that, when combined with his dimpled smile, illuminate his features like a sunrise. It was his smile that drew me to him in the first place, and I've never grown tired of seeing it since. Seven years married now, and I couldn't love him more.

"You baby him too much, Bay," he says. "We need to let him off the leash from time to time."

"The last time we did, he wound up with a chipped tooth, remember?" I recall the incident, Ethan running next to Noah on his Strider balance bike one minute, guiding him by the back of the seat, letting go the next. Noah, wheeling for the curb in a lazy arc, looking my way with a shout, "Look at me, Mama!" before flipping over the handlebars and skidding across the cement face first. We were in the ER twenty minutes later.

Ethan smirks. "Okay, point taken. But nothing's going to happen here."

"Famous last words."

He leans back and props his head against the wall, a dimple flashing as he watches Noah leap into the balls. "We did good, didn't we?"

"So good," I say, forgetting my exhaustion for a moment. Ethan's right. Our son is perfect in every way—the best thing we've done by a mile. And I'm thankful when he points it out. Ethan lives every day with gratitude. It's one of the things I love about him most. And he's also a wonderful father. Ethan's job as a part-time shift manager at Petey's, the corner grocery store four blocks from our house, allows him to spend most of his time hanging out and playing with our son. Which, in turn, has allowed me to pursue my career. He's the yin to my yang—my perfect match.

He reaches over and laces his fingers with mine. "So, what time did you get in last night?"

"Two."

"Jesus, Bay," he says as a trio of wrinkles form over the bridge of his nose. "Seriously?"

"Unfortunately. I feel like a zombie."

"I bet." He squeezes my hand. "You know how much I appreciate what you do for us, right?"

"You do? Why don't you ever tell me then?" I say it with a grin. He does. He tells me all the time. Still, I know my job can be hard on him, especially during tax season. It means four grueling months governed by client and governmental deadlines that rule my life with an iron fist. Sixty-to-seventy-hour weeks are the norm. But my position as a tax director at PricewaterhouseCoopers also provides us with the means to afford a very comfortable life. It allows us to live in our modern two-story home in Montlake, one of the premier neighborhoods in Seattle with access to some of the best schools in the entire state. My career is why we're able to eat organic meals and go on nice vacations and will be able to someday send Noah to whatever college he wants to attend. It's why I drive an Audi and Ethan drives a Lexus and both of us have closets full of nice clothes. All of this with money to spare, and I haven't even made partner yet.

Ethan gives me a mock wince. "Ouch. Probably because I'm such a terrible husband."

"That's the last thing you are," I say, leaning into him.

"Hang in there," he says, patting my knee. "Busy season will be over soon enough."

"You do realize it's barely getting started, right?"

"Yes, but—" he pulls me closer. "You have my permission to forget about it today. You can worry tomorrow."

I lean my head against his shoulder. "Deal."

"This is nice," he says, looking at the play area like it's a tropical oasis and we're parked on the beach near the water. I nearly laugh. Only my husband would find a place packed with shrieking kids like this relaxing. But he's right. Being here with him and Noah *is* nice. And Noah's having a blast. He's waving at me now from across the room, waiting for me to return the gesture. When I do, he smiles then turns and leaps into the balls.

Two more years.

That's all I need, and then I can devote more time to my family. Two more years of understanding from Ethan and Noah, and I'll be promoted to partner. After that, I—*we*—can do whatever *we* want. I'll set better boundaries with work. We'll take more of the vacations Ethan is always going on about. I'll spend more time at home. I will. I won't think twice. It will happen.

But not yet. Not when I'm this close to achieving what I've been working toward for so long now. Not after sacrificing my soul for nearly a decade to reach this point. And sacrifice is exactly what it's taken for me to be promoted to director by the age of twenty-nine. I'm one of the youngest employees in the firm to ever achieve that title, and as a woman no less. I haven't greased any wheels. I've done it all through hard work, blood, sweat, and tears with a vision toward creating a beautiful life for me and my family. And we're so close to realizing that dream. So close.

The thought dies when a cry fills the room. *Noah's* cry.

I spot him and another boy crumpled near the ball pit with their hands pressed to their heads, both of them wailing. A collision of some sort. Ethan jumps to his feet and rushes over. I follow, stopping when my phone buzzes in my pocket. My stomach clenches. I want to ignore the call, but I can't. Not if it's who I think it is. Not if I want to remain employed.

I pull my phone free and my stomach knots. It's him. Of course it is. Who else would it be? With a sigh, I bring it to my ear.

"Hey, Bob, what's up?"

"We have a situation," he says.

I tense, but it's not a surprise. There's always a situation, some urgent fire to put out for some pissed-off client. And at this time of year, they're all pissed off.

"What is it?" I ask, trying to mask the note of displeasure creeping into my voice. This is my first day off in the last two weeks, and I don't appreciate being disturbed—not that it matters. Inconveniencing me seems to be one of Bob Sanders' favorite pastimes. As the newest directing partner of the Seattle branch, Bob is deeply unpleasant at times. He pursues his goals with a blatant disregard for his personal health and that of his staff, but there's no arguing the man gets results. He's tripled our bottom line in a little over two years. So, when Bob Sanders asks you to do something, you drop everything and you do it, no questions asked.

"One of the seniors on the Miller engagement discovered a discrepancy in the cash account," he says. "It's not good. And it's big. I think we're looking at fraud, here. How soon can you get to the office?"

I hesitate, the words jamming in my throat as I study Ethan. He's kneeling in front of Noah, gingerly thumbing his forehead.

Two more years. Just two more years.

"Can you give me an hour?" I ask. "I'm at a birthday party with my kid."

"Sooner would be better."

I bite the inside of my cheek. "I'll do my best."

The phone clicks, Bob gone without another word.

I rub my eyes and groan, knowing this means we'll have to leave.

Noah and Ethan are going to kill me.

CHAPTER 11

"Bailey, come on," Ethan says as we push outside into a morning draped in fog. "Noah wants to stay."

"Please," Noah echoes, still rubbing his head. "I don't wanna go."

I lean over and ruffle his hair. "Another time, buddy."

"We'll take an Uber, Bay," Ethan says.

I resist the urge to roll my eyes. We just talked about this before coming outside. The Taylor Swift concert is kicking off at noon. Every Uber in the city is already backed up. The wait times are ridiculous—well over an hour—and so are the charges. Even then, I'd be happy to cave if Ethan could be trusted to properly install Noah's car seat, which he can't. Despite all of his strengths, my husband has two left thumbs. When he last tried, he missed one of the latches completely. And it wasn't the first time.

"Ethan, please don't fight me on this," I say as I stop. "I've already got enough on my plate as it is."

"Can you tell Bob no? You've killed yourself for that man. Surely he'll understand this once." He nods at Noah. "And we have the matinée later, remember?"

I suddenly feel very tired. My husband is made of gentler stuff than me. He doesn't possess the same constitution I have to claw my way through the corporate world. If I say no to Bob, someone else will say yes. And even at my level, it's still a race to the top.

"You know I can't do that," I say, annoyed, stepping forward to take Noah. There should be another option—the one where *I* grab an Uber and leave Ethan and Noah here with the car. But that option doesn't exist. Not after Ethan's DUI. Four months ago, he and a couple of his old high school buddies went to a Seattle Kraken hockey game and had a few too many beers. It was a much-needed night out for him to relax and unwind, a brief reprieve from watching Noah. And relax he did. Then he climbed behind the wheel and drove straight through a DUI checkpoint. It's one of the few major mistakes he's made in our marriage, and one we've already worked through—which is why I don't bring it up now, even though I'm tempted to. Doing so would be like pulling the pin on the grenade.

I head for the car instead, Noah dragging his feet the entire way. "No! Let me go! I wanna stay!"

"We'll come back next weekend, okay?" I open the back door to my blue Audi sedan and motion for him to get in. He goes slack in response, all of his weight hitting at once. It happens so fast, I nearly lose my grip on his hand.

"Stop it, Noah," I say, bending down to pick him up.

He nearly squirms free. "You stop it! You're being mean!" He bucks against me, thrashing and shaking his head as I pick him up by the armpits and set him in his car seat. "Let me go! Let me go!"

"Stop it," I repeat, then more firmly: "Noah, stop!"

Still he fights, his tantrum kicking into high gear. "Let go!"

I bend over and attempt to buckle him in. When I do, he swings his foot and the tip of his shoe connects with my chin. My teeth clack together painfully. I exhale and take him by the shoulders as I try again. "Noah Eric, you will behave right now! Understand? Right. Now."

"Bailey!" Ethan says behind me. "Calm down."

"A little help would be nice," I say, turning and pushing past him without another word.

Five minutes later, we're on the road with rain salting the windshield as I drive. *Whump, click. Whump, click. Whump, click.* Through the windshield, past the wipers, trees pass by in inkblot stains drizzled in fog. January in the Pacific Northwest is my least favorite time of year. The cloud cover is always bad, but at least in the summer you see the sun once in a while. Winter means going weeks without light. Sometimes months. It's a nice dose of seasonal affective disorder paired with all the work.

We travel in silence, the only sounds those of the highway mixing with Noah's sniffles. It's like this any time Ethan and I have a disagreement—a battle of the wills to see who will wave the white flag and speak first. I have a low-grade headache throbbing between my temples by the time he does.

"Hey, you missed the turn."

"No, I didn't," I say. "I'm not taking the interstate. There'll be too much traffic with the concert. Pioneer will be faster."

"No, it won't," he says. "It never is."

"Today it will be." I grip the steering wheel harder. "Are you trying to find a reason to argue with me at this point?" The statement comes out hotter than I intend. I tense for whatever Ethan's about to say in return, but he just runs a hand over his face and falls silent. He's right that Pioneer usually takes longer. It's a relatively empty stretch of road that winds through the rolling farmland near where Ethan's brother lives before dumping drivers back onto I-5. Most days it would add at least thirty minutes to the route but today it will save more than that.

"I wanna go back," Noah mumbles from the backseat through a heaving sob. "I didn't get to say goodbye to Luke."

I eye him in the rearview mirror. "We'll see Luke again soon, honey."

"Please can we go back?" Noah says with a whimper.

"I'm sorry, baby," I say. "I'll take you to do something fun as soon as I can, okay? But right now, I have to go to work."

"You always go to wook," he says, tearfully.

My gaze flicks to the rearview mirror. *Wook* when he means work. Noah's eyes glimmer with tears, his lower lip folding down in a full-on pout. "I don't want you to go to wook, I want you to stay. I love you."

My throat knots. "I love you, too."

"Hey, it's okay," Ethan says, rotating toward Noah to give him a fist bump. "We still have the movie later, okay? You're excited for that, right?"

"Is Mama coming?"

"No, I'm afraid not, bud," he says. "It's just you and me this time."

The knot thickens.

Ethan falls silent for a second and then turns my way. "Look, you know I'm all for your career, but ..." He stops mid-sentence. Hills pass by shrouded in mist, the fog growing denser, making it difficult to see. It feels like we're the only ones on this road—the only ones in the world.

"But what?" I say, prompting him, even though I know his response will be one I don't want to hear.

"Nothing. Never mind."

"No, tell me," I say. "What?"

"It's ... well, sometimes it feels like your job is all that matters to you."

"Come on, Ethan, you know that's not true."

He runs his fingers through his hair and chews on his lip. It's something he does when he's thinking about what to say next. "I'm sorry. That was unfair. But you have to find a way to gain some balance, Bay."

It's true and I know it. But I'm also running low on sleep and my nerves are completely fried. I don't have the bandwidth for this discussion at the moment. "Can we talk about this later?"

"Sure," he says with a nod before turning his attention back to the road.

"Take me back!" Noah says, his tone shrill. "I don't wanna go home!"

"Noah, please," I beg, my eyes burning now.

"I want Bear!"

"Bear's at home," I reply, trying to hold it together. "You'll see him soon."

"It's just that it never ends, you know?" Ethan says. "There's always another fire to put out, another emergency. And it's not good for you. I'm worried about your health."

"I thought we weren't doing this right now?"

"I know, but I really think we need to talk about it."

I tighten my grip on the steering wheel. *This* is the time Ethan picks to have this little spat? Right before I have to walk into a category-ten shit show at work with Bob Sanders swirling at the center? It's more than I can handle. "Ethan, I told you I don't have the bandwidth at the moment. Just because you're ready to talk doesn't mean I am. You're being selfish."

I don't mean to say it; the word just bubbles out before I can shut my mouth. He looks at me as if stung—his eyes wilting, his forehead collapsing into a series of folds. I want to reach out and grab the word and stuff it back in my mouth. *Selfish.* He isn't selfish. He's anything *but* selfish. He's always been one to put my needs and Noah's over his own—and all he really wants is for me to spend more time with them both. Which is something I want, too.

"Take me back," Noah cries. "Take me back, take me back!"

My eyes return to the mirror. "Noah, you have to stop—"

"Bailey, watch out!"

It happens in slow motion, the next few seconds slipping past like syrup.

My gaze coming back to the road.

The headlights slicing through the mist to our right, blowing past the stop sign.

The hot shriek of brakes.

The frantic thump of my heart.

And then we collide in a sonic boom of crushing metal and shattered glass. Noah's scream is the last thing I hear.

CHAPTER 12

GRANT

The woman who isn't my wife lies before me, moaning in a crumpled heap. I stare at her feeling completely gutted as my head spins in circles. If this woman is here, what does it mean for Avery? Is she hurt? Is she dead? Is she locked away in a cage somewhere scared and alone, wondering why I haven't come for her yet? And, *Jesus*, is the baby okay?

I rub my forehead. Why would they even do this if all they wanted was the money? They have it all now. So why don't I have my wife?

I don't have the answers, but maybe this woman does. I grab her shoulders and give her a gentle shake. "Hey, can you hear me?"

She winces, and her eyelids slowly flicker open. She blinks and fights for focus. Her pupils are dilated, at least twice as large as they should be. She's injured, probably concussed, but I don't have time to baby her. I need to know what she knows, and I need to know right fucking now. "Who *are* you?" I ask, as she squints at me and shields her eyes.

"Where ... am I?"

"It's hard to explain. First, I need to know who you are and why you aren't my wife. Then I'll tell you where you are."

"Your wife?" she parrots groggily.

I grind my teeth together. It's like I'm speaking Mandarin. I want to slap her and scream for her to focus. I want to shake her until she tells me everything she knows. But I can't. She's dazed, in shock. I can tell by the way her irises are swimming drunkenly through the whites of her eyes as she looks up at me like I'm nothing more than a waking dream.

I exhale long and slow and study her. From across the clearing, she looked exactly like Avery. She has the same slim build, the same cinnamon red hair. She's even wearing Avery's clothes—a black crop top and purple yoga pants—along with her shoes, a black and white pair of Merrells. There's no arguing this woman is a carbon copy of my wife, especially from a distance.

But this close, the illusion shatters. Instead of Avery's delicate cheeks and slender chin, this woman has a weak jaw and a face that is far rounder than my wife's. A heavy pair of frown lines tug at the corners of her lips, and her forehead is peppered with sunspots. She's older than Avery too—somewhere in her early forties if I were to guess. And her eyes are brown, not green.

"Here," I say, leaning forward. "Let me help you up." Her eyes widen at my touch, and she scoots back like she's just now seeing me for the first time. She looks dazed—no, more than dazed. She looks drugged.

"Calm down," I say, flashing her my palms. "I'm not going to hurt you."

"Who ... who are you?" she asks, squinting at me. "What do you want?"

"My name is Grant Wilson. I'm looking for my wife, Avery. She was abducted this morning. I thought you were her."

Her brow crinkles in confusion. "Wait, what? Why would you think that?"

"Because you look like her, and you're wearing her clothes."

"What are you talking about?" She drops her gaze, and her eyes widen again as she takes them in. "Why would I be ... oh ..." She trails off, her hand drifting toward her temple. "God, my head is killing me. What happened?"

"I was hoping you could tell me."

"I ... don't remember anything."

Her grimace deepens, like the mere act of thinking hurts. The panic in my chest swells. I need to find out what this woman knows, and I need to find out *now*. But I can't scare her any more than she already is, or she'll shut down.

"Okay," I say. "How about you start from the beginning. What's the last thing you can remember?"

Her eyes unfocus, and she gazes somewhere over my shoulder. "I was on my evening jog near ... near the park by my house and I heard this sound. An engine, I think. Something about it was ..."

"Off?"

She nods. "Yes. But I wasn't really paying attention. I had my earbuds in. I was jogging in place at an intersection when ..." She closes her eyes. "... when this van stopped right next to me, and—" Her eyes snap open again and go wide. "Oh god, I think I was kidnapped. Do you have a phone? I need to call the police."

A circuit breaker blows in my head. The police. *Gunn.* My gaze rips toward the thicket of trees in search of the man, but he's not there. All I see are branches and shadow. I spin a one-eighty toward the pile of boulders at the top of the road where I passed Officer Holston driving in. But he isn't there, either. There's just road, rocks, and sky. And absolutely nothing else.

What the fuck is happening?

"Are you okay?"

Startled, I turn back to the woman. "Yeah, fine."

"Your phone?" she prompts again with her voice trembling.

"Oh, right." I dig the burner from my pocket and tap the screen. Nothing happens. It's dead. "Shit," I mutter, showing her.

Her face crumbles. "I need to call my family. They have to be worried sick."

"We'll find a phone, I promise. What's your name? You still haven't told me."

Her eyes glaze over again, like she's having trouble remembering. "Elizabeth—Liz Gleason."

"Liz, who was with you in the van?"

"Men with masks on."

"How many?"

"I—I don't remember." She breathes faster, a tear cutting over her cheek. "All I know is I was pulled into the van and someone stuck a … a needle in my arm. And then I woke up here. That's it."

She's shaking now, rocking in place. I won't be able to push her much further. If I do, she'll shut down completely. But I *do* have to push some, because this woman is literally the only link I have left to Avery.

"Where do you live, Liz? Is your house close?"

She sniffs. "I don't know. I live near the golf course."

The golf course? I scour my memory of the town and come up with nothing. I don't think Ouray has a golf course. If it does, I haven't seen it.

My eyes narrow. "Which golf course?"

"Redlands."

A question takes shape in my head, and my stomach drops at what I think might be the answer. "Where is Redlands Golf Course?"

"It's off High Desert Road, right next to Ocotillo. It's—"

"No, which city?"

She pauses, frowns. "Grand Junction."

The name tumbles through my head like a boulder. *Grand Junction.* Grand Junction is nearly two hours away. This woman isn't even from here. Oh fuck.

"What?" Liz asks, taking note of the change in my expression.

"You're in Ouray."

Her eyebrows rise. *"Ouray?"*

"Yes." I rock back on my heels. "I need you to think very carefully. Do you remember anything else? Anything at all from the moment they took you until now?"

Her eyes flutter and she swallows. She looks at the ground and shakes her head. "No. I wish I did. But there's nothing."

I can't move. Can't focus. What the hell am I going to do?

Liz issues a soft sob and wipes her nose. The nostrils are pink. "Can you help me up, please? I can't stand with these things on."

It takes me a second to understand what she means, and then I realize she's talking about the zip ties binding her wrists.

"Of course," I say, bending to help her to her feet. "Are you good to walk? I have a car right over here."

"Yeah, I think so."

"Okay, let's go."

"Where?" she asks without moving.

"What you said earlier is right. We need to find the police."

CHAPTER 13

GRANT

I find an old Leatherman in the Yukon's glove box and snip the zip ties off Liz's wrists. Then we drive out of the quarry the same way I came in, up the hill and past the wall of boulders where I last saw Holston taking cover. The rocks are bare, like they've grown a mouth and swallowed him. Gunn is gone, too, nowhere to be seen.

Because they played you.

The thought is a firebrand pressed deep into the meat of my brain. But if they played me, why would they have left me with a car full of their fingerprints and DNA? Surely they know I'll take this thing to the cops. It doesn't add up. But nothing's added up since Avery was abducted this morning, so why should this?

A dull pounding comes from the base of my skull as I descend the road and ease back toward the quarry gate. I can't think, my thoughts congealing into a slippery bowl of spaghetti.

Did they really play me? Really? Why would Gunn do that? Why would Holston?

For the same reason as the men in the van—they wanted the money. Which I gave them.

So where is my wife? Where is Avery?

It's the only question that matters because Avery is the only thing that matters. Losing every penny I have to these men, whoever they are, stings. But I can recover. I can start over. What I can't replace is Avery. If I lose her—if I lose my child—I lose *everything*. Her face burns to life behind my eyes, her words whispering into my ear. *I love you ...*

"Who's that?" Liz asks, pointing up the road.

"I'm not sure," I say, squinting at the silver sedan idling beyond the gate. Alarm bells clang in my head and I bring the Yukon to a stop. The sedan is an older car much like the van, scuffed and dented in spots. But unlike the van, it doesn't contain any masked men. Instead, there's a guy wearing a polo standing next to it, holding a yellow manila envelope. He gives us a lazy wave, like there's nothing out of the ordinary going on. Like hanging out at the quarry to greet us after what just happened is the most normal thing in the world. There's no hint of threat in his posture, no menace, only boredom. That's what strikes me the most. The guy looks bored.

"I don't think we should go any closer," Liz says, her eyes wide. "What if he's dangerous?"

"He doesn't look dangerous," I say. "And we don't have a choice. You need to see a doctor and we both need to talk to the cops."

The real cops, I think angrily as I put the Yukon in gear and pull forward.

"Please don't get out," Liz says worriedly as I park near the gate.

"I'll be fine," I tell her. "Just wait here." And then I'm out of the car and striding toward the man, devouring the distance between us in ten quick steps.

"What do you want?" I demand.

"Are you Grant Wilson?"

The way my name rolls off his lips—his tone light and conversational—like he has no idea who I am or what I've been through today gives me pause. My anger ebbs. "Yeah. Why?"

"I have an envelope for you. Sign here, please."

He raises his hand and presents his phone. I study the screen. There's a company name printed next to a logo of a cartoon man running at a dead sprint wearing a red winged hat: QuickCourier. Beneath the words is a blank signature line.

"I don't understand," I say, confused.

"Look, man, I have a lot of deliveries to get to, so if you could just sign, I'll be on my way."

Instead of grabbing the phone, I take the envelope.

"Hey, you can't do that," he says. "You have to sign first."

But I'm already tearing the package open and reaching inside. When my hand comes out again, it's with a stack of photos. I stare at the first one and the world washes away. It's a picture of Avery bound to a chair. A length of rope is lashed around her chest, and there are two more tied around her wrists. She's naked except for her underwear. Streaks of grime trail across her collarbone and cover her breasts. And her face—*dear god*—is completely battered. Her eyes have been blackened. A dark band of purple runs over the bridge of her nose. The right side of her mouth is so swollen it's pulling her lips into a Joker-like sneer.

They beat her, I think, numbly. *They beat my wife.*

I flip to the next picture. This one is an overhead shot of a pair of grease-lined knuckles yanking Avery's face up toward the camera by the hair. Her eyelids hang at half-mast, revealing only the whites of her eyes. A gag winds around her jaw, looking tight enough to cut off her airway.

My stomach knots. I'm going to be sick. I can barely bring myself to shuffle to the next picture. It's another shot of Avery sitting in the chair, but with her head slumped forward this time, her chin planted on her chest. The crown of her head glows through her matted red hair, and for a sliver of a second, I wonder if the photo is fake, a picture of another stand-in actor like Liz.

That's when I spot the birthmark. It's stamped on her abdomen, hovering right above her waist. The same pale-pink shape I've orbited with the tip of my finger a hundred times. A thousand. Not only that, but I recognize the spattering of freckles around it. This is Avery. I have no doubt.

The pictures slip from my hand, and I stride toward the man. He says something, but I don't hear the words as I bunch my fingers into his polo and slam him hard against the car.

"Where is she?" I snarl. *"Where?"*

He sputters and chokes. Sputters again.

"Tell me! Where's my wife?"

A palm brushes my back. "Hey," Liz says. *"Hey!* Stop! Let him go!"

I loosen my grip, but only a little, just enough so he can speak.

"Shit, man, I don't—" The guy grabs my wrists and tries to push me back, but I only lean into him harder in response. "I don't know!" he finishes.

Liz grabs my arm. "Stop it! You're going to kill him!"

"Goddammit!" I say, releasing him.

Liz stares at me like I've lost my mind, her eyes bulging.

"Fucking psycho!" the guy says. I turn back to him. He's slithered away, is now standing on the other side of the car, trying to catch his breath. "What the fuck is wrong with you?"

"Who sent you?" I ask. I don't care that I've frightened this guy. I need answers, need to make sense of what's happening and find out why this guy has all these awful pictures of my wife.

He smooths his shirt, which doesn't do much to improve his frazzled appearance, not with his collar now ripped to mid chest. "No one. I was just trying to deliver a package."

"Yeah, I get that. But why?" I ask. "Why way out here?"

His face transforms into a shotgun splatter of confusion. "Hey, I go where I'm told. And my boss said to be at the quarry at three o'clock. That some guy named Grant Wilson would meet me here. So that's what I did." He runs a hand through his hair, trying and failing to work it back into place. "Fucking sure wish I hadn't now, though. Christ."

I gawk at him. My brain feels like an egg yolk cracked into a frying pan. For a brief second, I'd thought this nightmare was over. But now I can't shake the feeling it's just getting started.

"Who's your boss? Give me his address right now."

His brow wrinkles. "You want to talk to Frank? He won't know shit, either. He said this package came in via—"

"Oh my god," Liz breathes behind me. When I look her way, she has a fist pressed to her mouth, holding the pictures I dropped. "Is this your wife?"

"Yes," I say. It feels like someone else is saying it, like I'm no longer the one speaking.

Liz's forehead bunches and a crease forms between her eyes. "What's this?"

I edge closer to see what she's looking at. It's a note printed on a piece of white paper in generic Times New Roman font. I snatch it from her and devour the words at light speed.

HELLO, GRANT.

YOUR WIFE IS STILL ALIVE.
TO SAVE HER YOU MUST PLAY A GAME.
THE RULES ARE THE SAME:

IF YOU CONTACT THE POLICE, SHE DIES.
IF YOU TELL ANYONE, SHE DIES.
IF YOU DISOBEY US, SHE DIES.
RETURN HOME. YOU HAVE NINETY MINUTES,
STARTING NOW.

WE'RE WATCHING YOU.

I look up with my jaw hanging. Both Liz and the courier are watching me closely, waiting for me to say something. To do *something*. But

I don't. I can't. I'm too busy calculating the distance between Ouray and Durango. It's seventy miles of twisting roads and hairpin turns. Seventy miles of white-knuckle driving that doesn't lend itself to speed. It takes two hours on the best of days to make the trip, and that's without starting at a rock quarry several miles off the highway.

"What time is it?" I ask the guy.

He scans his watch. "Almost three."

Fuck. I need to be home by four-thirty. I'll be lucky to make it by five.

"I have to go," I say.

"Where?" Liz asks. Her voice sounds distant, like she's shouting at me from the bottom of a well.

"Home."

"Wait," she says. "What about me?"

I nod at the courier. "Go with him. He can get you help."

The man opens his mouth to tell me no, hell no, but I cut him off before he can say a word. "Look, I'm sorry for what I did earlier, but there are extenuating circumstances here. This woman was just assaulted."

He raises a single eyebrow. "You mean like you assaulted me?"

"Please." Liz turns toward him with more than a hint of desperation in her voice. I can already hear the tears forming.

He releases an exaggerated breath and rubs his forehead. "I mean, sure, yeah, why not. I'll probably get fired for this, but if it helps you two ..."

I step closer. "Can I borrow your phone? I need to make a call. It's an emergency."

He massages his brow and shakes his head. "Dude, you're killing me." But he reaches into his pocket and hands me his phone anyway.

I grab it and start for the Yukon.

"Hey, wait!" he says. "You said borrow, not *take*."

Which is true—but I'm already gone.

CHAPTER 14

BAILEY

I push into Noah's room and stand there. It's been two years since the wreck, and I haven't changed a thing. His toys lie right where he left them, scattered over the floor. His twin bed rests in the corner, covered by a rumpled Spider-Man comforter. The pillow on top still carries an indentation in the shape of his head. I sometimes trace my fingers over it and try to recall the feeling of tousling his hair or rubbing his neck. I lie there and ache to pull him close and smell the fresh vanilla scent of his skin—that sweet, sleepy fragrance of him. But it's long gone. In here, all that fills my nose is dust, and all I ever think of is his death. Especially on his birthday.

Today, Noah would have been six.

I trail across the carpet and the rainbow of Legos, creep past the toy trucks and Avenger figurines, and retrieve the love-worn bear resting on the foot of the bed. The fur is missing in spots. One eye hangs loose in its socket, the other scuffed from a playground fall. There's no doubt the thing is ugly. It always has been—a cheap, long-ago gift from Noah's first birthday party—but he loved it right away. Any time it went missing was cause for emergency.

Mama! Mama! Where's Bear?

Bear. That's what he called it. Nothing else. Just Bear.

He carried it with him everywhere we went—to the grocery store, the doctor's office, the playground, and the park. To the library, the beach, the zoo, and the mountains. It didn't matter the occasion, Noah always brought Bear along for the ride. He slept with the stuffed animal every night, wrapped tightly in his arms, holding onto it like I should have held onto him.

I set Bear on the comforter and grab the framed photo from the dresser. It's a picture of the three of us at Disney World. In it, Noah is wearing a Captain America mask with his arms cocked off his hips and his chest proudly aimed at the camera. Ethan and I stand behind him with our hands on his shoulders, trying to stifle a laugh. The branches of the Tree of Life stretch skyward behind us, outlined in a peach spray of light.

A perfect moment captured.

A perfect life gone in a blink.

Like I always do when I look at the picture, I study myself. There I am with my carefully styled hair and designer clothes, lost in the moment. It was one of the few times on the trip I hadn't been thinking about some pressing deadline at work or focused on how many calls I'd need to return when I made it back to the office. I was present—and I was happy, oblivious to what would come.

I want to reach into the photo, shake myself, and say, *Wake up, Bailey! This is what matters. Enjoy every second with them before they're gone.* I want to tell myself this is the last vacation I'll share with my family before they're taken from me, erased in an instant. But even if I was able to tell myself to soak it all in, it wouldn't have made a difference.

Back then, the last person I ever listened to was myself.

I shift my gaze to Ethan, my sweet husband who I berated for wanting to spend more time with me and our son. If I'd only let him stay at that party with Noah like he'd wanted, he'd still be here. If I'd only done what he'd suggested and told Bob I wasn't coming into the office, they both would.

"I should have listened," I whisper, staring at the picture. "I shouldn't have left."

If I'd waited another minute before leaving—one single, precious minute—before dragging Ethan and Noah outside, we never would have been hit by that car. But I hadn't, and we were, and now all that's left of my family are memories like the one I'm holding in my hand.

I blink and a tear hits the photo glass followed by another.

Two years. Noah and Ethan have been gone for two years now.

It feels like ten.

I threw up for three straight weeks after coming home from the hospital, unable to hold anything down. I sobbed until my eyes felt like open sores. I laid in bed for days at a time, lost in an ocean of grief so deep, I'd been unable to move. For months, the only moments of peace I had were those first few precious seconds when I woke every morning before the memories of what happened to my family came rushing back in a wave of pain.

Pain that's never once stopped.

I set the picture in my lap and gaze at Noah's superhero posters on the wall. Thor and Iron Man and Hawkeye and Black Widow—all of them draped in a shower of dusty afternoon light. Noah had wanted to be a superhero. He'd wanted to help people, and he would have someday. I'm sure of it. Maybe as a doctor or a teacher or a therapist. But he won't now. Those possibilities were stolen from him along with so much else.

The thrill of his first crush. The rush of his first kiss. His high school and college graduations. His first job and the career that would follow. Meeting the love of his life and witnessing his child smile. Every beautiful experience ripped away from him before they ever happened. My boy will never grow up. Instead, he'll remain forever etched in my mind, looking up at me from the Ocean Island parking lot as a red-faced four-year-old pleading for me to stay.

Mama, I wanna stay!

I should have let him. That's what my life consists of now: and endless list of what ifs and should haves. I should have spent more time with my family when I had the chance. I should have read Noah more books. I should have toured the vineyards and wineries in California like Ethan wanted to and taken him to more concerts in the park. I should have told him I loved him more, that I appreciated him. I should have done so many things with those moments before the wreck. But I hadn't.

I'd simply let them drift through my fingers like sand.

I can't bear it anymore. And I won't.

I wipe my eyes, place the photo neatly back on the dresser, and then leave my son's room for the final time.

———

The pills are waiting for me on the kitchen table. They sit in a single neat line that, once I swallow, will ensure I close my eyes and never open them again. It's exactly what I want. I can't handle the pain any longer, the lies. So many lies. The ones I tell myself: *You were just trying to build a life for them. You were only doing your best.* The ones others tell me: *Bailey, it wasn't your fault. You were a wonderful mom. How could you have ever known that would happen? There's nothing you could have done.*

I could have worked less.

I could have focused on them more.

I could have loved them as much as they'd loved me.

I could have stayed at that party.

But I hadn't. I made them leave early, instead. I'm the one who'd insisted we go. And it was me who'd buckled Noah into his car seat, so bleary-eyed with exhaustion that I'd done exactly what I was worried Ethan would do if he took an Uber. I didn't fully latch Noah's harness.

It's why he'd flown from his car seat at the moment of impact. The sheer force of it had snapped his back in four places.

My beautiful, perfect son gone just like that.

Ethan never stood a chance. He took the brunt of the collision, was killed instantly. He didn't suffer. That's what the surgeon told me when I woke up in the hospital, anyway. Neither did Noah. *Rest assured, they felt no pain.* The man saying it with a sad smile like it would somehow help me cope.

It didn't.

I'd suffered, though. Horribly. I'd nearly bled to death from a lacerated spleen in the ambulance. I'd shattered my collarbone and fractured six ribs. Four ligaments in my right shoulder ruptured and popped like rubber bands. I'd broken my ankle. The concussion I'd sustained left me with headaches so horrific, I wanted to die. Every single day I'd wished for it. And I still do.

My waking hours are a continual loop of those last few horrific moments with my family. I can see it all so clearly: The fear in Noah's eyes after I forced him into his car seat and told him to, *Stop it! Just stop!* The way Ethan's shoulders curved inward as I lit into him and called him selfish. The hurt in his face as he winced at the word. My eyes shifting to Noah in the rearview mirror when they should have been on the road. Ethan screaming for me to, *Watch out!* a second before the car sliced out of the fog.

The horrible shriek of brakes and the sound of rending metal.

The sick, empty blackness that followed.

Stop it, Noah!

He did stop. He'll never speak again. Neither will Ethan.

And now I'll join them.

CHAPTER 15

I grab the bottle of Ketel One by the neck and take a long, purposeful drink. The alcohol burns down my throat and coats my stomach in a warm bloom of heat. I set the bottle on the table and study the pills. Most of them are painkillers left over from my recovery after the wreck: Oxycodone, Percocet, morphine, and a bunch of muscle relaxers. I ate them like candy in the early days. I gladly welcomed their black-hole effect. They not only took away the physical pain, but the mental as well.

For a while.

Until I remembered the squeal of rubber and shatter of breaking glass. The relief never lasted long. The memories were always there, boiling just beneath the surface, ready to spill over as soon as the fog cleared.

Alcohol. Pills. Cannabis.

Running. Lifting. Yoga. Prayer.

Therapist after therapist.

None of it worked.

The only reason I'd even managed to hold on for this long was for my younger brother, Ben. He was my rock after the wreck. He did everything he could to nurse me back to life. Anytime I needed something, he was there. He slept on the pullout couch in the hospital for weeks, rushing to my side at the slightest sound, telling me he had me, that he wasn't going anywhere. And afterward, during all the excruciating months that followed, he was right there too, holding me when I shrieked. Comforting me when I cried. Telling me we'd get through this together like we'd gotten through all the hard times that came before. But even then, as I nodded along, I knew there was no getting through this. Not for me. Not this time.

"I'm sorry, Ben," I say as I sweep the pills into my palm. I know my death will break him, but he'll be better off with me gone.

Smack! Smack! Smack!

I jerk back and drop the pills on the table. They bounce and scatter. But I'm not looking at them. I'm staring at my brother—who is right there, staring back at me through the living room window. I'd closed the blinds, but apparently not all the way. I'd left just enough room for my brother to peer in and see *exactly* what I was about to do.

His palm smacks the glass again. "Bailey, open up!"

I shoot to my feet, trembling and unable to move.

He bangs again, and I startle. Lead lines my stomach as I drift toward the door. When I open it, Ben lurches past me, crackling with angry energy, his cane clacking against the tile like a drum.

"What are you doing?" he asks.

"Nothing. Why are you here?"

A deep V creases his brow, and he shakes his head. "Don't try to change the subject." He waves at the pills on the table. "Bailey, what the fuck?"

I raise my fingers and pinch the bridge of my nose, say nothing. I can't; I'm too tired for this, but my silence is answer enough.

His face falls. "Jesus, Bay ..."

"Ben, it's not what it looks like."

"Yeah? Because it looks pretty fucking bad."

"I'm just—"

"What?" he says, clicking closer. "Going to kill yourself?"

"No, I mean—"

"Stop it. You aren't the only one who's suffered here!"

I stiffen. "Don't you think I know that?"

"Do you?" he asks, drawing so close I can smell the coffee staining his breath. "Because what you're about to do says you don't. And I'm telling you ..." His voice splinters, and he shakes his head. "I'm telling you that you *do not* get to do this to me, *too*."

"I don't know how to go on anymore. I can't. I've tried."

Ben stares at me, the whites of his eyes going pink before he wraps me in a hug. I dissolve into him and sob against his shoulder. He cups the back of my head and pulls me closer. I feel his chest shudder. Neither of us say a word. We simply stand there, both of us crying, until he finally breaks free and leads me to the couch.

"Sit," he says, wiping his eyes. "I'll make us some tea."

He sets his cane on the couch and hobbles into the kitchen, returning a few minutes later with two cups of Masala Chai. He hands me one and then eases into the club chair on the other side of the coffee table and takes a sip from his mug.

I study him in a daze. Life hasn't been kind to my brother. At seventeen, he took a position as a construction hand downtown, working on a new high-rise. Three weeks into the job he fell through an unmarked skylight. He plummeted two stories and sustained thirty-three fractures as a result. The only reason he lived was because, after hitting a railing midway down, he flipped end over end and crashed into a pile of empty cardboard boxes that cushioned his fall. His surgeon said he was lucky, that if he'd landed two feet to the right or left, he would have died. I'm so very grateful for those boxes.

Until my wreck, watching him recover was the single most difficult experience of my life. He had brain damage—he didn't speak right for months. A single step was cause for victory. We all cheered him along. The fact he's sitting here with me right now, functioning normally after everything he's endured is nothing short of a miracle.

We've both lost too many people. Our father passed from a massive coronary a couple of years before my wreck. His death hurt me, but it hit Ben especially hard. He and Dad were close—more like brothers than father and son. They went fishing on the weekends, attended concerts and art shows. Growing up, Dad knew how to talk to Ben better than any of us, knew how to reach him when he was down. Any hole Ben fell into, Dad pulled him out of. And there were a lot of holes, especially after Ben's accident. When Dad died, Ben not only lost a parent, he also lost his best friend.

Our mother followed shortly after. With Dad as her anchor, her early-onset dementia was semi-manageable. She was forgetful but content. But after he passed, Ben and I were forced to put her in a memory care facility. We didn't want to, but neither of us could take care of her. Neither of us had the time or resources. Worse, without Dad, her good nature swung toward something darker. She became angry and bitter, turned her words into weapons: *You've never been a good mother, Bailey. All you do is work. You didn't learn that from me. I don't know where I went wrong with you.*

She died while I was in the hospital. Ben had to shoulder it all. He didn't even tell me she'd passed until several months later. And I didn't ask; that's how gone I was at the time. I didn't care about anyone else's pain. I was too lost in my own. When Ben finally shared the news, I didn't even shed a tear. I couldn't. I didn't have any left.

He takes another drink of his tea and appraises me.

"What?" I ask.

"I'm moving in with you."

I gawk at him. Ben lives in a mid-century modern home in the city with his longtime boyfriend, Owen Grayson, a prominent local architect. They spend their free time perusing art galleries and museums and their evenings attending plays and shows. A perfect weekend for my brother means evenings spent at wine bars and lazy mornings eating bougie breakfasts, not sitting here on my couch drinking luke-warm cups of Starbucks. The city fits him. The suburbs don't. Him moving in with me is out of the question.

"It's not happening," I say.

"Fine. Then you're moving in with me and Owen. You need a change, anyway.

I nearly snort. Their home is charming but small with barely enough room for the two of them. With me there, it would be bursting at the seams. "You know I wouldn't do that to you."

He gives me a hint of a smile. "Exactly—which is why I'm moving in with you."

"Ben, no."

"I'm not asking for your permission." His eyes flick toward the table and the snowstorm of pills spread over the surface. "Not after this."

"What about Owen?" I ask.

"He'll be fine by himself for a while. Besides, absence makes the heart grow fonder and all that."

It's not true. Despite what he says, I know being away from Owen for too long will drive him crazy. They're perfect for each other, and they don't need me getting in the middle of their relationship to screw it all up. I glance away and catch the edge of one of Noah's long-ago juice stains peeking out from under the leg of the couch. It made me so mad when it happened. We'd just recarpeted the entire house. Now all I want is for there to be more.

My eyes burn. I want to tell Ben I won't try to take my life again, that he simply caught me on a bad day. I want to gesture at the pills with a wink and a nonchalant wave of my arm and say, *What this? This is nothing, I was just messing around.* But I wasn't messing around. I *will* do something worse. And, selfishly, I don't want him to be here to stop me when I do.

"Seriously, what are you doing here, anyway?" I ask, lifting my gaze.

"You mean besides stopping you from doing what you were about to do?" He leans back in the chair and smooths a nonexistent wrinkle from his jeans. "I didn't think you should be alone today."

Of course. Noah's birthday.

"And there's another reason," he continues, crossing his arms.

I take a sip of tea. "Which is?"

"You need closure, Bay."

"Closure?" I nearly laugh. "There's no closure for me. There will *never* be closure."

He brings a hand to his mouth and massages the corners of his lips as though he's carefully considering what he wants to say next. Then he sighs. "I'm not so sure about that. I think it's time we talk about Evelyn Nash."

CHAPTER 16

REED
Scottsbluff, Nebraska
Age Ten

Reed stole the answers to the test on a Thursday.

He'd seen Mr. Matthews stash it in his desk on several occasions, plopped squarely in the center of the top drawer after he finished grading tests. Then, once lunch hit, Mr. Matthews would cap his red pen and take a stroll around the park behind the playground. So one day, after watching Mr. Matthews whistle past on his way outside, Reed slipped from the cafeteria, snuck into Mr. Matthews' room, and swiped the magazine-sized book. He slid it up his shirt and left. That evening, Reed copied the answers to every science test into a spiral-bound journal. He returned the key the next morning before Mr. Matthews arrived.

Reed didn't need the answers. He needed money.

He *needed* a pair of Air Jordans.

He'd first spotted them on Mikey Penbrook, a sixth grader, who wore the shoes to the neighborhood bus stop. Snow white with red trim and an outline of Michael Jordan in midflight stitched on both sides. Reed *had* to have them. There was simply no other choice.

But it wasn't the shoes Reed wanted so much as it was Mikey's confidence when he started wearing them. He seemed so confident and collected. So fun and cool. The girls noticed it, too. With his wiry mop of thick black hair and a pair of oversized glasses that swallowed his face, Mikey had never been all that popular. But that changed when he started wearing the sneakers. Girls talked to him now. They chased him around the playground. Mikey the nerd was now Mikey the cool.

Reed asked his dad for a pair of Jordans that night. When Reed told him the price, his father nearly spit out a mouthful of his beer. "One hundred and twenty dollars? Have you lost your goddamn mind? We don't have that kind of money."

Reed knew they didn't. They'd *never* had that kind of money. All Reed knew of fashion was what came from the Goodwill on Henderson Street. His wardrobe consisted of hand-me-down jeans from strangers that never fit him right and T-shirts that smelled like other kids. He hated that scent, hated the shirts with their peanut-butter stains and frayed collars. The clothes made him look poor and needy. Which is exactly what he was—one of the free-lunch kids with scuffed shoes and holes in his socks.

So when Reed's best friend, T.J. Reynolds, complained about their science exam—"I'd pay anything not to have to study for another stupid test"—the idea hit. Reed could steal the answers and sell them for five dollars a pop. Then he'd buy the shoes. Simple as that.

And it worked. Reed told T.J., who told Dillon Archer, who told Garret Thomas, who told Shane Velázquez, who told god knew who else. Yeah, it was dangerous, Mr. Matthews could find out. But Reed didn't care. Kids were palming him fives at a record pace. He'd have the Jordans in no time. But when Reed was called to see Principal Sparks, he'd only managed to collect sixty-five bucks. Not nearly enough.

Principal Sparks sat behind his desk, looking like a mountain with his arms crossed when Reed entered his office. The man was a monster. Seeing him sitting there like that, looking at Reed like he was considering swallowing him whole, made Reed quake. But that wasn't what scared Reed the most. What really made him want to turn and burst through the door wasn't Principal Sparks at all. It was the man sitting next to him.

"Sit down, Reed," his dad said.

Reed never felt smaller than at that moment, and never more scared. He sat with his cheeks flaming.

"Why do you suppose you're here, Mr. Aldridge?" Principal Sparks asked.

Reed knew *exactly* why he was here. But he didn't answer. He only shrugged and played it off like he had no clue. Maybe if he ignored this, it would go away.

It didn't work. His dad gave his shoulder a painful squeeze. *Go on. Speak.*

"The science test?" he said.

"Yes," Principal Sparks replied. "The science test. And what, exactly, about the science test got you sent down here?"

Reed squirmed in his seat.

Ten minutes later, Reed left Principal Sparks' office with a three-day suspension. His dad didn't say anything as they walked outside, never looked at Reed once. When they reached their car—an old Buick sedan with an engine that burped—Reed's father shoved him in so hard, his head nearly slapped the dash. Then they drove in silence.

Reed kept his eyes on the road. He didn't dare look at his dad. He didn't need to. He knew what the man was thinking. He'd have to take time off from work to watch Reed or pay someone to do it. And he'd make sure Reed knew just how inconvenient that was with a few swings of his belt. So, Reed sat there, sweating in the unconditioned air until his father pulled into a parking lot.

"Who did you tell about the answers?" his dad asked, turning his way.

"Only a couple of kids," Reed lied.

His father's eyes hardened to steel-gray orbs. "Did you tell any girls?"

"No," Reed lied again. He'd told Amy Richardson because she gave him Hot Tamales sometimes, and Reed was pretty sure she'd told Laura Freeling and Tara Smith. They smiled at him more after that. They gave him candy, too.

"The truth, Reed."

"A few," he mumbled, hanging his head.

"Even one is too many," his dad replied.

Reed frowned. "I know. I'm sorry. I shouldn't have told anyone."

"Not anyone. I'm talking about the girls. You shouldn't have told them." The corner of his father's mouth twitched downward on *girls*, and for a second, Reed was certain he was about to reach over the console and smack him. "Who is Ashley Parker?"

Ashley Parker was the prettiest girl in school. And the most popular. She hadn't even asked for the answers, but Reed had shared them with her anyway. She didn't seem impressed though, had simply shrugged her shoulders and skipped off.

Reed rubbed his jeans. "She's a friend."

"A friend, huh? She's the one who sold you out. Women will betray you, Reed. You can't trust them."

Reed wasn't sure how his dad knew this or why they were sitting here in the half-empty mall parking lot instead of going home. But as long as his dad wasn't yelling at him, it was fine by Reed.

"You remember what your mother did to us, right?"

Reed nodded. He still thought about that day, still wondered most nights how his mom had been able to walk right past him without giving him a hug or saying goodbye. He hated her for that. So much. But he also missed her sometimes. Not that he should. She was long gone, and Reed knew she'd never come back.

After she'd left, he'd waited at the window every night for months, watching for her car. He wanted to run outside and leap into her arms and tell her how much he'd missed her, even if she didn't say it back. Which she wouldn't. Reed had long ago realized you don't walk away from something you love. The only thing you walk away from is trash. And that's exactly what Reed was to his mom. Trash.

His dad gazed at him. "I think it's time we have us a man to man, Reed. I think you're ready for that. How about you?"

Reed straightened in his seat, paying attention now. They'd never had a man to man before. This sounded serious. "Okay."

"Your mother didn't just leave us," his dad said. "She stole from us. She took everything we had."

Reed rubbed the back of his head. He thought he knew a lot about his mother, but he didn't know this. "How?"

His father's face crumpled, and he suddenly looked much older than his forty-four years. "That bitch stole all of our savings. She cleaned out our accounts. Didn't leave us with a single fucking dollar. You'd think she'd at least have left me with enough cash to take care of you, but she didn't. She took it all for herself. Why do you think we had to move?"

Reed pressed his thumb into the center of his palm and thought about it. He'd loved their old house. His dad had built him a treehouse in the back yard where he'd played for hours. He'd loved the woods behind it, too, and splashing with his friends in the stream that curled through the trees like a snake. Riding bikes in the cul-de-sac was a daily ritual. He knew everyone in the neighborhood; they played football and tag and drank Cokes in the park. One of the worst days of Reed's life was when his father told him they had to leave. He'd pitched a fit until his father tossed him in his room and told him he had to stay in there until he got it together.

We're moving. Get used to it.

After that, *home* became a thing of the past. They had no home.

Not really. They chased work wherever his dad could find it. Home became a cheap collection of motel rooms and apartments that smelled of mold and dust and old, stale air. These rundown places stuffed full of rundown people. Everyone so jammed together Reed could hear every fight and moan through the cracked plaster walls. Reed *hated* those places. He hated the people there, too. And he'd hated his father for dragging him along. But Reed never realized until now—until this very second—that all of it was his mother's fault.

His father was telling the truth. He looked like he was about to cry. "Reed, if there's one thing I can teach you in life, it's this. You can never, ever, trust a woman. You might think you can. And you'll want to. Girls are pretty. I get it. But you can't. Do you understand why?"

Reed had heard this kind of thing from his father before, but the words had mostly drifted in one ear and out the other. Not this time. After hearing this about his mother, he did understand—he did, and he wouldn't forget it. He'd never trust a girl or a woman again. He nodded.

"Listen," his dad said, giving Reed's shoulder an attaboy squeeze, "I'm proud of you. What you did today was clever. It was industrious. Bold. You're an entrepreneur if I've ever seen one."

"What's that?" Reed asked, surprised. After the meeting with Principal Sparks, he'd expected to get grounded. Not this.

"An entrepreneur is someone who sees an opportunity and goes for it, exactly like you just did. C'mon," He said, opening his door.

"Where are we going?" Reed asked.

Reed's dad gave him a sly wink and smiled. "We're at the mall, aren't we? Let's go get you those shoes."

CHAPTER 17

GRANT

I tear down US 550, pushing the Yukon as fast as I can without running it off the Million Dollar Highway—a twenty-five mile stretch of hairpin turns and sheer cliffs named after the construction cost per mile combined with the priceless views. Most who drive it consider it to be a perfect slice of American heaven.

Right now, it's hell.

I can't think of anything other than the photos of Avery. They flash through my head one by one. Avery, with the crusted trails of blood pouring from her nose over her bruised and swollen upper lip. The shot of her gagged, the material sawing through the corners of her mouth like a knife. Avery sitting there, stripped naked, with her breasts covered in grime.

Did they rape her?

Tears fill my eyes and I wipe them clear. I can't linger on thoughts like that. Thinking about what these people have done to Avery won't help me right now—and it won't help her. I have to hit this deadline. I need to focus on getting home. I can't lose my wife.

She's already gone.

"Stop it!" I growl to no one. "Just stop already!"

I have ninety minutes and forty have already passed since I got the note. It's not enough time, and the line of cars in front of me aren't helping me ease my nerves. I know it's probably a bunch of tourists and retirees taking in a bit of countryside before dinner. Normally, I wouldn't begrudge them. Hell, I'd be going as slow myself. But right now, I need to pick up the pace. Only I can't. Not with thousands of feet of open air lying on one side of the road and a mountain on the other. And even if I could cut around them, driving like a madman up here will get me pulled over in a second. That can't happen.

Contact the police and she's dead.

It's all I want to do. But it would be foolish after their warning. It would—wait, maybe there *is* a way to reach them, especially if I'm not the one calling.

I have the courier's phone.

Steering with one hand, I pull it out and search for the number to the Ouray Police Department. A horn blares and I flick my gaze back to the road a second before I drift across the center lane and plow straight into an oncoming truck. My heart thrashes but I manage to jerk the wheel and guide the Yukon back into my lane. Then I punch in the number with my thumb and hit dial. The phone rings.

"Police department," a female voice answers in an overly cheerful tone.

"Yes," I say. "Officer Gunn, please."

There's a pause and then, "Who?"

"Officer Gunn," I repeat.

"There's no Officer Gunn here."

"How about an Officer Holston, first name Calvin?"

"No Officer Holston here, either. You sure you meant to call our department?"

My stomach twists even though I suspected this would be the answer. Now I know for sure.

"What's your name, sir?" the woman asks.

For a brief second, I consider actually telling her, but it would be a mistake. Calling with the courier's phone to confirm Gunn and Holston were impostors is one thing. Filling this woman in on all the details is another. Whoever took Avery has access to resources I don't. They might be monitoring the police station phone lines. Even mentioning Gunn and Holston's names was a big risk.

"Sorry, wrong number," I say, ending the call.

I toss the phone on the passenger seat. I had to know if Gunn and Holston were in on Avery's abduction. And they must be, but I still have so many questions, like why did Gunn leave me with his car? And is it even his car? Was the house it was parked in front of his house? How many men were involved in the operation? Four, at least. Maybe more. The fact that I still have no answers is terrifying. Worse, I no longer know what they want. They have our money. All of it—every fucking dollar. So why haven't they returned my wife? Why are they continuing to do this? That's the question that scares me the most.

A memory snaps through my head: Avery asking me about my biggest fear two months into our relationship. When I said heights, she'd tilted her head.

"No, really."

"Really," I'd answered with a laugh.

Her forehead had crinkled, her smile fading. "The truth. Out with it."

I didn't know what to say. I'd simply sat there hoping she'd let it go. She didn't, so I'd finally waved at the table, at her. "This. You."

"*I'm* you're worst fear?"

"No. Being vulnerable with you is. Letting someone in. That's my biggest fear."

"Why? Because you might get hurt?"

I'd nodded. *Because I've been hurt and swore I'd never let it happen again.*

"What about you?" I'd asked.

Her eyebrow had quirked higher. "What about me?"

"What's your biggest fear?"

She'd grinned. "I'll never tell."

"Hey, that's not fair," I'd said, momentarily hurt but playing it off with a laugh.

She must have noticed because she'd reached across the table to take my hand. "It's losing you."

"Come on, seriously."

She'd said nothing, just stared at me in such a tender way I knew she meant it. Dear god, she did. Part of me thought about running then—standing up and bolting for the door. It's what I'd always done in previous relationships when things got too heavy too fast. I'd run. But I was tired of running, and another part of me—a deeper part— recognized how special Avery was. What she'd just done took guts. No bullshit. No lies. Just the truth.

And there was something else lying beneath her expression in that moment. Something other than tenderness. She'd looked fragile in a way—like if whatever I said next came out wrong, it might cause her to shatter and break. Which meant she was as scared as me. And I remember staring at her, thinking, *I will never let anyone hurt you. I'll protect you with my life.*

A promise I'd just broken.

Not yet, a voice whispers as I scan the clock. *You still have a chance to save her. You still have time.*

But not much.

CHAPTER 18

GRANT

Our house rises in front of me, dusted orange by the late afternoon sun. I'm doing seventy as I rip down County Road 250, my eyes glued to the clock on the dashboard. It's 4:28 p.m., a mere two minutes before the deadline. When I hit the driveway and sprint for the door, it's exactly 4:30. It's an absolute miracle I made it without being pulled over. After I got off Red Mountain Pass, I sped the entire way back, tearing past car after car like a madman in an effort to get here on time.

"Avery! Avery! Are you here?" I shout, pushing inside.

The only response that comes is silence.

I search our master bedroom. Sticky beads of perspiration line my forehead as I bang into the bathroom and tear through the closet. There's nothing out of the ordinary inside. I race into the kitchen and check the pantry, then the living room. I frantically scan the space for anything different or out of place. Something I can latch onto that will let me know what I'm supposed to do next—a note, a phone, a package. Anything. But there's nothing. Which means I'm missing something.

I start over and go through the rest of the house at a slower pace. I scour the basement and the living room. I tear through every single bedroom and all of the bathrooms. I do the same with the entertainment room and the loft and find nothing that gives me pause or hesitation. The garage and the tool shed in the backyard offer more of the same—not a damn thing. The house is exactly as we left it.

By the time the clock hits six, I'm running on fumes. I haven't had anything to eat since breakfast. And even though I'm still not hungry, I head into the kitchen and pour myself a bowl of cereal. I don't have the energy to make a proper meal. But I need to eat because I need the calories to think. Every bite of cereal feels like swallowing splinters. *Grant, we're going to have a baby.*

I'd given up on the idea of becoming a dad. Sure, I'd flirted with the concept in my late twenties and early thirties. I'd considered what it would be like to start a family and live the standard American two-and-a-half-kids, white-picket-fence dream. Hell, I'd even played out those *Hey, Honey, I'm home!* fantasies a few times in my head, but I'd never truly considered it a possibility because I'd never met the right woman. I hadn't met Avery.

We were eating breakfast at Rupert's, our favorite greasy-spoon spot downtown when she told me why that could never happen. A chubby-cheeked toddler had wandered in with his parents. The kind of kid who looked like he'd been dropped from a cartoon into real life. A towhead with neon blue eyes and plump cheeks. The kid was a force of nature, pulling the tablecloth, grabbing the syrup, the saltshaker, wriggling and flinging his body back against her in a full, stage-effect flop. When I turned back to Avery, I expected her to be cracking up with me.

She wasn't.

She had her gaze aimed squarely at her plate, looking like she was about to splinter and crumble apart. Her expression paralyzed me for a second, it was that out of place. She looked so rattled and broken. I remember sitting there with veins of ice cutting through my chest, thinking she was about to tell me she had a few months left to live. I was certain the next sentence that came from her mouth would be,

I'm dying, Grant. I have cancer. But then she told me why she was so upset. "I can't have kids, Grant."

She had endometriosis. I'd never heard of the disorder, but I nodded along as she explained how scar tissue prevented sperm from traveling up the fallopian tubes. That wasn't the real problem, though. Plenty of people got pregnant despite endometriosis. There were solutions. The real problem for Avery was her diminished ovarian reserve. She didn't produce enough eggs, and the ones she did make weren't exactly viable, so even if her anatomy were perfect, it would still be difficult to conceive. Having both conditions made it next to impossible.

Still, when she told me all of this, I felt a wave of relief. I thought, *That's it? That's all?* I could live with this. *We* could live with this. And if Avery wanted children badly enough, we could adopt—not that I told her that right then and there. I knew that wasn't what she needed to hear. Look, I won't pretend to know exactly what she was feeling in that moment, or how she half-expected me to respond. I think maybe she was waiting for me to push back from the table and tell her we were through. I'm pretty sure she expected me to storm out the door. But it truly didn't matter to me.

"Avery, I don't care about that," I'd told her. "You're all that matters."

The way her face brightened when I said that, the way she looked at me with such intensity, like maybe she was seeing me for the first time—the *real* me—filled me with such a ridiculous amount of emotion, I couldn't speak. And neither could she. We both just sat there, staring at each other, the whites of our eyes dusting pink, sharing the same thought. If something this significant didn't divide us, nothing would.

The memory feels so distant now—like it belongs to another life and another man. The room blurs and I wipe my eyes. This shouldn't be happening. Avery and I should be eating dinner at the Brickhouse 737 in Ouray right now while discussing baby names. We should be guessing if we're going to have a boy or a girl and talking about what color to paint our child's room.

Instead, I'm alone and Avery and our baby are gone along with all of our savings. The question hits again, crashing through my skull. Why is this happening? Why haven't they returned her? I paid them millions. I complied with their every demand outside of meeting an impossible deadline, and I *still* don't have my wife.

Because she's dead.

It's an echo of the thought I had on the way back here, the one I'd immediately silenced. But I have to consider it at this point; there's no reason to believe Avery is still alive. If she was, they would have dumped her at the quarry instead of tossing a stranger out of the van. Which would make sense if it wasn't for the note from the courier. If Avery is dead, why are they continuing to string me along? Why risk interacting with me at all? It doesn't compute.

I bring the faces of "officers" Gunn and Holston to mind. Gunn's cut-from-granite features and Holston's squared-off chin and empty eyes—both of them actors in a show I didn't know I was in until now. I don't have their real names, but I have their faces. I could go to the police, *should* go to the police. Outside of the note, there's no reason not to. But the note is exactly why I can't.

If there's even a sliver of a chance Avery is still okay, I have to play along. Rushing to the cops right now feels like turning that sliver of possibility into a death sentence.

I limp to the liquor cabinet and retrieve a bottle of Macallan from the cupboard along with a highball glass. I pour two fingers of the straw-colored liquid over ice. I can't get drunk right now, but I can't stay completely sober either. Not with my nerves frying so hard I can practically smell them cooking. I need to take the edge off.

I take a long sip and then settle in at the kitchen table. The whiskey burns down my throat in a welcome trail of heat. I take another sip and then hammer back the rest. At this point, I don't know what else

I can do but sit here and wait for someone to contact me. The note the courier gave me said something about playing a game. At this point, I feel like I'm already playing it—a sick fucking game with rules I don't understand. A game I have no choice but to play until I know whether Avery is still breathing or not.

Feeling shaky, I set the glass down and wait.

Bang! Bang! Bang!

I whip my head up and grind my palms into my eyes. My gaze snaps to the clock on the wall. It's half past four in the morning. When I last looked at it, it was a few minutes before three. I must have nodded off at some point.

What did you hear?

I take in the room. The kitchen looks no different, a shower of jaundiced light bleeding from the ceiling over the countertops and floor. My highball glass sits empty in front of me on the table, the ice turned to an inch of cloudy water. Beyond it, the windows are black with night, everything the same. *So, what woke you?*

I'm not sure. I must have imag—

BANG! BANG! BANG!

The front door rattles. Three heavy thuds that send me shooting to my feet. My chair whips backward and cracks off the floor. I stand frozen for a millisecond and then I rush from the kitchen, through the living room, and toward the entryway. I don't hesitate, don't peer through the window, simply yank the door wide open and step outside to—

Nothing. Absolutely *nothing* except the breeze brushing soft over my cheeks along with the rolling chirp of crickets. My palms burn, and I realize I'm clenching my fingers so hard my fingernails are cutting into my skin. I'm coiled, ready for a fight, but there's no one out here. No cars in the driveway. No headlights or thugs waiting to attack. Only empty black night.

"Who's there?" I shout. "Show yourself!"

I wait for a reply, but none comes. With a final sweep of the yard, I turn back toward the house—and stop.

It takes a second for me to understand what I'm looking at. It's hard to see in the dim porch light, but it's there—a dark yellow square taped to the door. A manila envelope. I rip it free and rush into the house, slamming the door behind me. And then I'm back in the kitchen, dumping the contents on the counter. My blood turns to ice when I see what's inside. There's another cellphone and—*shit*—more photos.

With trembling hands, I pick them up. The first photo shows what looks like a basement with dirty concrete walls. There's a bar attached to the low ceiling. A woman hangs from it, her wrists bound above the bar, her knees buckled, her toes drifting over the floor. Her head is slack, her hair roping over her breasts in greasy strands—because she's naked. Fully naked this time. There's no mistaking the triangle of pubic hair between her legs or the birthmark on her abdomen.

A waterfall of panic races down my spine. It's Avery.

I fight the urge to vomit as I drop the photo and turn to the next. It's the same picture, but this time there's a man standing next to her. He's dressed the same as when I last saw him, clad from head to toe in black. In his hand is a knife. The tip rests against Avery's throat. My gut boils. I don't want to look at the last picture. *I can't.* I know what I'll see: the knife buried in Avery's neck.

With dread swelling in my chest, I flip to the final photo.

But I don't see the man slitting her throat. It's a zoomed-in shot of him pressing his masked face next to hers. I can't see much of Avery, can't make out her features through the limp hair, but I can see the dark trails of dried blood weeping over her lips. And I can see *him*, or rather his eyes—the same frost-blue eyes I first saw at the trailhead when he took her from me. The same eyes from the quarry.

Spots wheel through my vision like snowflakes. What color were Gunn's eyes? Or Holston's? I try to picture them. Gunn's were brown. Definitely brown. I'm sure of it. Holston's were ... shit, what? Brown, too? They definitely weren't blue like—

The phone rings, and I jolt, the pictures falling from my hands. I grab it and stare at the screen. It's a video call from an unknown number. I hit accept and an image flickers to life as the call connects. When the image comes into focus, I press a fist to my mouth. The woman staring back at me is all bruised flesh and dried blood. Her right eye is buried in a swollen mound of blue and purple skin. A clear trail of fluid leaks from the corner toward an equally swollen upper lip. Her features are all out of proportion—bloated on the right side but familiar on the left.

"Grant," Avery says in a voice so soft it's little more than a whisper.

"What have they done to you?" I manage to choke out.

"They ..." She swallows. "They won't ..." Her left eye rolls wildly in its socket and she blinks and shakes her head. When her chin tips toward her chest, I wonder if she's been drugged.

"Avery!"

She doesn't move.

"Avery, look at me!"

A gloved hand sinks into her hair and rips her gaze back toward the camera. She grimaces, and her good eye flutters open.

"Say it," a man growls off screen. "Tell him."

Avery swallows again and then speaks: "You have to ... you have to solve them."

"Solve what?" I ask, trying to comprehend what she means. "Baby, I don't understand."

"They said they'll—they'll kill me if you don't."

"Avery—please. I don't know what you want me to solve."

Her head tips forward again, but the hand in her hair jerks it right back into place. Her face buckles in pain. "The riddles."

I clutch the phone tighter. "*What* riddles?"

Her lips twitch as she issues a soft sob. "I can't hold on much longer."

"What riddles, Avery?" I repeat. "I don't know what that means." My eyes are burning now. I'm blinking back tears. "Just tell me what I need to do. Please, god, just tell me!"

A gloved hand holding an index card appears, placed right in front of Avery's face. The man's voice cuts through the speaker like a knife.

"Read it. Say the words."

And she does.

<h1 style="text-align:center">CHAPTER 19</h1>

BAILEY

I stare at Ben, wordless. The last person on earth I want to talk about right now is Evelyn Nash. It's a name that fills me with an unspeakable amount of sorrow and an equal amount of rage. It was Evelyn Nash who sliced out of the fog doing sixty in her luxury BMW X7 and killed my family. She ran straight through a stop sign and obliterated my car along with hers. And she did it while driving drunk.

Not a day has passed since the wreck I don't think of Evelyn Nash. She haunts my waking hours like a ghost. I see what she's stolen from me everywhere I look—in the dust coating the family pictures I took off the walls and piled in the corner of the living room face down. In the way Noah's swing hangs slack and still in the backyard. In the silence of my house where nothing ever changes unless I change it. All these holes punched into the fabric of my life by Evelyn Nash that will never close.

Why did you do it? Why did you get behind the wheel drunk?

Didn't you know how dangerous that was? Did you even care?

Do you know what you've taken from me? Do you know what you've done?

These are the questions I want to ask her. I want to sit there and listen as she tries to justify herself, and then I want to crack open my sternum, dig out my pain, and hand it to her black and dripping. *Here, take it. This belongs to you.* I want her to hurt like I hurt. I want her to suffer. Too bad she never will.

Out of the four of us involved in the wreck, I'm the only one who survived. Like Ben after his construction accident, I was intubated and placed into a medically induced coma. But unlike Ben, mine wasn't due to a brain injury. Besides my lacerated spleen, I had a severely punctured lung. I nearly drowned in a lake of my own blood on the way to the hospital. When I woke two weeks later, panting and sick, gasping for my child and husband, my first question after Ben told me what happened was: "Who hit us?"

"Evelyn Nash," he'd replied, his voice thick through the tears.

I didn't know the name, didn't have a clue who she was.

As I healed, I chased her down rabbit trails on Google. Evelyn Nash was the daughter of Donald Nash, one of Seattle's business elites. A plum-cheeked CEO already on his third wife—a serious-looking woman I saw dabbing her eyes next to him in the pictures of Evelyn's funeral. Donald had thinning hair and a Crest White Strip smile. He looked like the kind of guy who ate tender cuts of steak for dinner and drank expensive bottles of wine while complaining about cost-of-living raises for his minimum-wage employees.

I knew his type; I dealt with executives like him at every step of my career. A man whose favorite topic was himself. A high-cholesterol corporate warrior who'd go on for hours telling you about his golf swing and yacht club or any one of his five houses. There were numerous clips of him on the web doing exactly that. It seemed no topic was off limits except for his daughter.

On the rare occasion someone in the press asked a question about Evelyn even before her death, he shut down. *How was Hawaii, Mr. Nash? I saw you took your daughter.* Conversation over.

I studied those clips relentlessly. I wanted to understand her. I wanted to know who this woman was who'd destroyed all I'd held dear. She was a waifish woman with a penchant for tight ponytails and ill-fitting dresses who kept her gaze on her shoes in public and carried all the sparkle of a shadow. She had the kind of face that belonged in an anti-depression commercial. One of those women who couldn't bear to look out the window before she took the miracle pill: Sad, puppy dog eyes. Lips tied in a pout. Hair that was limp and dull.

After I got out of the hospital, I received a series of settlement offers from Donald Nash, which I tore up. I didn't want to think about the Nashes every time I went to the grocery store or paid a utility bill. I didn't want another reason for Evelyn to take up space in my brain. But more than that, I didn't want the Nashes to think my family had a price. There was no amount of money I'd accept to pacify their guilt.

Money.

As if that could ever buy me happiness. Ethan and Noah *were* my happiness; all I ever needed was them. In the end, I'd directed the Nash estate to make a contribution to Mothers Against Drunk Driving in Ethan and Noah's memory. I couldn't do anything about my loss, but I figured I might be able to help prevent others. It was the least I could do, and far more than I'd ever done with my life before the wreck.

After that, I tried to forget Evelyn, to forget the Nashes altogether.

Which is why I stiffen the second Ben utters her name.

I clench my teeth and shake my head. "Ben, don't."

He leans forward and his knee pops. "We're talking about her whether you like it or not."

I move to stand. I won't—can't—talk about her. Especially not now. Not today.

"Sit down!"

I freeze. Ben never yells. He's usually calm and soft-spoken. A steady hand.

I settle back into the couch.

"I'm not doing this with you anymore, Bailey! You've avoided talking about her for too long." He waves his hands at the room, at all the disarray and clutter. "All of this is because you've never dealt with what happened. You've never faced it." His voice softens. "Look, I can't pretend to understand what you've been through, but you need a purpose, and this"—he gestures at the room again—"is not purpose. It's the opposite. You don't go anywhere. You don't talk to anyone. You don't call *me*. You're supposed to call *me*, Bay. I'm your brother. It's my job to help you."

You can't help, I think miserably. *No one can.*

His eyes linger on mine, lightning still crackling at the edges. "I get it, though. And I don't blame you. No one should ever have to deal with something like this. But like it or not, this is your reality. You have to face it one way or another."

The pills sing to me from the table. I cross my arms and sink deeper into the cushion. "And how is talking about Evelyn Nash supposed to help me do that?"

"Because you've never heard her side of the story."

"She's dead, Ben. I can't."

He blinks. "That doesn't change the fact you need closure."

I sigh. "What are you suggesting?"

He raises his phone and scrolls, then holds up the screen and points at it, his fingertip coming to rest on a map—an address. "We pay the Nashes a visit."

"Absolutely not."

His gaze hardens. "We're going. Right now. Get dressed."

CHAPTER 20

BAILEY

"This is it," Ben says, pulling up to the gate.

I sit in awe, staring at the house beyond that isn't a house so much as a castle. Chimneys soar from a pitched clay-tile roof. The front is all stone and glass with an entryway that looks like it belongs on a luxury hotel. One we'll never be able to reach. The gate blocking the drive is solid wrought-iron—no way to get through. The sight fills me with relief. I'm not even supposed to be here right now.

I'm supposed to be dead.

"Looks like this is as far as we go," I say.

One corner of Ben's mouth kicks up into a half-grin, and my relief bleeds away. I know that look. He has a plan. He *always* has a plan.

"That's where I come in." He eases his Subaru Impreza forward and slides a white card from his pocket, rolls down the window, then presses the card to the electronic reader curving from the side of the road. The reader lights flash green, and I watch in shock as the gate retracts.

"How?" I ask, still staring at the now wide-open drive.

"Who do you think built the place?"

His architecture firm, I think. *Vertex Group. Oh no.*

"I have an appointment," he continues. "Mrs. Nash wants to

discuss a home renovation project."

"But we won't be doing that, will we?"

He shakes his head.

"Ben, you'll get fired."

"Yeah, probably. But it wouldn't be the worst thing in the world. I've plateaued there anyway."

"No, you haven't. You love your job."

"I do," he admits, chewing on his cheek in contemplation. "But not as much as I love you. Ready?"

I groan. "Not really."

"Too bad." With that, he pulls past the gate. The driveway is enormous. I can't tell if it's stamped tile or artisanal concrete. An expansive lawn skirts it, wrapping around the front of the home and descending toward a massive dock tethered in boats. Beyond it, Lake Washington sparkles with a surreal sort of light. It feels like I'm staring into a postcard.

We park near a perfectly sculpted bank of rhododendrons that fills the car with a sweet scent. It makes me sick. *Being* here makes me sick. The place reeks of money and excess. Every blade of grass is cut to the same exact height. The lawn is a ridiculous shade of green. The shrubs are expertly shaped everywhere I look, not a single stray branch out of place.

The home is worse—beyond opulent. Every inch of it looks custom built from the sprawling windows to the detailed brickwork. I turn my attention to the entryway and its gigantic oak doors. Donald and Paula Nash reside somewhere behind them. I've spent the last two years trying to scrub their faces from my brain. And now, here we are, about to pay them a visit like we're old pals.

But it isn't the prospect of talking to Paula that fills me with dread. She isn't Evelyn's mother. Paula Nash came along after Evelyn was mostly grown. Donald was the one who molded her into the kind of woman who got behind the wheel of a BMW so drunk she could barely drive. Donald is the man who raised the woman who killed my family. And it's Donald who deserves the blame. Not that I have any idea what I'll say to him if he's actually home. *Hi, I'm Bailey Nichols. My family's dead because of your daughter. Mind if I come in?*

A lump forms in my throat and I look away.

"Hey, breathe, okay?" Ben's fingers skim the back of my arm, and I realize it's trembling—that *I'm* trembling—my entire body shaking. Twin trails of warmth run down my cheeks and drip from my chin.

I sniff and take a deep, wet breath as I shake my head. "I can't do this, Ben." My vision blurs. Tears stain my shirt and patter onto my jeans. I don't know how I have any left at this point. I've cried an entire ocean's worth over the last two years.

"Bailey, look at me."

When I don't, he reaches across the console, places his fingertips beneath my chin, and tilts my gaze toward his. His eyes are glassy pink. "You've never fully processed what happened. You stopped going to therapy. You quit your job and shut everyone out. You shut *me* out." He tightens his lips and looks away for a moment. When he looks back again, his voice is thick. "You were about to ... Fuck, Bailey. You were about to kill yourself."

"I wish you would've let me," I whisper.

He winces. "How can you say that?"

I stare down at the backs of my hands and bite my lip. "Because I should have gone with them."

"But you didn't. You survived for a reason."

"Which is what?" I snap, suddenly angry. Anytime anyone tries to paint the wreck in a positive light, I see red. "Mom and Dad are gone! Ethan and Noah are gone! I wake up every single morning without any idea how I'll make it through the day. I'm not even living anymore, Ben. I'm just existing. I don't have anything left to live for."

"You have me."

The words slide into me like a knife. I gaze at him. His cheeks are wet. He's no longer trying to hold back his tears. He went through so much after his fall. It took fifteen surgeries to put him back together. He had to learn to talk again, couldn't eat, dress, or bathe himself without help for so long. He didn't take a single step for months, didn't walk on his own for a year. When faced with challenges like his, most people would have given up. But not Ben. Giving up isn't in his vocabulary. I've been so selfish, so lost in my pain, I've forgotten my brother has plenty of his own. He's right. If I can't live for myself anymore, I can at least try to live for him.

"Okay, fine," I say. "Let's go."

With that, I wipe my eyes and get out of the car.

CHAPTER 21

The memory of Avery's voice fills my head like a spiderweb; impossible to untangle. It took every ounce of my concentration to even understand her to begin with. I had to write the words on my arm in pen as she slurred away, and by the time I looked back to the phone to confirm I had it right, she was gone.

I'm a kingdom of tar,
Both vast and flat.
A place where travelers go tit for tat.

Come to me,
And you'll find your past,
Reflecting darkly, holding fast.

I have no legs, no feet,
No ears,
But still your weeping is all I hear.
What am I?

Be there at noon.

I take a sip of coffee and turn the words over in my head for the thousandth time, little bits of the riddle crashing against the inside of my skull like pinballs. *I'm a kingdom of tar, both vast and flat. A place where travelers go tit for tat.* A kingdom of tar means a highway or a street. It has to. Especially when paired with the tit for tat road rage clue. What else can it be? It makes sense ... until you take the second stanza into consideration.

Come to me, and you'll find your past. Come to me—as in a location. A place that apparently has some sort of meaning to me? But what exactly? I've never been involved in a road rage incident. I've never gone tit for tat with anyone in a car. And the last stanza? It's pure gibberish, the kind of bullshit line that always left me feeling stupid as a kid until someone smarter spouted the answer.

It's all so infuriating. And so ... bizarre.

Why did they make me rush home to meet a timeline that didn't exist? Why did they make me wait all night before contacting me? And why do they want me to run all over town now, doing this—whatever the hell *this* is?—chasing down the answer to some middle-school riddle in order to save my wife? I don't have the slightest clue. All I know is that from the moment they took her, I haven't had a second to catch my breath.

I pause and take another drink of coffee. It's almost 10:00 a.m. and I'm already on my fourth cup of the morning despite my sour stomach. I need the caffeine. It's all I can do to focus with how frazzled I feel, how strung-out. That, and the images of Avery won't stop flashing through my head every ten seconds. Her fist-blackened eye. Her swollen, distended lip. The way her head wobbled when she spoke, like it carried too much weight for her neck. And now, on top of all of that, I'm supposed to solve some fucking riddle in order to save her?

"Goddammit!"

I slam my fist on the table and send my coffee mug crashing to the floor. When it shatters, I don't bother cleaning it up. I have to figure this thing out. I *have* to. I don't have a choice. I close my eyes and try to slow my pulse, then summon the words. *Kingdom of tar, kingdom of tar.* Of all the clues, it's the clearest. But if it's not a highway or a street, then what can it possibly be? A parking lot? And if it is that, *which* parking lot? One that belongs to a store? There aren't thousands of stores in Durango but there are enough that I'll never be able to figure out the right one by noon. No way in hell. If it even is a parking lot.

Play it out. Narrow it down.

I grind my teeth. I might as well. I don't have a better lead at the moment. There's The Home Depot off River Road and the T.J. Maxx off Camino Del Rio. There's the mall, which is essentially one big parking lot. There are the downtown tourist traps. All the souvenir shops packed with T-shirts and trinkets and toys. There are dozens of restaurants. Fucking hell, I have no idea. My mind returns to the final line. *But still your weeping is all I hear.* Something about it feels personal. It's written like it's something that will happen to me. Or something that did. But what that is, I have no idea.

Until I do.

It strikes like a bolt of lightning, so clear, I don't know how I missed it before. *Here you fall.* As a kid, an elderly man ran me over while backing out in a Walmart parking lot. He came stumbling out of his boat of a sedan, burbling apologies, telling me he'd checked his mirror twice. *You sure came outta nowhere!* I didn't hear a word he said. I was too busy writhing on the ground with a broken arm. It took six weeks to heal and robbed me of the rest of my little league season.

It has to be it. It *has* to. Whoever wrote this knows me somehow. It means this abduction is personal—that either Avery or I have done something to someone. Exactly what, I don't know. But it would explain why they still have my wife despite taking all of our money. And that chills me to my core. It means there's a deeper meaning to all of this and I have to keep playing along, dancing like a monkey, until I find out exactly what it is. But I'll do it. I'll dance forever if that's what it takes to keep my wife and child alive.

———

The sky crackles blue above me as I sweep my gaze over the "kingdom of tar." And a kingdom it is. The Walmart parking lot stretches far and wide all around me. I don't know where to go even though I'm early—a full ten minutes ahead of the high noon deadline. Unless I'm wrong. What if I somehow misinterpreted the clues and I should be somewhere else right now?

What if I've already cost Avery her life?

"Stop it!" I hiss so loud that a gray-haired woman shoots me a disapproving look as she passes. I ignore her and keep hawk-eying the parking lot. This is the place. I'm certain of it. At this point, I don't have a better guess, anyway. My certainty fades when noon hits without incident and then ratchets toward panic when five more minutes slide past.

12:05.

12:08.

12:13.

What the fuck? I can't help the thought. Maybe I misread the clues after all. Maybe I'm not in the right spot. I've been standing by my car in clear view—a black Acura sedan I picked up a year ago on sale from a dealership in Denver—so my location should be obvious. I left the Yukon at home. Who it actually belongs to is anybody's guess. I tore through it this morning, searched the glove box and all the compartments and found nothing. Which means it's probably stolen. Continuing to drive it would be foolish. But is that the car they're looking for? Is that why no one has approached me yet? I check my watch for the thousandth time. It's now 12:17 and I feel like I'm about to slide out of my skin.

"Are you Grant Wilson?"

I spin around so fast I nearly fall. There's a kid standing behind me, maybe fifteen years old, with black hair curling out from beneath a red and blue NHRA racing cap. He's wearing the same slightly bored expression as the courier from yesterday, holding something I recognize—something that makes every hair on my body stand on end.

Another manila envelope.

"Yeah," I manage to choke out. "That's me."

"This is for you." He raises the envelope, and I snatch it from his hand so fast it nearly leaves a burn mark on his palm.

"Who gave you this?" I ask.

The kid shrugs. "I don't know. Some guy."

He moves to leave, but I'm on him before he can, seizing his arm and yanking him back. "What does he look like?"

The boy's eyes go wide, his gaze on my hand gripping his wrist.

"What does he look like?" I snarl again.

"I don't know, man. Like any other guy. Let go of me."

"Think," I growl, tightening my grip instead. "It's important."

"He had blue eyes, okay? He gave me twenty bucks to give this to you. Shit! Let me go already!"

"Let go of the kid."

I glance over my shoulder at a man wearing a flannel shirt, cowboy hat, and a pair of shit-kicker boots. He's shorter than me, and thinner. But he's got plenty of muscle, and I can tell by his stance and the way he's got his head cocked to the side he won't shy away from a fight. And I can't get into it with this guy. It will bring way too much attention, which is the absolute last thing I need at the moment.

I release the kid, and he scrambles away as I raise my hands. "It was just a misunderstanding," I say. "I don't want any trouble."

The man twists his lips to the side and sends a wad of tobacco juice to the blacktop. "It sure don't look that way to me."

I don't reply. Nothing I say to this guy will make things better. Instead, I slowly slide into my car and pray he'll be gone when I look in the rearview mirror. He's not—he's still standing there watching me with his arms crossed, his lower lip packed with chew. I start the car and pull forward, not stopping again until I've driven around the back of the building and he's completely out of sight.

And then I sit there, staring at the envelope resting in my lap, feeling like every nerve in my body is about to blow. I don't want to open this thing—I can't handle another visual reminder of what they're doing to my wife—but I have to. What choice do I have? Whatever's inside is my only chance of getting Avery back.

They won't give her back. Not after all of this.

It's another thought I instantly squash. I can't spiral right now. Not when I need to concentrate on what's in the envelope. Either way, after this, I have to find a discreet way to contact the police. I've already decided to. I can't keep doing this on my own. I need help.

I peel the envelope open and tilt it down.

Something rolls out and drops onto my lap.

Bile rises up my throat. I can't believe what I'm seeing.

There's a finger lying in my lap.

A fucking *finger.*

The world around me turns to slush. I gawk at it for a full ten seconds as blood from the severed digit seeps onto my jeans. It looks fresh, the skin tinged pink, the nail painted a light blue. A pale bit of bone extends from the base, roped in tendon. Above it, there's a wedding ring—one that belongs to my wife. My stomach rolls, and I barely get the door open before I vomit.

When I pull myself back into the car, the finger is no longer on my lap. It's lying on the floorboard. It's Avery's finger. I remember the pale blue nail polish from yesterday morning. And I know the ring by heart. I'm the one who gave it to her. I'm still staring at it when a familiar buzzing comes from the envelope. Another phone. I tear it out of the envelope and hit the green accept button.

"You motherfucker! If you—"

"Grant?" The voice snuffs out my anger like a cold wind.

"Avery?"

"Yes, it's me." She's crying as she says it, her voice thick.

"Why are they doing this to us?"

"They say ..." She sniffs and then starts again. "They say it's a warning."

"Jesus! For what? I've done everything they've asked."

"They think you'll go to the police. They told me they'll send more body parts if you do."

Warmth trails down my face. Tears hit my lips. *I'll kill them for this.* I will tear them apart. "I won't contact the cops," I say through gritted teeth. "I swear. I'll do whatever they want."

A man's voice rises muffled in the background, sounding angry. I can't make out the words. My heart thumps harder.

"Baby, where are you?" I ask. "Tell me where you are."

There's a long silence, and then: "They say I have to read the next riddle now. Grant, I'm so scared."

There's a shout, followed by the cold smack of a hand on flesh. Avery shrieks.

"Leave her alone!" I roar into the phone. "Hurt me instead!"

The scuffle ends and Avery returns, her voice quivering. "I—I have to start now. Do you have something to write with?"

I scrabble for a pen and pull a black ball point out of the console as she begins.

"Search for a place with ... with clinical air. Where worried souls bring their despair." She hesitates, and I can hear her sniffling, fighting through tears. "Inside, you'll find what's meant to heal, instead will leave a wound to fill."

Her voice fades, and I wait for her to continue, the pen hovering over the manila envelope. "Is that it? Is there more?"

"You have until one-thirty," she says. "I have to go now."

"No, Avery! Wait!"

But the line is already dead.

I stare through the windshield, gutted. I don't look at the finger.

What they've done to her is unthinkable. I can't begin to imagine her pain. I wipe the tears from my eyes and tell myself to get it together. I can't fall apart. Not when I have another fucking riddle to solve.

CHAPTER 22

GRANT

The automatic doors open with a pneumatic whoosh, and I'm hit with a cold wave of refrigerated air. The air is exactly why I'm walking into Mercy Hospital. It's the first line in the latest riddle from hell. *Search for a place with clinical air.* Clinical, a doctor's office or a medical facility.

A hospital.

What else can it be? There are over a dozen primary care and outpatient procedure offices located in Durango. Even with an entire day to blow, it would be hard to visit them all. With the time I have left—forty minutes now—it would be impossible. Surely Avery's kidnappers know that, so it has to be the hospital. The logic tracks. Hospitals are full of worried people. Hospitals heal. And if a procedure goes wrong, well, that happens frequently, too.

I march across the beige-tiled lobby with streams of afternoon sunlight spilling through the skylights above. Pastel naturescapes hang on the walls. Horses in mid gallop with their manes streaming behind them. Flowered meadows and sunlit, rolling hills. They're nothing but a distraction. The only image I can see is Avery's severed finger. The only noise I can hear is her voice leaking through the phone in tangled sobs.

I will kill whoever is doing this, I think again. *I swear it.*

There's a line at the reception desk. Of course, there is. But I don't have time to wait, so I cut right to the front where a woman is in the middle of telling the receptionist how she isn't sure how she's going to be able to afford her husband's treatment.

"We just switched our insurance and we're having trouble getting them to—"

"Excuse me," I say, interrupting her.

The receptionist, a woman with thick eyebrows and the underbite of a pug, looks my way.

"Sir, you'll need to wait your turn."

"I have an emergency."

"A medical emergency?"

"Yes. Has anyone left anything with you?"

"What do mean?" she asks, her eyes narrowing in confusion.

"Has anyone been in here in the last few minutes? A big guy carrying an envelope? Or a kid? Anyone who might have left something for me?"

She frowns, about to respond when a finger taps my shoulder.

"I was here first. We were in the middle of a conversation, and you interrupted me."

I don't bother to look at the woman, just raise my hand in dismissal as I continue to interrogate the receptionist: "It would be an envelope or a package—something with my name on it. Can you please check for me really quick?"

Grumbles rise behind me. The receptionist rolls her eyes. "What's your name?"

"Grant Wilson."

She leans over and digs through her desk as the people in line mutter with voices loud enough to hear:

"How rude."

"Who does this guy think he is?

"What a jerk."

Please be there, I think as the receptionist searches. *Please, please, please...*

She reappears, shaking her head. "Sorry. There's nothing here for a Grant Wilson."

I don't move. "Are you sure? There has to be ..." *What? What are you expecting?* "... something. You didn't check those baskets over there." I point at the two wire organizers overflowing with documents further down the desk.

"Those are intake forms," the receptionist says, her tone turning cold. "Do I need to call security?"

"Wait," I say, fighting for control. "Just wait. My wife is in trouble. It's very important I find her. I know it sounds strange, but I was given a clue that led me here." My voice cracks on the last word. I'm a few seconds away from a full-on panic attack. Because if this isn't the right place, I'm completely screwed—and so is Avery.

Her frown deepens. "A clue?"

"A ... riddle." Even in my panicked state, I know how stupid I must sound.

The woman releases an aggravated exhale. "Look, sir, I can tell you're upset. If you're worried about your wife, you should go to the police."

"You don't understand," I say, resisting the urge to scream. "I can't do that."

"What's the riddle?" a voice to my right asks. I turn and take in the woman I interrupted for the first time. She has curly, close-cropped black hair and is staring back at me through a ridiculously large set of purple-rimmed glasses, no longer looking annoyed but curious.

"What?" I say, taken aback.

"What is it? Your riddle. I'm good at them."

"Jesus H. Christ," the man directly behind us mutters.

I hesitate, but not for long. I'm out of options and I'm out of time. If this woman can help me, I'll take it. I speak the lines and the room falls silent, everyone listening in.

Her forehead puckers when I finish. She taps her foot.

"Say it again."

I do, and her lips move in an echo of mine, her eyes tilting upward as she thinks. "Hmm, you're right. A hospital does make sense. But obviously that's not the answer, since no one here knows what you're talking about. It has to be something else. That line about the wound, though. It doesn't really fit here as well as it would at ..." Her voice fades and her throat moves in a long, slow swallow. Her eyes wilt. "Oh."

"What?" I ask, peering at the clock on the wall, noting the time: Twenty-eight minutes left. I can literally feel the time flowing past, quickly closing on empty.

Her expression softens, the tips of her eyebrows rising slightly. She reaches out and places her hand on my elbow. "I'm sorry, but you might want to try the CARE Center on the north end of town."

"The CARE Center?" I ask. "What's that?"

She hesitates, and then says, "It's ... an abortion clinic."

CHAPTER 23

REED
Midland, Texas
Age Twelve

Reed and his father had been in Midland for a year and a half now—
the longest they'd been anywhere—and to Reed, it was starting to feel
like home. The people here were friendly and spoke with a rich twang
that warmed his soul. He liked the way the teachers took time to really
explain things to him in a way he could understand. Even better, the
kids were nice. They didn't make fun of his ripped jeans and worn
shirts like so many others had.

Reed and his father had rented a home on the eastern edge of
town that had paint-chipped cupboards, a living room covered in
stains, and two bedrooms the size of closets. His dad had taken the
larger one, of course. They didn't have much of a lawn, and what they
did have was covered in trash. Plastic sacks, mainly. No matter how
often they picked them up, the bags blew back in. They seemed to be
everywhere in Midland, scattered by the wind, clinging to the bushes
and their fence like tattered ghosts. Bags strung all over the street like
roadkill. But still, the place was better than their last by a mile, so Reed
didn't mind.

Most days went like this: Reed's dad would climb into his busted Chevy pickup and head out to his job as a roustabout in the oil fields before first light. Reed would wake to his alarm, grab a Pop-Tart, throw on his backpack, and head to school. The walk was two miles of dirt and concrete and endless sky, which gave Reed time to think about all the things he wanted to be when he grew up. A doctor or a teacher or a firefighter. Or maybe even a football player if was lucky. He was good at it. All the kids said so, and he loved playing. Really, he'd be happy with pretty much any job other than becoming a forklift driver or an oilfield guy like his dad. After school, he'd walk back home, do his homework, and then warm up two frozen pizzas. Dinner needed to be ready by six o'clock sharp because his dad came home hungry.

It was a rhythm he moved to well. Dad would stroll through the door smelling like dirt and grease. They'd talk about all kinds of things while they ate, like Reed's grades, his teachers and friends, and how he'd aced his math test. Reed's Dad would smile at that, clap him on the back, and tell him to keep it up. Then he'd complain to Reed about his day—tell him how Hank had wronged him, or Louis, or that sonuvabitch Jim or Bob. Reed had never seen these faceless men in person, but somehow he felt like he knew them. Guys who had it out for Dad were everywhere they went. When he got tired of talking about them, he and Reed would watch some TV together and then go to bed.

Reed loved those days. Those days were good.

There were other days, though. Thundercloud days. The days his dad came home late or didn't come home until long after Reed had gone to bed. On these days, Reed knew to take cover. He ate his dinner alone, cleaned the kitchen, and retreated to his room. There was no sense waiting up. He'd done it a few times and knew how it went. Dad would bang inside like an overheated engine at some point smelling like smoke and beer and talk in a way that didn't sound like him, his words slurred, his voice loud. Then he'd throw things, break things, tell Reed shit was about to hit the fan.

And shit had definitely hit the fan.

It had happened a month ago, on a Thursday. Reed had dinner ready as usual when his dad showed up, but when he came through the door, it was with bloody knuckles and a broken nose. Reed knew what it meant, he'd seen it before. *Pack up your shit, Reed. It's time to go.* His father even started grumbling about moving closer to his sister, which made Reed shiver. He did *not* want to move there.

His Aunt Beth was as thin as a skeleton and smelled like cigarettes and never seemed happy to see Reed. Mostly she seemed annoyed, waving him away with a flick of her fingers after a quick, one-armed squeeze hello. She'd only visited them a handful of times over the years, but it was enough that Reed remembered how he'd had to walk on eggshells around her and was relieved when she left. The thought of living anywhere close to Aunt Beth made his stomach hurt.

Thankfully though, when Reed had asked his father if they were going to move a week later, he'd simply replied, "We're not going anywhere."

"Really?" Reed had asked hopefully.

"I'm tired of chasing work. I'm done. There are other ways to make money." And then his gaze had settled on Reed full of a different kind of light. Instead of dull and defeated, it looked *alive.* "It's time I showed you how."

And he had. For the last three weekends, they'd visited the wealthy neighborhoods around town with Reed dressed in a Boy Scout uniform they'd found at the local Goodwill. They took donations for fake charities with names that fell out of his father's mouth at will. The Global Relief Initiative. Seeds of Change. The Foundation for a Better Tomorrow. The charities sounded real enough, but Reed knew they weren't because when people actually donated, they kept all of the money.

Reed felt a little bad about it at first, but not for long. He'd never seen his dad this excited before. He'd put on his gray suit, comb his hair, and it was like Reed was staring at a brand-new man. Even with his bruised face, he looked presentable. But it was the way he spoke when people opened the door that really blew Reed away. It was awesome.

"Hello, ma'am. It's a pleasure to meet you. If you can spare a minute, my son is in local troop five-twenty-nine, and we're out meeting our neighbors and raising proceeds for the Women's Empowerment Fund. They provide assistance to underprivileged women and girls who are trying to escape dangerous situations."

When his dad finished, is was Reed's turn. He would recite a few lines they'd rehearsed beforehand and paste a big ray of sunshine on his face. At this point, whoever was at the door would usually smile and say they were happy to donate a few dollars. Then Reed would hand them a pamphlet listing all of the charities that didn't exist and wait patiently until they paid. When they did, Reed's dad said cash was best, but if they needed to pay with a check, that was okay, too.

When Reed asked his dad how he turned a check into money, he told Reed it was called check washing. Reed didn't understand that at all because whatever weird chemicals his dad used to erase the charity's name didn't smell like soap. They just made Reed's nose burn and his eyes water. It didn't always work, either—sometimes his dad had to throw the checks away—but when it did, it made him especially happy, which made Reed happy too.

On those days, his dad would take Reed to Applebee's and tell him to order anything on the menu. He'd worked for it, after all. Reed loved those dinners. The food was amazing—and way better than frozen pizza. Even better than that, though, was how his dad had come back to life. He no longer sat on the couch and sulked like he used to when things didn't go his way at work. He walked Reed to school instead and played catch with him in the park on the way home. They went to the movies, and Dad would point at the people in the theater and laugh at how stupid most of them were. *Those idiots deserve to lose their money,* he'd say. *They have more than they need. Look at that guy's fancy watch. Losing a few bucks means nothing to him.* And in those moments, sitting next to his dad before the screen came to life, Reed agreed. Those idiots *did* deserve to lose their money. He and his dad needed it way more.

"I'm proud of you, Reed," his father would say before the movie started, looping his arm around Reed's shoulders. "You're a hell of a good son."

And in those moments, Reed truly loved his father. He hoped it would go like this forever. But this was the last weekend they would be pulling the Boy Scout scam. His dad told him you never wanted to do one thing for too long or people would catch on. Reed understood. It made sense. But it also made him sad. He'd gotten good with his speech, especially when it came to the Rwandan refugee crisis. He'd even managed to summon a few tears at the last house, which had led to an extra fifty bucks.

"Ready?" his dad asked, squeezing his shoulder as they stood on the sidewalk in front of the last home of the day. Reed knew this neighborhood. Everyone in Midland did. Grassland Estates was full of rich people, and this house looked richer than most. He'd make Dad proud, he told himself. He would no matter what.

He nodded.

They strolled up the walkway and rang the bell. When the door opened, it was to a woman with smooth blonde hair and a red-lipstick smile. Reed's heart leaped. The scam always worked best on women. And women were who they were really out here to get. Reed's dad had told him as much. Women were lazy. They stayed at home and spent their husbands' hard-earned money on fancy clothes and jewelry. *They steal from them, like your mom stole from us, Reed. It's really no different. They've earned what we're about to do to them.*

And to Reed, this woman, more than any of the others they'd come across today, looked like one of *those* women. The kind of woman that sat around all day eating chocolates and watching TV while her husband worked. She had big diamond earrings hanging off her ears and a bunch of rings shining from her fingers. It reminded Reed of his mother. She'd always wanted rings and necklaces. She'd bitched at Dad for them all the time. Then, when he'd told her no, she'd taken all of their money and run. The memory made Reed hate this woman. It made Reed want to make her pay.

He worked up the tears before Dad started talking about the Wounded Patriots Project. When his turn came, he gave the performance of his life. There were so many soldiers out there with missing legs and arms who really needed their help, and how could they even support themselves like that? He was about to hand over the donation pamphlet when he realized the woman was no longer looking at him. She was staring at his dad instead.

"Sorry, which troop did y'all say you were from again?"

"Five-twenty-nine," his dad replied without hesitation.

A deep line formed above the woman's nose. She frowned. "I don't think there's a troop five-twenty-nine in Midland."

His father hesitated, swallowed. "Oh, we're from the other side of the city, down in Belmont, actually. You probably haven't heard of us."

Her frown got bigger. "No, I would have, I'm sure." She glanced back over her shoulder. "Hey, Lloyd! Lloyd, come out here for a sec, will you?"

The door opened wider, and a man with a square head and a buzz-cut appeared behind her. His arms were bigger than his father's and so was his gut. He probably liked beer, too. "Yeah?" Lloyd said, his gaze still lingering on the football game blaring from the living room.

"These gentlemen say they're from troop five twenty-nine. They're asking for donations."

At this, Lloyd's attention sharpened. He squinted at Reed and his father. "There isn't a troop five-twenty-nine."

"See. That's what I thought," the woman said, proudly crossing her arms.

"Like I said, we're from across the city," Reed's father repeated, but his voice no longer held the same conviction. Something oily slid through Reed. This wasn't how it was supposed to go.

"Who's your scoutmaster?" Lloyd asked.

"Doug Waverly," Reed's dad replied, looking less confident by the second. "You wouldn't know him."

"Oh, I would," Lloyd said, stepping out onto the porch, "because I'm the district commissioner for all the Midland troops, and I'm telling you we don't have a troop five-twenty-nine." His attention fell to the pamphlet clutched in Reed's hand. "And we don't have any scouts doing donation drives, either."

"Okay, well it must be a misunderstanding, then. We'll be on our way." His father took a step back, pulling Reed after him.

The woman pursed her lips and narrowed her eyes. "Just what kind of business are you two up to?"

Reed felt his father bristle. "Nothing, ma'am," his dad said. "Thanks for your time."

"I don't think so," the woman said. "You better believe I'm going to look into this."

"You go on and do that," his dad said, then lowered his voice. "Bitch."

Lloyd's face, which until this moment had carried a look of mild annoyance, flashed to something darker. "What'd you say?"

Don't, Reed thought, peering up at his dad. *Please.*

He took hold of his dad's wrist and tugged him toward the street. But his father remained right where he stood. He didn't even look at Lloyd, simply stared past him at the woman, who was staring right back at Reed's dad the way Reed's mother used to before she laid into him.

"I said ..." Reed's father drew the word out. "That your wife is a fucking *bitch*."

Lloyd snarled. Reed had only seen his father in a fight once—at a pop warner football game when his dad had cursed at the ref after a bad call. Another dad told him to knock it off, and Reed's dad said to make him. So the man tried. Sure, Reed's dad took his share of licks, but he gave more than he got, and the blows he landed were dirty—scratching, biting, kicking the guy in the nuts. Nothing was off limits. So, Reed didn't doubt his dad would be able to handle himself against this man, either, even though Lloyd looked to be six inches taller as he shot forward and swung his arm.

Smooth as an eel, Reed's dad slipped to the side and ducked. Lloyd's punch hit nothing but air. And then his dad was on the guy—hammering a fist into Lloyd's stomach before swinging around him and leaping onto his back. His teeth sank into the man's neck like a vampire's. Lloyd barked in surprise and heaved himself backward, slamming Reed's dad into the front of the house with a crunch and a loud whoosh of air.

He slid down the wall looking dazed as Lloyd stumbled forward. The collar of his shirt was drenched in blood, his face white.

The woman shrieked, had been shrieking this entire time. "Stop it! Stop it! Stop it!"

For a moment, Reed thought they would. But then his father rose with a wild light in his eyes. Blood stained his lips. His fists were bunched. He rushed Lloyd and took flight, spearing Lloyd in the gut with his shoulder. They toppled together in a lazy, slow-motion arc. When the back of Lloyd's head connected with the cement walk it sounded like an eggshell cracking. The only thing Reed heard after that was the woman's screams.

CHAPTER 24

Ben rings the doorbell. When no one answers, he hammers on the Nashes' door with his fist.

"No one's home," I mutter, turning to leave.

He stops knocking and glares at me, his eyes pinning me in place as the faint sound of heels clicking comes from inside. A moment later, the door swivels open to reveal a woman with a face like a bird's. I recognize her from the photo I saw of Evelyn's funeral. Paula Nash has a nose like a hawk and eyes that are sharp and clear. Her brown hair is pulled into a tight bun on top of her head, and she has high-waisted cotton trousers on that run down to a pair of calfskin leather boots. She looks immaculate, like she's just stepped off the pages of *Elle.* But the dark circles under her eyes don't match her outfit.

She blinks at us in confusion. "Can I help you?"

"Hello, Mrs. Nash," Ben says, offering his hand. "I'm Ben Allison from Vertex. We're here to discuss your kitchen remodel."

"Oh ... right. I forgot that was today. I'm afraid now isn't a good time."

"I can assure you it will only take a few minutes," Ben says, pressing closer.

I eye him warily.

Paula shakes her head and gives him a polite smile. "I'm sorry, but something's come up. I'll have my assistant call your office and reschedule for next month." She moves to shut the door, but Ben steps forward and jams his cane in the gap before she can.

"What are you doing?" she asks, looking down sharply, then up again, her expression turning grim.

"Look, Mrs. Nash, I'll level with you. This is my sister, Bailey Nichols. Does that name ring a bell?"

Her eyes flick toward me and she studies me for an uncomfortable moment before her lips part with a soft gasp. "Oh."

"As you can probably guess, we're not really here about the kitchen," Ben says. "May we come in?"

Paula appraises me for a moment longer, then steps back with a sigh. "Today of all days. Yes, I suppose. This way."

The house unfolds around us like a castle as we trail after her. Everything is gleaming, the floor a river of polished hardwood. When we enter the living room, it steals my breath. A chandelier hangs from a sprawling ceiling thirty feet overhead, dripping with crystal. Expensive-looking pieces of art adorn the walls—landscapes painted in oils and pastels that look like they belong in a museum. A curving floor-to-ceiling sheet of glass across the room gives view to Lake Washington, the water glittering with dappled light.

"Please sit," Paula says, waving us toward a large sectional couch and several accent chairs. "I'll be right back."

I settle onto the sofa as she breezes from the room. Ben chooses a chair.

I pop an eyebrow at him. "I can't believe you."

"What?" Ben says with a shrug. "We're inside, aren't we?"

I roll my eyes. Paula returns a minute later carrying three bottles of San Pellegrino. She hands a bottle to me and one to Ben and then uncaps hers and sits. "How can I help you?"

You can't, I think bitterly. *No one can.*

Ben shifts next to me. "We'd like to talk about your daughter, Mrs. Nash."

She crosses her legs. "Evelyn wasn't my daughter."

Which I know is true. Evelyn Nash's mother, Donald Nash's first wife, had returned to her home country, Russia, a couple of years after their divorce, when Evelyn was four. I'd seen several photos of the woman—severe-faced with cheeks splattered in rosacea. A starter wife before Donald minted his fortune and traded her in for a Ukrainian supermodel. That marriage didn't last long, either. A couple of years maybe, before she cashed in and ran for the hills.

It explains Paula Nash, I guess. Attractive enough, but not ridiculously so. Intelligent. A worthy counterpart to someone like Donald. I know her type—someone who stands her ground when pushed. Ambitious but loyal. A woman who doesn't take any shit. Women like her made partner in my old life. Hell, before the wreck, I *was* her.

"Be that as it may," Ben continues, "I think it would help my sister and I find some closure if we understood her a little better. Is your husband home by chance? It would be nice if we could visit with him, too."

Paula's eyes dim. "Don's dead."

I straighten. *Dead?* Even as closed off from the world as I've been, the death of someone like Donald Nash would have wormed its way through my grief at some point. There's no keeping that kind of news at bay. But I hadn't heard a word about this.

"Dead?" Ben echoes, clearly as shocked as I am.

Paula picks a stray piece of lint from her pants and studies it for a moment then flutters her fingers. "Yes."

"I wasn't aware," Ben says.

"No one is," Paula says. "It happened a few days ago. We've had to keep it close to the vest. I'm sure you can appreciate what the death of someone like Don can do to a company if it isn't properly managed."

"So why are you telling us?" I ask.

"Because it's confidential. Not that I expect you'll run out and notify the press, but I'd like to keep it that way for now."

Ben blows out a slow stream of air. "Wow. Can I ask what happened?"

Paula folds her hands and places them in her lap. A flicker of affection flashes across her face mixed with a slash of grief. Emotions I know all too well. "He had a heart attack."

"I'm sorry," I hear myself mutter, even though I'm not.

"Thank you," Paula says. "But he's ... been dead for years."

"What do you mean?"

"He died when Evelyn did. He loved that girl with all his heart. When she passed, the spark went out of him. He wasn't the same man anymore." Her gaze settles on me. "He looked a lot like you do now. I want you to know how sorry I am for what happened to your family."

I open my mouth and close it. A thick clump forms in my throat, and I tell myself not to cry, not here in front of this woman. Ben gives my hand a squeeze.

"If you're here for closure," Paula says, "I'm not sure I can provide that for you. But I'll try. Even though Evelyn wasn't my daughter, I loved her like one. She was special."

I tense. *Special*. Noah was special. Ethan was special. Evelyn Nash was anything *but* special.

Paula tilts her head. "I can see that bothers you."

"Of course it does," I say. "She was driving drunk."

"There were ... extenuating circumstances. What Evelyn did wasn't her fault."

I blink and feel my lips go numb. "How can you say that?"

"Because it's true." Paula Nash leans back in her chair and takes another drink. "Make yourself comfortable. I have quite the story to share."

CHAPTER 25

BAILEY

"Evelyn had autism," Paula says. "She was funny in a lot of ways. Brilliant in others. But as you can probably guess, she wasn't always the easiest to connect with. Or to raise."

Autism. I don't know much about the condition other than what I've seen in the movies and at Noah's daycare. One of the kids there had it and always seemed to be melting down.

"That had to be difficult," Ben says.

Paula nods. "Very much so. It takes someone special to raise an autistic child. Not everyone is cut out for it. Evelyn's birth mother Nina certainly wasn't. Neither was Francesca."

"Francesca?" I ask.

"Don's second wife," Paula says. "She wanted everything to revolve around her. When Don prioritized his daughter, she left. I could have called that one from a mile away, but men will be men. Even someone like Don."

I want to roll my eyes. *Someone like Don.* Like the man is some kind of saint. "So why did you stay when the others didn't?" I blurt, annoyed.

Paula laces her fingers together and sets her hands in her lap. "I didn't meet Evelyn until she was sixteen. I didn't have the same challenges Francesca and Nina did. By the time I came around, Evelyn was mostly self-sufficient. That's not to say we didn't have our share of problems."

Ben leans in. "Like what?"

"Evelyn was always looking for connection. She wanted to fit in, to make friends. But that was difficult for her. Teenagers are mean, even at a private school. She was bullied. There were suicide attempts."

I feel Ben's gaze on me. I don't turn his way.

Paula continues: "Don was beside himself every time it happened. He didn't understand it. To him, Evelyn was perfect. Beautiful in every way. He blamed himself. He pulled her out of school."

"How many attempts were there?" Ben asks.

The question hangs there, Paula tapping her bottle of San Pellegrino before finally answering. "Three. One happened before I married Don and two after."

"I'm sorry," I say, struggling to process this new information, not sure how to reconcile it with my hate.

"It wasn't easy," Paula says. "Don took a sabbatical. We spent every day with her. I did what I could to cheer her up, but it was Don who really brought her back to life. He poured himself into her every chance he got."

I try to imagine Donald Nash in this light and struggle to do so. From the video clips I'd watched, he'd seemed so full of himself, so self-absorbed. But that doesn't mean it didn't happen. Maybe I'd misjudged the man.

"He truly believed he could save her," Paula says. "Though I didn't always share his optimism." She looks away for a moment, seemingly lost in a memory. When she turns back, her eyes are wet. "Evelyn walked in on me crying once, a few weeks after she came home from the hospital after one of her suicide attempts. When she asked me what was wrong, I told her what she did made me sad. I said I didn't want to lose her." Paula gives a sudden laugh and wipes her eyes. "Do you know what the girl did after that?"

I shake my head.

"She picked flowers. She hid them in these funny places only I would find. In my purse. In my makeup drawer. All around my closet. I even found one in the pocket of my jacket once. I sometimes spotted her in the garden picking them. Evelyn didn't always know how to talk to me, but she always made sure I knew I was loved.

"Evelyn seemed to improve from there, especially when Don fostered her creativity. She had real artistic talent. He helped her channel that talent. We flew to Italy a few times, and he introduced her to the greats. Botticelli and Caravaggio. Da Vinci. Raphael. After that, she really took off. She went to college and got a job in graphic design after graduation."

"She was able to do that?" Ben asks, before adding, "I'm sorry if that's a rude question. I don't know much about autism."

"Oh, yes. She was more than capable of living life on her own. And once she started to do that, it was a huge relief for Don. For both of us, really. Things settled down. It relieved the pressure. Evelyn flourished. We thought she was going to be okay."

"What changed?" I ask.

"She met someone."

I straighten. "Who?"

"A man. His name was Adrian Wallace."

"A romantic interest?" Ben asks.

Paula nods. "Yes. It wasn't the first time she dated someone. There were a few men before Adrian, but they never lasted. Adrian was different."

"Different how?" I ask, feeling myself being pulled into the story against my will. "He didn't treat her well?"

"Quite the opposite, actually. He treated her very well. They shared the same taste in music. Both of them loved art. Adrian was very attentive to her needs. He worshiped the ground she walked on. He was very kind to both Don and me. He seemed like a real catch."

Ben tilts his head. "And that was a problem, why?"

"It wasn't," Paula says. "Not in and of itself."

"What, then?" I ask, my impatience building.

Paula takes a drink of water, then sets the bottle aside. "I didn't trust him at first. Don didn't either. He seemed a little too eager to please Evelyn. He was a little too interested. It wasn't normal. Like I said, even though Evelyn wanted to connect with people, it was difficult for her. Especially when it came to men. She didn't know how to talk to them. She was, well, awkward. Most men weren't willing to put up with that aspect of her personality."

"But Adrian was?" I ask.

"Yes. He was quite taken with her. Don and I couldn't put our finger on it. The relationship moved really fast."

Ben shifts in the chair. "Honestly, a lot of couples move quickly. Besides Evelyn's autism, that doesn't sound all that out of the ordinary."

"That's what I told Don," Paula says. "It took a while, but Adrian grew on me. I could see why Evelyn was so infatuated with him. He was easy company. Very likable. But Don never came around. He was always a little suspicious of Adrian. Well, more than a little. A lot. I eventually had to tell him to calm down, especially after they moved in together." She shakes her head. "That didn't go well at all. We only found out because we stopped by Evelyn's condo for lunch and Adrian's things were everywhere. She told us then, just blurted it out. 'We live together now.' We were both shocked. They'd only been together for four months. Don flipped his lid."

I shift on the couch. I can't handle this any longer. As sad and complicated as Evelyn's story is, it doesn't change the fact that she killed my family. I need to know where this is going.

"What does any of this have to do with me?"

"Bailey," Ben says, casting me a mind-your-manners look. "Let her finish."

"It's okay," Paula says, surveying me. "If I was in your shoes, I'd ask the same question. But I'm not sure what I have to share with you will help you find much peace."

I feel my skin prickle, goosebumps rising along my arms. The way this woman is looking at me—like whatever it is she has to share will upend my world—sets off an internal alarm. For the briefest of seconds, I consider telling her to keep it to herself, but I know I can't do that.

"Please, just tell me," I say, bracing myself.

Paula raises her hand as if to rub her cheek, hesitates, and then returns it to her lap with a sigh. "The day your family died, Evelyn wasn't the one driving. Adrian was."

CHAPTER 26

GRANT

I jump out of the Acura and race for the front steps of the CARE Center. A sign hangs above the door, spelling out the abbreviation: Compassionate Abortion & Reproductive Education. I barely note it before looking at my watch to ensure I'm not late, that I still have time. And I do. It's 1:26. Four minutes. That's all.

I'm breathless as I fling the door open and bang inside. The doorknob slams into the wall. There's an office on the opposite side of the room with a long sheet of what looks like either laminated or polycarbonate glass and a steel door stationed next to it. Behind the glass is another receptionist. She's much younger than the woman at the hospital. Her blue-tinged hair is shaved on one side, revealing an ear studded in silver earrings and her eyes are rimmed in dark eyeliner. They're wide with worry as she takes me in, looking at me like I've lost my mind, probably wondering if I'm a psychopath seconds away from lighting up the place.

"Sorry," I say, raising my hands. "I didn't mean to scare you. I'm just in a hurry."

The woman visibly relaxes and leans forward to speak through a hole in the glass. "Yeah, I'll say. What do you need?"

The way she says it, the words rushed, her voice clipped—*What do you need?*—tells me she's already itching for me to leave. I need to tread lightly here. The last thing I want is for her to press some hidden panic button beneath the counter. I slide my hands into my pockets and edge forward slowly in a way I hope puts her at ease. "Has anyone left a manila envelope with you by chance?"

She gives me a *seriously, dude?* quirk of her eyebrow.

"A big guy maybe, with blue eyes? If he did, it would have been for me."

The woman's eyebrow rises higher.

Great, Grant. Way to calm her down. I cringe. I'm making it worse, talking about a big guy coming into an abortion clinic, right after banging inside like a maniac myself. But it's literally the only description I have. And it could be Gunn delivering the packages or Holston, or a dozen other people I have no chance of identifying.

"We don't exactly hand out descriptions," the woman finally says. "You do know where you are, right?"

Her question sits in the pit of my stomach like a stone. I know exactly where I am. I've been here before—a long time ago. The place has changed substantially. There are the new security cameras and safety features along with a fresh coat of paint and updated trim, but that doesn't stop me from instantly smelling the sharp antiseptic scent permeating the place. It doesn't change the weight of the air, so oppressive and thick that it feels like I'll suffocate if I don't get outside in the next few minutes. And it doesn't stop the specks of black from whirling through my vision as I speak because it's a place I swore I'd never visit again.

"Yeah, I do," I say. "I know this all must seem a little weird, but it's for a work scavenger-hunt thing. This guy would have left something for me in here." The explanation is beyond ridiculous but it's the only lie I can muster at the moment that makes even a sliver of sense.

The woman squints at me. "It's more than a little weird, guy. It's weird as fuck. But no one's left anything for you." She crosses her arms and just like that, the conversation is over. I glance at the clock on the wall behind her. It's 1:32: two minutes past the deadline and I'm completely screwed.

The room tilts and whirls.

"Hey, are you okay?" the woman asks. "You don't look so good."

"I don't ..." Saliva fills my mouth. My stomach churns. I take a lurching step sideways and barely manage to collapse into a chair before I fall. I don't even hear the receptionist as she exits the office, don't recognize she's crouching in front of me until she presses a bottle of water in my hand. "Here, drink this. I'm going to get a doctor."

I take the bottle and manage to uncap it. Water spills down my throat as my gaze settles on a framed poster on the opposite wall. It's a picture of a woman in a white dress standing on a hill overlooking a rolling forest. The words *Hope Lives Here* are stenciled over her head in a soft blue font. The last thing I feel right now is hope.

Heat stings my eyes.

God, I'm so sorry, I whisper, thinking of Avery, of my baby. *I failed you both.*

Bzzz bzzz bzzz.

I cock my head. There's a quiet buzz coming from ... *where?*

I wipe my eyes with the back of my hand and scramble out of my seat, follow the noise toward a side table on the opposite side of the room. The sound is muffled, hidden somewhere, but it's there, growing louder: A phone.

I yank open the drawer and find a pen and some birth control pamphlets inside. Nothing else.

Where is it coming from?

My eyes light on the plant resting on top of the table. A fern. Maybe it's buried in the pot? I'm about to dig into it when the buzzing stops.

No, no, no, no, no.

And then starts again, originating from somewhere lower. I drop to my knees and scan the carpet. Nothing. My gaze ticks higher—and there it is, duct taped to the underside of the table. It takes me a single second to rip it free, hit the green call accept button, and stand.

"Hello," I gasp.

"Cutting it a little close, don't you think?" The words drip through the speaker in a disguised slur, menacing and gruff.

"I'm here, aren't I?"

Across the room, the receptionist bursts through the door with an older woman, both of them heading straight for me, looking concerned. But I'm already moving away from them, angling toward the door.

"Why are you *still* doing this?" I hiss, pushing outside.

"Are you ready for your final clue?" the voice replies.

"Put Avery on right fucking now!" I'm vaguely aware of the women watching me through the window as I pace toward my car and get in.

Silence fills my ear, the sound of static.

And then: "You've talked to her enough."

I slam the heel of my foot into the floorboard. I want to scream. "How do I know she's still safe? After everything you've done to her!"

"You don't. But if you delay any longer, I can guarantee she won't be. Now pay attention." The voice crackles into my ear, revealing the final riddle. I memorize the words as they're delivered, mentally rehearsing the lines, running them through my head one-by-one. "Got it?" the voice asks after a moment.

"Yes," I growl.

"One more thing," the voice says. "Make sure you bring a shovel."

CHAPTER 27

When I reach the location, the sun is diving toward the San Juans. It highlights them in a dusty ribbon of pink I would normally find beautiful but right now doesn't even register. The entire world might as well be painted in black and white for all I care. The only important thing at the moment is whether or not I'm at the right spot.

> *Return to the place where love first bloomed.*
> *Where two hearts joined much too soon.*
> *You vowed a love without regret.*
> *But instead you broke, and your path was set.*
> *Be there at seven.*

I run the words through my head once more and then, with a hard swallow, I open the door and get out. Needles of apprehension lace down my spine as I grab the shovel from the trunk and yank it free. Questions churn through my head in rapid succession, one after another, none of them good.

Why do I need this? Is it to bury Avery? Or is it to dig a grave for myself?

Acid bubbles at the base of my esophagus and threatens to boil up my throat as I round the car. The meadow beyond the fence is as beautiful as I remember, swaying with tall banks of grass in between clumps of sagebrush and bunches of juniper. Beyond them, closer to the center of the field, is a tall stand of cottonwood overlooking a small pond. A rope swing hangs from a branch near the water where I used to sit and feed the ducks. I have so many memories of this place, so many recollections of good times. And it's chilling how staring at it now makes me shiver. *This is definitely personal.*

I cross the road and lean the shovel against the fence. And then I wait. This far out in the country, there aren't many cars or houses around. Outside of the odd McMansion every few miles, there's not much in the way of civilization. The only home I can see from here is the one beyond the meadow, looking sleek in the distance, fronted by a massive front lawn. It's a house I once loved because I loved the girl who lived there. A girl who's long grown and gone.

I turn my attention back to the pond, sweating even though the temperature has cooled to a comfortable seventy degrees. I don't know why I'm here. All I know is every moment since that van rattled out of the forest yesterday and swallowed my wife has led me to this place.

Where I continue to wait.

And wait.

Until the phone I took from the abortion clinic in my pocket finally rings. An overwhelming sense of dread overtakes me as I pull it out and hit answer.

"I'm here. What now?"

"Go to the center of the field," the robot voice orders. "Past the willows toward the hill. Keep the phone on."

"Why?" I ask. But no answer comes.

I toss the shovel over the fence and clamber after it, holding the phone in one hand. Even here this close to the road the grass is tall and wild, coming to my waist. The ground is lumpy and uneven beneath my feet as I walk. Every step is an effort, every movement feels like swimming through sand. It takes me five minutes to reach the willows and then another five to push my way through. When I finally break free, a wave of gooseflesh ripples down my back. There's a small white cross planted at the top of the hill—one I didn't see until now.

I raise the phone to my ear. "What is this?"

"This is where you dig." The phone clicks off.

Dig. The word leaves me shaken. They're watching me. I can feel their gaze boring through my skin as I trudge higher toward the cross. The man with the blue eyes is out there somewhere. Maybe Gunn and Holston, too. But I can't see them, can't see anything except the meadow draped in the soft light of the slowly setting sun.

I pause at the top of the hill, my palms sweating as I grip the shovel. I don't want to dig, don't want to uncover whatever they buried here for me to find. It takes everything I have to heave the first shovel full of dirt to the side. The earth is loose and comes free easily. I follow it with another shovel full, and another, digging as a floating sensation overtakes me. It's like I'm hanging above myself, looking down as the hole grows deeper and wider, the dirt rising to the side.

Thunk.

The shovel strikes something solid, and the vibration carries up my arms. I bend and scrape away handfuls of soil, heaving it out with both hands. Beneath the grime is a brown, mirror-smooth surface. Richly grained. Shining and wet. It's a casket. One that's too small to belong to Avery.

But not too small to belong to a baby.

Christ, help me.

I push back to my feet, frantic, and scoop free thick shovelfuls of clay until I can see the entire thing. My arms feel like rubber by the time I reach down and take hold of the casket and drag it free. And then I drop to my knees and stare at it—unable to move. The casket is about two feet long and one foot wide, with a silver plate stamped in the center. On the plate is an inscription partially concealed by dirt, which I brush off. And then I read.

To everything there is a season:
A time to weep, a time to mourn.
A time to lose, a time for war.
A time to kill, a time to hate.
A time to die, die, die, die.

It's a verse from Ecclesiastes and the lyrics to a song by the Byrds. I know them both by heart, but this—what I'm staring at right now—is all wrong. The words are garbled and out of order—no positive counterbalance to the negative. No, a time to be born or a time to heal. Not a time to laugh or a time of peace. Just a mangled version of the original verse repurposed in a warning. Especially the last line which doesn't belong at all. It makes me want to run and never look back because I know what I'll find inside when I open the lid.

But I can't run. I have to look. I don't have a choice.

I reach for the latch with trembling fingers, feeling sick, and it takes all the strength I have left to flip it up and lift.

The lid rises, my breath leaving my body as I peer at what lies inside.

There is a dark crimson pall.

And a snow-white satin pillow.

But there is no body. No alien-eyed, bleeding fetus the size of a plum.

No child.

Tears fill my eyes as relief pours through me. It means Avery is alive, that my baby is *still* alive. Maybe. I don't know for sure, but the thought is a lifeline I use to pull myself back to the moment. I wipe my eyes with the back of my hand and study what the casket contains. There's a stuffed bear with fur I can tell was once white but has gone brown with age. One eye is scuffed, the other hangs by a thread. Placed next to the bear is a child's Captain America mask along with several Avengers figurines. And there are pictures. Pictures *everywhere*—scattered throughout the coffin.

I pick one up. It's a photo of a boy with straw-blond hair and wide, bright eyes. He's looking up at the camera with a shy smile painted on his face and his hands stuffed in his pockets. There are more. A picture of the same boy on a swing set. Another of him eating a sandwich, his lips coated in jam. Several photos show the boy as an infant, and then as a toddler, his face shining like a star. There are images of him racing over a green lawn wearing the Captain America mask. There are pictures of him posing with the captain's plastic shield.

But these aren't the only photos in the coffin. There are shots of a man as well. He has the features of someone perpetually young. His thick brown hair swoops low over his eyebrows. His cheeks are full and dimpled, split by a straight but rounded nose. He has a smile that's wide and infectious. The smile of a guy who looks like he'd be fun to grab a beer with sometime. The same smile as the boy's. This man must be his father, and as soon as I make that connection, all I can think is, *what the fuck is going on?* I turn my attention to the last item in the coffin—a box resting on the pillow wrapped in satin-black paper and tied with a silver bow. There's a card in a white envelope pressed beneath the bow that reads, *Open Me.* I take it, slide it out, and read.

Hello, Grant.

Or should I call you Adrian? Or Logan or Miles? Lucas?
Or maybe I'll just use your real name, Reed.

Three and a half years ago, you took everything from me.
Today, I will take everything from you.
Everyone will know what you did.
The police are on their way.

Love, Bailey

Reed. The name rings like a bell in my head—cold and clear—and I can barely move, barely form a thought. It's a name I'd hoped to never hear again, tied to a past I'd worked long and hard to bury.

But someone found me.

And it's why they took my wife.

I scan the horizon again. There's still nothing out of the ordinary—just the sharp evening air in my nose and the gentle rustle of the breeze skimming through the grass. There are no sirens or man-made sounds of any kind. No police rushing forward with guns drawn, shouting for me to get on the ground. There's only that name— *Bailey.* It's a hook that sinks deep into my brain as I set the card down and unwrap the gift.

It's another picture. This one is a framed portrait of a family with an unnaturally large tree stretching away behind them toward a peach sky. I recognize the man from the photos in the casket along with the boy, who is once again striking a pose in his Captain America mask. But it's the woman in the photo that sends all the blood in my body rushing to my feet. She has blonde hair in place of the red I know so well, and her eyes are light brown instead of green. Her face is fuller than I'm used to, not as defined. And her nose is different, too. There's a bump in the bridge and it ends in a sharper tip.

But it's her. I know it's her.

The woman in the photo is Avery. The woman in the photo is also Bailey Nichols.

And *I know, I know, I know* what I've done.

And who I've done it to.

The earth shifts beneath my feet, everything spinning violently. It doesn't make sense. *None* of this makes any sense. Avery's ruined face in the pictures from the envelopes rip through my mind. The bruises and blood and the way her eyes lolled drunkenly in her head in the video call when we spoke. The severed finger wearing her wedding ring.

Was it all faked? And if it was, why? My brain smokes as I try to slot the pieces into place.

It had to be. There's no other answer. But again, why? Why go to all of this trouble?

To punish you.

It's the answer. It's why Avery did this. *All* of this. From the very beginning. From the first moment I met her.

I don't have long to feel the shock before the bullet slams into my back.

PART THREE
THE TURN

CHAPTER 28

REED
Durango, Colorado
Age Sixteen

Reed still couldn't believe his luck every time Taylor White took his hand. They'd been dating for three months now, and it still didn't seem real. *She* didn't seem real. The only reason she was with him was because he played football. Everyone at school knew it, but he didn't care. She stirred something in Reed he'd never felt before. With her light red hair and eyes the color of a mountain lake, something about her made him ache. But it was a sweet ache, like the fire in his core after a solid workout—an ache he wanted to feel again and again and again.

He was acutely aware of her presence everywhere he went. She was the first thing he looked for when he went to school or to a football game. He scanned the sidelines the moment he hit the field, hungry to see her smiling among the cheerleaders. Anytime she was near him, his skin tingled. They hadn't gone all the way yet, but they'd come as close as you could without slipping over the edge. Taylor said her dad would kill them both if they did, and Reed believed it.

Judge White hated him.

It didn't matter how many times Reed crossed paths with Taylor's father or how respectfully he spoke to him; he knew the man would never consider him good enough for his daughter. And Reed couldn't really argue with that. But it wasn't enough of a reason for him to stay away from her, either. And he didn't have a choice; being apart from her hurt. If Reed went for more than a day without seeing Taylor, it felt like a death of sorts—like she'd yanked out a piece of his heart. But when they were together, like they were now, things were perfect.

He'd convinced her to ditch eighth period, and they'd driven down to the river in her car. They came here sometimes to get away. Every time they did, all Reed wanted to do was kiss her, but today Taylor wanted to talk.

"Where do you think you'll go to college?" she asked.

Reed's heart dropped. He hadn't thought about college yet. And he didn't want to think about it now. They'd barely started their junior year. Didn't they have forever still? Besides, he couldn't afford college. His grades weren't anywhere close to good enough for him to land a scholarship. The only way he'd be able to go was if Aunt Beth paid the tuition, and there was no way in hell she'd ever do that.

That woman was hard—nothing but a collection of straight lines and edges. The only reason she'd taken Reed in after his father had been sentenced to seventeen years for manslaughter was because he'd begged her to do it. Begged and begged. Reed spent an entire year in the foster system before Aunt Beth finally relented. When she did, she made sure Reed knew how much of an imposition he was. She bitched at him every day. He made such a mess. He was so goddamn ungrateful. He took all her money. Blah, blah, blah. That's what Aunt Beth was to him at this point: nothing but white noise.

"Well?" Taylor prompted.

"I'm not sure," he said. "I don't know if I'll go."

Her perfect mouth pulled into a glossy knot. "What? Why?"

"I can't afford it."

"There are scholarships, Reed."

"Yeah, I know, but my grades aren't exactly great."

"There's still plenty of time to get them up."

"Maybe." The truth was, he *could* improve his grades. He just didn't want to. School was boring. And what was the point, anyway? Aunt Beth constantly told him he wasn't smart enough to go to college. Well, not exactly that, but she was always talking about how it made a lot more sense for him to become a mechanic or to go into a trade like plumbing where he could make money instead of wasting it on some worthless degree. But Reed didn't want to become a mechanic or an electrician or some shit like that. He wanted to play football.

"What do you mean 'maybe'?" Taylor asked. "There totally is."

He gave her a tight smile. "Yeah, you're right. I'll try."

They watched the river flow past for a while, quiet until Reed asked, "So what about you? Where will you go?" The question hurt. He didn't want her to go anywhere.

She bit her lower lip in the adorable way she always did when she was lost in thought. It drove him crazy. "Oh, I don't know. Probably Fort Collins if I stay in state. CSU has the best vet program if I can get in. Cornell or Ohio State if I don't."

"Really?" he asked. "That far away?"

Her nose bunched. "Aww, are you saying you'd miss me?"

He grinned. "Possibly."

She traced her nails down his arm and then slipped her fingers into his. "Come with me, then. You can try out for the football team."

Reed considered this. He'd scored more touchdowns than anyone else this season. He had good hands and rarely dropped a pass. And he was fast. *Really* fast. Reed might not get an academic scholarship, but if he kept playing like he was, Coach Halverson said he'd definitely be in the running for an athletic one. It wasn't a bad idea.

"You really think I could make it?" he asked.

"Totally," Taylor said, "but you'd have to study too. Have you thought about what you want to do for a career?"

"I want to play in the NFL."

She laughed in response—a single, quick giggle she immediately cut off when she noticed his wince. "The NFL isn't a real choice, Reed. No one gets to do that."

"I bet I could." He regretted how pitiful the statement sounded the second it left his lips.

"Maybe," Taylor replied, but he knew she didn't mean it.

"What does it matter?" he snapped back. "Why are you grilling me like this, anyway?"

"I'm not grilling you."

"Yes, you are. And it's not that easy for me. Not everyone has their entire life handed to them on a silver platter like you, Taylor."

Her eyes sparked. He'd crossed the line, and he knew it.

"Fine, whatever," she said. "Forget I asked. Let's just go."

She started the car, but before her hand hit the wheel, Reed sighed and took it. He had to fix this before it got out of control. "Wait. I'm sorry. I didn't mean to snap at you. It's just ..." He trailed off, thinking about what to say next. He could try to impress her, make up some bullshit about wanting to go to college to become an engineer or a doctor, but it would be a lie. When they'd first started dating, Taylor had made him promise to never lie to her. Even if the truth hurt, he shouldn't lie. If he did, it was over. Simple as that. So, he hadn't lied. Not once. And he wouldn't start now. He tried again. "The truth is, I've never really thought about going to college."

Her features thawed, the lines in her forehead smoothing. "Why not?"

"I don't know, I ..." He fumbled for the right words. "I guess I didn't think it was a possibility for me. I'm not sure I'm smart enough."

"Are you kidding?" She stroked the back of his hand with her thumb. "Reed, you're the smartest person I know. You can do whatever you want. I believe in you."

For a second, he thought she was joking, but her gaze told him she wasn't. She *did* believe in him. No woman in his life had *ever* believed in him. Not his mom who'd thrown him away when he was just a kid. Not Aunt Beth, who thought he wouldn't amount to anything and wanted him out of her house as soon as possible. Certainly none of his teachers, all of them women who looked at him with sour faces every time they handed him a C like an average life was exactly what he deserved.

Not Taylor, though. She'd never once stared at him like that. She'd only ever looked at him like she was looking at him now—holding his gaze in a way he knew she meant every word.

You can never trust them, Reed. They'll betray you.

His father's voice blew through his mind like a cold wind. He thought of the girl in third grade, Ashley Parker, who'd told on him for stealing the answer book. He thought of his mom and Aunt Beth and the woman in Texas who'd screamed for her husband to come outside and ruined Reed's life. In a way, they all had—every single one of them. But not every woman could be that bad, could they? Wasn't Taylor proof?

"Do you really mean that?" he asked.

She tilted her head, her eyebrows curling up like she couldn't believe he was questioning her. "Of course, I do. Remember our deal? No lying." Then she cupped his cheek and kissed him, and Reed decided to forget everything his father had ever said.

CHAPTER 29

A bell chimes as I breeze through the door of the Magnolia Café. The place is all black and white tile and kitschy art. There are posters of pastries on parade mounted on the wall, full of smiling pieces of toast and slices of pie marching with cartoon legs. An oversized set of forks, knives, and spoons hangs above the host stand, directly over a freckled hostess who's smiling my way. "How many?"

"I'm meeting someone, actually," I say as a bald man waves at me from a corner. "Thanks."

Zane Jenson rises as I near, towering over me by at least a foot and a half. He has a wide nose and a prominent brow and is dressed in blue jeans and a charcoal blazer. He stares down at me with dark eyes, appraising me with a clinical sort of intelligence. I can feel him cataloging me, pulling open an empty file drawer in his mind and slotting me in. Paula's voice fills my mind: *He's the best investigator I've ever met. He gets things done.* I don't know the man, but I can already see it.

"It's Bailey, right?" he says, offering his hand. I take it and watch mine disappear in his as we shake. "You find the place okay? Google always sends people across the street."

"I did. How'd you recognize me?"

"Lucky guess." He sweeps his arm toward the booth. "Please."

I slide into one side, and he settles into the other. I can't help but take note of the accordion file resting on the table near the edge.

"Thank you for seeing me on such short notice," I say.

"Don't thank me. Thank Paula. I didn't have much choice in the matter. As you may have guessed, when Paula Nash calls you answer." A smile cuts across his broad jaw, and he chuckles. "You didn't give me much choice, either."

Exactly three days had passed since Ben and I walked out of Paula Nash's house in a daze, and I'd spent every minute since thinking about Adrian Wallace. Before I left, Paula had pressed a business card into my hand with the words *Jenson Investigations* printed on the thick white stock along with a phone number. I'd called it five times before he finally answered.

"Listen," Zane says. "Before we begin, I want you to know how sorry I am for your loss. What happened to your family is tragic. I can't imagine how difficult that must have been."

The statement sparks a flash of irritation I have to mentally tamp down. I hate when conversations start this way. Since the wreck, it happens all the time—an inane condolence followed by some version of what Zane had just said. Something to the effect of "you poor thing," or "they're in a better place now," or "time heals all wounds." The worst ones are when people personalize my tragedy and tell me how they have kids, and losing them is their worst nightmare, like that will somehow help lessen my pain. It doesn't. Someone telling me about everything they have only reminds me of everything I've lost.

"It's why I'm here," I say, inclining my head toward the file. "Is that him?"

"Yes—what I have, anyway."

Before I can ask to see the file, a waitress in a short skirt appears next to the table, her fingernails and lips both matching shades of crimson. She smiles, sending a spray of cigarette lines shooting from the corners of her mouth.

"Coffee?" she asks, holding up a yellowed carafe.

"No, thank you," I say. "Water's fine."

"Sure thing, I'll bring a round for the table." She turns to Zane. "How about you, hon?"

He shifts his mug toward her in answer. She fills it and then strides away in a cloud of peach perfume.

Zane takes a drink, and I consider how to start. I've only been around him for a few minutes, but he strikes me as the direct type. I stare at the file.

"Paula said Adrian killed my family."

"That's never been proven."

"Paula seemed pretty convinced."

Zane nods. "She has good reason. The autopsy wasn't conclusive, but the injuries Evelyn sustained were … questionable."

"What do you mean?"

"Evelyn had significant head trauma to the right side of her skull, and her torso was twisted in a way that didn't make sense. The impact should have been more direct. She had minimal damage to the center of her forehead, no burn marks."

"Burn marks?" I ask, confused.

Zane grunts. "Airbags get hot when they inflate. There are chemicals released and sometimes fragments that can damage the skin. Evelyn didn't have those. And her neck was fractured laterally."

I set my elbows on the table. "Why does that matter?"

"It matters because it indicates she'd been looking to her left at the time of the crash instead of at the road—like she was talking to someone. Not to mention the position of the vehicle's steering wheel was much too high for her, and her legs didn't line up with the pedals."

My shoulders tighten. "Okay. Give me your opinion. What do you think happened?"

Zane readjusts himself, his eyes never leaving mine. "I don't think Evelyn was driving that day. There's no way. I believe Adrian was the one behind the wheel."

The room swims. If what he and Paula are telling me is true, I've spent the last two years hating the wrong person.

The waitress returns with our waters and takes our orders. A hamburger for Zane and a Caesar salad for me. I wait for her to leave before I speak again.

"If that's true, then why wasn't any of it in the police report? Why didn't they investigate further?"

"They didn't have a reason to. Evelyn was in the driver's seat. She'd been drinking. They had a toxicology report that showed she was well over the legal limit at the time of her death. And there weren't any witnesses. No one was around to question what happened."

"Including Adrian?"

He nods in agreement. "Including Adrian."

"Did the police look for him?" I ask.

"They did."

"And they never found him?"

"No." Zane takes another pull from his coffee and returns the mug to the table, then taps the file. "But it's not entirely their fault. It's hard to find a ghost. What else did Paula tell you about our friend here?"

I scratch my arm. "Not much. She said he took advantage of Evelyn, but she mostly talked about the accident."

One of Zane's eyebrows quirks higher. "Oh, he did much more than take advantage of her. He stole a couple million."

I'm about to take a drink of water and nearly choke. I set the glass down. "Paula didn't mention that."

"Evelyn's loss is a difficult subject for her. She doesn't like talking about any of this." He crosses his arms. "Let me ask you a question. What do you think killed Donald Nash?"

"A heart attack," I reply.

"Go deeper."

Paula's voice whispers in my ear. *He's been dead for years.* "The death of his daughter."

"Yes. I've known Don for a long time. I worked a lot of corporate cases for him early in his career. He was one of the most focused individuals I've ever met. Calm. Cool. Levelheaded. That all changed when he hired me to investigate Adrian Wallace."

I lean in. "How so?"

"Don's a man who's used to getting results. He was always the kind of guy to throw money at a problem until it got solved. Well, that didn't work in this case. Besides me, I'm guessing he hired a half-dozen other investigators to track this guy down, but no one could. I've never seen someone vanish so completely. Literally no trace.

"Anyway, after a few months of this, Don went nuclear. He turned up at my office unannounced, demanding answers I didn't have. He was red-faced and pissed off, pacing around the room covered in sweat, asking where the fuck Adrian was. Telling me I'd better find him or else. Threatening me. Saying he'd end my career if I didn't. I kid you not, every time Don came in after that, I could feel my blood pressure rising. He wanted nothing more than to make Adrian pay. Don loved his daughter. Evelyn meant the world to him. She—"

He stops suddenly and pulls a buzzing phone out of his pocket. "Give me a second, will you? I have to take this." He punches a button and brings the phone to his ear as the waitress returns with our meals. I pick at my salad and listen to Zane's one-sided conversation.

"She fell again?" Pause. "How bad is it this time?" Pause. "Okay, good, but you should still take her in to be safe. I'll be there as soon as I can. I'm almost done."

He ends the call and runs a hand over his face.

"Do you need to go?" I ask.

He considers it. "In a bit. I'll eat first. Unfortunately, this happens a lot. My daughter's sick. She falls sometimes. But this one doesn't sound too bad. She'll be okay. I'm not so sure about my wallet, though." He shakes his head. "Health insurance isn't cheap when you're self-employed." He picks up his hamburger and digs in. "Where were we?"

"You were about to tell me what happened to Adrian."

"Right. After a year of searching, I finally turned up a few leads. I put my other cases on hold and went all in. When I finally located Adrian, the first call I made was to Don. The guy lost his mind. He said he was packing his bags. Told me we were leaving that night. He said he'd kill Adrian himself. Said he'd strangle him to death." Zane picks up his hamburger and takes a bite, chews. "It sounded like he was having an aneurysm. I'd never heard him so angry before. He died two hours later. He never made it to the airport."

"And then what?"

"Then nothing."

I do the math. Donald Nash died a week ago. Which means finding Adrian is recent. My pulse ticks higher. "Paula isn't going to go after him?"

Zane laughs. "Seriously? The woman is in the middle of burying her husband. And no. The case is officially dead. She told me to drop it."

The answer leaves me cold. "Why would she do that?"

Zane sighs and returns the hamburger to his plate. "Put yourself in her shoes. Evelyn wasn't her kid. Sure, they mostly got along, but it was Don she really loved. It took years to get Evelyn on her feet. Once they did, she and Don had a normal marriage for a while. They were happy. But then all this shit with Adrian happened and she lost him again. First, she watched him deteriorate in real time, and then she had to watch him die. She was there when he had his heart attack. It happened in their living room. She gave Don CPR for twenty minutes before the paramedics showed up."

Jesus. I imagine it. Paula crying, spilling tears in between breaths and chest compressions. *Come back to me!*

"That's terrible. But I still don't understand why she'd let Adrian get away with this?"

Zane shrugs. "People process grief differently. And she saw what happened to Don. He was hellbent on making this guy pay. Obsessed with it. It poisoned their marriage. It poisoned *him.* Then it killed him." Zane drags a fry through the ketchup on his plate and pops it into his mouth, chews. "I mean, sure, maybe she'd be able to make a case with the evidence I have and bring Adrian to trial, but that would mean she'd have to testify. She'd have to see his face every day in court. On the news. Cases like this can take years. Paula just wants to move on. Sometimes justice doesn't mean much when you've already put everyone you love in the ground."

My vision blurs, a tear breaking free before I can stop it from rolling down my cheek. I wipe at it angrily and look away. Someone laughs nearby. Dishes rattle. The noise of the restaurant muffles to a din. I've put the people I love in the ground. But unlike Paula, I can't just walk away from this. There's no moving on for me. I have no life without Noah and Ethan. That future doesn't exist.

"Where is he?" I ask, attempting to regain my composure.

Zane wipes his mouth with a napkin, then pushes the folder over. "It's all in here."

I peer at it, zeroing in on the name printed on the label. "Who's Reed Aldridge?"

"That's his real name," Zane says. "Adrian Wallace doesn't exist."

CHAPTER 30

REED
Durango, Colorado
Age Seventeen

Taylor quit speaking to him on a Monday. All week, Reed had tried to talk to her. He looked for her at lunch but only found an empty seat where she usually sat. In the halls, he'd spot her from a distance, but the second he'd start her way, she seemed to disappear. Anytime he bumped into one of her friends, they stared at him like he'd done something wrong, like he'd hurt her somehow. But he hadn't. Reed loved her and she loved him. They'd been saying it for months now.

I love you. The first time she'd told him was after a party at Jason Callahan's house. He thought it was because she'd had too much to drink. But then she'd said it again the next day during a movie. She'd whispered those three words into his ear and it felt like a spark coming to life in his chest. When he said it back, the spark whooshed into a flame. Reed loved her, he did—so why wouldn't she speak to him? The question left him in a panic.

"You need to leave that girl alone," Aunt Beth said on Wednesday, looking up from painting her nails at the table after he'd tried to call Taylor three times. "She clearly needs some space."

He *had* given her space. Or rather she'd taken it. His phone bore witness, the screen awash in his one-way texts:

Where are you?
Why won't you talk to me?
Did I do something?
Taylor, I need to see you.
What's the matter?
Just write back already. Please.

By Friday, he'd had enough. That night, he showered, shaved, and put on his best outfit—a plaid button-up dress shirt and a dark pair of blue jeans—then headed for the door.

Aunt Beth stopped him. "You're going to see her, aren't you?"

"No," he lied.

"Reed, don't do it. Sometimes a woman has a reason for what she does, and right now, that girl doesn't want to talk to you. Give her some time and she'll come around."

Something about the way the kitchen light framed Aunt Beth made her look soft in the moment, like she might actually be concerned. Like she might actually care about him. But Reed knew she didn't. She never had. She'd only grudgingly taken him in out of obligation to his father. What she thought didn't matter. He'd be gone soon enough anyway, and she'd never have to think about him again.

He turned and pushed through the door.

Thirty minutes later, he sat in front of the White ranch, which wasn't really a ranch at all. There weren't any animals or crops or anything. But it was way out in the middle of nowhere and it was easy enough to imagine a herd of cows roaming over the twenty-acre spread, grazing on wild buffalo grass or a stretch of wheat growing somewhere on the property. Everyone called it a ranch, though, so that was how Reed thought about it—as a ranch. One he tried his best to avoid if Judge White was home.

When Judge White wasn't around, he loved this place. The

basement held a massive theater where he and Taylor would make out ... and sometimes do more than that. They'd spend entire days lying in the sun on the front porch, drinking beer and screwing around when no one else was home. If they grew bored, they'd ride ATVs around the property or wander down to the pond near the cottonwoods and feed bread to the ducks. Everything about the house was great, but what Reed loved most about it was that it belonged to Taylor.

She was home now. He could see her red Toyota Camry sitting on the driveway next to her father's Mercedes. The sight filled him with anxiety. Maybe Aunt Beth had a point. Maybe he shouldn't be here. Taylor was definitely pissed off for some reason. He just didn't know why. But whatever it was, she would get over it. They loved each other. They just needed to talk.

No time like the present, Reed thought as he got out of his car. By the time he reached the front door he felt tight and nervous, already sweating through his shirt. He rang the doorbell. A sound like a gong came from inside the house, followed by footsteps.

Hard footsteps.

Deep footsteps.

Judge White's footsteps.

Shit.

He flung the door open and looked down at Reed like he was a fly skittering over glass—something to be squashed.

"What are you doing here?"

"I was hoping to talk to Taylor, sir."

"She doesn't want to talk to you. Hasn't she made that clear?"

Reed didn't know what to say to that.

The judge scowled, the sunspots on his cheeks darkening. Reed felt frozen beneath the man's glare, unable to move. Hate rose off the judge like steam. The man had always disliked Reed, but this was different. Reed could practically see the judge's disgust coiling through the air as he spoke. "That you actually have the nerve to step foot on my property after what you've done is—"

"Daddy, stop!" Taylor's voice swam toward Reed like honey. She appeared next to her father and placed a hand on his arm. "Let me talk to him."

Judge White's gaze remained on Reed. "That's not a good idea, punkin."

"Please," she said. "Ten minutes."

Her father pulled a breath in through his nose and exhaled. "Fine. Ten minutes, but no more."

Taylor slipped past him and shut the door, then took Reed's hand and pulled him toward the corner of the covered patio. They settled onto the porch swing. The sun bathed the horizon in orange and pink light. Reed took Taylor's hand, but she immediately pulled it free and returned it to her lap.

"What's wrong?" Reed asked. "Why are you mad at me?"

"I'm not mad."

"It doesn't feel that way."

"Reed, I need to … tell you something."

"Okay," he said, waiting for her to continue. But she didn't speak. She just sat there, staring at the mountains, shaking her head. When a tear cut from the corner of her eye, across her cheek, Reed had to resist the urge to pull her into his arms. Seeing her like this was absolutely killing him.

Finally, she spoke. "I'm pregnant."

A churning sensation filled his gut. Had he heard that right? *Pregnant?* It was the absolute last thing he'd expected her to say. He'd thought maybe he'd said something bad about one of her friends or had accidentally insulted her the last time they'd talked. But this? *Pregnant?* Never this.

"I don't understand," he said, scratching his head. "We've been careful." And they had. They'd been having sex for six months now, and Reed always used a condom. Except for the last few times because

Taylor had gotten on birth control.

She brushed her fingers over the back of his hand. "I know." She chewed her bottom lip and shook her head. "But it happened. I've taken the test three times."

"Three times? And you're only telling me now?" Reed's shock swung toward anger. "Why didn't you tell me sooner?"

"I ..." She turned away from him and hung her head. "I should have. I'm sorry. When it happened, I was so devastated. I didn't know what to do. My mom saw me crying and I just blurted it out."

"But you told your friends, too," Reed said, still reeling. She must have. They'd been staring at him like he was the devil all week long, shooting daggers his way like this was his fault and Taylor carried none of the blame.

A tear dripped off her chin and landed warm on Reed's wrist. "No, I didn't. My mom called Laura's mom. Word got out." Her shoulders slumped. "I should have told you sooner, though. I'm so sorry. I didn't know what to do. I still don't." And then she was sobbing, crying and shaking her head.

Reed pulled her close and cupped her warm, wet cheeks and tilted her gaze to his. Her dark walnut eyes glimmered in the fading light. "Hey, okay. Yeah, this is serious. It is. But we'll be okay. Taylor, we can do this together."

"What do you mean 'do this'?" she asked hesitantly.

"I can find a job, something that pays well. You can still go to college. We both can. Everything will be fine."

She wiped her eyes with the back of her hand. "You ... want to keep it?"

He hesitated, stunned by her words. It felt weird to hear her call their child *it*. But he brushed that aside and said, "Of course, I do. Don't you?"

"Reed, I ..." Her voice quivered. She looked up at the sky, as if deep in thought. Her lips tightened.

A dark cloud of doubt spilled over Reed—like someone had

released a vial of ink in his blood. "Wait, you don't want to?" He couldn't believe it, but he knew she didn't. Already, he knew.

"It's not that I don't want to," she said. "We're just so young. I'm not ready to be a parent."

"That doesn't matter. This is our baby." Reed could already see his face outlined on the child's, could already hear its gurgling laugh. He'd never wanted a kid before—hell no, not at his age, it was the last thing on his mind—but if it was with Taylor, it was okay. More than okay. It felt right. And he'd sworn to himself if he ever *did* have a kid, he'd never abandon it; not like his mom had abandoned him.

"It's not your body, Reed," Taylor said. "This isn't your choice."

"What are you saying?"

She closed her eyes and bowed her head. "I'm not keeping it. We *can't*."

Her words felt like a ball of ice landing in his lap. She moved to stand, but he grabbed her hand and held her there. "Wait, please don't do this. Think about it at least."

Tears streamed down her face. "I have. I'm sorry. If you truly love me, you'll come with me tomorrow."

"Where?" he asked, fighting for something else to say that would keep her there.

"To end it." And then she pulled her hand from his and rushed back into the house.

CHAPTER 31

BAILEY

"This is unbelievable," Ben says, gawking at the contents of the accordion file spread over the kitchen table in front of us. "He had all of this?"

"Yes," I say, still struggling to believe it myself. My entire life, along with everything I thought I knew about the death of my family, had been flipped upside down in a matter of days.

"Unbelievable," Ben says again. He's repeated the word at least a half-dozen times since getting home from work. When he asked what I was doing, I passed him Reed's file. It was the first one I read after returning from lunch with Zane. He'd organized everything into five smaller sub-folders full of detailed reports, photographs, and background information, one for each of Reed's victims and a folder for Reed himself. I'd already studied that one for hours.

Reed's upbringing was admittedly a tragic one. As a child, he was abandoned by his mother and left to his convict father to raise. Jack Aldridge dragged Reed all over the country searching for work: Pennsylvania, Nebraska, Arizona, Texas. They never stayed anywhere for long. Jack's employment records were littered with terminations. There were run-ins with the law. Mostly petty stuff—bar fights and DUIs—until Jack killed a man on his front porch in Midland when

Reed was twelve years old.

Reed spent a year in the foster system after that, racking up behavior complaints until his aunt, Beth Aldridge, adopted him and brought him to Durango, Colorado. Reed seemed to level out from there. He got decent grades and managed to land a spot on the high school football team. His yearbook photos look like those of all the other boys his age—Reed staring empty-eyed at the camera, attempting to look cool. Reed perched on a bench with some friends, managing to appear both bored and agitated at the same time. Reed on the football field caught in mid-flight, leaping for a pass. In those pictures, he never smiled. His smiles were reserved for Taylor White.

It's why I'd keyed on her to begin with. There they were, sitting side by side on the gym bleachers, Taylor giving Reed an *oh you!* flap of her hand. There they were huddled over a classroom table, Taylor focused on a project, Reed focused on her. Just look at the two of them caught in conversation at a cafeteria table, so cute together, so in love. Zane hadn't provided many photos of her and Reed on the flash drive he dropped into the file, but there were enough to let me know Taylor mattered. In those pictures, Reed's smile was real.

"These are the women? The ones he conned?" Ben says, pulling a photo closer. I've arranged Reed's victims in a single row at the top of the table by name: Rachel Dawson, an Etsy queen who designed cheap handbags and cutesy home decor. Lacey Grayson, a fitness buff whom Reed conned using a fake fitness franchise. Jennifer Stewart, a Montana realtor with a killer smile who made the mistake of adding Reed to her business bank account. And finally, Evelyn Nash—the payoff Reed had been chasing for years.

"Yep," I say. "The ones we know about, anyway."

"Fucking hell," Ben says, returning the photo to the lineup. He takes one of Reed and whistles low through his teeth. "He dresses so differently in all of these. I'd never guess he was the same person."

"I know," I say. "It's unreal."

Beneath the women, I've positioned pictures of Reed as he appeared in each relationship. He was good. *Really good.* His wardrobes. His hairstyles. Even his posture. Every look expertly curated for his targets.

I study the different versions of Reed again, one by one.

There's Lucas Pierce for Lacey Grayson, a tattooed gym bro fond of tank tops and full-body tans. Lucas is well built with muscular arms and wears his hair short in a buzz cut. He has a strong jawline and a V-shaped torso and looks like he belongs on the cover of *Men's Health*.

Next comes Miles Baxter for Jennifer Stewart the realtor. In these photos, Reed is freshly slacked and polo'd. He has a head full of investment-banker hair—perfectly parted to the side. His eyes are slightly magnified by a set of thick-framed glasses and he's wearing a fake-as-shit smile I want to punch.

I shift my gaze to Logan Thompson. This version of Reed tends toward baggy clothing. Logan is a hoodie enthusiast who wears his ball caps backward and buries his hands deep in the pockets of his jeans. He looks like the kind of guy you'd find hitting vape pens behind a gas station. He's not exactly my type, but he's definitely Rachel Dawson's.

The picture Ben holds is of Evelyn Nash's Romeo, Adrian Wallace, a long-haired hipster in a denim jacket and slim-cut jeans. This iteration of Reed looks far less assured than the others—but purposefully so. I have no doubt he presented this way in order to not overwhelm Evelyn.

"It's not just how he's dressed, either," I say, taking the photos of Reed and re-arranging them in a line, based on the dates of his cons, from the earliest to the most recent. I point at the first one, Logan Thompson—Rachel Dawson's version of Reed. "Look at his face. See the fullness of his cheeks?" I move my finger to the right and set it on Lucas Pierce. "They're slimmer here."

Ben's eyes narrow. "He lost a lot of weight, didn't he?"

"Yes. And he went even further with the next girl." I pull the picture of Miles Baxter closer. "Look at his nose. See how it's been contoured?"

Ben picks it up and squints. "Surgery?"

"I think so. But nothing that looks unnatural. Just enough of an alteration to change his appearance when combined with the new haircut and wardrobe."

Ben sets the picture back on the table. "So, what name is he going by now?"

"Grant Wilson." I dig into Reed's file and pull out another picture and hand it to Ben. It's a faraway shot of Reed sitting on a wraparound porch with a beer in his hand, gazing out at a spectacular view.

"Nice place," Ben says.

"Yeah. The guy's been enjoying his retirement."

Ben studies me, then pops his elbow onto the table and leans forward. "You're taking this to the cops, right?"

"No," I say. "What would I tell them? That Reed was the one to hit my car instead of Evelyn? There's no proof he was involved. Nothing solid, anyway. There weren't any witnesses."

Ben frowns. "So find these other women, then. Get them to file a report."

I snort. "They already have. Zane looked into them. It didn't matter. None of these women had his real identity. Reed's good, Ben. He's been doing this a long time. If I go to the cops, he'll get spooked and disappear again."

"You don't know that."

In all actuality, my brother is right. I don't, though I suspect it's true. But either way, I'm not about to hand Reed over to the police. I don't simply want Reed arrested. Reed Aldridge is the reason I'll never again feel the brush of Ethan's hand against my own or hear him whisper *I love you* as he pulls me close from behind. Reed is the reason Ethan and I won't grow old together or travel the world like he wanted to; backpacking across Europe had been his dream. And that's exactly what it will remain. A dream. A *what-if,* forever buried in the past along with my husband and my child, all because of Reed.

He took so much from me that day. He obliterated every beautiful memory my family will never share. All of the birthdays and holidays and family vacations, gone. Because of Reed Aldridge, I'll never attend Noah's high school and college graduations and never get to see the man he'd become from there. Because of Reed Aldridge, I'll never get to meet my daughter-in-law or hold my grandchildren in my arms. The day Reed barreled into the side of my car, he took *everything* from me. Just like he's taken everything from so many others.

Which is exactly what I'm going to do to him.

"So, if not the cops, then what?" Ben asks.

I turn my attention back to the table and the photographs of the women. "Look, he has a type. Pretty but not untouchable. Slender. The girl next door." I set my finger on Jennifer Stewart, the realtor. "Like her. Petite. Medium height. Cute build." I move my finger to Lacey Grayson's picture. It's a shot from her fitness franchise website, Lacey glistening with sweat as she directs a HIIT class. "Just like her."

"I'm not so sure about that," Ben says, nodding at Rachel Dawson. "She doesn't exactly fit. And neither does Evelyn."

I'd noticed the same thing. "No, she doesn't. But Rachel was Reed's first target. He needed money. He made an exception. And Evelyn was his big score. Here, look." I snatch the yearbook photos I printed and hand one to Ben. "See the girl next to Reed?"

"Yeah. Who's that?"

"Taylor White. An old girlfriend."

"How do you know?"

"It isn't hard. See how she's looking at him? It's obvious." I pass him another photo—this one from Reed's yearbook. "Notice anything else?"

Ben massages his mouth. "She's cute."

"Besides that."

He sighs. "Okay, yeah, I'll give. She looks like the others. And that hair. Wow."

I study it—a flowing, strawberry mane closer to red than blonde, framing a pair of light green eyes.

"Like I said. He has a type." I reach over and set my hand on his arm. "Ben, look at me. Tell me what you see."

He smirks. "My sister?"

I roll my eyes. "No. Pretend I'm a stranger. Who do I look like? Who do I remind you of?"

He rubs the back of his neck and shrugs. "I don't know. I'm not tracking."

I sweep my hand toward the photos. "Them. I look like them."

His brow furrows, his gaze pinballing between the photos and my face. "I mean ... maybe. Sort of. Why does it matter?"

I hesitate. I've debated long and hard about this. I could keep Ben in the dark or I could tell him what I plan to do. In the end, I know there's no way I can lie to him. Besides, I don't need him worrying when I disappear, thinking I've decided to take another run at ending my life. And I certainly don't want him filing a missing person report. No, if I'm going to do this—and I absolutely am—Ben has every right to know.

"It matters," I say, swallowing. "Because it means I'm his type."

The crease over his nose deepens. "His type? Bailey, what exactly are you getting at here?"

"I'm going to meet him."

Ben recoils. "*What?* Why the hell would you do that?"

I stiffen. "Because I'm going to do to him what he's done to all these women, to me. I'm going to destroy him."

The color drains from his face. He blinks. "Oh, Jesus, Bailey, no ..."

"You're the one who said I needed closure."

He gives me a *what-the-fuck-are-you-smoking* kind of look and shakes his head. "How is getting involved with this guy closure? That's not closure. What you're talking about—shit—it sounds like madness."

Heat hits my eyes, the tears already rising. I stand and grab the picture of Reed sitting on his deck, beer in hand, and shake it. "This man has destroyed so many lives, Ben. So many! You want to know what closure is for me?" I slap the photo back to the table and stab it with my finger. "Ruining him. Taking back what he stole and returning it to his victims. Doing to him *exactly* what he's done to others. I want to make him hurt. I want him to suffer. That's closure! It's how I stay out of the ground. And you can either support me in this, or you can walk away. I wouldn't blame you if you did. But you don't get to stop me. I'm doing this with or without you. Do you understand? With or without."

He stares at me with his eyes glossing. His lips tremble, and I know he's fighting tears, too. But there's something else buried in the look—a flicker of understanding. He's been here before in his own way, when the doctors told him he'd never walk again, that living a normal life would be difficult. He didn't listen to them, either. He simply turned their words into motivation and proved them all wrong. He did it his own way, just like I have to do this mine.

After a moment, he nods. "I'm always with you. You know I'm not going anywhere."

"I know," I say, leaning over and pulling him into a hug. "I know."

When we separate, he's crying, no longer holding the tears back. He runs the back of his hand over his face and laughs. "You're out of your goddamn mind, though. There's no way you can do this alone."

I retake my seat. "I'm not going to. Zane's going to help me. He just doesn't know it yet."

CHAPTER 32

REED
Las Vegas, Nevada
Age Twenty-Four

The bachelorettes were fucking obnoxious. They couldn't be much older than Reed—he guessed them to be somewhere in their mid-twenties—but they were screeching like they were at a college frat party.

They'd stormed into Frankie's five minutes ago in a drunken mash of pink and white skirts and proceeded to swarm through the bar like a cloud of mosquitoes. They danced and giggled, shrieked and nuzzled, barely managing to stay upright on their way to the bar.

"Shots! Shots! Shots!"

They took them down together, the bride-to-be closing her eyes before throwing her head back in a howl.

Reed sighed.

He knew their kind. They filtered past him every day at the Wynn, paying him about as much attention as the luggage he carried. Women who snapped their fingers at him like he was their own personal servant and complained about their lives all the way to their rooms.

"You would not believe how bad Marcus dented the BMW. It just looks awful now."

"My manicure is already chipping. It's so embarrassing."

"Am I fat? I'm getting fat, right? It's all the fried food out here, I swear."

These women who acted like their lives were the equivalent of a suburban concentration camp. None of them had struggled. Not by a long shot. Not like Reed had struggled when Aunt Beth kicked him out of her house after graduation. She'd paid for a single semester of community college before pulling the plug. A single fucking semester.

"I told you I was done if you get Cs."

One C in math. That's it. A single, goddamn C—which would have been a B if his bitch of a professor hadn't docked him for showing up to class late after pulling a double-shift changing oil at Mac's Garage. Traffic had been bad on the way over. He'd explained this. He'd told her he had to have a job to pay rent. It wasn't his fault. He'd even managed to summon a few tears in the process, but she hadn't cared. She'd simply told him to take his seat. That was it. College over.

He took a long pull of his beer. It was why he was here now, struggling to make ends meet. Reed thought he might make a few professional connections in Vegas and find a job that paid well. But between rent and the outrageous living expenses, the city was a sewer that seemed to suck every single dollar he made right out of him.

At least he had Frankie's. The bar was a neon-soaked respite where he could toss back a few beers and unwind with the locals comfortably far from the strip. It was his sanctuary in a way—a place to get his head straight after a long shift. Yet, here they were, these women dusted in sashes and glitter, ruining the vibe while reminding him of exactly where he stood in the social pecking order.

One of them—a chunky blonde with a helium-balloon voice— was honking at the bartender for another round of drinks a few feet away while the two behind her giggled and swayed.

"Jesus Christ," the guy next to him said, slapping a twenty on the bar while rising to his feet. Reed was about to do the same—needed to get the fuck out of here—when something one of the women said cut through all the clatter.

"… made over two-hundred thousand last year! Can you even believe that?"

He rotated toward the voice and spotted the bride-to-be in conversation with a brunette who had her lips rounded into a red-lipstick O. "You're kidding me. That's amazing!"

"It's crazy, right?" the brunette replied. "Who knew candles would sell so well."

The bride set her chin on her hand and her eyes seemed to slosh in place. "I did. Girl, wasn't I the one who told you to go for it? I always knew you'd go places."

Reed groaned. *Girl.* Like the brunette was an eighth grader instead of a woman pushing thirty.

"You *totally* did, girl! Oh my god, I don't know how I'm going to keep growing it though, you know? It's, like, getting so hard to do on my own now." The brunette's voice dipped weepily toward the end of the statement, like continuing to make two-hundred grand would be the worst thing to ever happen to her.

"You'll figure it out." The bride squeezed the brunette's arm and gave her a little squeal. "I'm just really happy for you, Rachel!"

The brunette screwed her face into a happy pout, then pulled the bride into a hug. "Not as happy as I am for you."

Oh, good god, Reed thought, about to vomit. Luckily, the bartender returned with the drinks and set them on the bar. The bachelorettes scooped them up one by one and scurried away toward an empty table—all of them except for the brunette named Rachel who pointed at the empty space on the bar in front of her. "I think you missed one."

The bartender frowned. "Sorry about that. What did you order again?"

"A chocolate martini."

"Be right back."

"So you sell candles, huh?" Reed asked, cutting in.

Rachel startled at his voice and then looked at Reed like he was a mushroom that had grown out of the stool beside her; an unpleasant thing better suited for the dark. Her gaze warmed the second it reached his face. A handsome face, he knew. Reed didn't have much going for him, but he had his looks. They were about the only good thing his mother had ever given him.

"Are you spying on me?" she asked.

He feigned a good-natured laugh. "Overheard, actually. I'm a home-goods distributor."

"A ... what?"

She gave him a lazy blink, first one eyelid, and then the other, like she was trying to dial in his resolution. Reed had no clue what a home-goods distributor was or why he'd said it. But he'd lugged a trolley full of suitcases up to a two-thousand-dollar-a-night luxury suite for a guy with that title the other day. They had to make good money. Besides, what did it matter? He'd already jumped into the deep end with this conversation. Might as well see how far he could take it.

But where was he taking it? He didn't know. He finally decided to go with, "Someone who helps people like you achieve scale."

She blinked again, looking confused, so he added: "You know— connect you with more customers. Do all the busy work while you rake in the sales."

Her eyes brightened at that. She was attractive enough, pretty even, with her full lips and olive skin, but definitely not a supermodel. Although Reed could tell she thought she was. Add another five years and twenty pounds and she'd be chasing down her glory days in an endless series of nips and tucks.

"Wait, seriously? I've been looking for someone like you. I—" She hiccupped. Giggled. A pair of pendant earrings hung from her ears and glittered as she laughed. "I am *sooo* drunk. Good lord."

Reed grinned. "Big night, huh? Where are you all in from?"

"Here, actually. Summerlin."

Here? Reed hadn't expected that. Vegas was mostly transients and tourists. But people did live here. Especially rich people. People like this woman. Summerlin was full of them.

He realized she was still talking and tuned back in as she flapped her hand. "Bridgette's getting married in Tahoe. She's flying me and the rest of the girls up there in a couple of months for the wedding. Her family's loaded. It's going to be ridiculous." Her voice stalled on the last word before it finally tumbled out in a slur: *ree-digulis.*

"What's your name anyway?" she asked.

"Logan," Reed said. "And you're Rachel."

"How did you—"

"Know?" He tipped his beer toward the table where two of the bachelorettes were trying to call her over.

"Rachel, what are you doing?"

"Yeah, come on, bitch! Get your ass over here!"

"Oh my god, give me a minute!" she hissed over her shoulder.

The bartender returned with her martini and set it on a napkin.

"I'll get that," Reed said to the man.

Rachel smiled. "And a gentleman, too."

"Already paid for," the bartender said.

Reed knew this. He'd seen another one of the women open a tab.

"The next one, then," he said, winking at Rachel.

She reached over and smacked his chest. "How cute are you? So, tell me more about this big job of yours, city boy."

Reed started to, spilling terms like *just-in-time inventory* and *supply chain management*, rattling on about cost efficiencies—shit he'd picked up listening to the businessmen around the hotel—when he realized her eyes were glazing. She hadn't *really* wanted to hear more about him. Why would she? She just wanted to talk about herself. It pissed him off, but he was the one in control here, even if she didn't know it.

He stopped, leaned in, and brushed his knee against hers. "It's boring stuff. Not nearly as fun as candles." He couldn't believe he'd just said that, but it did the trick.

She came back to life. "Oh, it's more than candles."

So much more. She made handbags and coffee mugs and a bunch of other tacky crap she sold on Etsy to soccer moms and suburban housewives. Daddy had given her the seed money and—*voila!*—the business simply took off like a rocket. Of course, it had—everything handed to her on a silver fucking platter.

It made Reed's blood boil, not that she could tell. Ever since the bullshit with Taylor, he'd clamped down on his emotions. There were times she still haunted him even now, times he lost himself in memories of her and what could have been. But he'd never let them linger long before he squashed them. He'd cried for a week after the abortion, actually fucking cried, breaking into tears like some sad-sack little bitch at inopportune moments until he finally got it together. And when he did, he swore he'd be damned if he ever let a woman gain that kind of control over him again. Hell no. That was pathetic. Those days were through.

He turned his attention back to Rachel, who was still droning on about her stupid candles. It was clear she'd never worked a single day in her life. Not *really.* Etsy didn't count as work. She'd never had to scrub dirty toilets like Reed had or begged for change at an intersection just to afford her next meal. She'd never had to dig a ditch with her bare hands while standing waist-deep in slop.

No, for Rachel, things simply worked out.

"Girl, c'mon, we're going dancing!" Three of the bridesmaids had wandered over, one of them already tugging Rachel by the arm.

"Wait," she said, shaking free to grab a pen and a napkin. She wrote something on it and passed it his way. Reed couldn't help but notice the diamond sparkling on her finger as he took it. "I gotta go," she said. "Call me, okay?"

An idea bloomed as he stared at the phone number. Reed would call her. He *definitely* would.

It was time something worked out for him.

CHAPTER 33

Jenson Investigations is located on the fourth floor of an office building that was once cutting edge but now swims with plastic surgeons and billboard lawyers hungry for car wreck insurance cases. Zane's office matches his business card: efficient and organized. Minimally decorated. Decidedly male. A couch rests next to an accent wall painted in a cool gray tone. A black-and-white portrait of Mount Rainier draped in a blanket of mist keeps watch over a glass coffee table layered in magazines. *Time* and *Life* and *Forbes*. No celebrity gossip. No *People* or *Us*.

The couch is where I'm seated now. Zane is stationed across from me in a white leather armchair, looking at me in much the same way Ben did yesterday evening when I filled him in on the details of my plan—eyes wide, eyebrows arched. His reaction is more muted than Ben's, though, a momentary flicker of surprise before his face returns to normal.

"It's not possible," Zane says.

"Why not?"

"This guy's a pro. He'll see you coming from a mile away."

"Not if you help me."

A shadow of a smile curls over his lips. "I'm not the one who has to sleep with him."

"I can handle it." My stomach lurches. I have no idea if I can—the thought of being intimate with the man who killed Ethan and Noah makes me physically sick—but that's a problem for future Bailey to solve. Right now, I need to focus on getting Zane onboard.

"I'm not so sure about that," he says. "And even if you could, we're talking about a man who manipulates women for a living. It's hard to con a con."

"Not when they're rusty. Reed hasn't done a job in two years, right?"

Zane crosses his arms. "Not that I'm aware of, no."

"Exactly. He thinks he got away with it. He's retired."

"Guys like Reed don't get rusty, and they don't stop. He'll be back at some point."

I shake my head. "I don't think so. According to the file you gave me, he's been stringing these jobs together for what, close to a decade now? At most he goes dark for a year. That's it. That's as much time as he ever takes. Then he's back at it. He's never been out this long before."

"He's never killed people before."

I flinch. *My people.*

"And that right there is why this will never work," Zane says, taking note of my reaction. "If I can read you, he'll be able to as well. The second he triggers you it's over. You aren't ready for something like this."

"I can get ready."

"I seriously doubt it. And even if you could, you'd still have to find a way to connect with him. A way to give him something none of these other women ever could. He doesn't operate like other people. He's a narcissist. He only loves himself. And you're talking about making him fall in love with you. You won't be able to do that."

"Yes, I will."

Zane groans and rubs his temples. "Okay, I'll bite. Tell me how, then."

I pull the yearbook photo out of my purse and place it on the coffee table, tap it once. "I become *her*."

Zane picks up the photo and studies it. "Taylor White. Why?"

"Because she was important to him." I retrieve another picture from my purse—this one of Reed and Taylor standing next to a bank of lockers, Reed gazing at her as she laughs—and slide it over. "Look at his face. That's no act. He's capable of love."

Zane studies the photo, rubbing the corners of his lips with his thumb and forefinger. "Maybe, but this was a long time ago. It won't be enough."

"It will if I pair it with a story. *My* story."

Zane sets the picture down, his eyes clicking back to me. "I'm not sure I follow."

I cross my legs. "You're right. I won't be able to hide my emotions. Not fully. So, I'll use them. I'll tell Reed I was in a wreck and I killed someone. I won't be able to talk about it without breaking down. Reed won't be able to tell me he did the same thing, but he'll see himself in my story. It's why he'll bond with me. Even a narcissist has feelings."

"You sure?" Zane asks. "Remember, this guy pulled a dead girl into the driver's seat after draining her bank account. And besides, you still haven't addressed the biggest issue.

"Which is?"

"You. He killed your family. What if he recognizes you?"

I'd considered this. I don't know if Reed looked into me after the wreck. If he did, he wouldn't have found much. Besides a few photos on the corporate website that were deleted after I left Pricewaterhouse, I don't exist. In my previous life, I was too busy to focus on social media. I never saw the point of sharing images of what I had for dinner. But I know there *are* pictures of me on the Internet. Old photos from yearbooks. A few pictures of me out with friends. Shots of me with Ethan and Noah on Ethan's Facebook page, which Ethan kept private.

Despite my low public profile, it's likely Reed's seen me online at least a few times. But would he recognize me if he saw me in person? I doubt it. Someone like Reed who makes a career out of ruining other peoples' lives probably doesn't spend a lot of time regretting his actions or living in the past. And if for some strange reason he does, I have a plan for that, too.

"He won't," I say. "I'll change my appearance."

Zane steeples his fingers and places them beneath his chin. "You've certainly thought this through, haven't you?"

"It's all I've thought about. But I can't do it alone."

"Well, you won't be doing it with me," Zane says. "It's too risky. And it would take too much work. I have other clients to consider."

"That's unfortunate," I say, my gaze drifting behind him toward the photo sitting on the corner of his desk—a picture of Zane with his arms slung around his kids. A boy I peg to be close to eighteen and a girl who looks at least ten years younger. She has sleek black hair and a face like her father's, although much narrower, the hollows overly pronounced. And while Zane's skin is a warm tan, the girl's is as pale as milk.

I clocked the picture the second I entered Zane's office along with the stack of medical bills piled in the basket near his computer. I instantly recognized the Harborview Medical logo in the upper left corner of the topmost envelope. After the wreck, I'd received plenty of bills from Harborview of my own, though none of them had the red past-due stamp Zane's has. And it's that stamp, along with Zane's comment from the other day about the cost of health insurance, that I'm banking on to help me change his mind.

"How much would it take?" I ask.

Zane doesn't hesitate. "More than you can afford."

"Don't be so sure about that. How much?"

He taps his fingers on the arm of his chair. "I don't know. I'd have to crunch the numbers."

"Ballpark. I won't hold you to it."

His lips curl into a half-grin. "You're tenacious, I'll give you that. A million, minimum."

The number feels like a slap to the face. I'd expected him to demand a substantial amount, but not seven figures. I have Ethan's life insurance settlement, sure—what I haven't already used, anyway— every dollar of it drenched in blood. And I have what I'd managed to save for retirement before the crash still sitting in my 401(k). All in, I can come up with close to six-hundred thousand—so there's no way I can afford Zane's number. But I can't let him know that, either.

"How about five-hundred thousand up front, and another five hundred once we're done?"

His fingers stop tapping. His gaze sharpens. He says nothing, probably wondering if I'm serious, which I am. I'm not lying. I'll find a way to get him the money. I can take out a home equity loan if I need to.

I lean in and set my elbows on my knees. "Zane, what's your daughter's name?"

He stiffens. For a moment, I don't think he'll answer. Finally, he does. "Cora."

"That's beautiful. I know you mentioned she's sick."

He frowns. "Don't bring her into this."

"She's already part of it. I can see the bills on your desk. I lost my child. Let me help yours. What exactly does she have?"

He tenses, and I can practically hear his spine crack. I know focusing on his daughter is risky, especially after his warning, but I don't have a choice; she's the only leverage I have. My pulse thumps harder as he continues to stare at me, his eyes shining like bullets. I can't tell if he's actually considering my offer or if he's seconds away from telling me to get out of his office.

Finally, he reclines in his chair and lets out a long breath. "Have you ever heard of MLD?"

"MLD?"

"Metachromatic leukodystrophy. Cora has this fatty substance accumulating in her brain. We all have it, actually. But hers ... it builds up. It doesn't get eliminated like it does for the rest of us. It's slowly strangling her nervous system. It affects her ability to walk, to communicate. It diminishes her hearing and sight. The best way I can describe it is like watching someone drown in quicksand, but there's nothing you can do to help them."

"Jesus," I whisper. "That sounds terrible."

"It's awful," Zane says, his eyes dimming. "My wife, Maria, and I ... we've been to so many specialists. Tried so many treatments, but nothing's worked." A brief tremor runs through his voice. He pauses then says, "And it's expensive. You wouldn't believe how much the drugs for this disease cost. The procedures. It's backbreaking."

"I can only imagine," I say. "But surely what I'm offering to pay you will help."

"Not as much as you think."

I fold my hands and set them in my lap. I don't know what else to say.

He pushes his tongue against his cheek, his gaze never leaving mine. A muscle pops near his jaw. His eyes turn to slivers. "If I were to consider this, and I do mean *if*, you would have to agree to do it my way. There would have to be no deviation. A guy like Reed is as slippery as they come. If you fuck it up, he'll bite back. He won't play fair. And he won't only come after you. He'll come after me, too. And I refuse to put my family in jeopardy."

Something resolves in my chest. For the first time since I lost Ethan and Noah, I feel something other than grief, and something deeper than rage. For the first time since the day my world exploded in a ball of glass and metal, I have a purpose. And that purpose has a name: Reed Aldridge. I can absolutely do what Zane asks. And I will.

I nod. "Understood."

He leans back in his chair. "One point five, and I'm in."

My stomach knots. "You just said a million."

"I said, a million *minimum*. And you said you wouldn't hold me to it. One point five. That's my number."

I attempt to swallow past the sudden lump in my throat. It's unsettling he's asking for this much cash. It either means he's greedy or under severe financial stress. My guess is the latter based on what he just said about his daughter. I don't like it. If there's one thing I know from my career in tax, it's that people with a lot of debt will often do unpredictable things. Sometimes dangerous things. But Zane's a professional, not to mention the only resource I have who can reasonably help me pull this off. There's no doubt I need him. Still, I can't even swing his first figure, much less this new one. But there might be a different way I can play this—another option.

I sigh. "I can't afford that."

"Then I'm out."

"Wait," I say, raising my hand. "Hear me out. I still pay you a million, but you get thirty percent of what I take from Reed. He's stolen a lot of money from a lot of people. Whatever he has squirreled away will be substantial."

Zane's eyes narrow as he considers it. "Fifty."

"Forty," I shoot back. "And that's *my* final number. Whatever's left of Reed's money won't change what happened to my family, but it will go a long way in improving the lives of his other victims. It's a big reason why I'm doing this. After what he put them through, they deserve as much as they can get. I won't budge. If you're out, I'll find another way."

Zane rubs his chin. His eyes remain locked on mine, as if he's trying to get a read on my thoughts, wondering if he can push me higher. He can't. And my bet is he won't.

After what feels like an hour has passed, Zane finally grunts and gives me a single nod of his head.

"Deal."

CHAPTER 34

REED
Cincinnati, Ohio
Age Twenty-Five

Reed and Lacey pulled up to the curb outside of Ironwood Commons. The redeveloped industrial complex was home to several boutique businesses, including a coffee shop and a vegan café. Lacey's brand-new franchise, Soul Fitness, clung to the corner of the property which overlooked an abandoned auto shop across the street. It was an ugly structure full of rust and busted cars, surrounded by a ring of oil-stained pavement, and a sagging chain-link fence. The body shop was an eyesore. It was also the only reason Reed could afford to pay the first month's rent on the three-thousand square foot Soul Fitness lease. The location was just close enough to Walnut Hills for him to cultivate the *soon-this-neighborhood-will-be-booming* vision Lacey needed to believe.

Lacey straightened in her seat with a groan. "Oh my god, he's here again."

Reed followed her gaze toward the homeless man sleeping in the recessed entryway near the Soul Fitness door. From here, he looked more like a pile of rags with a face than a human.

"I've had to shoo him away three times now," Lacey said. "I don't know why he keeps coming back. Do you think we picked the wrong location?" Her eyes crimped with worry as she said it, and Reed knew if he didn't soothe her quickly, she'd burst into tears.

"No, not at all, babe," Reed said. "They're developing the entire area. This is exactly the right spot. Just wait until you see what the painters did inside. Come on."

They got out of the car, and Reed moved to wrap Lacey in his arms, but she was already gone, marching toward the man.

"Sir, you can't sleep here," she said the second she reached him.

The man didn't move. "Sir," she said again, prodding him with her toe. "Hey, wake up."

She toed him harder, and the guy groaned and looked up at her with a pair of bloodshot eyes set deep within a pile of wrinkles. A mostly white beard framed his gaunt chin, and his joints crackled like popcorn as he pulled himself into a sitting position.

"Come again?" he said, blinking hard, trying to get his bearings.

Lacey planted her hands on her hips. "I said, you need to leave. You can't keep sleeping here. This isn't a hotel."

"This place ain't even open yet. I ain't botherin' anyone."

"Not yet," Lacey said with a voice that dripped from her mouth like a melting popsicle, sweet and cold. "But this place is my place, and it's opening a week from now. So you're going to need to find somewhere else to go, okay? There are plenty of shelters downtown. I'd hate to have to call the police."

The man heaved a sigh and slowly, painfully, pulled himself to his feet and tottered away. The stale scent of cigarettes hung in his wake. Reed turned to Lacey to ask if they should at least offer him a bottle of water, but she'd already breezed into the gym.

He followed her inside and found her staring wide-eyed at the exposed red brick walls and polished concrete floors. It was the first time she'd seen it like this. The space was bare but honest, crackling with potential. A single squat rack sat in the corner near the group exercise room. Several sets of pull-up bars were mounted on the wall directly across from the entrance, centered beneath an artfully stenciled passage from Philippians. It was Lacey's favorite verse—a surprise Reed hoped would hit home.

I can do all things through Christ, who gives me strength.

They'd shared that message many times, both in text and in conversation. It was their creed. A code to live by. Their pillar in the storm. When things got tough, they turned to the Bible.

Lacey's gaze remained locked on the words, and she took in a sharp breath.

"What do you think?" Reed asked.

"Oh my god, Luke, it's perfect."

Reed knew it was. He'd crafted every inch of the space around her. From the natural light spilling through the skylights above to the pops of color everywhere you looked: A purple Soul Fitness logo hung over the entrance. A pair of mint green and white battle ropes were secured to the floor. Powder blue foam rollers and purple exercise balls sat on a shelving unit placed against the wall. A cream-colored reception desk rested near the front along with a jade area rug and a furniture set—a place for members to relax while waiting for their next class.

Outside of that, the gym was empty, although Reed had marked the floor with locations for all of the cardio equipment along with the weight racks and exercise equipment that would remain permanently on backorder. There wouldn't be any dumbbells delivered, no benches or machines to offload from a truck. Everything would remain as it was now—nothing more than a dream.

Lacey Grayson's dream.

———

Rachel Dawson had been the perfect con. Stealing from her had been a piece of cake. The woman was oblivious; she had no idea he'd been casing from the start. The moment he'd stepped foot in her house, he knew he'd hit the lottery. She had jewelry *everywhere*. On the shelves of her closet, piled in the back of her dresser, scattered throughout a bathroom drawer, jammed into a jewelry case on the kitchen counter. Rachel didn't even have a safe. Reed couldn't believe it. But why would she need one? She lived in Summerlin, after all, fifteen miles from Las Vegas. And no one got robbed in Summerlin.

A month into their relationship, Rachel flew to Phoenix for a craft convention. She'd begged Reed to come with her, had talked about it for weeks. He'd told her he wanted to, really he did, but he had to work. Too bad. So sad. Then, he'd slipped into her house at two a.m. using the door code she'd been dumb enough to give him and cleaned her out. Thirty grand just like that.

It would have been more—a *lot* more—but he had to pay Rhonda, his contact at Hidden Gems Pawn who had the face of a truck driver and the voice of a two-pack-a-day smoker. Reed didn't care that she smelled like an ashtray or talked his ear off anytime he came by. All he cared about was that she sold the shit he stole. And she did every time. The only problem was she took a sixty percent cut. "You try and offload it if you don't like the terms," Rhonda had told him with a rasping laugh when he'd complained.

Reed took the money. It was more cash than he'd ever made by a long shot.

He'd pulled more jobs after that. Started dressing better and refined his approach. What he said initially didn't really matter as much as identifying the right mark: Women with average looks starved for attention. Women with spray-on tans who wore obnoxious dresses and brightened at the approach of a good-looking man. In a city like Las Vegas, it was like fishing with dynamite—the marks floated up everywhere. All he had to do was drop a quick line, and he was in:

Excuse me, I'm afraid I'm lost. Are you from around here?

Wow, I love your shoes. My sister's birthday is next week. Can I ask where you bought them? I'd like to get her a pair.

Hey, didn't I see you at Cirque last night? What a show, right?

Unfortunately, most of the marks weren't as careless as Rachel; even the dumb ones kept their valuables locked up. But Reed still managed to do well enough. All he had to do was wait for an opportunity to present itself. And it always did. Credit cards. Watches. Necklaces. Rings. High-end handbags. Furs. It didn't matter. If he could sell it, he stole it. And he stole a lot. Then he'd disappear for a couple of weeks before doing it again. All in, he'd cleared nearly eighty grand before Rhonda shut him down.

"I'm done, kid. The cops are asking around. You gotta find someone else."

Reed didn't know anyone else. He'd come back anyway. He'd parked nearby and was about to get out of his car when the front door to Hidden Gems slammed open to a pair of burly cops shoving Rhonda outside in handcuffs. The sight froze him, memories of that fateful day with his dad in Texas crashing through his head like shotgun fire.

Bang! "Wake up! Wake up! Oh god, Lloyd, please wake up!" The woman's cries mixing with all the wailing sirens as she knelt next to her dead husband and cradled his head.

Bang! The police as they arrived, guns drawn, shouting at his father to, "Get the fuck down, get on the ground!"

Bang! His father's ashen face and bloodshot eyes aimed at Reed, his cheek smashed against the pavement. He looked so pathetic in that moment, so hopeless and broken.

Reed had promised himself right then and there he'd never go to jail, never get arrested. No fucking way. And this—what had just happened with Rhonda—was *way* too close. Two days later, he packed his bags and moved to Ohio.

He'd buzzed his hair by then and started working out at a local gym. That's when he'd spotted Lacey Grayson—a slice of blonde heaven clad in tight blue yoga pants and a white halter top. Every guy in the gym ogled her. They had good reason to. She was beyond gorgeous. Worse, she knew it—and she drank it up.

Reed hated her immediately.

The other guys didn't. Most took a shot, especially the meatheads. She turned them all down. Reed guessed it was because she went to church. He'd overheard her talking about it to a friend. It was a place called Timberline Hills. One of those massive nondenominational spots where people showed up in flip flops and shorts, clutching cups of Starbucks. Reed didn't know why he hadn't thought of going to one of these churches earlier. It was the perfect place to hunt. Especially *this* kind of church; a place large enough he could blend in while he scoped out a fresh target.

He'd spotted the flier on his second visit.

Build with a purpose. Connect your business with faith.

Are you a small business owner or entrepreneur?

Do you want to honor God in pursuit of your purpose?
Do you want to network with others who do the same?

Then come join us for Christian Business Fellowship!
Every Thursday at 7 p.m. in the Garden Room.

Reed hadn't planned on seeing Lacey there, he was simply looking for an easy mark. But there she was, planted in the middle of the second row, dressed in jeans and a sweater, looking hot as fuck. He sat two chairs down and pretended to listen as a guy wearing a twenty-year-old sport coat dropped a bunch of Christian catchphrases about perseverance and integrity and how you needed to let go and let God. It made sense to Reed because God's power was exactly what it would take for a guy like this to ever make a dime on his own.

"Don't you work out at The Spot?"

It had taken Reed a second to realize Lacey was talking to him. He'd nearly fallen asleep in his chair.

"Yeah," he'd replied, rubbing his eyes. "Do you?" He'd said it like he didn't know, like he hadn't had to tear his gaze from her at least a dozen times.

The corners of her lips had kicked up into a pair of dimples. "No, I'm just stalking you."

"Do I need to call the cops?"

"Probably. But you'll need my name for the restraining order. I'm Lacey."

Reed had laughed at that. Couldn't help it. "Luke. So, what brings you here?"

She wanted to start a yoga studio, but the property prices in LA were outrageous. She had family in Ohio and had moved here after graduating from UCLA to save up. Reed told her he'd done the same, though he'd migrated from the East Coast. And then he'd surprised himself and asked her out. One second, they were there talking and the next—*bam!*—he knew exactly how to play her. That's how fast his plan hit.

They'd dated for two months before he set it in motion, Reed listening as Lacey droned on about all things Lacey most of the time: Her devotion to eating vegan. Her exercise regimen. How she microbladed her eyebrows and preferred vintage handbags to modern. Her faith. Dear god, her faith. The church food drives she organized but never volunteered for. The Bible studies she dragged him to, which were nothing more than thinly veiled social clubs full of women who gossiped about the people who weren't there and talked about problems that weren't really problems: Sick pets. Kids who didn't get into the local charter school. Bullshit campaigns to modernize the already modern church.

It drove him crazy. But he'd endured it ... he'd played along for Lacey's sake. Their shared Christian morals were what they'd bonded over in the first place, after all. They were both in search of something higher than what the world had to offer. And they both steered clear of temptation—which was code for no sex. Reed hated it, hated how Lacey was forever toying with him, teasing him, edging closer but pulling back at the last second with her lips brushing against his ear. *I just want it to be special, you know?*

Reed did know. He'd told her he felt the same way. Of course, he did. He was different than the other guys at the gym constantly trying to get into her pants. Unlike them, he wasn't chasing her body; he was pursuing her heart. He wanted to know her. The *real* her. Sex could wait. And then, when he was certain she believed that, Reed had baited the hook and dropped the line.

"I need to tell you something."

They'd been sitting at a Mad Greens, eating salads for the thousandth time, and she'd given him an *oh-here-it-comes-I-knew-this-was-too-good-to-be-true* expression, her lips curling down as she asked, "Should I be worried?"

He'd played into the question, hesitated for effect—like what he had to say next would change her life. "No, it's a good thing, actually. Remember how I told you I work in accounting?"

"Yes—for the health club chain."

"Well, I do a little more than that. I'm not really supposed to share this, but the reason I'm in Ohio is because Soul Fitness is looking to expand. I'm here conducting a market study for the company."

"Why is that a secret?"

"The competition. We don't want word getting out. We want to be the first to market."

"Oh," she'd said with a shrug before going back to her salad, her interest already waning, exactly like it had any time he'd mentioned anything about his "job" in the past. He'd dropped hints along the way, telling Lacey how Soul Fitness was a faith-based franchise focused on expanding across the country with the purpose of providing exercise locations where believers could gather and workout together. He'd said Soul Fitness was committed to building fitness centers where followers could worship through the beauty of exercise and movement together, and how beautiful was that?

In case Lacey bothered to verify his story, Reed had created a sleek website that would back him up. He'd even filed all of the appropriate business paperwork and backdated it five years to make it look like the chain had been around for a while. But despite this, Lacey had only asked about his job once. Reed had been surprised she'd even remembered what he did when he mentioned it now.

"Well, that's exciting," she said in between bites.

"It is. But the real reason I'm bringing it up is … well, I'm wondering if you'd be interested in running a location?"

Her eyes returned to his and widened. "Are you serious?"

"Yes. I think you'd be a perfect fit."

———

Reed watched Lacey bustle around the room, looking like a kid on Christmas, her face so bright it seemed to glow. "This is incredible."

"I'm glad you like it," Reed said.

"Like it? Are you kidding? I love it." She neared the squat rack and cocked her head. "This looks a little old though, doesn't it?"

It was. Reed had picked it up off eBay for four hundred bucks. A quality rack could easily run into the thousands, and he'd had to stretch to cover all the costs as it was. The most difficult hurdle to clear had been the first month's rent. The landlord had wanted ten grand a month, but Reed had been able to talk him down to six—an amount he'd covered with part of Lacey's twenty-thousand-dollar "franchise deposit". The rest of the bogus franchise fee—$180,000—was due today.

"Don't worry," Reed said. "It's temporary. The new squat racks take a month or so to fabricate, but they'll be here soon. I just wanted to make sure we had one on hand in case the rest don't arrive before we open."

He suppressed a grin. *We.* Like he'd be here cutting the ribbon with her instead of lying on some beach in Mexico, shit-faced instead.

She neared and slipped into his arms and draped her hands around his neck. She smelled like lemon and sugar. "I don't know what I did to deserve you."

He tucked a strand of hair behind her ear. "I ask myself the same question about you all the time."

"I love you, you know."

Reed smiled. "I love you, too."

She leaned in and pressed her lips against his. They remained there, locked in the embrace until she took his hand and led him toward the windowless fitness studio in the back, her hips swaying.

"Where are we going?" he asked.

Without answering, she entered the room and slipped out of her top and slid off her leggings. When she turned to face him, she was naked.

"Wow," he whispered. She was absolute perfection.

Lacey stepped closer and set a finger on his chest, then pulled it lower toward his belt. "I think you've waited long enough, don't you?"

Reed nodded. He had. This was the one thing he had yet to take from her. It made him feel bad for a second. But not bad enough to stop.

CHAPTER 35

"Not bad," Zane says, appraising me from across the table. "You clean up well, Ms. Carter."

I feel my lips curl higher in response.

"Thank you."

Coming from another man, I might take the statement as flirtatious. Coming from Zane, it's nothing more than a fact. My transformation has taken six months and several procedures to achieve. My eyelids are wider and brighter as a result, the skin beneath my eyes fresh and firm, the bags gone. Thanks to the laser depigmentation, my irises are no longer a deep hazel brown, but rather a stunning light green. My nose looks better too, the tip contoured and the bump in the bridge smoothed in a way that brings more harmony to my profile. My entire face has a certain vitality I didn't realize was missing until now.

I've never been a fan of plastic surgery—hadn't given it much thought before all of this, really—but now I understand why people pursue it. The results are stunning. When I gaze in the mirror, I barely recognize the woman looking back at me—especially after dyeing my hair. My mop of dirty blonde has blossomed into a lush mane of red. Unlike my eyes, the color change isn't permanent. I'll have to keep after it. But I can manage that. Even if Reed catches on, it won't be a big deal. Lots of women dye their hair.

Zane takes a swig of his beer. "Are you ready for this?"

"I think so," I say.

He frowns. "That's not good enough."

"Fine," I say, smacking my vodka tonic against the table. "Put me in, coach. I've never been more ready."

It's true. My change isn't just a physical one. Over the last six months I've felt myself coming back to life little by little. With each passing day, I've sensed my resolve going stronger. I'll admit I was on shaky ground at first—especially after paying Zane the initial five-hundred grand we'd agreed on. I'd constantly questioned how I'd come up with the rest of the money. But I've never questioned my decision to go after Reed. In fact, my conviction to crucify him has only grown stronger. Lately, I've even managed to log eight hours of sleep for a few nights in a row instead of waking in a panic from my usual sweat-drenched nightmare. So yes, I'm ready. In a way, it feels like I have a new lease on life.

Zane tilts his bottle and clinks the neck against my glass. "Much better."

We're heading to Durango, Colorado tomorrow, Reed's adopted hometown, and Zane suggested we grab a quick drink and review the last few details of the plan. That, and we both need a break from all the preparation. I've been living as Avery Carter for nearly half a year now. I've memorized every detail of her life.

Born in Sioux City, Iowa to a single mother, Avery had a decent upbringing. She and her mom bounced around the Midwest until settling in Des Moines, where Avery played soccer for several years at North Polk High School. She wasn't exactly a star, but good enough to think about a scholarship or two before a knee injury sidelined her. A few years at the University of Kansas followed, until a fatal car accident took that away too—Avery the one behind the wheel.

She spent a year behind bars. Then two years of probation, Avery off to a local community college to finish her finance degree after that. Some hard years from there: Her mother's cancer. A funeral. A long stretch spent moving around the country, chasing work, before finally settling in Durango where—

Oh, hello, there.

—she'll meet Reed Aldridge.

A transient childhood. A single parent. A tragic car accident and a fatality.

A history of isolation.

A fake past tailored with enough similarities to Reed's to evoke empathy. A past that will remind him of his own—all of it available with a few clicks of a mouse thanks to Zane and his contacts. Newspaper articles, database records, paper trails; when it comes to Avery Carter, it's all there.

As for my actual past, Zane obliterated it. You can't find a mention of Bailey Nichols anywhere. I don't know who he hired to do it, but they did an incredibly thorough job: all my high school and college records, every business article I've been a part of, my time at PricewaterhouseCoopers and all my client presentations are gone. There are no stray images of me still floating around the Internet. Even the articles about the wreck and the deaths of my family have been wiped clean. It's like the crash never happened at all.

I take hold of my drink, the glass cool against my palm. "So, everything's good to go, then?"

Zane sips his beer and deadpans me. "What do you think?"

"I think Paula was right."

"Yeah? About what."

"She said you were good."

He gives a nonchalant shrug. "You get what you pay for."

I have. Zane is good. Very good. After taking the job, he gave me an entire library's worth of books on adaptability and persuasion.

He spent days educating me on compartmentalization and how to maintain my composure in tense situations. We role-played various scenarios for hours. Any time I said or did something out of character, he stopped and explained exactly what I did wrong and why.

There can be no slips. No mistakes. Not with Reed.

I have to be different from his prior targets: a confident woman, strong enough I can't be manipulated, but not so strong I scare him off. A fun, flirty, fresh, cool-ass woman who challenges him in the best of ways, all while validating his grandiose sense of self-importance. I'll need to connect my past with his and remind him of the girl he once loved. But I'll have to be different from her, too. I'll need to make him believe that, unlike Taylor White, I won't abandon him—would *never* abandon him. Not when I'm meant for him.

"Listen," Zane says, "I know you think you're ready, but you never really are. You have to be perfect. There's no room for error when you go undercover like this. You say the wrong name, you mention something from your past—your real past—and it's over. You forget your backstory for a second, it's over. You act in a way that isn't congruent with who Avery Carter is, and it's over. I know you know this, but what you're about to do is dangerous, Bailey. It's dangerous as hell."

I tilt my drink toward him. "You did it, didn't you? And you're fine."

"I worked in NARC. I never had to sleep with my targets. And I still found ways to fuck up at times. It's incredibly difficult to act against your instincts in high-pressure situations like this. You have to ignore every emotion screaming at you to get the fuck out of there. But that's exactly what you have to do. Ignore them. Once you commit, you need to go all the way. There can't be any half measures."

"That's fair. But I can handle it."

He assesses me for a long moment, his eyes turning clinical again. I fight the urge to shrink back. His gaze is a fearsome thing. One minute everything's fine, the next you feel like you're sitting across from him in an interrogation room, guilty of murder.

He runs a hand over his chin, then gives me the ghost of a grin. "You know what? I actually think you can. You do everything exactly like we practiced, and you'll have your shot."

My cheeks warm as I smile. I can't help it. Zane's compliments are as rare as shooting stars—blink, and they're gone.

"Thank you for doing this."

"Trust me," he says with a quick laugh. "It's not out of the goodness of my heart. Now come on, let's get out of here. We both need to get some sleep."

Zane calls the waitress over and pays the tab. We're nearly halfway to the door when something catches his attention.

"What is it?" I ask.

He doesn't answer. Instead, he stares at the bar, which is crowded with people—some seated, some standing. Nothing seems out of the ordinary. Nothing but Zane, who suddenly heads for a man with thinning hair and glasses wearing in a salmon-pink polo. He looks up from his stool as we draw near, his eyes slowly widening in recognition when they land on Zane.

"Hello, Doctor," Zane says, coldly.

"Oh—hello, Mr ..."

"Jenson," Zane finishes.

"Right," the man mutters. "Sorry. Mr. Jenson. How's your daughter?"

"Still very sick."

"I'm ... sorry to hear that."

"Are you? You referred her to a shrink," Zane replies. "You told us she had ADHD." A vein throbs near his temple, and the man shifts back on his stool.

"Listen, Mr. Jenson," he says, after a quick swallow. "Why don't you call the office and schedule an appointment, and we can talk about this further there?"

A dangerous light flashes through Zane's eyes—something I haven't seen before in him—but his voice remains as even as ever. "And wait another three months to see you like last time? I don't think so."

I lay my hand on his back and feel the muscles tense beneath my palm. "Hey, let's get out of here."

"She has MLD," Zane says, ignoring me.

The man pales at this, but he doesn't say anything. I can feel the tension rising off Zane like a heatwave.

"Zane," I say more firmly.

But he still doesn't move, just stares at the man and says, "You're a specialist. You should have known better. You'll be hearing from my lawyer."

With that, he moves past me and heads for the door.

CHAPTER 36

REED
Seattle, Washington
Age Twenty-Nine

The coffee shop buzzed as Reed approached Evelyn Nash. She blinked up at him when he neared, and he nearly took a step back. Her round, owl-framed glasses were too large for her slender, almost gaunt face. Her eyes were as dark as her hair, her pupils lost in her irises. She had a flat nose that hung over a pair of thin lips and a jaw that tapered into a sharp point. Standing this close, something about her features seemed insect-like to Reed—like he was staring at a human grasshopper.

"Not all who wander are lost," he read aloud, nodding at the sticker plastered to the back of her computer. "Aragorn, right?"

"Are you a fan of Isildur's Heir?" she asked.

"Sorry?"

"The rightful king. Strider of the Wilds. The one who wields the Flame of the West."

Reed coughed, unsure how to respond. He opened his mouth and shut it, then opened it again. "I—"

She tapped the sticker. "Aragorn. Are you a fan?"

"Yes, sorry. I love *The Lord of the Rings*." He'd prepared for this, knew she was into Tolkien. He'd even spent some time brushing up on all things Middle Earth over the last few months in preparation, but her direct question and clipped, monotone caught him off guard.

"I don't see how that can be the case if you don't recognize his many names." She waited for his reply, her face an expressionless mask as her insectoid eyes clicked over him in a series of slow blinks.

Reed hoped she liked what she saw: a man a few years older than her wearing scuffed jeans, a blue denim jacket, and a black T-shirt showcasing her favorite band, The Strokes. He'd grown his hair out and tucked it behind his ears, pairing it with two days' worth of scruff. Like her, he wore a pair of framed glasses, except his carried no prescription. He looked ruffled but not homeless, just distressed enough to be her type.

"It's uh, been a while since I read the books," Reed said, placing his hand on the empty chair across from her. "Mind if I sit?"

"This is a public space, isn't it? The chair is available."

Nope, he thought, about to break for the door. *No way.* But he forced himself into the seat anyway, and Evelyn spoke the second he did.

"I met Julian once. He's an introvert. He's also highly intelligent. Some would classify him as a genius."

Reed nearly flinched. The change of topic felt like machine-gun chatter, her words spitting into him in a way that made him want to duck. But this time he knew exactly who she was talking about: Julian Casablancas, the lead singer of The Strokes. She'd noticed his shirt—was staring at it now like he'd hoped she would.

"He's very smart," Reed said. "Did you know he can communicate with crows?" Reed didn't know if it was true, but he'd read something about the man attempting to do that somewhere on the Internet.

Her eyebrows inched higher, and her lips bloomed into a smile that transformed her entire face like a flick of a switch—a dark room suddenly bright with light. Her eyes crinkled at the corners. Her cheeks rose and flushed with color. The expression was so welcoming, so warm, he couldn't help but smile back.

"I did not," Evelyn said. "How very fascinating. Are you certain it's crows? It might be ravens. They're technically more intelligent."

"I'm pretty sure it's crows. I'm Adrian by the way." Reed stretched out his hand and she took it, pumping it vigorously.

Just one more, he told himself. *One more and I'll be done.*

Evelyn Nash would be the last.

———

He'd spotted Evelyn while sipping a martini in the Plaza in New York City of all places. He'd been relaxing before attending a charity gala for neglected animals or homeless kids in Africa—he couldn't remember which, only that it was some bullshit event where women with too much money went to play at being philanthropic—when he'd noticed her on the television screen hanging over the bar.

Evelyn clung to her father, Donald Nash, as he hollered at a bunch of reporters to clear away from his car. She had limp, dull hair and hands that were swallowed by the sleeves of a too-large sweater. Her eyes were glued to her feet as her father tugged her through a swarm of press shouting questions about the latest Nash Logistics earnings report, Donald roaring right back, red-faced. Reed hadn't known her name at that point, had only known the woman appeared terrified and awkward, but the gears in his brain were already turning as he googled her.

The daughter of a shipping tycoon.

A woman with sad eyes who seemed empty and lost.

Someone who looked incomplete.

I can complete you, he'd thought. *I can do that. And then I'll disappear forever.*

Reed didn't know exactly when it had happened, but he'd grown tired of conning. There had been so many women: Tara Knowles, the fashion boutique owner who'd financed her Main Street Kentucky store with Daddy's money because she'd been too lazy to go to college and make something happen herself. Jennifer Stewart, the high-end realtor who cut deals on closing costs for her rich friends but charged full price to everyone else. All the others. The Rachel Dawsons and Lacey Graysons of the world who thought the universe revolved around them and expected every man in their orbit to do the same.

There had been so many identities, too—all the driver's licenses, passports, birth certificates, and credit cards. All of the names, the changes to his appearance and mannerisms. The surgeries. He was forever running, constantly waiting for someone to recognize him and shout for him to *stop!* Waiting for the police to pound on his door in the middle of the night and order for him to *open up!*

All the personalities. All the lies.

So many lies Reed didn't even know who he was anymore, knew only that he was tired. The game—which was exactly how he'd thought of it until now, as a game—had lost its appeal. But that didn't change the fact he still needed money, still had to survive. So he kept going, kept telling himself the next job would be his last.

It never was. The paydays didn't last long enough. The people he contracted to help him disappear and then be reborn—*Happy Birthday, Reed! Welcome to the new you!*—were incredibly expensive to employ. Nothing about what he did was cheap. But it was the only thing he knew how to do. And the only thing he did well. So he kept doing it, but he was done.

It was time to move on, time to start a new life and do something different. He'd thought about it for so long now. Maybe he'd open a bookstore somewhere and spend the rest of his years lost between the pages. Or maybe he'd start a coffee shop where he could listen to his customers talk about all the small, unimportant problems in life as he forgot about his own. That sounded nice. Anything other than this. But first, he needed one more score. A *big* score. One last target he could really sink his claws into and tear free enough cash to set him up for life.

Someone exactly like Evelyn Nash.

CHAPTER 37

"It's not too late to change your mind, you know."

Ben's words fill my ears as I gaze through the windshield at the terminal. A thrum of traffic surrounds us, airport shuttles and buses buzzing past in rapid succession. My body aches with the sound. Something no one tells you about surviving a car wreck is this: Getting into a car hurts. Literally. Any time I do, I feel my ribs pulse along the fracture lines like they never healed. Any time my foot touches the floorboard, I hear the snap of my shin and crunch of my ankle. My shoulder aches whenever I reach for my seatbelt like my tendons are about to tear all over again.

After the wreck, I did everything I could to avoid driving. In the early days, I relied on Ben to get me to my PT appointments. When he couldn't help, I called an Uber. I had all of my groceries and alcohol delivered. All of my pills. Back then, I couldn't imagine ever driving again. The first time I tried, I wound up sitting at a stop sign with a barrage of horns piling up behind me for who knows how long. All I could see in that moment were the headlights of Evelyn Nash's black BMW X7 heading straight for me, ready to re-break my bones.

After a wreck as bad as mine, getting into a car is war.

What I'm about to do is worse.

"Seriously, Bailey," Ben says. "Say the word, and we'll go. I'm here for you. You don't need to do this."

I twist toward him, his face tender, his forehead dimpled in concern. My heart cracks. I want to be able to tell him he's right, that he can help me through this. But he can't. And he shouldn't have to. Since my suicide attempt, things have been rocky between he and Owen. I've overheard their phone calls, heard the strain in Owen's voice muffled through the speaker when they talk. The two of them are a rubber band pulled to max tension; if I stay between them any longer, I have no doubt they'll snap.

Besides, I need to do this. I *have* to. If I don't, I know the darkness will pull me back in just when I'm starting to glimpse the light. And that light is Reed's destruction.

"My baby brother, always looking out for me," I say, reaching over to place my hand on Ben's cheek. "I'll call you as soon as we land."

"You'd better. Every night."

I pop an eyebrow at him. "You know I won't be able to do that."

"Once a week, then."

"I'll try."

He frowns. "I'm serious, Bay. If I don't hear from you at least once a week, I'm going to the cops."

I tense. Bringing the police into this is one of my non-negotiables and he knows that. We've only discussed it a dozen times. No cops no matter what happens. But with what I'm putting him through, I suppose I can give him this. "Okay, fine. Once a week. But do me a favor, will you?"

"What's that?"

"Go home and focus on Owen for a while. I'll be fine."

"I wish I could believe that," he says before pausing like he has something else to say.

I wave my hand. "Go on. Out with it."

"It's just ... I don't know if I'll ever get used to that."

"What?"

"Your new face."

I mime a pained expression. "You don't like it?"

"I love it, actually," he says with a grin. "With your ugly mug, I can't believe you didn't do it sooner."

"Oh, shut up," I say, laughing as I slap his shoulder before pulling him into a hug. "Bye, Ben."

"Bye, Bay," he says, squeezing me. "You be careful. And don't forget to call me."

"I will," I say, squeezing him back. "Love you."

"Love you, too."

He gives me a final wave as I pull my suitcase from the backseat and shut the door. And then he's gone, his car swallowed in the traffic. I'm hit with a sudden rush of sadness. My brother is about all I have left to love in this world. Even if something happens to me, I hope he'll be okay.

I turn away from the curb, and a man barges past me, banging his suitcase into mine without a word.

Somewhere to my left, someone barks out a laugh.

"You're shitting me!" a woman screeches behind me into her phone. "You can't be serious!"

Her voice blends with other conversations—people laughing and shouting and clacking by in shoes that smack against the cement like jackhammers. I haven't flown since the wreck, haven't ventured to the airport once. Just being here, standing in this crowded space, makes my skin crawl.

I suddenly wonder if Ben was right. Maybe I shouldn't be doing this. It feels overwhelming—all these people, all this noise. My heart flutters, and I take a deep breath and try to slow it, but it only beats faster in response. How can I navigate the complexities of a relationship with the man who killed my family if I can't even walk into an airport without suffering a nervous breakdown?

It's not too late, Ben's voice whispers. You can still change your mind.

My fingers drift toward my pocket and my phone. All I have to do is dial his number. All I have to do is call and ask.

And then I see her.

Zane crouches in front of Cora several yards ahead. He's holding his daughter by the shoulders, speaking softly with his head in a tilt. She trembles in place as her mother, Maria, stands behind her, biting off a sob. Zane says something that makes the girl laugh, and then she half-thrusts herself, half-falls into his arms. He holds her there and runs his hand over the back of her head.

I draw closer and take her in. Cora's eyes are a deep, liquid brown. One tracks slightly outward while the other battles to focus through a slow series of blinks. Her face is pale and slack, and her lips move as if caught in a constant mumble. She tilts forward when Zane pulls back—like she's about to collapse—but Zane steadies her and then presses her forehead to his. They remain like that for a long moment before Maria swoops in and helps Cora into the car—something infant-like about the girl's motions, something so ... helpless.

Zane watches them go as they pull away, and my heart breaks again for the second time in five minutes. Seeing him with his daughter like this is gut-wrenching.

"She's beautiful," I say, easing next to him.

He nods, but doesn't turn my way, just remains there looking as broken as I've ever seen him, staring at the traffic like he's about to shatter.

"That she is," he says, clearing his throat. "Come on."

Thirty minutes later, we're seated at a table in the food court, both of us with cups of coffee in hand. Zane stares into his with half-lidded eyes. "Sorry about that. It gets harder to leave her every time."

"I can only imagine."

He lifts his gaze. "You're one of the few who can. Not many people know what it's like to lose a child.

He falls silent, and I don't press him. Instead, I change the subject.

"So, are we going to talk about last night, or pretend it didn't happen?"

"What about it?" he asks.

"That little altercation of yours with the doctor."

"Peter Wainwright. Yeah, he was one of Cora's specialists."

"Was?" I prompt.

"Correct. No more. He's a neurologist. We were told he was the best. Maria and I had to wait months to see him. The day we did, Cora was fairly alert but did have a few behavior problems in his office. She threw a fit and knocked some stuff off the shelves. He didn't even spend thirty minutes with us before he referred her to a child psychologist for behavioral therapy. He wanted us out of there, said to come see him again in a month if things didn't change."

"I'm guessing they didn't."

He shakes his head. "No, they got worse. Cora started falling all the time, had trouble communicating with us. With everyone really. So we booked another appointment with Wainwright, but we had to wait longer than a month like he promised. Maria and I told him how concerned we were when we were finally able to see him again. We laid out all the symptoms. But he didn't listen. He ordered the wrong tests and then referred us to a bunch of other doctors that couldn't help. He didn't seem to care. It delayed Cora's diagnosis by almost half a year."

His eyes glimmer, and he shakes his head and takes a long sip of his coffee. "That girl means everything to me. I wanted to do things right this time around. She's supposed to be my second chance."

I wrinkle my brow. "What do you mean?"

"My son, Sean. I … well, I fucked up with him to be honest. I was on the force back then. Worked way too much. Ignored him when he needed me the most. I had a bit of a gambling problem back then. That and the job were all that mattered to me at the time. By the time my priorities changed, it was too late."

An ache like poison spreads through my stomach. I know this kind of regret. It's a blade that cuts deep.

"Anyway," he continues, "Sean was always getting into trouble. Bullying kids. Acting out. Looking for attention. My first wife, Samantha, did her best with him, but she was working too. Neither of us were around enough to keep Sean in line. He got into a lot of trouble."

"Like what?" I ask, curious. Zane's never opened up like this before, and it's a strange kind of relief to realize I'm not the only one struggling here.

"The usual stuff," Zane says. "Pot. Drinking. Running with the wrong crowd. Playing the tough guy and getting into fights. Stealing things. Sam and I did what we could. We tried to get him involved in sports and extracurriculars and all that, but it was too late. You have to start young with kids. We waited too long."

"How old is he now?" I ask.

"Twenty-one. He helps me out with my cases sometimes. I keep waiting for him to turn it around, but I don't know if he ever will. He's still on a pretty bad track." Zane takes another drink of coffee and returns the cup to the table. "Anyway, after Sam and I split, I swore if I ever got another chance to be a father, I'd do it right. And now that I have, I can't even get my little girl the help she needs."

My heart softens, and I reach across the table and set my hand on his. "Hey, what's happening with Cora isn't your fault, Zane. None of this is on you."

He wipes his eyes and shakes his head. "Yeah, maybe. I don't know. But either way you don't need to hear about any more of my shit. You've got enough of your own to worry about." He checks his watch. "You ready? This is your last chance to back out. We board in fifteen minutes."

I nod. I am. I just hope he is too.

CHAPTER 38

REED
Seattle, Washington
Age Twenty-Nine

"Look at the form here. It's a tondo," Evelyn said.

"A tondo?" Reed asked, studying the Botticelli—a painting portraying the Virgin Mary surrounded by angels with an infant Jesus sitting in her lap. It was one of many such paintings in the Seattle Art Museum they'd been examining for the last few hours.

"Correct," Evelyn said. "A circle. It creates a sense of harmony. It's an efficient use of space. It adds to the warmth of the piece. Can you see it?"

Reed *could* see it. Something about the portrait felt more inviting than the others. At some point, they'd all started to blend together to him. Painting after painting of figures wearing serene expressions while standing in gardens or posing in churches. The colors were all too similar, the scenes interchangeable. He was bored in minutes.

But then Evelyn walked him through the differences, and the paintings came to life. She pointed out the way the impressionists used loose brush strokes while the Baroque artists employed a more energetic style. She noted the atmospheric effects utilized by the

Renaissance painters and the playfulness of the scenes of the 18th century masters. These little things Reed would have never noticed on his own, but were blindingly clear once Evelyn highlighted them, like he'd been handed a fresh pair of eyes.

She did that. The way she looked at the world continually surprised him. Evelyn didn't simply hear music—she felt it. The way a bass drum throbbed in your chest. How the sound of a violin filled you with a warmth like air. She saw stories in the mundane. A scuffed doorknob was an opportunity to question how many hands had worn away the paint. A crack in a ceiling was a home's slow-motion war against gravity. The color of the sky was never simply blue but rather cerulean or cobalt or teal. Her observations were one of the things he loved about her, which was troubling because he shouldn't love anything at all.

He slipped his hand into hers and caught the scent of ink and paper mixed with that of violet. Evelyn never left home without a few spritzes of a fragrance she'd found online called Paperback. When he'd asked her about it, she'd simply shrugged and smiled. *Books are my favorite smell.* They were his now, too.

"Come on," he said, pulling her away from the piece. "We're going to be late."

"My father can wait."

"Maybe for you he will," Reed replied. "But he won't for me."

"He'll have to," Evelyn said, looking perplexed. "We'll arrive in the same car."

"No, I mean ..." He trailed off with a chuckle. "Never mind. Let's go. I want to be on time."

Evelyn struggled with anything that moved beyond the literal. Implied meanings were lost on her. Reed thought of statements like the one she'd just made as Evelyn-isms—quirks of speech that should annoy him but didn't. After all the mind games women had put him through over the years, it was refreshing not to have to second guess everything she said. Evelyn told him exactly what she was thinking.

Her father did the same, but nothing about what Donald Nash said was endearing. He grilled Reed like he was some fresh-out-of-prison felon any time he saw him. No matter how supportive he was of Evelyn, no matter how kind or polite or respectful, Reed couldn't seem to win the man over.

Not that Reed could blame him.

———

The Nashes were already seated by the time he and Evelyn arrived. They lounged at a table in the back corner of the restaurant next to a wall of glass overlooking Lake Union. The sun set in the distance, draping the Cascades in a blanket of pink light.

Paula rose as they neared, first hugging Evelyn, then moving to Reed. Donald remained in his chair and watched. He had a chin as hard as a dam and eyes that sparkled with all the shine of wet asphalt. He clutched a half-empty tumbler of amber liquid which Reed guessed to be a Manhattan based on the cherry and the large block of ice. The man had an affinity for all things whiskey, something Reed enjoyed himself, not that it had helped them connect. Nothing Reed did or said elevated him above the man's suspicion.

Reed extended his hand across the table. "Hello, Donald." Donald, never Don. He'd made that mistake once early on. *My friends call me that. You can call me Donald.*

Donald stared at Reed's hand until he pulled it back, then gestured at the empty chair across from him with a tilt of his glass. "Are you going to sit, or are you going to stand there all night, making me uncomfortable?"

"Be nice," Paula said, slapping her husband's arm as Reed sat. "So, Adrian," she asked, "was the SAM everything you imagined?"

"It was," Reed said. "Evelyn was a great tour guide."

Paula set her chin on her fingers. "She always is."

"We spent most of our time studying the European artists," Evelyn said. "Adrian was especially interested in the transition from the Renaissance to the Baroque."

"Is that so?" Paula asked, winking at Reed.

Reed smiled. "I didn't even know the difference between the two before today."

Donald leaned in and set an elbow on the table, his gaze coming to rest on Evelyn. "Did you find the Reni?"

"Oh, yes. The Atalana. It was there like you said."

"You remember seeing it in Naples, don't you?"

"Of course, I do."

"I'll never forget that trip," Donald said, his face softening in a way that made Reed wonder if he was looking at a different person—a gentler, kinder man hidden somewhere beneath all the rock and stone. "It was incredible."

"It was a very enjoyable experience," Evelyn agreed, smiling brightly.

Reed had no clue what trip they were talking about which was fine. The more they talked, the less he had to. Unfortunately, Paula pulled him right back into the conversation after taking a sip of her wine. "When Evelyn was younger, Don took her on an art tour of Italy. They stopped at all of the big museums. She came back a brand-new person. It was a real turning point for her."

"A turning point?" Reed asked, curious. "How so?"

Donald shot Paula a glance. "Don't."

Paula opened her mouth, but it was Evelyn who replied first. "Why not?"

"Because," Donald said with the cement flowing back into his face, "it's a family matter. And there's no need to rehash the past."

"It's fine," Evelyn replied, brushing him off as she turned toward Reed. "When I was younger, I struggled with depression. I was ...

unkind to myself at times. Art helped me heal."

"I said, don't." Donald cleared his throat and waved his empty tumbler at the waiter, who quickly came over. "I'll take another of these. And then we'll be ready to order. Everyone pick out your meal."

The waiter nodded and disappeared. Evelyn remained undeterred. "No. I want to talk about this. We can discuss anything in front of Adrian. I love him."

Reed coughed, nearly choked, and drowned it with a quick drink of his water. Love was a weapon he liked to employ as quickly as possible when it came to a con. Love impaired a target's ability to think clearly. Love allowed him to manipulate well. Love had earned him hundreds of thousands of dollars over the years. And love would help him take much more from Evelyn. But for her to drop the L-word here for the first time, right in front of her father, was dangerous. It jeopardized everything.

When Reed looked up, he fully expected Donald to be glaring at him, ready to leap over the table and tear him in half with his bare hands. But he wasn't. Donald was staring at Evelyn instead, his lips parted, his forehead ashen. Paula gaped at her as well, a fine tremor running through the wine glass in her hand before she set it down. "That's ... well, it's wonderful. Isn't it, Don?"

"You don't love him," Donald said.

"I do," Evelyn responded bluntly, as if she were commenting on the weather or the score of a baseball game.

"No, you don't," Donald repeated.

Evelyn stiffened. The reaction wasn't much, but Reed saw the slight tightening of her jaw and the way her lips pressed into a thin line before she spoke. "I'm sorry, but are you implying that you are me?"

Donald's brow crumpled. "What?"

"You just said I don't love him. In order for you to know something like that, you would need to have access to my feelings—which you don't. You aren't me. I love him. Don't presume to tell me otherwise."

"But, Livy, you don't even know him." Donald's tone had turned pleading—the kind of voice Reed knew he never used with anyone but her.

She crossed her arms, a flush coming to her cheeks. "Incorrect. I know that he's kind and inquisitive and listens to me when I speak. I know I'm his top priority. I know we share many interests, and I know that he loves me. He's already said so."

Reed had—several times now, but Evelyn hadn't said the words back, had simply blinked at him and gone back to whatever she'd been doing at the time without a word.

Donald groaned and rubbed his head. "Oh, for fuck's sake, Evelyn. I don't care what he says. He doesn't *love* you." He flapped his hand at Reed like Reed was nothing more than a mosquito to shoo away. "He's using you. Can't you see that?"

"Donald, stop," Paula warned with a slight shake of her head. Others were looking now, heads all around the restaurant turning their way.

"No. This guy drops into my daughter's life out of nowhere like some goddamn magician, moves in with her a few months later, and suddenly they're in love just like that? My ass." Donald shot Reed a quick glare. "He barely even exists, Paula. Zane hasn't been able to dig up much on him besides a birth certificate and a few odd jobs, and—"

Evelyn cut him off, her face darkening. "Wait. You're *investigating* him?"

Reed's insides churned.

"Of course, I am," Donald said. "To protect you. This is moving too fast."

"No, it isn't!" Evelyn raised her hand and extended a single finger. "You just can't stand the fact that someone other than you might make me happy."

He raised a hand. "Livy, that's not it at all."

"Yes, it is!" Her voice climbed toward a screech. Reed had never seen her like this before—it was like she was transforming into a wild animal before his eyes. "I'm not a teenager anymore! I'm an adult. You don't control my life. And you certainly don't control Adrian's. I refuse to let you ruin what we are building together. If you persist in interfering like this, I will have no choice but to sever our relationship!"

Time seemed to slow and then stop all together. The ropes in Reed's guts knotted tighter. Spiders skittered across his neck. He couldn't breathe. He was going to be sick.

"Excuse me," he said, jerking to his feet and stumbling toward the bathroom. He crashed through the door and made a beeline for the sink and turned it on. He splashed cold water over his hands, over his face. He was overheating, his pulse hammering in his ears. The ground undulated beneath him, rising and falling like he was on a boat.

Stop it! What's wrong with you?

Reed didn't usually feel this way with cons. Sure, the circumstance was extreme—one of the worst he'd endured to date, especially the part about Donald investigating him—but Reed prided himself on his calm, his cool, and this reaction was anything but cool. He was on the verge of a panic attack. No, he was having one.

But why?

Because she's different than the others.

Because she actually cares about you.

Because you just might care about her.

The bathroom door slammed open before he could absorb the last part. Reed felt the hair on the back of his neck rise. He knew exactly who was standing behind him.

"What are your intentions with my daughter?"

Reed slowly rotated. Donald Nash stood a few feet back, fuming, his hands clenched. Reed half-expected to see two coils of smoke rising from his nostrils. "What do you mean?"

"Don't play stupid with me. I know what my daughter's like. Answer the question. Why are you with her?"

There were so many things Reed wanted to say in that moment, so many bullshit reasons he could give the man. But Donald Nash would see through every one. So, Reed said the only thing he couldn't argue with.

"I know you might not see it, but I love her, sir. Truly. She's one of a kind."

Donald Nash scowled, and a road map of wrinkles imprinted on his forehead. His eyes boiled like hot pools of tar. "I don't know what you're up to, but there's something off about you. Something I can't put my finger on. But I will. And I want you to listen to me carefully. I am not a forgiving man. And I'm not a kind one. There is nothing more important to me in this world than my daughter. If you hurt her, if you damage her in any way whatsoever, I will destroy you, Adrian. And I'm not just talking legally. No, I'll make sure you never walk again. That's a promise."

Reed stood there, shocked. He didn't need to feign it; the threat left him shaken. "I would never hurt her, sir," he managed. "You have my word." Then, before the man could say anything else, Reed pushed past him right through the door.

CHAPTER 39

AVERY
Day One

If you need me, I'll be there.

Zane's words echo in my mind as I kneel next to the silver Honda Accord. He's concealed himself in a stand of pine a ways up the hill from my location, looking down on me through a pair of high-powered binoculars, ready to spring into action if I need help. The thought doesn't give me much comfort. If that happens, it means everything I've done to reach this point was for nothing. If I need him, it means I've failed before I've even begun.

Ten minutes ago, he placed a quarter inch nail in front of the Accord's driver's side tire and I rolled over it, planting it deep within the rubber. Then, I made my way down County Road 250 and parked a half mile from Reed's ranch-style home, directly along the route he travels every evening on his five-mile run. It usually takes him thirty-five minutes to reach this spot, but I'm here with fifteen minutes to spare just in case.

At exactly 5:20 p.m., I pull the nail from the tire with a pair of needle-nose pliers and wait for the tire to deflate. Then, I crouch next to the vehicle and pretend to struggle with the lug wrench until I hear the *crunch, crunch, crunch* of Reed's shoes hitting gravel behind me.

I don't need to look to know it's him.

I crank on the wrench again, my hands shaking. My heart stutters and climbs into my throat. My entire body is about to slip into a violent tremble if I let it. I bite my lip, pairing the action with a phrase. *Break it!* It was one of the methods Zane and I'd practiced; a visualization tool to regulate my emotions when they got out of hand. We'd spent entire days with him trying to trigger me and provoke a reaction.

Do you even miss Noah and Ethan? You don't act like you do.

The wreck was your fault. You know that, right? You're the reason they're dead.

Do you regret how much you worked? How much you ignored them?

Think of your family, Bailey. Picture their faces. Visualize how much you let them down.

At first, Zane succeeded more often than he failed, turning me into a hot puddle of tears. I'd stormed out of his office more than a few times with a *Fuck off, I'm done,* only to return the next morning, ready to do it all over again. It took time, but eventually I learned how to ground myself, to focus on my senses like Zane instructed. *Find something to latch onto. The temperature of the room. The way the couch molds to your body. The air filling your lungs. Anything to pull you back to the present moment.*

It mostly worked. And when it didn't—when things escalated too fast—there was another option. I'd force myself back to the present with a physical reminder. A pinch of the arm or a sliver of cheek pulled between my teeth paired with an image of a brick wall slamming down and crushing all the anxiety flooding my mind.

Break it.

"Do you need a hand?"

I whirl around and press a palm to my chest. "Oh god, you scared me!"

"Sorry about that," he says, breathing deeply as he plants his hands on his hips. His hair is ruffled, his cheeks tinged pink. There's no arguing Reed Aldridge is handsome—I've seen it over and over again in his pictures. His looks are a weapon he wields well. But the version standing in front of me, wearing the beginnings of a salt-and-pepper beard, looks older than the others. His sins are finally catching up to him, burrowing into the lines of his face. He looks nothing like his last iteration, Adrian Wallace, who seduced Evelyn Nash with a man-bun hair and tortoiseshell glasses. This version, Grant Wilson, would barely even pass as Adrian's brother. The change is startling.

"So," I ask, trying to control the tremor in my voice. "Are you going to help me, or are you just going to stand there and stare?" I smile as I say it, forcing my lips to form the warmest shape they can make. I practically beam at him, thinking, *I hate you, I hate you, I hate you. I will make you pay.*

"Yes, of course, sorry." He wipes his hands on his shorts. "Let me take a shot."

I stand and hand him the lug wrench. "You're a lifesaver. I'm not getting anywhere with this thing."

He takes it with a grin. sweat dewing on his forehead. "It's not easy. They really screw these bolts on tight. Do you have a jack?"

"I think so? I'm not sure. If I do, it's in the trunk."

"Mind popping it for me?"

"It's open."

"Oh," he says, flustered. "So, it is." He ambles over and makes a show of scrounging through the space even though I don't have any-thing else in there and then returns with the jack and takes a knee.

A vision of ripping the lug wrench from his hand and bringing it down on his skull flashes through my head. The urge is so sudden and strong, I'm forced to grab my wrist.

"What happened?" he asks as he works.

"I'm not sure. Everything was fine and then the car started rattling."

"It was probably a nail. There's a lot of new construction going on. Lots of people building homes."

"I can see why. It's so gorgeous." And it is. It's why Reed came back here—to find a place that once felt like home and try to reclaim an unspoiled piece of his past. A place where he thinks he can live out the rest of his days in peace. That's my guess, anyway, and one I hope is right, because I'm going to turn this little sanctuary of his into the biggest nightmare of all.

"It's wonderful." He takes the spare, which I've already pulled from the trunk, and bolts it in place, then lowers the car and stands, brushing his hands. "There you go. All done. You're good to go. You'll want to get that flat fixed soon though. Take it to Gills downtown. They'll treat you right. And you'll want to drive slow. These donuts aren't built to last."

I screw up my eyebrows even though I know exactly what he means. "Donut?"

"The spare. Sorry. That's what they're called. Here, let me get this stuff for you." He scoops up the tire and the jack and returns them to the trunk.

"Thank you," I say. "You didn't have to do that."

"It's nothing." He shuts the lid, and then turns, looking proud of himself. "I don't think I caught your name. Mine's Grant, by the way." He offers his hand.

I take it and my skin ripples when it touches his. "Avery."

"So, are you new to the neighborhood? I don't think I've seen you around before."

"Yes. Just moved actually. But not here," I say. "To Durango. I've got a place in town."

His gaze sharpens. "So, what brings you out this way?"

You do. "Just doing a little sightseeing. I thought I'd take a drive. It's such a pretty area." I cast a mournful look at the spare. "I guess I should have stayed home, though. Figures this would happen. I have bad luck."

"Oh, I don't know about that," he says, gazing at me in a way I hope means he's staring straight into his past.

We remain like that for an awkward moment before I say, "Well, I'd better get going. I've kept you long enough."

Reed gives a slight shake of his head and blinks. "Right, yes. Of course. It was nice to meet you."

"You too." I reach out and set my hand on his forearm. "Thank you. I seriously don't know what I would have done if you hadn't come along."

"No problem. Happy to help."

I let my hand linger a beat longer before stepping past him toward the car. I have to play this right. I can't come on too strong. If I do, I risk rousing his suspicion. He needs to think he's the one in control here. Not me. If he doesn't ask me out now, I'll make sure to bump into him again soon, in a week or so. It's only a matter of time before it happens. Time, I realize, I don't need the moment he speaks.

"Avery."

I turn back. He looks flustered, one hand cupping the back of his neck.

"Would you maybe want to grab a drink sometime? I'd be happy to show you around town."

My lips curl into a smile again—one I don't have to force.

"Sure. I'd love that."

CHAPTER 40

REED
Seattle, Washington
Age Thirty

Reed strode through the parking garage toward Evelyn's BMW X7. She was gone, attending a graphic design conference in San Francisco. She'd flown out last night. It was why he'd picked today to leave. He'd planned it meticulously. He'd had the date marked on his mental calendar for weeks. An easy exit like always. And out of all the jobs he'd ever pulled, that's what he needed with this one. An easy exit. Because what he was about to do to Evelyn would devastate her, and he knew it.

He opened the BMW's trunk, placed his luggage inside, and stared at it. His entire life fit into a single suitcase. At thirty years old, it didn't seem fitting. And after what he'd just done, it wouldn't anymore.

Eight months. That's how long it had taken Reed to uncover the investment account. With Donald breathing down his neck a little more every day, Reed knew he was running out of time. He should have left town already.

He hadn't counted on the trust.

Evelyn's inheritance sat inside the financial equivalent of Fort

Knox. Reed figured she'd be swimming in money—and in a way she was. She received a monthly stipend of thirty thousand for living expenses. A good amount of cash, sure, but nowhere near the retirement money Reed had counted on when infiltrating her life. Still, the monthly distributions seemed like more than she needed by a long shot. And she didn't buy shit.

So where was all that money going?

"I invest it," she'd told him one day when he'd asked her off the cuff, looking at him like it was the dumbest question ever—like there was no other alternative.

"Really?" he'd said. "I didn't know you were into the stock market. It's a passion of mine. I invest all the time."

"Why haven't you disclosed this before?"

He'd shrugged. "I didn't know you were interested."

"What are your primary sources of information?"

"I'm a big fan of Buffet."

She'd snorted then. "Being a fan of someone isn't a reliable way to make an investment decision, Adrian."

She was right, so he started leaving investment books on the kitchen table, in the bathroom, near the mail. He slipped market analysis into their conversations. They spent hours discussing the S&P 500 and which ETF was the cheapest. They yammered about value stocks and P/E ratios. It was the auditory equivalent of watching paint dry, but Reed acted like he loved every second.

It took a month for her to show him her portfolio.

It took him another month to hack her password.

Evelyn Nash had accumulated a little over two million dollars.

Reed took it all.

He shut the hatch and got into the X7. It was pure luxury. With all the upgrades, the vehicle was worth close to two-hundred grand. He wouldn't get that much for a hot car, but he had a contact downtown who said he'd take the BMW off Reed's hands for eighty thousand. It would be a nice cherry on top of everything else.

Will it, though? Do you really want to do this?

The voice filled his mind like a sudden rush of wind, and he had a strong impulse to get out of the car, walk back into the building, and take the elevator up to the condo he'd shared with Evelyn for the better part of a year. He could simply stay. In a strange way, he could see it; he didn't love Evelyn in a romantic sense, not in the same way she loved him, but he cared for her. He cared for her more than he wanted to admit. She wasn't like the other women who'd been scattered throughout his youth like a minefield, waiting to explode. She never manipulated his emotions or lied to get what she wanted. She never used her station in life to her advantage like most women with money did. Being with her was easy. That was the best word for it. *Easy*. She made him—he didn't know, happy maybe? Or at least if not that, close.

He *could* stay. He really could. It would be a better life than he deserved.

But Donald Nash would never allow it. He'd seen through Adrian Wallace's mask from the start. He was always picking at it, chipping the paint and trying to pull it free. If Reed stayed, it would only be a matter of time before the man exposed him, and he couldn't have that. He had to leave. He didn't have a choice. So he'd take the money. But this was it—his last con. He'd never do something like this again.

"Just go already," he muttered to himself as he fired up the BMW and pulled up to the parking garage gate.

The passenger side door opened.

Evelyn got in.

Reed's heart carved through his chest. She wasn't supposed to be here. But here she was sitting next to him, reeking of ... booze? He'd never seen her take so much as a sip of alcohol before. It couldn't be that. But then the scent hit him again—the sickly-sweet odor of alcohol-infused sweat—and he knew she *had* taken a sip. More than a sip. A lot more. She smelled like she'd been swimming in a pool of tequila.

He gaped at her. "I thought you were—"

"Out of town? Yes, I'm quite aware. Where are you going?"

You'll never know, Reed nearly said. He scraped his brain for a lie, hesitated for a split second, then said, "Oh, just out for a drive. I've been feeling a little cooped up. Figured it might be nice to see some countryside."

Evelyn turned toward the windshield, her glasses flashing. "That sounds nice. I will come with you."

A fist formed in Reed's gut. "Aren't you tired? Why don't you go upstairs and get some rest. I'll be back in a bit and we can grab some lunch."

"Just drive." It was an order, Evelyn's voice devoid of warmth. *Shit.*

It's okay, he told himself. *It's only a bump in the road. You can figure this out.* He did the math. His flight left at four. He'd been planning to sell the BMW and arrive at the airport a few hours early to have a beer before boarding. He still had time. He simply needed to find a way to get her out of the car first.

He drove. The buildings passed by in silence beneath a dark scoop of gray sky. He angled south out of the city, Evelyn sitting next to him not saying a word, just staring out the windshield as motionless as a human statue. It was how she got when she was upset about something, and it always made him want to crack her out of her shell.

"I'm glad to see you," he said, reaching for her hand.

She pulled it away.

"What happened to the conference?" he asked.

She didn't respond, and the smell of liquor hit him again, so sweet and thick it hung in the back of his throat like glue. "Why didn't you tell me you were coming back?"

Still no answer—which meant she knew something. He could feel it. But what, exactly? And how? He'd been rigorous in his planning, hadn't slipped up at all.

But you did. Somehow you did.

Find a way to get her out of the car.

He had to. That was the only choice he had left. Get her out and then bolt.

Another urge rose then, a sudden insane need to do the opposite, to come clean with her about everything and beg for her forgiveness. A need he quickly choked down.

Goddammit, Reed, stop it already! Just get it done.

Miles passed. He drove aimlessly. They were somewhere close to Snoqualmie now, but he wasn't sure, not through all the patches of fog that hung in the air like ghosts. The trees were becoming steadily less visible by the minute, the traffic thinning. In fact, he hadn't seen another car for several miles now. Only mist.

The gears in his mind rattled and churned. He had to find a place to stop.

"Are you hungry?" he asked.

Evelyn didn't turn his way, didn't even move.

He continued. "Why don't we grab a bite to eat, and we can—"

"You've been dishonest." The word came out in a slur: *dish honest.*

Every hair on Reed's body rose. He kept his eyes on the road. "Why would you say that?"

"Do you think I'm an unintelligent person, Adrian? Do you consider me stupid?"

"What? No. Of course not."

"Your actions lead me to believe otherwise."

He looked at her. She sat stiff, her shoulders straight, her hair piled on top of her head in a tangled mess that made her appear like she'd just rolled out of bed. Her eyes were pink and wet.

"Livy," Reed said, using her pet name—a tool he often employed when he needed her to soften. "You show up out of the blue when I think you're away, and then you sit there without saying a word while I drive. And now this. Will you please tell me what's going on?

Whatever it is, we can talk it out."

She tilted her head toward her lap, her chin clicking lower in a stilted, almost animatronic way. "I did well in my classes growing up. Math, science, geography. It didn't matter how hard the subject was. There were rules to follow. Patterns. I could always figure them out, even when the other children couldn't. They asked me for the answers, and I helped them. Then they mocked me. They imitated the way I spoke. They pretended to be robots. For a significant portion of elementary school, I thought it was a compliment. I thought they did it because they wanted to be like me. For an intelligent person, I was quite stupid."

"You're not stupid," Reed said. "Not at all."

"Yes, I was. In middle school, I let two girls cut my hair. They were popular. They told me a new hairstyle would help me fit in. When I let them do it, they chopped most of it off. Then they attempted to shave my head with a pair of electric clippers. I ran home in tears. I looked incredibly foolish. I wanted to die after that. I tried."

She tried? What did that mean? His stomach lurched. "That's ... horrible."

"Correct. It was. And it continued into high school. No matter what I did, or how kind I was to my peers, they continued to torment me. During my sophomore year, a girl stole my clothes from the locker room while I showered. A girl I'd thought was my friend. All I had was a towel. More girls were waiting for me when I came into the hall, and one of them snatched that, too. Then they laughed. They called me Naked Nash." Her tone went high and biting. "'Here comes Naked Nash!' 'Watch out, everyone, Naked Nash is on the loose!' Every day, they called me that, day after day after day, until I cried so hard my father withdrew me from school."

She blinked and shook her head, her lower lip trembling.

"He told me it was for my protection. And perhaps it was to an extent. But his actions weren't congruent with protection. He rarely took me out in public. He didn't take photos with me, or videos. It didn't make sense to me then, but it does now. He didn't want to be seen with me. He had a legacy to protect, and I was an embarrassment."

"He loves you," Reed said, stunned at her interpretation. "There's no way he—"

"Do not interrupt me, Adrian!" Evelyn's voice cut through him like a sheet of ice. "I *know* he loves me. And I'm answering your question. I'm telling you what's going on."

A weight formed in Reed's gut. He returned his gaze to the road.

"As I grew, I came to realize I was different. And people don't like people who are different. They like people who are the same as them. It made sense to me. I understood then I was meant to be alone. It took me some time to accept that, but I did. And I was fine with it until you came along and changed my mind."

The weight in Reed's gut swelled and expanded until it felt like his skin would rip. He tried to say something, to assure her everything was fine, to tell her he didn't know where this was coming from, but when he opened his mouth to speak, all that came out was a slow stream of air.

Evelyn turned her expressionless face toward him, her eyes drilling straight through his skull. "You wanted to see some countryside, did you? In this weather?"

Reed's mouth went dry. The blanket of fog surrounding them was growing thicker by the second. At this point, he had no clue where they were, only that they were rolling down some random country road with his heart beating so fast he thought it might explode.

"How long have you been planning to misappropriate my money?"

Reed was right. She knew—which meant he was in danger. But not from her so much as from whoever she'd told. Forget lunch. He needed to ditch her right now. And he needed to lose the BMW as soon as possible after that. Then he'd need to get the fuck out of town.

No way he'd risk the airport at this point—too much attention—he'd need to take a bus.

"Why would you say something like that?" he asked, eyeing the road, looking for a spot to pull over. There weren't any, and the fog was making it increasingly difficult to see.

"My money is gone, Adrian. All of it. I know it was you. I installed cameras in the condo. I saw you packing. I saw you retrieve your phone. Give it to me. I need to turn it over to my father." Before he could stop her, she swiped the phone from the cup holder.

Reed nearly choked. He'd dumped his burner. This was his real phone full of all of his contacts. Packed with his personal information. He'd kept it hidden from Evelyn in a small hole he'd cut into the wall near their closet and covered with a blank wall plate until now. Until today.

She couldn't have it. It would ruin him.

He lunged for it, snapping it out of her hand before she could stuff it into her pocket. She unbuckled her seatbelt and came at him, her features a blur of rage as she tried to take it back. Her fingernails carved five hot trails from his forehead to his chin as they raked over his face. Her sudden weight on his knee forced his foot into the accelerator, and he ripped the wheel left in an attempt to keep the car on the road. He barely had time to register what was happening as she clawed for the phone, shrieking for him to, "Give it back! Give it back!"

"Evelyn, stop!" He took her by the shoulder and flung her into her seat. Blood dripped into his eyes as he went for the brakes. He saw the intersection with the stop sign—and the car beyond it—too late.

CHAPTER 41

Snaps of light flashed behind Reed's eyelids. The acrid smell of smoke filled his nostrils. A groan came from ... somewhere.

Came from him.

Reed's eyes flipped open to a spider web of glass. Tendrils of fog swirled beyond it as he pressed the pads of his fingers to his forehead and groaned. He struggled to remember what had happened, why his face was covered in ... something sticky. Something warm.

Blood. The smell of iron hit him along with the harsh tang of burning metal. He'd been driving. It came back to him now; he'd been heading ...

Where?

To the airport. He'd needed to get away. *Was* getting away when ...

Oh god, Evelyn.

He cranked his head right with a wince—and he saw her. It was as if the entire world stopped in that moment. A high-pitched ringing filled his ears.

No, no, no, no, no, please, god, no.

He shot toward her and placed his hand on her cheek. It was already growing cold. A stream of blood creased her nose like candle wax. He snapped his fingers in front of her face. "Look at me! Please, Evy, look at me!" he begged.

She didn't. He already knew she'd never look at him or anyone else again. Not with the way her head rested on the dash in such an impossible angle. He had no doubt she'd broken her neck.

A sob crawled up his throat and he started hyperventilating. *Why? Why had this happened? Why hadn't her airbag gone off?*

He couldn't remember. They'd been driving one moment, arguing about something, and then—

His phone. She'd tried to get his phone. She'd leaped at him, and he'd shoved her off, right before they'd hit.

Hit ... *what?*

Another car.

Ice filled his veins. Smoke rose in front of him through the splintered windshield—or was it the fog? He didn't know. He eyed Evelyn again and bit off a sudden sob. He had to get out of the car.

Get out! Get out now!

The voice that screamed at him felt disembodied—like it was coming from someone other than him. He fumbled out of his seatbelt and tried to open the door. It wouldn't budge. *Go! Get out! Get out!* He pulled the handle and then rammed his shoulder into the door. It didn't budge, so he did it again. A bolt of pain surged up his arm this time, but it was enough. The door swung open with a metallic *bang!* And then he was tumbling out of the BMW and lurching into the wet blanket of mist outside. His head swam as he spun a slow circle. Flashes of green farmland floated through the fog along with—

Oh, fuck. Oh, Jesus.

Crumpled blue metal.

Reed felt like he would come apart then, like he would disintegrate.

The sedan, or what remained of it, rested on its side at the base of an embankment beneath the shoulder of the road. The entire length of the passenger side was a canyon of crushed metal. Shards of glass littered the road and the grass. Both the front and back windows were blown out, and through the front passenger side, Reed could barely make out what looked like a man's face.

He hung in place, still strapped to his seat, perfectly motionless. His head was cranked to the left and dangled in a way that obscured most of the driver. All Reed could make out of the person was a single arm resting on the steering wheel, the fingers deathly still. His gaze shifted to the backseat, and a moan bled off his lips. The ground spun beneath him. There was a silhouette there. A small, familiar shape that soaked him with dread.

No, he whispered. *Lord, please, no.*

It was a car seat.

But it was empty.

Reed exhaled long and slow, his legs going weak with relief.

He took a step forward to be sure—and he saw the child. A boy just past toddler age with his hair matted in blood, and his eyes dull and wide. He'd somehow been thrown free of the seat and sat wedged beyond it, near the door. The left side of his skull had caved in.

Reed turned away and choked back a mouthful of vomit.

A thought clawed through his panic, frantic and hot: *Help him. He could still be alive.*

But Reed already knew he wasn't, none of them were. Not the child, not the people in the front of the vehicle. And not Evelyn. No cars had passed them yet, but they would any minute now. And when they did, he had to be gone, had to be anywhere but *here.*

He turned and took a single, lurching step away—and stopped. He couldn't leave. Not yet. They would hunt him for this. *Donald* would hunt him. They would track him down unless ...

Unless he painted a different picture.

Acid stung the back of his throat. He knew what he had to do.

Reed moved, his shoulder still tingling, his fingers numb as he stumbled back to the BMW and cranked the door wider.

You did this to me.

It was as if Evelyn was speaking to him with the empty look in her unseeing eyes, her skin nearly as pale as the fog outside. His vision instantly blurred. "I didn't mean to," he croaked. "This wasn't supposed to happen."

But it did, she said, *and you're the reason.*

"No," he mumbled, running the back of his hand over his face before leaning in and curling his arms beneath her armpits. He heaved, and she came toward him, jerking to a stop before he could free her lower body from the crushing weight of the dash. He tried again with the same result, her head flopping forward onto his shoulder this time when she caught, her hair skimming his cheek. A scent filled his nose; something warm and woody. The sweet must of ink and paper. The smell of books.

Tears burned to life in his eyes.

"Come on!" he shouted in anguish, tugging harder—"Come on! Come on! Come on!"—yanking until she finally came free with a wet, ripping sound. He nearly tumbled back onto his ass but managed to catch himself then leaned in and forced Evelyn upright in the driver's seat. Things he couldn't name cracked and popped inside of her. In the distance, he heard the whoosh of rubber slicing over the road, coming closer.

Hurry up!

He took the seatbelt that had saved his life and roped it over Evelyn's chest and clicked it home, then scrambled for his phone. It was jammed in the corner of the floorboard. He grabbed it and slid it into his pocket.

And then he stopped and stared at her. Everything melted inside of him. Every last bit of hatred he'd ever felt for a woman, every stinging abandonment and betrayal at their hands—it all liquefied and rushed away. None of it had been worth what he'd done to Evelyn. None of it had been worth this.

Never this.

"Livy ... I'm so ..." Reed's voice cracked and whatever word he meant to say next snapped off in his throat. What was it? Sorry? Sorry was such an insignificant word for what had just happened. Sorry wouldn't change what he'd done to her or the people in that car. The kid and his parents who'd never take another breath. All of them dead.

Because of him.

He gazed at Evelyn. He looked into her lifeless eyes and felt his heart crack.

Reed knew he'd never come back from this.

The car was so close now—he could distinctly hear the engine. If he was going to go, he had to go *now.*

He moved, his knee clicking beneath him like a latch as he popped the trunk and seized his suitcase. Then he ran. Every step hurt like hell. His entire body did. But the pain was nowhere close to the anguish boiling in his chest. The shame. It would never stop. He knew this. It would last forever. But it didn't have to.

Of course, there was another way.

You can end this right here. You can stay and turn yourself in.

Reed wanted to. He did.

But he just kept running.

PART FOUR
CHECKMATE

CHAPTER 42

BAILEY

Three years.

That's the thought that runs through my head as Reed Aldridge pushes through the willows and stops at the base of the hill. Zane and I are parked a ways off the road, hidden beneath a thick patch of Douglas fir a quarter mile away from the White property. We're watching Reed through two pairs of military-grade binoculars that provide a surprising amount of clarity from this distance. We can see him perfectly, but there's no way he'll spot us.

Three years, I think again. I've waited over three years for this moment. I've poured all of my rage into what's about to happen, every ounce of my grief and pain. My hatred for this man and what he's taken from me is a fire that's burned inside of me without end. Every blistering minute without my husband, every scorching second stolen from my child, has led me right here to this place and time.

I love you.

You're my forever.

I'll never leave you.

We're having a baby.

Every one of these statements a lie. There have been so many, but none more important than the last. The icing on the cake. I knew it from the way Reed's eyes filled with tenderness the moment I told him I was pregnant. I saw it in the way his lips tightened when I handed him the fake ultrasound. I felt it in the way his fingers trembled and shook. There was so much awe there. Such beautiful shock. A miracle! His chance at redemption. God's hand reaching down from the clouds to hover over my womb. *Let there be life.*

I gave him everything.

My heart. My soul. My life.

A child.

And now, here where Taylor White once lived—a place that held such importance to Reed—I'll tear it all away and leave him with a hole so deep nothing will ever fill it again. A hole exactly like mine.

"Here we go," Zane says in a way that reminds me of "Officer Gunn", the persona he played to absolute perfection with Reed, his voice low and clipped.

It's all gone to plan so far: My "abduction" and attempted "rescue". The unstable timelines and the riddles I created. Reed craves control. He prioritizes order. So, taking them away and watching him unravel before my eyes has been particularly satisfying. And now, after my curated tour of the darkest moments of his youth, he's ready for the grand finale.

Ten minutes ago, Zane sent an email containing phone records, transcripts, photos, money trails, past identity documents, and every other bit of information we have on Reed to every major news outlet in Colorado: Who he is. What he's done. Who he's done it to.

Tonight, Reed Aldridge will be local news. Tomorrow, he'll be national. That's my hope anyway. I'm banking the story of a con man flushed out of hiding will be too juicy to resist. Sure, I could have called in a tip to begin with. I could have turned Reed in right away and skipped all of this; it would have achieved the same thing. But it would have been too easy. Too benign. A simple arrest and prosecution was never going to be enough. Not when Reed deserves to know what it feels like to have a life he loves—along with everyone and everything in it—ripped away in an instant.

Right now, Sean, Zane's son, is in the middle of removing my belongings from Reed's home. I don't relish the idea of the kid going through my things alone. Something about Sean Jenson has always given me chills. There's a certain cruelty to him. The way he intimidated Elizabeth Gleason, the fake version of me, during her brief abduction seemed a little too real, and a little too enjoyable for him. But when it came to Reed's takedown, Zane insisted we "keep it in the family", especially this last part. Despite his unstable past, Zane assured me his son was someone we could trust. And I have to admit he's lived up to that label so far. Despite his age, he slipped right into the role of Officer Holston. Reed didn't have a clue.

So, I agreed, and we left him there, alone in the home, to remove every happy picture of Reed and me together, along with all of my clothing and jewelry and makeup. Every last trace of me will be wiped from Reed's life like I was never there at all. Like Reed has done to so many of his victims before this, Avery Carter is about to become a ghost. And now that I'm finished, the public can have him. They'll devour a story about a misogynistic piece of shit who hates women brought to justice.

Except that's not the Reed you know.

The thought cuts through me like a bitter wind. I can't let myself go there. Not now. Not ever. It doesn't matter the man I've spent the better part of the last year with doesn't match the monster I'd imagined in my mind. I'd expected a selfish man. A man without a conscience. A manipulative narcissist and pathological liar so full of himself he's able to ruin the lives of innocent people without a second thought. And not only that, but a sadist and a murderer. A man who turned an autistic woman into a corpse and then rationalized pulling her into the driver's seat to take the blame for killing my family.

Yet from the moment I met Reed Aldridge, all he's been is polite, respectful, and kind. He remembers the small things about me even Ethan didn't. Like that I prefer my coffee with two spoonfuls of cream and one packet of sugar. He knows I take my eggs over medium instead of easy. He serves my drinks with straws because my teeth are sensitive to cold, and he's the first to pour me an evening glass of wine after a long day. He's attentive. He actually listens when I talk. When I'm frustrated with him about something, he tries to do better.

These are the things, I've had to remind myself, he's done for all of his victims. Because Reed Aldridge isn't actually a good man. He's just good at what he does. He's a con man for a reason. One who I'm going to make sure never harms another woman again.

It's why five minutes ago, I called the Durango police department using one of Zane's burners. *There's a man trespassing on Judge White's property. He's about to break into the house! Please hurry!*

The judge isn't home. He and his wife are vacationing in California wine country. And although I'd give anything to see Reed arrested in front of the father of the girl who refused to have his child, it had to be this way. We had to prepare things for Reed without the Whites taking note. And now that we have, Zane and I can simply sit back and watch as Reed is arrested and put away forever.

"A few more shovelfuls and he'll be there," Zane says.

I don't respond. I can't. I'm too busy staring through my binoculars at Reed. It's like he's been sucker punched as he pulls the coffin from the earth and drops to his knees. He brushes the dirt off the lid and reads the inscription. I know the scrambled verse will hit him like a truck—his father's favorite song, except all wrong, the words a warning. *Don't look inside.*

But he will.

He wavers for a moment and then finally reaches for the lid.

Relief floods his face when he pulls it open. So much relief. It's clear in the way he exhales and runs a hand over his forehead. Thank god. His child isn't inside waiting for him. But mine is. And while his is a phantom, mine is real. *Was* real, I have to remind myself.

Was. Because Reed took him away along with Ethan, and every precious moment with both of them that should have come after.

Reed's relief fades and turns to confusion instead as he plucks a photograph from the coffin and stares at it. He blinks, then returns the picture and reaches for another. I can read his thoughts. *Who are these people? Why am I looking at them? What do they have to do with me?*

Nothing at all. And everything you can imagine.

Zane adjusts his binoculars and leans over the steering wheel. "Okay, showtime."

Reed has the gift in his hands now, the picture of the three of us at Disney World. He stares at it for what feels like a full minute before ripping it open. When he does, his face cycles from confusion to understanding, and then from understanding to shock. He snaps his head up and looks around, his features twisted with pain. I can tell he's fighting back tears, which means he knows who I am. The anguish in his face is so intense, I'm overcome with an unexpected slash of guilt. But it doesn't last long before the anger rises, and I remember everything he's taken.

No, I tell myself. *No.* He deserves this. Every last bit.

Fuck you, Reed. I think. *You did this to yourself.*

And that's when I hear the gunshot ring out.

CHAPTER 43

REED

With the bullet come the memories.

―――――――

"Let's get out of here. My place isn't far."

Those are Avery's first words to me on our third date before our drinks arrive. Her eyes are the green of fresh leaves, the green of spring, and I can't help but cough as I set my water down on the table. I open my mouth to say something, but she's already standing and taking my hand.

I try to fill the silence as she drives, but any time I'm about to speak, she presses a single finger to her lips and shakes her head. We arrive and she's on me the second we spill through her door. We're hot skin and hungry lips. We are need and desire, lust and want. We are two bodies clawing at each other for the first time, both of us hungry. But there's something else in her eyes, too, a flash of pain swimming right beneath the surface—there and gone in an instant. It's a glimpse to some deeper part of her—a part I'm suddenly desperate to know because I carry that kind of pain, too.

When we finish, she rolls off of me and threads her fingers through her scarlet hair. "Okay, now we can talk."

"That's all it took?" I say with a laugh.

"I had to see if you were worth it first."

"And?"

"I'd say you passed."

And then she's kissing me again, and I'm already in love.

But not real love. Not yet. I've been here before. I've made that mistake, and I swore I never would again. Which is fine, because it's easier this way. The flirting. The games. The way we can't seem to keep our clothes on when we're around each other. How, with one look, we wind up in bed. Or on the couch, or the floor, or the table.

But this, whatever *this* is, is more than sex. I can feel her seeping in. Avery is supposed to be a quick break from my self-imposed seclusion. My "simpler" life. Except, now that I've met her, I can't imagine not seeing her again, can't envision spending the rest of my days staring out at the horizon alone. It's ridiculous to think I deserve anything other than that, especially after the things I've done, but it's nice to dream. So, I decide to keep her around, if only for a little while.

We talk. She tells me about her life: a good life with a mostly idyllic childhood. She grew up in Iowa and played soccer in high school until she shredded her knee in state semifinal her senior year. Then came college in Lawrence, Avery a Jayhawk. Two years spent majoring in finance before she plowed into a pregnant woman downtown after a night at the bars.

"There's something you need to know," she tells me a month in. Her voice drips with pain as she tells me about the accident. She wasn't even drunk, just distracted by her friends who were when the woman wandered onto the crosswalk. It happened in a split second. The baby died and Avery spent a year behind bars—but the regret she feels is a life sentence.

When I don't reply, she mistakes my silence for agreement and stands to leave. But what she doesn't understand is that I can't speak. Her words are razors that have sliced me to the core. "Wait," I say, taking her by the wrist and tugging her back to the couch. "Everyone deserves a second chance."

"Do you really believe that?" she asks through the tears.

"Yes." And I do—for her. Never for me. There's no forgiving what I've done.

Still, a part of me wants to tell her about Evelyn. The prospect of sharing my pain with someone feels like a ray of sunshine after a lifetime of rain. But it's dangerous to tell her the truth. Especially *that* truth. And there's no point: I've already buried Reed Aldridge. He's long dead and gone.

———

I look into Avery. Of course, I do. After all the sins I've committed, something about her feels too good to be true. I have to be certain there's nothing I shouldn't be aware of—not that I expect there is. She's never given me any reason to doubt her. But I need to be sure.

I reach out to an old contact and provide him with the specifics: Her name—Avery Carter. Her driver's license number. Her date of birth. And then I wait, terrified I might lose this small slice of good.

But when the file arrives, it all checks out.

Avery Carter was indeed a teenage soccer player in Des Moines with an impressive slew of stats. There's a slice-of-life piece in the local newspaper about her time with the team and her injury. A picture. The doctors tell her she won't be the same. Avery tells them she won't give up on her dream. She'll never give up. And she doesn't. But it's not enough. She's no longer the same.

Off she goes to Kansas University as a finance major. Two years at the dorms. Her grades are impressive. She's on her way. And then comes the incident with the woman and everything stops. The court records confirm her story. There's a mugshot, Avery staring at the camera with eyes cupped in dark circles. A year in Topeka Correctional. Besides the death of her mother, it's quiet from there. There are no marriages. No divorces. Just a trail of addresses with the last one leading to Durango.

Avery is exactly who she says she is.

Unlike me.

But I can change. I *have* changed. I'm not the man I once was—a selfish, misguided hypocrite who spent years blaming everyone else for his problems but himself. I won't give Avery that man. I'll give her the version I'm working to become. An honest man. A good man. The man she deserves.

And then it's the little things ...

We both prefer spending time at home together instead of going out. Our mornings are lazy beautiful things spent having sex and drinking coffee. We take hikes and spend hours exploring the trails around Durango. Avery points out the flowers. There are so many—flowers everywhere, blooming in all kinds of shades and colors. She sees beauty everywhere she looks, and I see the beauty in her.

She moves in. I'm nervous at first, but she's easy to be around. She leaves me notes. Post-it's stuck to the mirror with sweet sayings like, *You are my world!* And, *I don't know what I did to deserve you.* And, *Your laugh is my favorite thing.* I leave the same notes for her. I hide them beneath her pillow and tape them to the inside of the refrigerator door.

I love your face.

I love your smile.

I love you.

On a bitter morning in February, I slip from bed early, trail into the living room, and head for the coat closet. The phone is on the top shelf, buried in the far corner, hidden beneath a pile of gloves and hats. I fish it out and power it on for the first time, and then I wait for it to ring.

Today is my birthday. I'm thirty-three years old. Two months ago, I sent my dad a letter. In that letter I gave him this number spelled out in code. At eight o'clock sharp, he will call like he does every year, and we will spend fifteen minutes talking about nothing. He will complain about the prison food and ask how I'm doing. I will say fine, just fine, and tell him a little about my life. This year, I'll tell him I met a girl. We'll have a few laughs after that and then he'll tell me he has to go.

It's been twenty-one years since the Midland incident, and this June he will finally be freed. It should have happened five years ago, but my old man's a fighter who decided to beat up two prison guards. One of them wound up with a broken arm. Jack Aldridge has never been one to do things the easy way.

I've only seen him a few times since he went to prison. Once, at his sentencing and twice after, both around Christmas. The last time I went was right before I moved back to Durango. It was a foolish thing to do. A moment of weakness. After losing Evelyn, I needed to lay eyes on someone who would look at me with something other than the disgust I felt for myself.

It had been so long since I'd last seen him. He looked the same, only older, grayer. And softer somehow, a kindness in his eyes that was never there before. We talked for an hour. He told me he was looking forward to getting out and starting fresh. He wanted to do something right with what was left of his life. And he wanted me to visit him again soon. I made sure he understood why I couldn't. Why showing up in person in a place where I might be identified was dangerous for me. He nodded but he made me promise him something.

"Be here when they let me out, Reed. You gotta help me get back on my feet."

And I will. I'll be there. I can't wait—which is exactly what I'll tell him when he calls. But he doesn't. Eight o'clock comes and goes without the phone ringing. He's never missed this call, not once. Still, I convince myself he's fine, that there must be some reason for the delay. But when the clock hits nine, I know there's a problem.

"Clements Unit," a woman answers when I call the prison.

"Hi, I wanted to check on an inmate. Make sure they're okay."

"Name?"

"Jack Aldridge."

"One moment." Through the phone, I hear the clacking of a keyboard, and then a pause followed by, "Oh … I'm sorry, but I can't provide any information on his status. We have privacy regulations."

The room around me turns to mist. She doesn't need to say what I already know. I heard it in her hesitation, and the way her tone went flat when she spoke. My father is dead. I can feel it in my bones.

"Sir?" she says. "Sir, are you there?"

I end the call and Google his name, but nothing comes up. There is no obituary, no death notice. There's no news anywhere. But there are other ways to find what I'm looking for. I search for funeral homes and start making calls. It only takes three—my father was buried a month ago, a man with a weak voice tells me. The phone clicks, and I stare through the window. The lawn is bristling with ice, everything covered in white. I don't know how long I remain there, staring outside, but when I turn around, Avery is standing behind me, stretching with a yawn.

"What's the matter?" she says when she sees my face.

"My dad … he's …" The tears come before I can finish.

She glides across the floor and pulls me into her arms. I cry for an hour.

I don't move the rest of the day.

I don't leave the house for a week.

And I mourn. Avery doesn't leave me once, even when I tell her to, even when I say I know this is too much. She stays right there with me the entire time and that's when I know I truly love her.

CHAPTER 44

BAILEY

"What's happening!" I shout as Reed whips forward and slams to the earth.

Zane still has the binoculars to his eyes, staring intently through the windshield.

"Hey!" I slap his shoulder, but he ignores me.

"Watch."

I raise my binoculars. There's nothing to see at first—just the meadow swaying in the breeze, the grass rippling. Then I spot it: a shrub rising in the shape of a man. *What the hell?* I blink and try to make sense of the image. It's someone wearing one of those camouflaged army suits, the kind made to look like leaves and grass. The man's face is concealed by a hood covered in foliage. I can't make out his features, but I can make out the gun in his hand—the long black rifle he used to shoot Reed in the back.

I sweep the binoculars back toward Reed's still form. He's lying prone with both arms splayed to his sides, his right leg cranked at an odd angle. Beside his head is a dark splatter of blood.

This shouldn't be happening.

Reed is supposed to be arrested. He's supposed to be paraded through the news as a callous, reprehensible con man who targets and exploits vulnerable women. He's supposed to be sentenced to decades in prison and live out the best years of his life in a cold gray box alone like his dad did before him. This—whatever just happened—isn't the plan. It's something else entirely.

I watch as the man in the camo suit stalks through the grass and draws closer to Reed. It feels like everything is unfolding in slow motion as he climbs the hill and pulls out a pistol. One he raises and aims at Reed's back.

Crack! Crack!

Reed jerks twice in response. The gun rises toward the back of his head, but I'm already leaping out of the car with a scream.

"STOP! DON'T!"

The man whips around, searching for my voice. From this far away, he looks terrifying, like a creature from the earth—something born without a face.

A radio squelches to my left as Zane speaks. "No more gunfire. It'll draw attention. Just finish the job."

The man holsters the gun and then pulls something from his waist and brings it to his lips. "Ten-four."

I recognize the voice. *Sean's* voice.

I turn toward Zane who's watching me from the other side of the car. He waves at my open door. "Get in."

"You weren't supposed to kill him," I say in a daze.

"Just get in." His voice is sharper than normal. Cold. I hesitate. We should be hearing police sirens by now.

Bees buzz through my chest, and I take a step back.

He shakes his head. "Don't."

"Why not?" I manage.

"Two reasons, the first being this." He raises a gun and sets it on the roof of the car. "And the second is your brother."

My legs go weak. "What does Ben have to do with this?"

"Nothing at all. And I'm guessing you want to keep it that way."

It's all he has to say. I get in.

We drive.

Zane keeps his eyes on the road. His usual calm demeanor is gone, replaced by something harder, darker. His fingers flex on the wheel every few seconds, his knuckles bleaching white. The sun bleeds pink in front of us, draping the outside world in a canvas of pastel tones. It's beautiful—a scene that doesn't match what just happened. The bees in my chest buzz harder.

They killed him.

They killed Reed.

It's what I say, my lips parting before I can stop them. "You killed him."

"Yes," Zane replies.

"Why?"

"Because you wouldn't."

"We agreed there wouldn't be any violence," I say, trying to remain calm. "This isn't what we planned."

"Plan's changed."

My forehead crinkles. "I called the police, though. They'll arrest Sean."

"You called who I wanted you to call."

My heart plummets. I've been using burners for nearly a year now. It's a practice Zane insisted on. No calls from personal phones ever. We can't risk being traced. And every phone I've used has been supplied by Zane. The guy has a connection for everything. Fake documents. Cars. Weapons. People. Which means the woman I spoke to over the phone doesn't work for the Durango Police Department. She works for Zane.

Veins of ice bleed down my legs. "And the email?"

"Never sent," he says.

I don't know why he's doing this. I've paid him handsomely,

exactly as we'd agreed. I never lied to him, never strung him along. Sure, we've had a few disagreements along the way, made a few changes to our approach, but we've always been able to work things out, especially in regard to the critical things, and *especially* as they relate to the last few days. We'd planned it all with precision, mapped out every single detail. We made sure everything was perfect before initiating my abduction. And it was—it went off without a hitch. So why would Zane betray me now? After all this time? It doesn't make sense.

But it does, I think. *You just don't see it yet.*

We continue to drive, Zane winding down a series of county roads I don't recognize, pushing further into the remote countryside. He feels like a stranger right now. The way he's sitting there, strangling the steering wheel, without saying a word is disturbing. It makes me wonder if this is the persona Zane painted for Reed when he arrested him as Officer Gunn, wearing a hairpiece that looked so authentic, I would have never guessed the man was bald if meeting him for the first time.

Or did he treat Reed like he treated me when he threw me in the van? The blue-eyed menace with the colored contacts who oozed the threat of violence. His anger had been so authentic when he'd taken me, so physical, it had left me shaken for hours.

I'm sorry for that. It had to look real.

Is this real? Panic swims down my spine. Zane may be a chameleon with his emotions when he has to be, but this—the way he's acting now, pulling a gun on me and threatening my brother, taking me somewhere in his car—feels different than anything that's come from him before. It feels dangerous.

"Where are we going?" I ask.

"To a place we can talk."

"How about we talk here?"

He doesn't reply, just continues to drive. Finally, after what feels like an hour, we pull off the road and onto a long gravel driveway concealed by a dense wall of pine. One of those blink-and-it's-gone turnoffs most people never see. Zane follows the road until a log cabin with a red tin roof comes into view through the trees. There are no neighboring houses, no other cars. Just the two of us and this place.

"Now what?" I ask when he cuts the engine.

"Now," he says, drawing his gun, "we go inside."

CHAPTER 45

Don't move.

That's all I can think as the sound of footsteps crunching through the brush comes closer. *Don't. Fucking. Move.* Every instinct I have is screaming for me to leap to my feet and bolt. But I can't. Whoever shot me is too close, nearly on top of me now. If I move, they'll kill me for sure.

The footsteps stop. Blood seeps from my hairline and into my eyes. Blood that isn't from the bullet but rather from the stone I hit as I fell—a single glancing blow to the forehead that had me seeing stars. Whoever is there is standing directly behind me now, studying me. I can feel their gaze burning over my neck. I don't move an inch, don't breathe, just lie there motionless and pray they'll think I'm dead. For a second, I think that's exactly what will happen, that they'll turn and walk away. But they don't. Two more gunshots come instead, the bullets punching straight into my back.

The pain is sudden and scalding. I feel something crack. A howl tears up my throat, but I bite it off and lock it behind my teeth. I can't move even though I'm in absolute agony. And I don't. I simply lie there, waiting for the final bullet. The one I know will end me. I can already feel the gun moving higher, centering on the base of my skull.

Just get it over with. Make it quick.

But instead of another gunshot, I hear a distant scream. A cry for whoever is hovering over me to—

"STOP!"

I sense a shift. A hesitation.

A radio squawks. There's mumbled conversation. It's static to me, nothing more than noise through my still ringing ears. Then it's gone, and I can hear the dry crunch of grass once more as the man—I know it's a man now based on his voice—moves closer. If he's smart, he'll take that final shot. If he isn't, he'll get close and try to roll me over.

Roll me over, I think. *Please, roll me over.*

A pair of camouflaged knees come into view.

A hand hits my shoulder and pushes.

I take the rock—the one I've been cupping in the palm of my hand since I fell—and swing it upward as hard as I can. The man's eyes widen a second before it connects with his chin. That's all I can see of him. His eyes. The rest of his face is covered with a camouflage face mask. His head whips back with a satisfying crunch. And then I'm up and slamming into him with my shoulder. We tumble down the hill together. My ribs crackle like broken glass when we hit level ground.

The gun flies from his hand and lands a few feet away. We both scramble for it.

He's fast.

I'm faster.

My palm lands on the grip a half-second before his. And then I'm rolling away from him, bringing the gun up. But not high enough because he's already on me, one hand clawing at my eyes, the other grabbing my wrist.

I pull the trigger.

He goes stiff and then topples onto his back. I jump to my feet with the gun still in my hand and rip off his mask.

"No more shooting!" he cries. "Please!"

My mouth falls open. Even through all of the grime on his face, I recognize him immediately. The round cheeks. The buzz-cut blond hair. The empty eyes which are now filled with fear: Officer Calvin Holston.

"Who else is here?" I growl.

"No one." He winces as he says it, and I see the blood seeping through his fingers, both of his hands cradling his gut.

I level the gun at his head. It's a Sig Sauer nine-millimeter. I know this because I own a Sig myself. A 44 ACP. I don't like guns, never have, but after the crash, I decided it would be wise to learn how to protect myself. Pistols like this are one way to do that. Bulletproof vests are another.

I'm wearing one right now, strapped to my torso beneath my hoodie. It's a level-four tactical combat vest designed to stop even the most high-powered rounds. It's the only reason I'm not the one lying on the ground in Holston's place, trying to keep my blood in my body. After the wreck, I grew paranoid, certain Donald Nash would eventually track me down. And when he did, I knew he'd hire someone to take me out. It's why I wore the vest beneath a collection of baggy sweaters and pullovers for months anytime I left the house. I was certain every stranger I passed would pull out a gun.

When no one did, my paranoia faded, and I started to relax. After a while, I stopped wearing the vest altogether. The only reason I have it on now, is because I'd thought to grab it when I swung by the house to get the shovel. And I'm glad I did. The vest is the only reason I'm still alive. But that doesn't change the fact my ribs feel like they've been hit with a parade of sledgehammers. Every breath hurts.

"No one?" I ask, glancing around. "I don't think so. Lie to me, and I shoot you again. Who else?"

A vein bulges near the kid's temple. "I swear! My dad was here, but he left! He thinks you're dead."

I should be dead. It's a miracle I'm not. "Your dad is Officer Gunn, I assume?"

He gives me a weak bobble-head of a nod. "Yes."

"What's his real name?"

He doesn't hesitate. "Zane Jenson."

"And who does that make you?"

"Sean."

"Okay, Sean, last chance. Who else is in on this? Because I know there are more than two of you."

"There aren't. I promise. Fuck, man, you have to help me. I'm dying here!"

He is. The blood bubbling through his fingers is a dark crimson that almost looks black in the fading light. The color likely means the bullet hit an internal organ. Maybe his liver.

"Answer my questions, and I might call an ambulance. If there were only two of you, who was driving the van at the quarry?"

"I was. We ... we parked it back in the trees before we brought you there. We had to circle back to get it after you drove to the meet-up point. It took me longer to get there than ..." He screws his eyes shut with a grimace and then opens them. "Than I thought it would. It's why we were late to the exchange."

I let his explanation simmer in my brain. What he's saying could feasibly make sense. They would have had to change out of their cop uniforms first. And they *were* late. Besides, the kid is seriously wounded, and he's scared. If he's lying to me, he's one hell of a good actor. Still, there's something bothering me—something that doesn't add up.

I lean forward and position myself directly over him. "Do you think I'm stupid? You must, because your father has brown eyes. The man who took Avery had blue eyes."

"No," he says, shaking his head rapidly. "He does that. He's really good at changing his appearance. And changing other people's. All those pictures of her looking hurt ... it was all makeup."

His words settle like stones in the pit of my stomach. All of my worry for Avery, all of my fear about what was happening to her, my absolute panic over what they were *doing* to her—all of it was for *nothing*.

I realize Sean is still speaking, his lips turning blue. "When he abducted her, he was wearing colored contacts. It was him. I fucking swear it was!" He blinks again. He's shaking now, going into shock. I tear off my hoodie, crouch next to him, and press the shirt against the wound.

"Here, use this."

He winces and takes it.

I wipe a fresh ribbon of blood from my forehead. "Why did you try to kill me, Sean?"

His lips quiver. "We—we needed your money."

"You already *have* my money!"

He blanches. "No, we don't. Bailey does. My sister, Cora, she's—she's sick. We need the money for a procedure … or she'll die. The account you transferred the funds to belongs to Bailey, and she won't give it to us. She's the one who did this to you. All of it. You know her as—"

"Avery," I finish.

He gives me a weak nod, and my heart plummets. Avery did this. Avery who is Bailey. Bailey who set this in motion the day I met her on the side of the road nearly a year ago. The realization rolls over me like a tide. She studied me. Manipulated me. Used me. Convinced me to pool our money and invest in crypto so she could steal it all.

The staged abduction.

Her pregnancy, which I realize now—*Jesus*—was as fake as her name.

The mad scavenger hunt designed to take me on a tour of the dark corners of my past. Like the Walmart parking lot, which was a reminder of the insurance scam I ran with my father when I was a kid. He'd station me behind cars as they backed out of spaces and then sue whoever was driving when I was hit.

And the abortion clinic, which was a nod to the day Taylor killed our baby and burned our future together. Even the place where I'm standing now—*Taylor's* property—is a reminder of the life I had before everything went to shit. Every moment from the last two days was engineered to inflict as much pain on me as possible.

I look at Sean. "You still haven't answered my question. Why did you shoot me? Did Avery tell you to do that, too?"

"No," he says, trying to speak through a bubble of blood. "My dad said we couldn't let you go. He said you'd eventually find out what we did. He … said you're …" He swallows, and his Adam's apple inches up his neck. "A liability."

"Where did they go, Sean?"

His eyes flutter. He doesn't answer. I'm losing him. I reach for his chin and give it a shake. "Sean! Where is your father and Avery?"

He smacks his lips and squints. "At a … a cabin."

"What about your vehicle?"

His eyelids flutter, his gaze drifting over my shoulder. "That way—a half mile down the road. There's a pullout near an old barn. Please … don't let me die. I don't want to die."

His eyes roll into his head, and I give his chin another shake. "Sean, give me the address to the cabin."

"14 … 54 County—County Road 213."

It's the last thing he says.

I stare at him with everything inside of me twisting into knots. This didn't need to happen. *None* of it. A hollow weight forms in my gut. I did what I had to do. I defended myself and fought back. So why do I feel so guilty?

Maybe it's because Sean is so young. Maybe it's the fear I heard trembling in his voice with every word. Or maybe it's because he never should have been put in this position in the first place. Whatever the reason, I can't help but feel like his death is my fault—an echo across the years coming from my old life. A life I was done with. A life I now know will never be done with me.

A liability. The word smokes through my head, hot and blistering. I wasn't one.

But I am now.

CHAPTER 46

Zane orders me into the cabin, gun still in hand, and directs me toward the living room where the bust of a twelve-point buck hangs over the fireplace, mounted next to a pair of stuffed pheasants.

"Sit," he says, nodding at a heavy oak chair stationed in the middle of the room. There is a thick length of chain wrapped around the left arm. Secured to the chain are steel handcuffs. The sight makes me shiver.

"Put them on."

Run. The thought hits like a firework. I need to *run.*

Except I can't run. Not after what he said about Ben. I won't place him in danger. And even if I do run, even if I somehow manage to escape before Zane stops me, it won't matter. This is a man who, when I asked him to, procured a human finger from a cadaver without so much as raising an eyebrow. This is a man who effectively erased my old life online and created a new one in its place—one that almost feels more real than the last. More importantly, this is a man who finds people for a living. People who can't be found like Reed. He'll find me, too.

So, I do what I'm told, and I sit. The handcuff is cold as I latch it shut around my wrist, my gaze lingering on the handgun Zane has strapped to his waist. It's the same gun he told me he was bringing to Judge White's property for our protection. *It's only for self-defense. You can't be too careful when dealing with someone like Reed. We need to be safe.*

Safe. The word feels ironic because, until Sean shot Reed in the back, that's exactly how I felt: Protected. In control. Safe.

Which I now realize I'm not.

I'm anything *but* safe. That much is glaringly clear, as is the fact that I made a mistake. I missed something. I still don't understand what. This isn't like Zane. Or at least that's what I thought until he and Sean murdered Reed instead of turning him in to the authorities like we'd planned to. No, like *I'd* planned to. Zane was never going to go through with this.

The image of Reed crumpling to the ground fills my head, of Sean standing above him a moment later and raising the gun.

Crack! Crack!

I'm hit with a sudden swell of sorrow. Reed deserved a lot of things, but he didn't deserve that.

Zane pulls a chair over and takes a seat directly across from me. He doesn't say anything, just stares at me with an intensity that's unnerving. Not that I've ever felt particularly comfortable with his eyes on me, but right now they're like cold chips of ice.

"Why are you doing this?" I finally manage.

He crosses his arms. "I need the money."

"What are you talking about?" I ask, incredulous. "I've already paid you." And I have. I wired him five hundred thousand when he took the job last year and another five-hundred thousand just yesterday after we conned Reed. That, and he still has more coming. A *lot* more. Forty percent of Reed's fortune or one point six million to be exact. Which is what I tell him.

"It's not enough. I need *all* of the money, Bailey," he says, without blinking.

My mouth goes dry. I don't know what to say. "Why?" I finally mutter.

He closes his eyes and rubs the bridge of his nose. When he looks up again, he seems older, the lines in his forehead deeper—like he's aged ten years in the last ten seconds. "There's an experimental gene-therapy drug in Europe with incredible results. But insurance cut me off a year ago. Everything Maria and I have, we've put into Cora. I took out a loan on my business to pay for her last therapy. I've completely leveraged our house. We're close to bankruptcy. I've even gone to the casino a few times, chasing a miracle. That's how desperate I am at this point. I'm chasing miracles."

He went to a casino? His words from the airport flash through my head: *I had a bit of a gambling problem ...*

Is that it? Does he *still* have a problem? Is he the reason they're in debt? Is this partially because of him? I have no idea, but this is exactly the kind of unforeseen circumstance I'd initially worried about when I hired him. And it's exactly why I'd retained full control over all things financial, including access to the account now holding Reed's funds—even when Zane had insisted otherwise. *You'll get your money,* I'd told him when he said we should have a redundancy plan in case something went wrong. And he will.

"I've already paid you a million dollars, Zane," I say. "And you still have the rest of your cut coming. You're nowhere close to bankrupt."

"You have no idea what I'm up against!" he replies angrily. "No idea. MLD costs more to treat than any other disease in the world. What you've paid me isn't enough. It hasn't even helped me crawl out of the hole I'm in after what I've spent to keep Cora alive."

I gawk at him, stupefied. "How is that possible?"

"Because the system is broken. Because my daughter has a disease that's incredibly rare and insanely expensive to treat. Because life isn't fair. It doesn't matter how it's possible. It just is, and I'll do whatever I have to do to give Cora a fighting chance."

I stiffen. "You know what's left is for Reed's victims. I was clear on that."

He slams his fist onto the arm of his chair. "I don't give a fuck who it's for! This is my daughter we're talking about here! My *daughter*. She's almost ten years old and she's back in diapers! This gene therapy costs more than two and a half million per infusion. Two and a half million! And that doesn't even include the hospital and all the recovery costs. The long-term care. But it works. It actually fucking works. And Cora is going to get that drug."

My mouth falls open. I can't help it. The number is staggering. "I ... didn't know it was that much."

"Why would you? You don't pay me to make my problems yours." He falls silent for a moment, a muscle in his jaw twitching. His eyes remain locked with mine. I look away and he leans back in his chair and crosses his legs. "So, tell me, now that it's done, how does it feel?"

I grit my teeth. "You know I never wanted to kill him."

"Never? Don't lie to me, Bailey. We know each other too well for that."

He's right. I wanted to kill Reed the moment Zane first said his name. I've dreamed about it more times than I can count. I've woken with visions of tearing his face to shreds so real I expect to see strips of his skin wedged beneath my fingernails. But even more, I wanted to punish Reed. I wanted him to spend the best years of his life alone, rotting behind bars like his father.

Then I met him—and there were moments when all of that stopped. These brief flickers of hesitation when I'd catch Reed looking at me with such genuine affection, I'd question what I was doing—until I remembered why.

Noah and Ethan were my real life. My *true* life.

What I had with Reed was nothing but a lie.

"You knew the plan," I say.

Zane appraises me and sighs. "I didn't have a choice. He's too dangerous."

"That wasn't your decision to make."

"Maybe not, but it's done." With that he stands, goes into the kitchen, and returns with a laptop and sets it in my lap. He raises the screen, and the cryptocurrency exchange flashes to life.

"Log in to your account."

I don't move, and he sets his palms flat on both arms of the chair and leans forward. He's so much bigger than me it gives me chills. His bulk is a literal weapon I've seen him use against Reed in frightening ways when he posed as my abductor. His entire body is coiled in a threat, from his slightly tilted head to his massive shoulders and muscular arms. Something about him in this moment reminds me of a grizzly bear rising to full height, about to charge.

A question rises up my throat—one I'm not sure I want to ask. "What happens if I don't?"

"You don't want to find out." His expression flattens, but I don't miss the heat in his eyes. The promise there.

"Why now?" I ask, attempting to stall. "Why didn't you take the money when Reed first transferred it?"

He doesn't reply, but his jaw tightens.

"Zane," I prompt. "Why?"

He threads his fingers together and leans forward. "Because we had a deal. And because I know what it feels like to lose a child. This is what you wanted, and I owed it to you to see it through to the end." He glances away with a shake of his head. It's a barely-there motion. A brief flicker that I've landed on some deeper truth he doesn't want to reveal—something that pains him.

And then his meaning hits: *He's going to kill you.*

The voice doesn't sound like mine as it rushes through my head, but I know it's true the moment I think it. He owed it to me to see it through to the end. *My end.* My entire body turns to a canvas of gooseflesh. Like Reed, I'm dangerous, too. I'm a loose end, and Zane is a man who doesn't leave loose ends. Not when it comes to his family. It's why Reed is dead and why I'm next.

"Oh, fuck," I whisper. "Please don't do this."

He pulls his lips between his teeth and looks away. "You saw my son shoot Reed."

Not only shoot Reed, I think with a chill. *I saw Sean kill him.* Which makes me a witness.

"Zane, I won't say anything. You have my word."

He leans back and exhales, looking weary. "Bailey, I've been in this profession for a very long time. I've seen people do a lot of surprising things. But one thing that always holds true is this: People are unpredictable. They change their minds. Only the dead can truly keep a secret."

Panic fills me. I need to find a way to get through to him, to convince him not to go through with this, but I can't think of a single thing to say.

His face hardens. "Now, log in."

I feel every drop of blood in my body drain into my feet. "No."

He doesn't take his eyes off me. "You will. You're going to transfer that money. It's just a matter of what I have to do to you first."

CHAPTER 47

Zane doesn't reply, just stands and crosses the room and retrieves a black velvet pouch from the kitchen counter. He returns and sits again, setting the pouch on his lap. It's sleek and nondescript, the velvet soft and luxurious looking, but something about it sends a hard shiver racing from the tip of my head all the way to my toes.

"Would you be surprised to learn more prisoners of war died in Japan than in Germany during World War Two?" he asks.

The question leaves me spinning, my mouth dry.

"It's true. Approximately one in four. Do you know why?"

I can't speak, can only shake my head. I have no clue where he's going with this.

"There were many reasons," he continues. "Malnutrition for one. Disease for another. The soldiers were neglected when they were sick, or forced into labor. They often worked until they collapsed. If they did, they were left to rot."

I swallow, my pulse thumps harder.

"My grandfather fought in World War Two. He was a pilot. His plane went down in the Sea of Japan. He was one of those prisoners. He never said a word about it, though. Anytime anyone mentioned the war, his face would go white. He'd shut down, conversation over.

It was easy to forget he'd fought at all." Zane pauses, his eyes never leaving mine. "But there was one time he talked about it. It was just the two of us. Me and my grandfather on a camping trip. He'd had a few drinks, and I gathered the courage to ask him about it.

"'Zane,' he'd said, 'you don't want to know.'

"'I do,' I'd said. 'Tell me.' So he did. The Japanese pulled him out of the water and shoved him into a cargo hold with a thousand other men. There wasn't enough space for them all to lie down. It was boiling hot. No water. No air. They grew so thirsty they bit each other in an attempt to drink each other's blood."

My stomach turns at the description.

"A lot of men died on that ship. My grandfather didn't. They put him to work in the mines. The things they did to him there were unspeakable. I don't know how he survived. They tortured him. They beat him and broke his fingers. He lost over half of his teeth. But there was only one thing he said he'd rather die than face again." His hand settles on the velvet pouch and my heart climbs my throat.

"Zane, whatever you're thinking of doing ... please, don't."

Time slows as he unties the ribbon and unrolls the pouch to reveal several metallic pins that look like oversized sewing needles. He pulls one free and rolls it between his fingers. "Did you also know the Imperial Japanese are credited with creating many forms of modern torture? One of their most effective devices in the camps was the use of bamboo splinters. They shoved them beneath the fingernails of the prisoners if they thought they had information. They thought my grandfather had information. It's what they did to him." His eyes click toward mine. "I don't want to do this to you, Bailey. But I will. I'll do it for Cora. Things will be so much easier for you if you just give me the money."

I would. I'd happily give it to Zane to avoid this. My life means nothing to me anymore.

But Ben's does. Zane already threatened him.

And Ben knows everything.

"If I transfer the money, you'll kill my brother," I say.

"No, I won't. It isn't necessary."

"Didn't you just say people are unpredictable? That they change their minds?"

"I don't. And I won't have a reason to. Your suicide will be hard on Ben, but it will make sense. You've attempted it before. And this time you'll succeed. You got too close to Reed. This plan of yours was too painful. You couldn't handle it. The logic will track. Do we have a deal?"

I don't nod, don't move, don't respond, just stare at him, feeling like I'm balancing on the edge of a cliff about to fall over. *Do we have a deal?* How can I trust him after this? How do I know he'll leave Ben alone?

I expect more words, for Zane to try to fill the silence and convince me what he's saying is true, but before I know what's happening, he slams his hand over mine and plucks a pin from the pouch. I try to pull my arm free but he's far too strong. He places the tip of the needle against the delicate flesh beneath my fingernail. He's so close I can smell his sweat.

"Do we have a deal, Bailey?"

The point presses into the skin ever so slightly, feeling more like a splinter of sun than a bit of metal.

"Swear to me you won't hurt him," I say. "Swear on your daughter's life."

Zane smiles, but it's a sad smile, the corners full of weight, with no matching crinkle of the eyes. "I want you to know this is the most difficult thing I've ever had to do. I don't relish this. And I won't betray you. I won't harm your brother. I swear."

"Okay," I whisper. "Okay."

The pressure in my fingertip releases, and he stands and gestures at the laptop still sitting in my lap. I tap the mouse and it flashes to life, the crypto exchange login screen glowing once more in front of me.

"Do it," he says.

It's not easy with one hand cuffed. It takes me four tries before I'm able to enter my password correctly. When I do, Zane passes me my phone. An authenticator question is there waiting for me. Am I trying to login? My finger hovers over the yes button and my heart falls. Once I click it, it's over. Zane won't need me anymore.

But the truth is, he's already won. I won't be able to resist this kind of torture. If he *is* planning on hurting Ben, he's going to do it no matter how much I struggle. At this point, all I can do is give him what he wants and hope he keeps his word.

I click the button. The account loads and Zane goes to work on the transfer. His fingers move rapidly as he keys in the amount and then enters his crypto wallet address—a combination of several dozen alphanumeric characters that will swallow what's left in my account forever.

He's just about done when his phone buzzes. A split second later, there's a knock on the door. Hope butterflies through my chest. Maybe it's a delivery man or some distant neighbor—someone to hear me scream. And then I glimpse the image of the front door on Zane's screen, and the hope dies. It's Sean, still dressed head to toe in camo.

"Idiot," Zane hisses through clenched teeth setting the computer aside before stomping toward the door.

"What's wrong with you?" he asks, swinging it open. "Why are you still wearing the ghillie suit? Get inside before you attract attention."

What comes next happens in a blur of motion I struggle to follow. Sean bursts through the door with his gun drawn, telling Zane to, "Get the fuck back!"

Except it isn't Sean's voice.

It's Reed's.

Zane's eyes peel wide. He doesn't obey. Instead, he lunges for the gun in Reed's hand, and three of his fingers disappear in a shower of bone and meat.

Bang! Bang!

My ears ring from the gunshots as Reed takes a step forward and slams the heel of his boot into Zane's stomach. Zane flies backward into the kitchen counter. He somehow manages to keep his balance, but Reed is already on him, bringing the butt of the pistol crashing down between his eyes. It's like watching a tree fall the way Zane tilts and slams to the floor, his head cracking hard against the tile.

He doesn't move as Reed pulls out a long length of black nylon rope and winds it around Zane's wrists and ankles. It's clear he's unconscious, but I'm no longer watching him. I'm thrashing in the chair, straining to free my hand. My wrist erupts in a bright bloom of pain. The handcuff goes slick with blood. It's agonizing, but I don't care. I have to get out of this room, *have* to get away from Reed. I stand and jerk harder, yanking with everything I have. My palm slides higher, the steel ring tearing skin as it nears my knuckles. One more pull and I'll—

"Stop!"

The world blinks and wavers. Blood drips from my fingers to the chair. When I look up, Reed is standing a foot away, no longer wearing the ghillie mask. His mouth is pressed into a thin razor blade slash, his hair matted with dirt and blood. The gun in his hand is aimed at my stomach, but it's the way he's staring at me with his eyes baked in hate that fills me with dread.

"Hello, Bailey," he says. "It's nice to finally meet you."

CHAPTER 48

REED

"Hello, Reed."

She spits my name at me like a bullet. The fear that swept over her face when she first saw me recedes like a wave, leaving nothing but stone. Blood seeps from her wrist and pools on the arm of the chair. It looks like it hurts, but it's nowhere close to the level of pain Officer Gunn will be in when he regains consciousness.

Officer Gunn, whose real name is Zane Jenson.

Zane Jenson, who's the father of Sean Jenson, aka Officer Calvin Holston.

Sean who told me how to get here for this little reunion with my wife Avery Wilson, real name Bailey Nichols.

All of it lies. A happily ever after I should have known better than to ever think I could achieve.

Or deserve.

"I saw you die," she says in a voice so low and cold, so full of hate, it feels like she thinks I'm the one who tried to kill her rather than the other way around.

"I'm sorry to disappoint you."

"How are you still alive?"

"Does it matter? Your plan failed."

"It wasn't my plan." Her gaze ticks left toward the kitchen. "It was his."

Which I already know, Sean's weakened voice scraping through my head in a slur. *My dad said we couldn't let you go. He said you're ... a liability.*

I spent a few minutes considering my approach before I left the White property. I could break into the cabin or cause some sort of distraction to draw Zane outside, but either option would put him on alert and lower my chance of taking him by surprise. And then it came to me as I stared down at his son. A third choice I hadn't considered, and a simpler one. After seeing me take three bullets to the back, Zane likely wouldn't hesitate to open the door to someone dressed in the ghillie suit. Sean and I were approximately the same height. Zane would assume I was his son. It was an easy choice to make. But this—sitting across from Bailey who is still Avery in my mind—is the single hardest moment of my life.

I recline in the chair, and it's all I can do to mask the sudden flare of pain the motion unleashes. My entire back feels like a pane of shattered glass. "How did you find me?"

"I didn't."

"Who then?" I nod at Zane. "Him?"

"Yes. But you helped." She glares at me and for a moment I don't think she's going to continue, but then she says, "Zane managed to work through your aliases. I don't know how he did it, but he did, and he uncovered your real name. He didn't know where you were though, or who you'd become. You gave that to him yourself."

"How?"

"Does it matter?" she says, spitting my line back at me.

"Yes. It does."

She leans back in the chair, her eyes smoldering with hate. She's trembling, but I know it's not with fear. It's with rage. "Your father."

The statement is a fist to the gut. *My father.* I know immediately.

"He had someone watching the prison, didn't he?"

"Every day until you came."

And then I led them right here.

I run a hand over my face in an attempt to keep it together. "Was any of it real?"

She smiles, and there's something cruel in the shape, something sharp, like if I touched her lips they might cut. "What do you think?"

The words are concrete pouring over my heart. She's shaking harder now, her entire body a clenched fist.

"You and I aren't so different, you know," I say.

Her nose wrinkles in disgust. She pulls back like I slapped her. "I'm *nothing* like you."

"You're *exactly* like me!" I say, leaning forward. "I was your target, your mark. You studied me. You built a profile. You looked for a way in. You saw I was isolated and alone and in need of connection. And then you exploited those things to get what you wanted. It's exactly what I would have done."

Her smile returns. "How does it feel?"

I wilt, the anger rushing out of me. I know what she wants me to say. That I'm gutted. Devastated. Ruined. Which I am. I'm absolutely cored right now. But she isn't innocent in all of this, either. Not after what she's done.

"My son's name was Noah," she says. "He loved superheroes and playing with toy trucks. When he turned three, I painted his ceiling in glow-in-the-dark stars. I hung planets. We'd lie on his bed, looking up at them, and he'd tell me that's where he wanted to live someday— among the stars. He wanted to be an astronaut. He wanted to be so many things. And you stole them all." Her eyes meet mine, and I want to tell her to stop, that I can't handle this right now, not after everything I've been through the last two days. But I can't speak, can't do anything other than listen.

"My husband's name was Ethan," she continues. "He was an

incredible father. You should have seen the way he poured himself into Noah. They went fishing on the weekends. He spent hours in the backyard teaching him how to hit a baseball. They were so happy together. I loved watching them. But what I miss most is the sound of their laughter." Her voice thickens. "Ethan was such a wonderful husband. He brought me flowers all the time. Lilies. They were my favorite. Anytime I needed to talk, he was there for me. Anytime I felt down, he'd find a way to cheer me up. He was the most giving person I've ever known." She wipes her eyes. "I should have told him that more. I took him for granted."

"Avery ..." Her fake name sounds alien as it rolls off my tongue, but I can't pull it back before she continues.

"Do you know what the last thing I said to him was?"

No. And I don't want to know.

"I told him he was selfish." A tear rolls down her cheek. "Do you know how many times I've relived that moment? How badly I want to take that back? All I want is to tell him I'm so sorry for not valuing him like I should have. I want to tell him how much I love him just one more time. But I can't. I'll never get to say that because of *you*."

Her words are arrows that punch into me so hot and deep I can barely breathe. "I never meant for any of that to happen to you." The statement feels weak as it leaves my mouth—a spoonful of soup spit into a fire.

"No, you only meant to target certain women. But what you did to Evelyn destroyed my life!"

The memory hits with a rush: The intersection and the car beyond it. The burning scorch of rubber as I fought for the brakes. The impact, so brutal I felt it in the roots of my teeth. The smoke and silence that followed. The blood in my mouth. Gushing from my nose. The ringing in my ears. Evelyn lying next to me in a broken tangle of limbs, looking like she'd been throttled at the hands of a giant.

"You framed a dead woman, Reed. A *dead* woman. You took

everything from her. Exactly like you took everything from me! Everything! So, when you ask me if any of this"—she gestures at me wildly, then at herself—"was real, I want you to understand none of it was. Not a single fucking second."

And then she leans forward and spits in my face.

I don't bother to wipe it off, *can't* wipe it off. All I can do is sit here spinning in the wake of her anger as it drips from my chin and onto my lap, gasping for air beneath her waves. Avery was supposed to be my chance at redemption. My fresh start—a way to finally and forever leave my past behind. But now I know I'll never be able to do that because Avery never existed. Only Bailey did. And that's exactly what Bailey is: my past. One I was foolish to ever think I could escape. I'm ruined. I can see that now. And so is she. I know what I need to do. The only thing left for both of us.

I take the gun and stand.

CHAPTER 49

BAILEY

Reed rises from the chair, and I know—I *know*—he's going to kill me. I can see the hurt painted in his eyes and the anger splattered all over his face along with my spit. I've bathed him in my rage. I've lied to him, used him, and manipulated him just like he's done to so many others. I've taken everything from him: his money, his pride, his trust, his heart.

His child.

But that isn't why he's about to shoot me. No, he'll do that because I broke him. Any hope he has of living a normal life is gone. Even if it's not in jail, he'll spend the rest of his days isolated and alone. He'll never be able to trust anyone after this, never be able to give his heart to someone else—not in the same way he gave it to me. That's what I've taken from him. It's exactly what I wanted.

So why do I feel so empty inside?

Because it won't bring them back.

The thought burns. It's a truth I've buried for so long now. This revenge of mine—this crusade against Reed—has always been a way for me to keep from letting go of my family. To make it feel like they mattered. To keep their memory alive—if only for a time. Because I can already feel them fading away a little more every day, their edges dulling, their faces blurring like the lines of a chalk drawing washed away in the rain.

It's like I'm losing them all over again, but in a way that feels more permanent than before, one grain at a time. I can no longer clearly picture the perfect curve of Ethan's smile or hear the bright chime of Noah's laugh. I can't recall the soft weight of my son as I wrap him in a morning hug or feel the heat of Ethan's palm against mine when he takes my hand. Their smells, their touch, the way they so effortlessly filled the small spaces around me, all of it gone.

Since the wreck, my grief had only grown steadily deeper and ever wider. Grief like tar forever pressing in, choking me until I could no longer breathe. Grief without end. And then I found out about Reed. And in that moment, when Paula first spoke his name, I was finally able to feel something other than grief: Hate. Hate has carried me for so long now. Hatred is why I'm still alive. And hatred is why I'm going to die.

Reed stands in front of me looking like a zombie, his eyes two empty holes, his face all but drained of life. It's like I've sucked his soul from his body and spit it on the floor. The gun twitches in his hand and I flinch. I can't help it. I drop my head and wait for him to pull the trigger.

Do it. Get it over with.

I want him to. I'll finally be free. From the hurt. From the pain.

From the memories of that day that will forever burn through my mind.

But the barrel of the gun doesn't rise. Reed takes no forward step, makes no sudden movement. Instead, he rotates and heads toward the kitchen, snatches something from the counter, and returns with a ring of keys.

"You're right. I've hurt a lot of people," he says. "For a long time, I didn't regret my actions. I had my reasons, or at least I thought I did. I told myself the women I targeted deserved it. That all changed with

Evelyn. I knew she was different. I knew from the beginning. I could have stopped at any time. And I should have. I wanted to. But I didn't. I'll never forgive myself for what I did to her. It hurts. I think about it every day. What I did to you, though—that hurts even more."

He looks away and closes his eyes, like whatever he's about to say next will come with a chunk of his heart. "I ... saw your family that day. After the wreck. I saw what I did to them. To you. I could have stopped then. But I didn't. I ran. It's what I've always done. But no more." With that, he leans forward and fits a key into the cuffs, and I'm free.

Thoughts storm through my head.

Bolt.

Go for the gun.

Attack him.

But I do none of these things because there's no time. Reed is already kneeling in front of me and handing me the pistol, pushing the grip into my palm. I take it, stunned, unable to understand what's happening as he leans in and presses his forehead against the barrel. "Do it."

Flickers of Noah whoosh through my head. His dinosaur-themed birthday party, Noah flashing me a gap-toothed smile after opening his present—a cheap, plastic race car that made him squeal with joy. *I love it! I love it!* Another memory of him dashing through the house in a red cape as Superman. Me holding in a laugh and pretending to be in awe as he cocks his arms off his hips at the top of the stairs in a perfect super-hero pose. Noah and I reading a book about astronauts together on the couch with his body so perfectly molded to mine, as if I was created only for this moment, for him, as we talk about the stars.

Do you think anyone lives up there, Mommy? Could I?

A billow of heat fills my chest, and it's Ethan I see now. My husband-to-be casting me a shy smile over a plate of pasta on our first date. He's all bluster and nerves as he laughs and knocks over his glass of water. He's flaming cheeks and apologies. He's so beautiful in this moment. Dimples that look like crescent moons. Eyes that are light brown and free and always return to me.

Every time they do, they are full of love. On a trip to Stevens Pass, Ethan smiling as he teaches me to ski with snow fluttering down around us like cotton. As we kayak in Seacrest Park with the sun spraying the Seattle skyline a soft yellow orange. On our wedding day, the two of us promising each other our forevers, Ethan never dropping his gaze once. And all the times that come after. The highs and the lows. The stupid fights and tearful reconciliations. Every single moment filled with love.

Always with love.

More memories hit: Noah's first steps as Ethan and I laugh and clap and cheer him on. Our weekend trips to the beach with the three of us looking for shells beneath the waves. Saturday afternoons spent at the movies staining our fingers yellow with popcorn. The way Noah's laugh bubbles from his throat when tickled. It's a sound I'd give anything to hear again. *Anything.* A sound forever taken by the man kneeling in front of me now.

Beads of sweat erupt along the nape of my neck. My hands shake and tremble. Hate spills down my arms like fire. My lungs boil and char. I want to force all of the heat from my body into Reed's. I want him to ignite and burn and turn into a lazy spiral of ash.

My finger wraps around the trigger.

My palms go slick against the grip.

The gun shakes. All I have to do is squeeze and Reed will be erased from this world. A quick pull of the trigger, and the man who stole everything from me will be gone. Reed, who I lied to, because there *were* moments our relationship was real. These split-second slivers of time when I lost myself in his smile or the way the sound of his laugh filled the room before the memories of Ethan and Noah would come howling back like a storm, and I'd remember *exactly* why I was there.

"Do it!" he says again, louder, his voice breaking.

I blink, and he comes back into focus. His thick, brown hair. His pale skin. The silent tears spilling from the corners of his eyes. Eyes that, like Ethan's, have never looked at me with anything but love.

Stop it! I hiss into my boiling brain. *He killed your family! He destroyed your life!*

His palm slides over the back of my hand, Reed nodding now, speaking. "It's okay. Let me give you this."

A buzz fills my skull. A sound like a saw biting into wood. A bright metallic whine.

The pressure in my finger tightens. Just a millimeter more.

A final squeeze and he'll be gone.

It won't bring them back. It won't change anything.

A wail claws up my throat. I lift my gaze toward the ceiling. The sound that pours from my lungs is alien—a voice I don't recognize as my own. Tears pour down my cheeks. I grind my jaw so hard, it feels like my teeth will crack. Reed and I are two ships tethered together in the same storm. Waves rise and crash down all around us. We boom together and come apart in a fury of metal and wood. Destroying this man has been my purpose for so long now; it feels like all I've ever known.

It. Won't. Bring. Them. Back.

The hole in my chest widens and I know if I pull the trigger, if I kill him, it will swallow me too.

The gun slides from my hand and thuds to the floor.

I slump back into the chair. And I cry.

I sob so hard it feels like blood is pouring down my face in the place of tears. I shake until I'm about to come apart. Somewhere in front of me a shadow forms as Reed rises. How long he remains there, I'm not sure, I know only that at some point, I manage to stand, grab the car keys, and rush out the front door.

CHAPTER 50

My heart dissolves in my chest as I watch Bailey go. I've destroyed her.

Exactly like I've destroyed myself.

I'm sorry, Bailey. I'm so fucking sorry.

The words snap through my head like a wall of dust—hot and worthless. Sorry won't fix everything I've broken. Sorry won't heal all the women I've shattered. Sorry won't bring Evelyn back to life or resurrect Bailey's family. Nothing will. And nothing I do can ever change that. But there is still something I can give her. Zane Jenson planned to hurt her. I'm certain of that. And I can make sure it never happens.

I turn toward him—and I freeze.

Because Zane is no longer lying unconscious behind me. He's pushing to his feet instead, the ropes around his wrists and ankles severed.

How?

My eyes track behind him toward an open pocketknife lying on the floor, the handle smeared with red. In my rush, I didn't think to pat him down, didn't search his pockets. His damaged hand hangs by his side, the stubs of his fingers dripping blood like a leaking faucet. And in his other hand is a gun.

I move for mine.

"Don't," he says, as I shift forward. His voice is like iron. The same voice the masked man used during Bailey's staged abduction. I return my gaze to his. His eyes are those of Officer Gunn's, brown, not blue. But they carry a new emotion compared to the last time they looked at me: Hate. I can feel it radiating off of him like a furnace. This man hates me now.

"Where's my son?" he asks.

Lies surge up my throat in rapid succession: *Outside in the van. Gone, he took off. Injured, but he's okay. He's at the hospital. You can find him there.* Even now—after everything—the lies come so naturally. So freely. But I won't let them. At this point, I've told enough lies to fill an ocean.

"Dead," I say.

A cord ripples in his neck. "How? I saw him shoot you."

I press my fist to my chest. "I wore a vest."

"And then you shot him."

"Yes."

Zane winces, the statement a slap to his face. He takes in a slow breath then exhales in a slow hiss through his teeth. "I should have taken you out at the quarry when I had the chance." He shakes his head, his face paling as it ropes into a snarl.

"Why didn't you?" I ask, after a second.

"Because this—" he stabs the gun at me "—doing all of this to you is what she wanted. And I owed that to her after everything she's been through. After what *you* put her through."

Her, I think. *Bailey.*

"Why?" I ask. "So you could feel better about betraying her?"

His eyebrows slant down, and he takes a single step forward, the gun wavering dangerously in his hand. "You of all people dare to judge me? Fuck you! You have no idea what kind of hell I've had to endure, you selfish prick! You'll never know!" His eyes dust red and he shakes his head. "I did all of this to save her. All of it! And I still failed."

Her—but this time I know he isn't referencing Bailey. The anguish splashed over his face as he says it is too raw for that, the pain too real. He's talking about his daughter. I don't respond. Anything I say right now is likely to get me killed.

You're dead already.

It's true. It's just a matter of time. Still, I don't speak. I simply stand there and wait for Zane to continue. When he does, it's in a mutter, his face cycling through a storm of emotions: An angry flare of his nose. A quick flash of his teeth. A painful downturn of his lips. I realize he's no longer talking to me.

"He shouldn't have been there. I shouldn't have put him in that situation."

He's talking to himself.

"I failed him. I failed them both."

Go, I think. *Move.*

I'm about to, but his gaze snaps to mine as if reading my mind. "Don't even think about it."

I raise my hands.

His lips tremble. The gun wobbles. His complexion has faded to a pale, sickly yellow I know isn't just from the blood loss but also from what I've done to his son. He looks so bad, I don't know how he's still able to stand.

"This is all your fault." He jabs the gun toward the open door through which Bailey fled moments earlier. "She was Cora's last chance."

And mine, I can't help but think, bitterly.

He continues to stare at me, and his eyes clear. He raises his chin. "Live or die?"

"What?" I ask, confused.

"It's a simple question. Do you want to live, or do you want to die?"

His words slam into me with a terrible weight. *Do I?* After everything I've done, after everything I've taken and lost, what's the point?

"Live or die!" he growls again.

It should be so clear, but even now I don't know the answer.

But I do know what I deserve.

"Kill me," I say.

He appraises me for a long moment before the corners of his lips curl into a sad grin. There's no light in his eyes, no relief at my answer. All I see are two empty black holes leading to a bottomless pit of despair.

My heart thuds as he draws the gun from my chest and levels it at my head. His grip on the weapon tightens, his knuckles blanching white. He blinks, and a single tear slides over his cheek. "If that's really what you want, you'll have to do it yourself."

And then he brings the gun to his temple—and pulls the trigger.

CHAPTER 51

I spend hours sanitizing the cabin. By the time I'm done, the place is sparkling.

A three-quarter moon hangs overhead when I step outside, draping the world around me in a sick, pale light. I stare at the van in the driveway, and a thick wave of revulsion rolls through me. In the back, wrapped in a tarp I found in the garage, is Zane.

It took me a while to figure out what to do with him, but when the answer hit, it was clear; I know exactly where he needs to go.

It's almost three in the morning when I reach the field. I park beneath a bank of trees that mostly conceal the van. It's possible someone might see it if they're paying attention. But it's highly unlikely. No one will be out at this hour, and if they are, the last thing they'll care about is a stray vehicle.

It takes me ten minutes to find a gap beneath the wood fence large enough to pull Zane through, and another twenty to drag him toward the hill. I'd be able to move faster if I had more light, but I don't dare use my phone. Even with how remote and isolated the White property is, I don't want to risk being spotted, not with what I'm about to do. The light from the moon will have to be enough.

The shovel is waiting for me, right where I left it.

I pick it up and widen the grave, then make it deeper, sweat pouring off my brow as the dirt piles up. It's hard work, and I have to dig fast, but the soil is already loose and I'm able to get the job done. When I finish, it's just past four o'clock.

I roll Zane in first and then follow him with Sean. The kid lands face up with moonlight glimmering in his eyes. It's like he's staring at me, judging what I've done.

I'm sorry, I think again. At this point, they feel like the only two words I know.

I turn my attention to the casket, which sits next to me, empty. After all the digging, cleaning it out is easy. I take everything—the pictures, photos, and mask—and dump them into a garbage sack. Then I push the casket in and fill the hole with dirt. I spend a few minutes restoring the earth and concealing it with brush. When I'm done, the area looks undisturbed. Not that anyone would notice if it didn't.

Even in my youth, Taylor's parents never spent much time out here. And now that they're in their seventies, there's little risk they ever will. It's not a perfect plan—it's possible some stroke of bad luck will reveal what I've done—but I'm short on time, and this is the best plan I have. With any luck, Zane and Sean will simply disappear.

I survey my work for a moment longer and then hustle back to the van. When I reach it, the sky is beginning to blush.

And then I drive.

The trees slide past like ghosts dressed in white. Through the van's open window, the clean, sweet scent of sagebrush and the sharp tang of pine fills the air along with the rich scent of earth. I breathe deep and pull them into my lungs. I love these smells. I always have. If I could ever call someplace home, this would be it.

The ache within me grows with every passing mile. What I did to Evelyn was unforgivable. What I did to Bailey was worse. I'd been recovering from the crash in Mexico when I'd forced myself to read the article. It was a brief piece about a Seattle socialite who'd barreled drunk into a family of three and killed two of them—a man and a child—along with herself. Only a woman by the name of Bailey Nichols had survived. I remember how my stomach dropped in that moment, how I'd rushed to the ocean's edge and thrown up until a member of the resort staff drifted my way and asked if I was okay.

"No," I'd replied, wiping strings of vomit from my lips. "Not at all."

I'd spent the rest of the day doing the same—drinking and puking until it felt like my stomach lining would come up. How had it happened? How had all of my decisions gone so wrong? Three people had died because of me. *Three.*

And yet I was still alive.

I swore right then and there I would change and become a new person. I'd bury what I'd done forever. I'd never think about that day again. I knew it was far too late for redemption, but maybe I could find a way to survive. I thought I could heal if I returned here to Durango—the one place I'd ever truly been happy, if just for a time. I told myself I'd find a way to impact the world in some small positive way.

So, I did what I did best. I ran and I hid.

From myself.

From what I'd done.

And then I met Avery ...

I can still feel her spit on my face, can still see the hate steaming in her eyes. The absolute devastation I never knew was simmering there, right beneath the surface, waiting to boil over because I erased her entire world in an instant.

Just like she's erased mine.

———

I park the van behind a hardware store and leave it unlocked with the keys on the seat. I've sanitized it as well, scrubbed it front to back with bleach. I can't do much else, except hope someone steals it. If they do, great, and if not, oh well. Knowing Zane, there's no chance the thing will lead the cops back to him or anyone else in his circle. Neither will the contents of the casket. It's gone. I burned it all, and I dumped the guns in the river.

I take my time as I stroll up the street. I'm wearing a new set of clothes I purchased from a truck stop where I took a shower before heading into town. The shirt is a size too large, the jeans too small, but I pay them no mind as I walk slow and enjoy the cool morning weather. Blocks pass along with people. Some of them smile at me. Others walk right on by. It's strange how these last few moments feel so normal.

When I spot the building ahead, I stop. It isn't much to look at: a brown stucco blob hulking on the corner of East 2nd Avenue and 10th Street downtown. I've only been here once before, on an ancient high school field trip, but I remember the place well. I know what I'll see when I walk through the doors. An expanse of dull, clay-colored tile floors planted beneath a ceiling long gone yellow with age. The lobby will smell of burned toast and old coffee and long-expired dreams.

And that's okay, it's exactly where I deserve to be—but there's something I need to do before I enter. I pull the phone out of my pocket, surf to my email, and login. I'm not sure how long it takes me to write the email, but I'm having trouble seeing clearly by the time I hit send. Bailey might not ever read it, but my guess is at some point she will.

I wipe my eyes, power off the phone, and toss it in a dumpster, then walk the rest of the way, pausing when I reach the doors.

It's not too late. You can turn back.

It's true. There are so many places I could go. I still have money stashed away in a number of rainy-day accounts. I have drop boxes stuffed with cash at several banks across the country along with a storage shed in New Mexico full of everything I'd need to start over again: fake IDs. Passports. A safe packed with jewelry and gold. I can make it happen. A new life. A different name. A fresh start.

I let out a sad chuckle. *Yeah right.* I'm done running. It won't work. Not when I'm the problem. No matter how fast I run, I'll never be able to outrun myself.

And after this, I'm too tired to take another step.

I make the decision and enter. The lobby is just as I remember it. Not a damn thing has changed. It's empty except for a single row of orange plastic chairs stationed near the window and a man in a uniform sitting behind a wooden desk. He yawns as he looks up from his computer screen.

"Can I help you?"

He's young—has the same kind of face as Sean Jenson, except his cheeks are fuller and still rosy with baby fat. But unlike Sean, or Officer Calvin Holston as I first knew him, this man is an actual cop.

"I need to report a crime."

His shoulders straighten and draw back. His gaze sharpens. I have his attention now. "Yeah? What's that?"

I only hesitate for a second, just long enough to take a deep breath and let it out before I say, "Mine."

CHAPTER 52

BAILEY
One Year Later

Cora moves easier than when I last saw her. Freer. Her legs don't shake with every step. Her feet no longer flop like she's wading through a foot of wet cement. Her gait isn't perfect—one foot still turns in, and she wobbles if she walks too fast—but there's a steadiness that wasn't there before. A rhythm.

The biggest change is in her expressions. Her lips curve in a way they didn't before. Her eyebrows rise, and her dimples crease. When she smiles, it's like her entire face glows, and it's so good to see.

It's not the same for her mother. Sure, Maria Jenson doesn't look at her daughter like a leaf that might blow away at any minute like she used to. She doesn't clutch Cora's hand as tight. Yet there's a weight in her gaze that wasn't there before. A grief I understand all too well. She misses her husband. And Zane is gone because of me. I needed to give her something in return.

It didn't take me long to make the decision.

The more I studied MLD, the more I tilted. Just like Zane said, it's a disease like quicksand; it swallows its victims slowly, inch by horrible inch until they're nothing more than a shell with a soul trapped inside. All of this is due to a gene mutation that swamps the brain in a coating of fat it can't break down. The nerves die. Brain signals can't get out. To lose your child in this way is a horror I can't imagine.

Even after losing my own.

Noah died without warning—there one second, gone the next—ripped away in the blink of an eye. His loss along with Ethan's was, and always will be, the very worst moment of my life. But I didn't have to watch either of them suffer before they died. I didn't have to watch them fight for movement or struggle for breath as they went deaf and blind. They were simply ... gone.

Yes, it's true Zane betrayed me, that he cuffed me to a chair and threatened to jam steel splinters beneath my fingernails if I didn't give him Reed's money. He took advantage of my desperation and used it to relieve his own. He did what he thought he had to do to save his child in the same way I'd done what I thought I had to do to avenge the death of mine. It made him dangerous. But he's not anymore.

You're safe now. They won't bother you again.

I read Reed's email a week after returning to Seattle. I'd told myself I was done with Avery Carter, that I'd never go back to her again. Which was why I'd opened my inbox in the first place—to erase the account. And there it was, the subject line sandwiched between a bunch of junk mail halfway down the page.

Bailey, please read this.

I nearly deleted it, but I couldn't. I had to know what it said. And it nearly tore my heart out. There were no justifications in his words, no excuses, only pain for what he'd done. Pain I could literally feel bleeding through the screen with every word. I read it with tears in my eyes, and when I reached the end, I almost didn't register the meaning behind the final line. *You're safe now.* When I did, I nearly dropped the phone.

Zane and Sean were never coming home. It's why I hadn't heard a word from either of them since I'd fled the cabin. It's why I hadn't woken in the middle of the night with a gun to my head or wound up bleeding out in an alley. They were dead—both of them. Cora wasn't, and I could do something to keep it that way.

I looked into the European gene therapy. It appeared promising. More than promising. Zane was right. It actually seemed to work. I watched video after video of MLD parents weeping with joy when their kids walked again and talked again. Kids whose paralysis melted away like butter. I could withhold that from Zane, sure. After what he'd done to me, I despised the man. But how could I withhold that from his daughter? How could I withhold that from his widow? If someone had the power to bring back my son, wouldn't I give anything, *do* anything, to make that happen? I knew I would—but I didn't have the power to save Noah.

I did have the power to save Cora.

I established a confidential trust and named Maria as the sole beneficiary. Then I sent her the money. Three million in total—two-and-a-half million for the treatment and another five-hundred thousand for the recovery. I left a single anonymous note in the remittance line: *Save your daughter.*

And she did.

I split what was left between Reed's victims. There were the ones I already knew about—Rachel Dawson, Lacey Grayson, and Jennifer Stewart—and two I didn't, both revealed by Reed in his email. Five women in all: two-hundred thousand each. It wasn't enough to erase the anguish of what Reed had done to them, but it was a start.

Just like today is a start. A new beginning.

I return my attention to Maria and Cora. They're at the park, having a picnic. Cora sits at the table as Maria covers it with a checkered tablecloth. Maria pulls sandwiches from a wicker basket and sets them on two plates and then hands one to her daughter while saying something that makes Cora throw her head back in a laugh.

"She's doing so much better," Ben says in awe as he stares at the girl.

We're sitting in his car across the park near the playground watching them. Any time I tell him I'm going to check up on her, Ben pleads for me not to, just like he pleaded with me not to go through with my plan with Reed. Too bad I've never been good at listening.

It's strange how things worked out. In a way, Reed saved my life. If I hadn't found out about him when I did, I would have ended things for sure. He gave me purpose when I had none. And that purpose was to make him pay for what he'd done.

To the women he conned.

To Evelyn Nash.

To Noah and Ethan.

To me.

And he had paid. I knew it the minute he walked into Zane's cabin and saw me sitting there. It was like he'd been hit by a truck. When I told him nothing between us had been real, it was like I'd plunged my fist through his ribs and ripped out his heart. It was everything I'd hoped for and everything I'd imagined. But instead of vindicated, his pain left me feeling empty. And when he knelt in front of me and offered me his life in apology, that emptiness expanded into a chasm.

I didn't want to see it then, but Reed had already suffered—in his own way. Abandoned by his mother. Left to a father who'd raised him wrong. Robbed of the chance to raise a child with the girl he'd loved. Haunted by the death of Evelyn and my family. He'd suffered at my hands, and I'd suffered at his. It didn't make me feel better. It didn't bring Ethan and Noah back. It's true what they say, that hurt people hurt people, and that hate only leads to more hate. I can see that now.

Hate is what led me to do what I'd done to Reed.

But hate isn't what forced him to walk into the Durango Police Department and confess to his crimes that day. It was ... something else. Guilt? Repentance? Remorse? I wasn't sure. The press picked up the story exactly like I'd hoped they would. A good-looking man who spent his life manipulating women before confessing to his crimes out of the blue was too juicy for the media to resist. It made national news.

During the coverage of his trial, I noticed something in Reed I hadn't expected. Besides the obvious—the shame in his eyes, the agony and humiliation—there was something else. He almost looked at peace in a way, like a weight had been lifted. It's strange, but I think jail is where Reed finally gained his freedom. And Cora Jenson is where I'd finally found mine.

"Okay," Ben says, watching her as she helps her mom. "I'll admit it. You were right to give them the money."

"Does that surprise you?" I ask.

"Don't push it," he says, grinning. "I only have so much humility to offer."

I return my gaze to Cora, and we both sit there, watching as Cora curls into her mother in the same way Noah used to curl into me—her head planted on her mother's shoulder, their arms intertwined. I close my eyes, and it's like I can feel my son there sitting next to me with his torso pressed warm against my side.

I'll never forget you, I think. *I'll never let you go.*

Ben's fingers brush the back of my arm.

"Hey, are you going to be okay?" he asks.

A laugh I didn't know I was holding back bubbles up my throat. I wipe my tears and take his hand, give it a squeeze—my brother, the rock. "Yes," I say with a smile.

And for the first time in as long as I can remember, it's not a lie.

WAIT, BEFORE YOU GO ...

Want to read the email Reed sent to Bailey before he turned himself in?

Want to know what he couldn't say before she fled?

Want to discover the surprise guest who pays him a visit in prison?

Grab the bonus epilogue, "After What I've Done," right now to find out! Just scan the QR code below to get instant access.

I love connecting with my readers. When you sign up for my newsletter, you'll get insider news, book updates, and behind-the-scenes stories—never spam, just the good stuff. Also, I'd love for you to join my reader group on Facebook, where we can hang out, connect, and talk about bookish things!

One last favor: **reviews keep authors alive.** If you enjoyed this book, please post a quick review on Amazon, Goodreads, The StoryGraph, or your favorite review site. It makes a huge difference.

Thank you for your support—I'll be back with more books soon!

AUTHOR'S NOTE

As an author, one of the questions I'm asked most is this: "What's the hardest part about writing a book?"

There are so many answers to that question, and all of them are valid:

They often take years to complete.

You spend a ridiculous amount of time alone.

It's emotionally draining. You have to give a piece of yourself to the work; a good book requires that you tear out a piece of your heart.

People will tell you that you can't do it—and even if you do it, that you can't do it well.

You tell *yourself* you can't do it or do it well.

You wonder if it's a waste of time, and if anyone will ever read your work.

And on and on.

Again, all valid answers, but for me, the answer is plotting. Coming up with a fresh, nuanced story full of twists that make sense is incredibly difficult. I'm talking waking-up-in-the-middle-of-the-night-panicked-you-screwed-shit-up difficult. If the plot doesn't work, the book falls apart. If the twists don't make some semblance of sense, the book falls apart. If the story you are telling is old and tired and rehashed, well ... you get it.

Once you have an idea, you have to craft characters with

motivations that fit the plot—and again—make sense. Their actions must organically lead to a fresh, yet inevitable twist, or it will feel contrived. One of the main twists in *You'll Never Know* is fueled by Zane's desperation to save his daughter. Cora's disease needed to be one that felt insurmountable. One that would force him to do anything.

Metachromatic leukodystrophy, or "MLD", is a rare, neurodegenerative disorder that affects the brain and the nervous system. It's a truly insidious disease, and I hope I portrayed it accurately. If I didn't, and you or someone you love suffer with it, please accept my apology. There's no way for someone who hasn't lived with or experienced the effects of MLD firsthand to fully describe the affliction, but when I did the research, it seemed to be to me exactly as Zane describes it in the book—like watching someone you love drown inside of themselves, fading away bit-by-bit, until they're gone. It's heart breaking.

And it's horrifically expensive to treat.

Writers take certain liberties when crafting a story. We often have to bend the truth to fit the narrative. And that's exactly what I did when Zane says the MLD therapy is $2.5 million per infusion. It's not. At the time of writing *You'll Never Know*, the wholesale acquisition cost for this particular drug, Lenmeldy, in the United States was a whopping $4.25 million! In Europe, the price ranges between $2.3 million and $3.9 million, depending on the country.

It feels unbelievable, which is exactly why I reduced the cost in the book. But for those stricken with the disease, it's their reality. And in reality, dealing with the financial burden of a disease like this is far beyond the financial means of most people. The annual healthcare costs for someone struggling with MLD can easily approach a hundred thousand (or more) a year as it progresses. And worse, it's a disease that mostly affects children. It's a diagnosis with little hope.

But in life, there is always hope. And there are always ways to help.

The MLD Foundation does just that. They provide family

support and advocacy as well as fund MLD-focused research to advance MLD care. And you can donate to them via the QR code below.

I have. Will you join me?

If you do, thank you for caring.

ACKNOWLEDGEMENTS

Writing a book is a wild thing. It's starts with a single idea. A sole what if that plants itself in your mind like a seed. Some seeds die and some seeds take hold. And when it's a good idea, it's a seed that won't let go and grows. That's when you know you have a potential book on your hands.

The idea for *You'll Never Know* was one that wouldn't let go—more so than anything I've ever written. I had people tell me it wouldn't work, that it was too complex, that it didn't make sense, but it didn't matter. The idea had other plans.

So, I wrote the thing.

Like every book, it wasn't easy—don't let anyone tell you that writing a book is—but this one poured out of me a little smoother than the rest. It was a bit more magical. I loved writing this book. Even when I was panicking that I'd screwed things up as all writers do with every novel, I loved it. I fell asleep trying to solve plot problems and woke with the solutions the second my eyes clicked open the next morning. Okay, it wasn't quite that easy, but you get the gist.

I poured myself into this story. I *lived* in this world. At times when writing, you see the world through a character's eyes and feel their emotions. You inhabit their world—and I spent more time inhabiting the minds of Grant, Bailey, and Reed than I would like to admit. Which is why it takes someone special to share a life with an author. Writers are constantly lost in their imagination, spending time with people who don't exist. So, my first and biggest thank you goes to my wife, Jen. I can't tell you how much I appreciate the countless hours you spend fielding my questions and brainstorming plot. And not only that. You literally make me a better person each and every day. There's no doubt I married well. You are an incredible mother, and I'm so lucky to have you in my life. I appreciate you and what you do for me and our family more than you know. In fact, you'll never know!

Thank you to my girls, Harper, Riley, and Addie. Watching you grow has been one of the biggest blessings of my life, and I'm so proud of who you are and who you are becoming. Thank you for lending me your imaginations and putting up with my stories. I can't wait to see the people you will become.

To my family, especially my parents, my sisters, and all of my wonderful in-laws. Thank you for your love and support. I know life hasn't always been perfect, but you're all perfect to me. I wouldn't change a thing.

And speaking of support ...

To all the Booktokers, Bookstagrammers, bloggers, and readers—where would I be without you? No, seriously. Where? Unknown is where. Invisible. Over the last couple of years, I've been humbled by all of the kind souls who've picked up one of my books, taken the time to read it, and then shared it in a video or a reel. Writing has been a dream of mine for so long now—and that's exactly what it would remain without you—a dream. Here's the crazy thing, because of you, I'm close to living that dream. I'm at a point where I can think about writing fulltime, and to me, that's an absolute miracle. You've helped make my dream a reality, and I am so very grateful for your time and support. If I could name each and every one of you, I would, but I would surely miss some very important people, and I would hate to do that, so I won't try. But you all know who you are. And *I* know who you are, and I won't forget. A quick shoutout to Dani Bueno for all the marketing help. You absolutely rock!

A special thanks to my early readers. Faith Gardner, I appreciate your willingness hold your breath, dive into a messy first draft, and surface with some brilliant suggestions. They helped so much. Charles Dunphey, thank you as always for all the time spent reading multiple iterations and chapters of this book and helping me round out both the characters and the story. Chatting plot with you is one of my favorite things to do. Noelle Ihli, you're a brilliant reader and friend. Your read was a crucial one, and this book is so much better because of you—thank you. Steph Nelson, thank you for helping me polish this one and for your infectious independent author spirit—it helped spark my own, and for that, I'll always be grateful. And finally, Jennifer Patterson, thank you for reading and providing feedback on later drafts of this book. I needed that final gut check to make sure the story (mostly) worked—and you provided that. I appreciate you!

To my agents, Ezra and Ethan Ellenberg—thank you for taking a chance on me and on this book. Your approach to hybrid publishing, and belief in the power of independent authors, has been refreshing to say the least. Jason Pinter, the same thing can be said for you. Thank you for supporting me, believing in me, and bringing the audio version of *You'll Never Know* to life in such a powerful way. I'm honored and excited to be a part of Simon Maverick!

Patti Geesey, thank you for your incredible editing skills and for helping me publish the best books I can. And thank you to Molly Halstead for the expert formatting and design. You are a magician with a keen eye, and I appreciate your work.

A quick shoutout to all of the people who've helped me grow as a writer over the years: C.B. Jones, Brett Mitchell Kent, Alex Wolfgang, Chris O'Halloran, Solomon "Lord Mordi" Force, P.L. McMillan, Carson Winter, Ivy Grimes, Christi Nogle, Ai Jiang, Jenny Kiefer,

Shane Hawk, Tina Alberino, T.J. Price, Erik McHatton, Patrick Barb, Chelsea Pumpkins, Jennifer Collins, Bridget D. Brave, Ryan Marie Ketterer, Lindsey Ragsdale, Pauline Chow, Timaeus Bloom, Michelle Tang, Jessica Peter, Peter Ong Cook, Eliza Broadbent, Evelyn Freeling, Angela Sylvaine, Andrew Sullivan, Rae Wilde, J.W. Donley, Joe Radkins, Antony Frost, Emma E. Murray, Mob, Sylvia Langille, Laura Pritchett, Heather Webb and all the others I've surely missed. Thank you for reading and believing in my stories before I did. You gave me the confidence to think I could tackle this whole writer thing to begin with, and I'm forever grateful.

I have one more thank you. And it's to YOU, the person reading this right now. Thank you for picking up my book. If you would have told me I'd have people I didn't know reading my work just a few years ago, I wouldn't have believed you. Thank you for doing so.

I can't wait to see where we go from here.

—Caleb

ABOUT THE AUTHOR

Caleb Stephens is an award-winning thriller author based in Denver, Colorado. He's the author of the psychological thrillers *You'll Never Know, If You Lie,* and *The Girls in the Cabin,* and a two-time Colorado Book Award finalist. When he's not writing, Caleb enjoys spending time with his wife, kids, and his furry son, Bodhi—easily the most spoiled member of the family.

To learn more about his work and grab a free story, check out his website www.calebstephensauthor.com, and follow him on TikTok and Instagram @calebstephensauthor.

Read a thrilling excerpt from Caleb Stephens' psychological thriller If You Lie.

CHAPTER ONE

Sounds came.

The steady ping of rain drumming against steel.

The muted whoosh of wind. The high whine of rubber kissing asphalt.

I was moving.

Why am I moving?

Air clawed up my throat and slid back down again—slowly, painfully—my lungs pulling harder than my esophagus would allow, my chest rising and falling in uneven shifts. I couldn't breathe.

I should be able to—

My eyelids snapped open to darkness. Pure black. I tried to scream and couldn't. My voice was gone, lost in my burning throat. Another sound came instead—this one closer, directly overhead.

Clack. Clack. Clack.

I raised my hands and brushed a loose rod, then pushed past it and felt cool metal press against my palm. I followed it lower, the metal curving behind my head until it terminated in a rubber seal.

A car, I thought. *I'm in a trunk.*

Oh, God ...

Oh, fuck.

It's why my knees were jammed in a fetal position, why a rough pad of carpet burned against my cheek and scratched my neck. A shot of cold panic swam down my spine. Time stuttered, and I wheezed for oxygen. It felt like I was breathing through a straw. I was going to pass out if I didn't get it together and fast.

Focus, Olivia. Stay calm.

And then: *He thinks I'm dead.*

It's why my hands weren't bound, why my mouth wasn't gagged. It's why my ankles weren't slung in an interstate of knots. The man who'd done this to me thought I was dead. I could still feel his fingers squeezing, digging into my neck, could still hear his voice burning hot in my ear.

Fucking die, already!

Those words pouring over me in a shower of sour breath.

Clack. C-Clack. Clack.

Think, Olivia! You have to think!

I slowed my breathing and forced my mind to calm. There had to be a way to open the trunk or signal another car. A wire to rip free from the brake lights or a latch to pop. Didn't all the newer cars have those specifically for situations like this? For women who, like me, simply disappeared?

And I *would* disappear if I didn't find a way to get out.

My heart sloshed in my chest, and I rolled to my right, toward the sidewall of the trunk, and extended an arm. My fingers brushed over objects I recognized. Jumper cables, and a can of gas. Coiled rope and boxes. A hard plastic case. Duct tape. Nothing else.

Jesus, no latch.

I tried the other side, muttering a prayer as my hands crawled through a graveyard of clinking bottles, my fingers scraping over the dry brush of cardboard and through the crinkle of plastic sacks. Dust tickled the back of my nose, and I nearly unleashed a sneeze before I bit it off. *Don't! He'll hear you.* Then I tried again, moving slower this time, feeling for what *had* to be there.

And it was—nestled a few inches above the floor of the trunk.

A trunk release. A lever to pull.

Reality wobbled. My heart fluttered and crashed.

Work, I thought. *Please, God, work.*

I pulled.

There came a click, and the world exploded into a fireball of light. A gray sky moved above me, swollen with thunderheads, trees sweeping past on either side. Headlights coasted behind the car in a sea of rushing metal. Cold rain lashed against my neck. I forced myself upright, and the brakes slammed and sent me hurtling backward as the car screeched to a stop.

Move! Move! Move!

I scrambled from the trunk.

One foot connected with the ground. The other slipped. I crashed to the road, and the sound of rain filled my ears along with the heavy thunk of a door opening. Two boots hit asphalt.

His boots.

Air scabbed over my lips. The world swam.

Go! I pushed myself upright—and I ran. Across the white line on the shoulder of the road and into traffic with brakes shrieking all around me. Horns tearing past. Rain pelting my face. Wind hissing in my ears. Behind me came a full-throat roar.

"Stop, you fucking bitch!"

My lungs burned for air, everything smearing to a blur.

"I said, stop!" Louder this time. Closer.

But I didn't stop, *couldn't* stop. I kept running—pushing through the fire in my chest, ignoring the pain in my throat—until I stumbled off the road and tumbled down a grass-slicked descent.

Rolling now. Everything spinning. Gasping for air.

I splashed into a pool of muddy water and came up coughing, wiping my eyes to a sight that filled me with terror. The man stood above me on the hill, looking down with one hand balled into a fist and the other holding a knife.

You're dead, I thought. *He's going to kill you.*

A cloud of blue and red light rose behind him followed by a voice. "Remain where you are! Drop the knife!"

But the man didn't. He just stared down at me with his breath turning to mist.

And took a step. Took another.

Then the gunshots rang out.

CHAPTER TWO

I woke with a start, my eyelids snapping open without warning or hesitation; a flashing, *Bang! Hello, Olivia, welcome back!* Outside the plane's window, a wet slice of jungle flashed past. Palm trees interlaced with deep pockets of shadow.

My phone buzzed on my lap. I knuckled the sleep from my eyes and grabbed it, scrolling past the unread text messages and news alerts flooding the screen in favor of the envelope icon at the bottom. An email I'd already read at least two dozen times since it hit my inbox two weeks earlier. The email that had me sitting on this plane now.

My thumb hovered over it—and clicked.

> ***To:*** **SurvivorPodmail; livmiller;**
> ***From:*** **QMiller@gmail.com**
> ***Subject:*** **I'M GETTING MARRIED!!!**

Via — Hi! How are you? Doing well, I hope? It's been far too long. Look, I'm not really sure how to start, other than to get right to it—I'm sorry for how everything ended with us. We both said a lot of cruel things we didn't mean. *I* said a lot of cruel things. I didn't know how to deal with my life back then. I couldn't make sense of it. I couldn't cope.

Which is why I ran ...

I paused and thought of Quinn. I hadn't laid eyes on my sister in what, four years now? Five? I pictured the last time I saw her, the Las Vegas scarecrow, throwing me out of her Section 8 house with her cheekbones sawing beneath her skin like knife points, her voice leaking out in a tight rasp.

You're dead to me, Olivia! I don't ever want to talk to you again!

Then she'd slammed the door in my face, leaving my plea for her to return to Columbus with me and get her life together rotting in my throat. And now here she was, diving straight out of the blue, bomb-shelling me with an engagement announcement and an invitation.

I sighed and continued to read.

> I needed some space to heal, you know? I just needed time. But that doesn't make what I did right. I'm sorry for vanishing like that. It was an awful thing to do. I can see that now.
>
> I've met the best group of people, Via. The *best*. I've grown in so many ways because of them. The past only controls us if we let it. And I'm done living in the past. I'm ready to move on, and I hope you are, too.
>
> Which is why I'm writing ...
>
> I'm getting married! My fiancé's name is Bryce. He's intelligent, kind, hot, and *very* funny. We have so much in common. He proposed last month, in St. Martin. Of course, I said yes! (In a place like that, coming from that man, how could I not?) And you know who I wanted

to tell first?

You, Via. I wanted to tell *you*.

Listen, I think it's time we patch things up. Bryce has scheduled a cruise, and I want you to come. It's going to be amazing. Please say you will. Call me, and I'll fill you in on the details. I can't wait to hear your voice.

Love, Q.

I slipped the phone back into my pocket. It didn't even sound like Quinn, the letter written with the cotton-candy cadence of a sixteen-year-old. I could practically hear her sing-song pitch dancing up from the letters. *I said yes! How could I not? Let's go on a cruise!*

"First time to Puerto Rico?" The question came from the guy in the seat to my left. He sported a heavily veined nose and the watery gaze of a functional alcoholic.

"Yes," I mumbled.

"You have to try the pernil," the man added. "It's delicious."

"Mm," I replied, glancing out the window again, telling myself, *do not engage.*

Something about my face invites conversation: With wide eyes, and an easy smile, I'm approachable—no resting bitch face here!—which made men like this one think they actually stood a chance. Honestly though, even if he looked like Ryan Gosling, I wouldn't be interested. After what happened to me, I had issues with men. Being strangled and stuffed in a trunk will do that to you.

A tinny voice announced our arrival through the speaker and I returned my attention to the phone. At first, I thought the email was a joke. A cruel hoax by someone in the media looking to make a few bucks off an emotional response. A quick, *fuck off, asshole,* they could splash over the gossip sites, or sell to some B-level media outlet. It had happened before, especially after my autobiography dropped.

But *Fighting for Air: The Olivia Miller Story* released years ago, and I couldn't remember the last time someone reached out for an interview. Besides, tragedy has a short shelf life in America, and mine was long past the expiration date.

A sudden *ding!* extinguished the seatbelt light, and fifteen minutes later I stood near the baggage belt, waiting for my suitcase with a cup of dark roast. I took a sip and closed my eyes. The Quinn I'd left in Vegas five years ago was the definition of a hot mess. What would she look like now? She'd long ago obliterated all of her social media accounts, so I had to imagine her face—a perfect pair of lips drowning in a nest of frown lines. Nostrils scabbed pink from drugs. Eyes cupped in dark circles. Hair pulled back into a tight ponytail greased with neglect. My sister, the burnout. How she fit with Bryce Cullen was beyond me.

Finding her fiancé online wasn't hard. A quick Google search after my call with Quinn revealed a diamond-handed finance bro with pearl-white teeth and a body that looked like it had never ingested a single gram of sugar. Polo shirts without a single wrinkle. Olive skin and dimples. A cleft chin. Sandy blond hair thick with product. Hot was an understatement because Bryce was beyond perfect. Which, I guess, was the other reason I'd decided to come. Simple curiosity. How the hell had she snagged this guy?

I trashed the coffee and retrieved my suitcase, then wheeled it to the doors and took a deep breath. *You can do this, Olivia. You can do hard things.* It was my father's favorite expression, one I'd adopted long ago, thinking it would give me courage, but it never did. It only made me feel worse; he'd never been great at doing hard things.

Outside, the humidity hit me like a fist, instantly teasing beads of sweat from my pores. People rushed past, *way* too many people, Ubers and taxis and bodies mixing into one big wall of noise and light and sound.

And no Quinn.

"You want a ride?" a man with silver teeth called through an open window. "I take you where you wanna go."

"Thank you. No, I'm fine."

"Oye. Get in. I'll cut you a deal, mami."

"No, really I'm—"

"Via?"

I turned toward the voice. A woman stood behind me, wearing a sleek black skirt and a white fitted top. A waterfall of strawberry-blonde hair fell over her shoulders and pulled my gaze lower toward a set of bronzed legs and toned calves. She tilted a pair of oversized sunglasses toward the bridge of her nose and stared at me with eyes the color of spring grass, eyes I'd recognize anywhere.

My mouth fell open. "Quinn?"

Her smile widened and she closed the distance between us.

"Oh my god, it *is* you," she said, enveloping me in a rib-crushing hug. I hung slack in the embrace, limp. This woman looked nothing like the shuffling zombie I remembered, staring out at the world through a pair of filmy, pill-addled eyes. This woman was vibrant and gorgeous. This woman was *alive*, looking like the A-list actress Quinn had always aspired to be. And she was hugging me—not exactly the welcome I'd expected.

I slithered from her grip. "You look great, Quinn. Really."

"Thank you." She set her hands on her hips and appraised me, her head tilting to the side. A diamond the size of a beetle winked from her ring finger; I guessed three carats. "And you haven't changed a bit."

I peered down at my frayed jeans, scuffed Converse, and vintage Nirvana shirt which clashed aggressively with her dress. My cheeks flared. An apology crept onto my tongue but I wouldn't let it out. What did I have to apologize for? Still, I wanted to. It's what felt natural in the moment. A way to break the ice. *I'm sorry, Quinn. For everything.*

"God, it's good to see you, Via! So good."

"It's good to see you, too."

"C'mon. I can't wait for you to meet Bryce."

I reached for my suitcase, but Quinn took my hand and tugged me forward before I could grab the handle. "Don't bother. Javier's got it."

A man with sand-colored skin I hadn't noticed until that moment stepped past me and took the bag with a curt nod. I stared at him, confused. *Quinn has staff now?*

"It's fine, Via. Let him do his job."

"Olivia," I corrected.

"What?"

"I go by Olivia now." I hated my nickname—Via. Only two people had ever called me Via: Quinn and my father. And my father was dead. Via died with him.

Quinn frowned. "Okay, I'll try to remember that. Come on."

I followed her in a daze, watching her walk, still attempting to connect this Quinn to the hollow-cheeked version who lived rent-free in my mind. I couldn't reconcile the two people—it looked like she'd aged in reverse.

She came to a stop in front of a white stretch limo parked a few feet from the curb.

"We're taking *that*?" I asked.

Quinn's forehead bunched like it was a stupid question, like everyone in Puerto Rico took Maserati stretch limos from the airport.

"I told you this trip was going to be amazing." The tone of her voice rose on the last word, matching the flowery cadence of her email. My sister, who'd communicated in monotone for as long as I could remember, was now speaking in uptalk. When did it happen? When had she changed?

I hesitated and she cocked her head. "Hey, are you okay?"

I blinked. "Yeah, fine." My throat constricted. I couldn't move. Being here, with this new version of Quinn, after so many years apart, suddenly felt overwhelming. I didn't know if I had it in me to wade back into our past.

"Quinn, I—"

"Listen, Olivia," she interrupted, "before you say anything, hear me out. I know this is a lot for you. It is for me, too. I must have rewritten the email I sent you at least thirty times. I almost didn't send it at all. But I meant what I said. I want you in my life, and I think you want the same. Let's give it a chance, okay?"

For some reason I couldn't pin down, I wanted to say no. I wanted to dash back into the airport while I still had the chance. But the way she was looking at me, with so much sincerity in her eyes, so much need, prevented me from replying with anything other than, "Okay."

"Good. And truly, this is going to be so much fun. Just wait. Bryce has so many activities lined up for us. You're going to love every minute of this trip, I swear." She held up her little finger in an echo of our long-ago childhood ritual: *Pinkie swear?* My hand moved on its own, and I watched my finger twine with hers.

"Promise?" I heard myself say.

Quinn smiled. "On my life."